The entire condo started rocking, tilting up and down. The walls buckled, the floor cracked apart and jutted up in large sections, like pieces of ice.

The ceiling lobbed huge chunks of itself to the floor. Glassware shattered. The tiles on Giles's stairway popped off, and the bannister collapsed.

"It's the big one," Faith yelled.

"Willow!" Buffy shouted. "Willow, tell Kendra to run!"

Then up from a fissure in the floor, a swathed head jutted upward. A torso followed, then arms. It was holding a box. It rose into the air as the apartment shattered and split apart around it.

As the condo blew to pieces with the force of an explosion, a second covered head appeared.

The ceiling collapsed, trapping Buffy, Faith and Giles in mounds of rubble. Buffy struggled, horrified, as the creatures pulled out axes and started gliding straight for Giles, who was pinned.

And who stared helplessly back at them.

Buffy the Vampire Slayer™

Buffy the Vampire Slayer (movie tie-in)
The Harvest
Halloween Rain
Coyote Moon
Night of the Living Rerun
Blooded
Visitors
Unnatural Selection
The Power of Persuasion
Deep Water
Here Be Monsters
Ghoul Trouble
Doomsday Deck
The Angel Chronicles, Vol. 1
The Angel Chronicles, Vol. 2

The Angel Chronicles, Vol. 3
The Xander Years, Vol. 1
The Xander Years, Vol.2
The Willow Files, Vol. 1
The Willow Files, Vol. 2
How I Survived My Summer
   Vacation, Vol. 1
The Faith Trials, Vol. 1
Tales of the Slayer, Vol. 1

The Lost Slayer serial novel
   Part 1: Prophecies
   Part 2: Dark Times
   Part 3: King of the Dead
   Part 4: Original Sins

Available from ARCHWAY Paperbacks and Pocket Pulse
Child of the Hunt
Return to Chaos
The Gatekeeper Trilogy
   Book 1: Out of the Madhouse
   Book 2: Ghost Roads
   Book 3: Sons of Entropy
Obsidian Fate
Immortal
Sins of the Father
Resurrecting Ravana
Prime Evil
The Evil That Men Do
Paleo
Spike and Dru: Pretty Maids All in a Row
Revenant
The Book of Fours
The Unseen Trilogy (Buffy/Angel)
   Book 1: The Burning
   Book 2: Door to Alternity
   Book 3: Long Way Home
The Watcher's Guide, Vol. 1: The Official Companion to the Hit Show
The Watcher's Guide, Vol. 2: The Official Companion to the Hit Show
The Postcards
The Essential Angel
The Sunnydale High Yearbook
Pop Quiz: Buffy the Vampire Slayer
The Monster Book
The Script Book, Season One, Vol. 1
The Script Book, Season One, Vol. 2
The Script Book, Season Two, Vol. 1
The Script Book, Season Two, Vol. 2

Available from POCKET BOOKS

THE BOOK OF FOURS

A Historie of the Four Slayers
This Being Their First Adventure

as told by The Watcher of the Fifth Slayer

to

Nancy Holder

POCKET BOOKS
New York   London   Toronto   Sydney   Singapore

Historian's Note:
This story takes place during the third season.

An *Original* Publication of POCKET BOOKS

POCKET BOOKS, a division of Simon & Schuster, Inc.
1230 Avenue of the Americas, New York, NY 10020

Originally published in hardcover in 2001 by Pocket Books

ISBN: 0-7434-1241-9

First Pocket Books paperback printing February 2002

10 9 8 7 6 5 4 3 2 1

No question about it, Lisa Clancy—
this one's for you.

Acknowledgments

No writer is an island:

Thanks so very much to Joss Whedon, Caroline Kallas, and the cast and crew of *Buffy the Vampire Slayer*, to George Snyder of Mutant Enemy, and Debbie Olshan of Fox. All you Bronzers out there, especially Allie Costa and Angela Rienstra (and mom Pat), you are superfun! My undying affection and gratitude to the Merry Pocketeers: Micol Ostow and Liz Shiflett. Dear, dear agent mine, Howard Morhaim, *aloha pumehana*. Same to Stacey Schermerhorn. And big aloha to John and Shannon Tullius, Liz Engstrom, and her sister, Cheryce; Katherine Ramsland, John Saul, and Mike Sack, and all the other MWRetreaters, especially my students: Phyllis Melhado, Penny Buckely, Debbie Viguie, John Oglesby, Bill Duke, Skip Shockley, Kelly Watkins, Hillary Buckman-Palmer, Diane Button, Ruscha Robbins, and Joan Sawyer. Thanks for all you have taught me.

Lee Sigall, you rock. So do you, Rev. Andy Herron-Sweet. Karen, Neal, and Rachel, Grace, *je vous aime*.

And more love than can be expressed to the Mariotte-Hart-Holder-Jones continuum: Jeff, Maryelizabeth, Holly, Belle, and David; Leslie and Will; Elise and Hank, Richard, Teresa, David, and Sandra and Bill.

And of course, to Dot, Sasha, David, Sugar, Spice, Muffin, Gray Mouser, and Grenaldine—what's life without total chaos?

I have seen no more evident monstrosity and miracle in the world than myself.

—MONTAIGNE, 1533–1592

Prologue

The town of Sunnydale could no longer contain the forces—natural and not so much—that had tried for nearly a century to tear it apart. Hellmouth ground zero had reached critical mass. The air was saturated with energy; wind and rain blew at hurricane force. The soaked ground shook and ruptured, trapping houses, cars, and people in flows of mud. Beneath the weight, men, women, children, and yes, even vampires, froze into statues like the ash-coated victims of ancient Pompeii. Fires raged everywhere, burning whatever lay in their paths—buildings, people, and the entire population of the Sunnydale Zoo.

As the forces of nature and the beyond mounted, each rock, each tree, each atom of each cell flew apart in a bacchanalia of destruction. More people had perished inside the cursed city's perimeter in the last twenty-four hours than in the previous twenty-four years. Buffy knew that as she stood high atop Dead Man's Point with the others, death was the victorious gladiator parading down below on Main

Street, a clutch of skulls in his waistband, his sandals sloshing through a river of blood.

The ground raged beneath the feet of Buffy, Faith, Cordelia, and Willow, whole chunks of the summit soaring into the air as others smashed into the wind and the waves. Blocks of stone and brick—the remains of the lighthouse—catapulted through the storm as deathdealing projectiles. From below the Point, flames of crimson, scarlet, and brilliant orange geysered toward the heavens, as if to burn the very stars themselves.

All that had gone before—the fires, the quakes, the floods, and the windstorms—were an unspeakable promise of what was to come. A mere taste of what hell on Earth would really be like.

If we fail.

We have to stop the Gatherer, and we don't know how.

This was the last battle, and they all knew it, felt it, were as ready as they could be for it. Cordelia's chin was up, her fists balled, and Buffy, though very tired, was primed. But Faith was badly injured and could barely stand; and Willow had staggered from her bed in the intensive care unit at Sunnydale Medical Center to be here.

"Thought I knew what the end of the world was gonna be like," Faith shouted, at the opposite end of the row of four.

Standing to the left of Buffy, Willow yelled, "But it's worse."

Cordelia bellowed, "No small talk! Stay focused."

Buffy remained silent, but her mind was racing. She was strategizing. They desperately needed a plan other than the current one of fighting until they died.

If the Gatherer gets both Faith and me, it will com-pletely suck up our primal Slayer force and there won't be any left . . . There will never be another Slayer again. Ever. And this demon will destroy the planet without any opposition.

But the portent says there must be four to kill it. We are the Four, Faith and me and the other two. But . . . last-minute substitution okay? Or not?

She hazarded a glance behind herself, taking in the others of the good side, about twenty feet away. Brave friends to the end, they had fought their way through the cataclysm to be here on the summit for the battle: Giles, Xander, and Oz, who were crouching to avoid being blown away, and Angel, who stood with his feet planted wide apart, his duster soaked with rain as it flapped in the gale. Their faces covered with mud and soot. And blood. No one had made it this far without his share of damage. No one had died yet, either, and Buffy's throat tightened as she thought of how things could have turned out.

Kneeling slightly apart from the others, dark-haired Kit Bothwell, grim and determined, was speaking, praying, or chanting an incantation. The young Watcher was an accomplished sorcerer, and he had coura-geously joined their ranks, despite the fact that their fight looked to be a lost cause.

Angel's dark eyes caught Buffy's, held them. She could almost read his mind: *Don't think like that. Don't think that all is lost.*

Buffy, damn it, kill that thing and live through this.

Slowly, she nodded. Angel nodded back. Her heart hurt from loving him, and in that moment, she under-stood a lot more about self-sacrifice than before, and she found it in her heart to forgive India Cohen.

When I die, will the pain stop? Or will my love for him keep me wandering on the Ghost Roads, forever?

The sky exploded. It shook, rippling from a sonic boom that threw Willow to the ground and sent Faith reeling. The others grimaced with pain and covered their ears.

Here it comes.

Buffy took a deep breath. Quickly regrouping, the other girls looked at one another, then at her, a little less steady, a great deal more frightened. Faith was on the other end of the row; on her right was Cordelia, and then Willow, who stood beside Buffy.

Then, as Buffy locked gazes with each one, they grew taller, more solid, surer. In turn, each favored Buffy with a smile. Faith winked and Willow made as if to shake her hair out of her face, although she was as bald as a billiard ball.

As if on cue, the four young women joined hands.

"We are the Four," Cordelia yelled.

"We band together," Willow cried.

Faith whooped. "And we're gonna kick some ass!"

Buffy was proud to stand with them; their backs straight, their chins high. Despite terrible odds, they were there to do what was right. What they must do, even if it demanded worse than their deaths.

We are warriors. We are protectors.

Another tremendous skyquake boom shook Buffy, rattling her bones as if she were a string puppet. Clouds and smoke whirled and eddied, so thick the hurricane-force winds and rain couldn't blow them away. The earth shook with renewed force; bolts of lightning shrieked through the clouds and landed inches from Buffy and Faith on the outer points of the line. Neither one of them flinched as they rode out the eruption of giant fissures in the earth. There was nowhere to go, nowhere to hide. This was it.

Then the fires rose all around Dead Man's Point, even on the sea side. The ocean waters themselves were burning. Smoke began to circle the summit, rushing, moving, becoming a spinning dervish, whipping up faster and faster until it whistled like wind. It formed a cone that shot upward, to a point so distant Buffy couldn't see it.

Far above them, a single pinprick of light burst into a ball of light; the sphere expanded across the black sky, lighting up their surroundings as brightly as a summer's day. It was as if the sun had come out in the middle of the night.

"Angel, be careful!" Buffy shouted, turning toward him.

Her vampire love was running for cover. Despite the wind and the rain, the back of his duster was smoldering and tiny flames danced along the hem.

Suddenly, without warning, Willow let go of Buffy's hand and broke from the line. She wheeled around as if she were going to tackle Angel and throw him to the ground.

"No! Willow, we have to stand together!" Buffy shouted.

But it wasn't Angel Willow ran to; she zigzagged crazily toward Kit Bothwell, struggling against the storms. The wind knocked her injured body like a giant taunting a kitten. She fell, got to her feet, and stumbled onward.

Cordelia screamed, "Come back here!"

Willow paid her no heed. No one else ran after her. Transfixed, they watched her racing toward the newcomer.

They had their orders: to stay and fight; not to break ranks for any reason.

Not *any* reason.

"I saved you once," Willow cried, running toward the man. "Kit, Kit I love you!"

She flung herself into his arms, then turned around and faced the other three, and the vast, penetrating brilliance. "Take me back!" she shouted. "Take me back, fully, and leave them all alone!"

Before Buffy realized what Willow was doing, the redhead had raced to the edge of the summit. She tottered there a moment.

Buffy whispered, "No. *No.*"

Willow's last look was saved not for Buffy, or Oz, but for Kit. Then she threw open her hands and let the wind tear her off the precipice. For a moment, the wind buoyed her up, and then she fell.

Everyone was mute with shock.

Then the brightness was extinguished like a fragile candle flame, and through the darkness—strangely— Buffy caught her first full view of the Gatherer. Her mouth went dry; her face went numb; and she thought, *It can't be this horrible. I must be seeing things.*

But it was there. This was no dream, no waking nightmare. This was really happening.

"I walk," it proclaimed.

The stars shook.

Rigid with terror, Buffy thought of how they had gotten here, and wondered how they would ever leave this place alive.

The Book of One

Prologue

The Ghost Roads, in Timelessness

For India Cohen the Vampire Slayer, her return to awareness came like the switch of a light. One instant off, the next on:

I've been dead.

I'm not dead now.

I was the Slayer, and I died. That sucker killed me. That gross mummy-guy found me and opened his disgusting container of skin and bones, and that demon-in-a-box jobbie leaped out of it. It had an axe, and it hacked me to shreds, cut off every part it could, and emptied my body of everything inside it like a hotel maid dumping out an ashtray.

The bummer is, I let it.

The whole time I fought it, while Kit was screaming at me to run and Mariposa was barking, I knew I was going to lose. It was the worst moment of my life, to realize that I wasn't going to pull it off. You're the Slayer, you fight long enough, you think no one can beat you.

I slayed for three years. In my line of work, that's a long time. But I could have kept going, and I know it.

Maybe I didn't try hard enough because I knew there'd be another Slayer to take my place. I'd never kidded myself that I was indispensable. As soon as Kit explained the whole Slayer system to me, I realized I was just one of many Slayers, fully interchangeable, engaged in a battle that was never going to end.

When he told me I was the Slayer, he tried to make me feel special—"one girl in all her generation"—but that's not really true, is it? Because when that one dies, there's another. And another. And another. So much for one per generation.

It's just one per lost battle. And we seem to lose fairly often, don't we?

Still, there is the matter of being Chosen. No one else could take my place until I lost my place.

As the old saying goes, "Fools rush in where angels fear to tread."

Yeah, but they get the best seats.

What I hoped for was to stall the demon long enough for Kit to grab my puppy and get himself the hell out of there. Kit, my Watcher, would be the first one to tell me that I violated my duty, which is to survive. I am—I was—the Slayer. Watchers are much easier to replace.

But oh, Kit, I hope you made it. I hope you're still alive.

All right, truth: I sacrificed myself because I loved him. It's as simple as that.

Kit, I wish . . . no, I don't wish you were here. I'm glad you're not.

It's no fun being here.

There's another Slayer, isn't there? Of course there is. The new girl in town. My replacement's certainly been activated, and she's fighting the good fight. And when she dies, someone else will pick up where she left off.

Like a pet white rat on a wheel in a cage.

Who knows how long I've been here? Maybe there have been fifty Slayers since my death. Maybe everybody's left Earth and there's a Slayer on Mars.

As for Kit, my dearest love: I don't know if I managed to save you, but if I did, my defeat was worth it. Slayers are replaceable, and Watchers, too, but there will never be another man like you. You are—you were?—my life, my soul. The way we two meshed was beyond supernatural.

If I had ever needed proof that magick exists and that Slayers' dreams come true, you were that proof.

But dreams end, too, and nightmares take over. That thing that attacked me . . . I don't think I ever saw anything more grotesque. Did that crazy British vampire conjure it up? When she started screaming about it back in Spain, was she foreseeing my death at its hands?

My death. When the creature was cutting me apart, and the pain stopped, I knew that that was the precise moment of my death. It stopped, and I stopped, and I was . . . gone. I have no idea how long I've been gone. Apparently, there is nothing after we die, in spite of all the discussions Kit and I had about souls and vampires and demons and portals into other dimensions, some of which are like our version of hell.

Which now, I'm thinking how horrible, creepy. After all that effort and sacrifice to save the world from the ultimate evil, the answer is that after we die, we just circle "none of the above"? That the afterlife—the results of all that battling between good and evil—is an absolute zero?

I feel incredibly stupid. And used. I can't believe what a waste it all is. Right now, I'm willing to believe that hell is better than nothing. That it's better to suffer in agony than to be nothing.

Because I've been nothing. Nothing at all, and that sucks. I guess the universe had no more need of me, so I got shoved in a trunk and left in the great cosmic attic with the divine dust bunnies of the hereafter and the cobwebs of time and space, et cetera, et cetera, et cetera.

But if that was where I was, why am I back?

How am I back?

Who brought me back?

Oh, my God.

Pain is shooting through me now. Unimaginable. Unbelievable. It's worse than when I was hacked apart. It's searing me like a piece of meat. It's skewering me. It's shredding me.

I can't escape. I can't make it stop. I can't even tell where it's coming from. And if I have no body, how can I be hurt like this?

I must be in Hell after all.

I can't stand it. I have to stop it. I have to fight it.

But there is nothing to fight. I'm alone. I don't know how to escape. Must make a plan . . . I am the Slayer.

Oh, God, if I could trade this for oblivion, I would. I'd choose to climb back into the trunk. I would. This is past enduring. I can't take this.

Hello? Whoever? Wherever? Make me nothing again. Only, stop this!

No. No, I don't mean it. I would rather take this pain than feel nothing. I'd rather be tortured than cease to exist.

But it hurts. It hurts more than I can take, and I'm a Slayer. I have the highest pain threshold of any human being on the planet.

Or, maybe I was a Slayer, and this is the pain other damned souls suffer.

But why would I be damned?

Because I pretty much committed suicide?

And now I'm being pulled away, or yanked, or shoved; I don't know how I know that, because I have no sense of space or distance, and I don't know where I am. I have no body, no surface, no border. Physically, I'm still nothing except for the sense of touch.

Now I have sight. But there is nothing but formless, vast gray all around me—above, below, on either side. I could be upside down or spinning like a top, and I'd never know it.

There's shadow, of a sort: the dimmest of light against the flat, nickel-dull gray stretching before me. Now there is light as well, but indistinct and very distant.

Wait. Can it be? Yes! Someone or something else is here. Some distance away, I see a shape. It's a circle. An oval. It's a face. A human face, floating without a body? If that face means there's something living present here, then I'm no longer alone.

Or am I creating what I want, need to see? They say if you go long enough without your five senses, you begin to hallucinate. Is that what's happening to me? Is my mind feeding me a mirage?

She's a young woman. I see her body now, hovering in the gray. Her hair is swept back into a bun, and she's wearing dark, old-timey clothes. Her dark blouse is high-necked and long-sleeved, and over that she wears an equally dark jacket of some sort. It's all quite tight. She appears to be wearing a bustle. Her black skirt covers her feet, but I can easily imagine high-button shoes.

She is holding a bouquet of dead roses, and they, too, are black.

I'm seeing her in black and white, like an old movie.

She's a ghost.

And I don't know how I know this, but there's no doubt in my mind that she's a Slayer.

Like me.

Am I a ghost? Does she see me?

She must be able to see something. She's looking straight at me. Her lips are moving. Every so often, she bobs her head. She's speaking, and yet I can't hear a word she's saying.

She must realize that she's wasting her breath. If she breathes.

She's closing her eyes. Her lips are still moving.

And now there's even more pain. Unbelievable pain. Oh, no, stop. It can't be like this. Pain this bad cannot be real. It can't actually exist. No. Stop. I can't suffer like this another second . . .

Now I can hear her voice. She's chanting. I can't understand her.

Is she doing this to me? Because if she is, I'll kick her ass—

I'm washed over with more pain. More, and more. Oh, God! Stop it! Slayer, I'm like you! If you don't knock it off, I'm going to destroy you. You will not believe what kinda hurt I'll inflict on you.

I'll freakin' annihilate you.

She's speaking.

She says, "Buffy needs you, desperately. Faith, too."

And I think I'm speaking to her. I think I'm saying, "Who's Buffy?"

She's still there. I know her name. Why do I know her name? She is Lucy Hanover, she was a Slayer, too, and she died a hundred years before I did.

Lucy says, "You are the only one who can stop the Gatherer. The only one. You have to help her, India."

My name is India Cohen the Vampire Slayer. I was called in 1993, and I died in San Diego in 1996.

I say again to her, "Who's Buffy?

"And why does she need my faith?"

Chapter One

The Arabian Desert, the Past

There are sacred places in the body of the parched desert, which are bountiful gifts from the One Lord, which is Allah, May He Be Praised for His Unending Mercy and Generosity.

When a Bedouin is wandering the sands of the ages, and the sky and the earth are parched and dry; and his soul and his body cry out for sanctuary, Allah provides. He gives His faithful nomad a glimpse of the Paradise that is to come, a miniature window, on Earth.

These tantalizing views are the famed oases, where rounded dunes of velvety sand and the gentle slopes between them promise delights. Sensual and inviting as a *houri*, luxuriant reeds fan above fresh, sweet water. Succulent fruit dangles from swaying, lacy palms. Cooling shade caresses sunburnt skin.

There are other places much like this also, but they have nothing to do with Divine Mercy. They are lies. And why they exist, no man knows, save that it is said that the evil *djinn* feed off men's despair.

These lies are the legendary mirages. Where no water ripples, thirsty people on camelback stare at verdant pools. Where no figs hang, miserable nomads trudge hopefully, stretching their arms to pluck sweet fruit.

The skeletons of these deceived travelers are discovered years later, reaching for what was never there.

In an oasis in the heart of the Sinai, a mirage was born, so long ago it was before Slayers walked the world. Good and evil had just begun their endless feuding, and the finger of destiny had not touched a single hero, nor crushed an unlucky martyr. At least, so it was in the Arabias.

The mirage began as a thickness at the bottom of the oasis pool, and where and what it was before then, no one has ever known.

The thickness had no function, but it had a quality: it was pure and unknowing evil. It existed for no other reason than to express its nature. A dark shard of badness, it remained that way for eons. The sands shifted around the oasis, and its evilness endured. Its essence never altered for what men call centuries. Millennia.

Then one day, the tiniest of sand fleas bobbled beside the water's edge. What possessed the nimble creature to venture too close, and fall in? And how did the thickness know it was there, and draw it down, down into the depths, and consume it?

The flea's life energy transformed the thickness into something slightly more than it had been before. Previously unknowing and unaware, now it was dimly conscious. At a very primitive level, deep within its matter, bloomed the vaguest, most unformed sense that it was one thing, and everything else was not whatever it was.

That disturbed it. There should be nothing more than itself. It had always been the center of its universe, though it did not really understand its own assumption, and it should remain so.

Centuries passed. The first Slayer walked. Evil fought back.

Then a brown sparrow happened by the water. How it got there, no one could say. The Hand of God decreed that it should be, and it was not for any lesser being, angel or person, to know.

But when the bird pecked at the sparkling wet diamonds reflected in the surface of the water, the thickness lurking below pulled at the creature, and yanked it in, and sucked it under, and devoured it.

The sense of "self" and "that not yet consumed" grew. Energy galvanized its impulses: it must have more.

As endless time unfolded, the thickness grew into a pasty glob, fuller now, like the fanned head of a cobra.

And then it devoured a cobra, and it knew itself one bit more. It knew itself as a consumer of energy, which made it increase, multiply, thrive. It experienced the sensation of life, and of power.

As is the natural order imposed upon this world by Allah the Most Wise, the thickness wanted still more.

It waited to receive more, and the experience of wanting something that was not itself bestowed upon it more self-awareness. It began to understand lack, and that allowed it to make comparisons based on having and not having.

Ambition was the perfect breeding ground for covetousness, which grew into frustration, which became anger. Anger unanswered: seething rage. And rage allowed it to devise schemes to get what it wanted.

Goats came next, then an antelope, then a camel.

Then one desert night, a foreign man rode there to

meet a woman he could not, should not have. He had come from far away, and he had the right to travel. She, a veiled concubine of a ruthless and powerful pasha, did not. If her absence from the harem was discovered, she would be boiled in oil.

If her infidelity was so much as suspected, even worse would befall her.

Of the man, it was better left unsaid what would happen to him.

Beneath the scimitar of the moon, their lives hung by a thread. But their love was stronger than their fear, and they embraced. Lips, arms, sighs; perfumed hair, oils, and scents; languor and ecstasy.

Heartbeats.

And then hoofbeats shook the desert floor. Fearfully, she looked up, and strained her gaze across the starry night. The pasha's men! She and he were lost!

At her lover's urging, she plunged into the water of the oasis. With the splendid battle-axe at his belt, he cut her a reed to breathe with underwater. She put it to her lips and sank beneath the surface.

What he never knew, as he held the axe in his hand and stood firm for the fight, was that the thing in the water curled around one slender ankle, and then the other. Inexorably, it pulled her down, swallowing her up as she struggled, screaming beneath the water, unable to be heard.

The curved tips of her shoes; the jingling coin bracelets around her ankles. Her gossamer pantaloons, her sash, her blouse. Her veil. Her circlet.

Like the burp of a fat, happy merchant after a feast, the thing disgorged her skull. It had been picked clean.

It bobbed to the surface and floated for a second, empty eye sockets posed as if watching the massacre of the woman's lover. Within seconds, the man was hacked to pieces.

His axe landed at the water's edge. Evil, which had spread into the water from the killing of a human being, licked the blade, and it was tainted for all time. But the pasha's guardsman, who plucked up the axe and hid it in the folds of his clothes, did not know that.

He had three more such axes made, brothers to the weapon he had plundered from the dead man—one for each of his sons. Singly, they were exquisite; as a quartet, their splendor was unmatched. Proud and acquisitive, rather than gift his male children as he had planned, he kept the four axes together in a beautiful wooden box in his quarters in the city. And how the evil transferred from one piece of metal to the others, no one knows.

That is not the point.

The point is, that it happened.

Chapter Two

Sunnydale, the Present

Being the Chosen One sucks, Buffy decided, as she fell on her butt and with her hand crushed a poor, innocent snail oozing peacefully along a chunk of scraggly ice plant. *Giles goes on and on about how great it is to have a destiny. Me, I'd rather have a future.*

She was fighting for her life on Dead Man's Point. The highest point in Sunnydale, the summit had been named in honor of one Armando Lewis, who had leaped off the cliff to his death in 1902, after claiming that his wife had risen from the grave and tried to suck his blood. Buffy knew that if she didn't keep track of the edge of the sandy cliff, the jagged rocks below would slice and dice her before the waves gathered up the pieces and dragged them into the ocean. Self-preservation dictated that she keep track of where she was at all times, even though she also had several other things to keep track of, and they all wanted her dead.

The abandoned lighthouse was to her right. All the little kids claimed it was haunted by Armando, but Giles had chalked up the reports of clanking chains and ghostly groans to vivid, youthful imaginations.

Buffy was fairly certain it was where the Baffles had been sleeping between bouts of eviscerating large dogs, deer, and unfortunate coyotes. As usual, the Sunnydale Police Department had mounted a search for a pack of wild dogs; as usual, a few people made noises about a serial killer or an escaped lunatic from a nearby insane asylum. That there was no nearby insane asylum never seemed to occur to them.

The clifftop was saturated with fog, more so even than the city itself. Sunnydale in autumn was always foggy, but this had been peculiarly thick. She and Faith had noticed it while on patrol for a missing girl named Holly Johnson. The girl's mother was frantic, and Giles shared Buffy's fear that whatever lurked in the fog had finally decided to sample human prey. She hoped they both were wrong.

So far, on the cliff, the death count was four and rising.

Which, as Martha Stewart says, is a good thing. However, we're not quite finished with tonight's special project.

We sure could do with a recipe to get rid of pesky fog banks, though.

Buffy had no idea if the unusual fog had conjured the things that were hiding in it. Or if the creatures had used the fog as a cover to go on a rampage, savaging everything that came their way.

After all, Sunnydale was originally called *Boca del Infierno* by its founders. For those who slept through Spanish class or preferred the more amusing torment of learning about French irregular verbs, that translated as "the Mouth of Hell." So Buffy could never be sure if the fog was real fog or, if it was, well, the devil's bad breath, spewing out the supernatural versions of plaque, tartar, and the gum disease known as gingivitis.

The Devil's bad breath. I gotta remember that line. Xander will love it.

"Yo, Faith!" Buffy shouted, as she rammed the heel of her boot into the face of her attacker. Or what passed for a face. Or maybe it was its stomach. Her boot sank up to the ankle in the putrescent outer coating, cracking something hard beneath, then continuing through to gelatinous grossness.

Yuck. This is not your father's Snickers bar.

The thing wheezed or started deflating or who knew what, and lurched backward. The smell was sickening and Buffy tried to hold her breath. Not the easiest thing to do when one had been fighting for fifteen minutes or more.

Maybe it's shrinking.

Maybe it's reproducing.

Yuck to the power of yuck.

The fog made it difficult to see anything, not that Buffy particularly wanted to. These creatures—there had been at least six of them when the checkered flag was dropped—were nasty-looking. Vaguely—emphasis there—human-shaped, they were covered with a sort of translucent skin of slime green, beneath which oozy, red and yellow pustules clumped in groups.

I'll never eat Jell-O with fruit in it again.

After the tense moments during which Oz took center stage as a suspect in the brutal killings, a homeless man who called himself Carlos New Mexico had provided a description of the monsters to the local news affiliate. Carlos New Mexico had insisted he had seen three ten-foot-tall, hairy upside-down ice cream cones rampaging through a Dumpster with hooked tentacles that sliced cleanly through the metal sides.

Everyone figured Carlos was on the Sterno again—until Devon, the lead singer for Dingoes Ate My Baby, casually mentioned to Oz that the description matched the ghost story he'd once heard while working as a summer camp counselor.

"They're called 'Baffles,' " Oz had reported to the group, and Giles had found a picture in a book. It matched the description one Officer Dickinson had provided in the police report Carlos had insisted be filed, and which Willow Rosenberg, Buffy's best friend, expertly hacked into.

"I saw that movie," Xander Harris had volunteered, when they discussed the sitch in the school library.

The room was typically murky and the stacks gave off a musty, unused odor, which made sense; hardly anyone at Sunnydale High School ever actually used the school library. That made it the ideal headquarters for Slayer Central. Buffy, and now Faith, trained there with Giles, who kept their weapons stored in the book cage. Xander, Willow, and Oz dropped by at least once or twice a day to see if they could help with anything. Cordelia, though she had officially turned in her Scooby Gang badge, still showed on a frequent basis as well.

Everyone was seated around the study table after classes, sipping their drinks of choice, and in Xander's case, munching astonishing amounts of junk food. He popped clusters of Raisinettes and Nacho Doritos in his mouth. "It was incredibly bad cinema, even by my standards." Xander's love of bad movies was the stuff of legend, if not a career in the film industry.

"Also, Frank Zappa wrote a song about it," Oz had offered.

Everyone moved their munchies out of harm's way as Giles staggered toward the table with a tower of his big, weird occult books. "It's called 'Cheapness,' " the librarian offered.

Oz looked sadly at Willow. "Zappa. Late. Great," he murmured.

"I swear, that new girl at my salon does *not* know how to shape eyebrows," Cordelia contributed, as she stared at herself in a hand mirror pulled from a designer purse she did not buy at the "low-rent" Sunnydale Mall, she had already made sure everyone knew.

Giles moved on. "Now, I've expanded upon the description Mr. New Mexico gave the police."

"Hairy ice cream cone," Willow offered helpfully.

"Quite."

"To what, extremely hairy raspberry sorbet in a sugar cone?" Xander suggested.

"Please." The Watcher opened a heavy bound volume. Dust rose and Buffy waved her hand in front of her face, coughing.

"Actually, 'Cheapness' was about a giant poodle named Frinobulax," Oz added.

"Why is his name 'Carlos New Mexico,' anyway?" Cordelia asked. "I mean, what's up with that?"

"A man of the streets," Oz observed. "Has a street life, carries a street name."

"Gives him street cred," Xander added, tearing open a bag of Skittles. He popped a handful in his mouth and chewed. "Not my thing, frankly. Very few people leave bags of candy in the Dumpsters. Just fried chicken and rolled tacos, stuff like that."

"Absolutely no ice cream," Buffy added helpfully.

"Please," Giles begged. "All of you, please listen to me."

"Aye, captain." Buffy saluted. "I'm all ears. Which, we have on occasion, found in Dumpsters. Fire away."

Giles fired. First the mutilated corpses had been those of small animals—cats, dogs, raccoons—and, as usual, the good—and extremely indifferent—people of Sunnydale chalked it up to packs of wild dogs. Given how often that excuse was used, there were more packs of wild dogs per square inch of Sunnydale than there were movie stars in Los Angeles.

The grisly deaths had arrived with recurring episodes of heavy coastal fog, and everyone seated around the table of Slayer HQ—the murky, dusty, otherwise unused Sunnydale High School library—had seen that movie before. But when larger animals such as deer started showing up on the outskirts of the forest, disemboweled more thoroughly than a disgraced Japanese samurai warrior, it was time for Buffy—and Faith—to don their Superslayer capes.

They had been patrolling for a whole week, and found nothing except for a few vampires here and there. If anything, Sunnydale was enjoying a relatively demon-free first semester of senior year.

But then the little girl—Holly Johnson—went missing, and Buffy and Faith pumped up the volume.

And tonight, we got lucky.

So to speak.

They'd both noticed that the fog was extra thick up around the lighthouse, and had gone to see what was what. They still didn't have an answer, but Buffy had a feeling the what was what they'd been looking for—the thing that had invented new ways to slice and dice.

* * *

The something that was probably "the thing" smeared her back and she whirled around, slamming her fist into yet more gunk.

"Faith? How you doing?" Buffy yelled again.

"Five by five," Faith shouted back. "Man, I'm gonna need a shower! With a fire hose!"

"Tell me about it."

Buffy followed through with a good, solid uppercut, her left fist sliding in up to her wrist. With another backward kick, she caught her first assailant off-balance. It shrieked, the signal—which the Slayers had learned the hard way—that its tentacles were emerging. Buffy didn't give it time to whip 'em good; she flung herself at the towering mass as hard as she could.

It shrieked again. One tentacle shot free of the gooey outer layer; it sliced through the leather of Buffy's brand new boot and tore into the flesh across her arch.

"Hey! I just got these!" she protested.

She leaped into the air and whip-kicked it with her other boot.

Its answer was a sickening thud and then a loud splash. The creature had tumbled off the cliff, hit the rocks, and landed in the Pacific Ocean.

Panting, she assumed her fighter's stance, alert and ready for more. Her foot hurt like crazy. But she couldn't afford the luxury of agony at the moment—*which is so often the case in my life, both here and in math class. So many Scantron bubbles to fill in, so little time.* There were more of these things lumbering around in the fog, and she knew from finding the bodies that their tentacles could disembowel a deer in seconds flat—never mind slicing off a human hand or ripping someone's head off.

She couldn't see Faith, but lucky for them both, the

two Slayers had spent the earlier part of the evening patrolling at the Sunnydale Mall, just to take a breather before another long, boring night of a stake here, a stake there, and nothing much to report back to the gang except the occasional discovery of the extremely disgusting remains of another victim of the Night Stalker.

At the mall, Faith had sprayed herself with about two gallons of perfume at the Robinson's-May fragrance counter because "they have to let you do it for free." Now she left a wake of cloying fragrance so strong Buffy could almost see it, like Pepe LePew in a Warner Brothers cartoon.

"Ah, woo! Got you, suckah!" Faith bellowed, as a shape flew past Buffy and back into the fog. There was another thud, another splash, and Buffy mentally painted another kill on the side of her own personal version of Snoopy's World War I flying ace doghouse.

Shades of some old ghost movie; musk and notes of floral came on very strong, like the earthbound spirit of someone's dead grandma. Buffy triangulated with her Slayer radar to raise her hand at the precise moment to connect with Faith's upraised hand as Faith smacked her palm in a victorious high-five.

"Yo, we bad!" Faith chortled.

"The baddest," Buffy agreed, and sneezed. Faith's perfume was giving her a headache.

"Bottom of the ninth?" Faith asked, winding up for more killing. She was like Rocky on angel dust. "Or are we ready to leave early to avoid the traffic?"

"Moving into overtime. There should be at least two more," Buffy said. "I counted six when we won the coin toss."

"Knew you'd keep track of the yardage, B."

"Someone has to, F," Buffy shot back, vaguely aware that the two of them were mixing up their sports metaphors. Then, sensing a presence to her right that did not smell at all expensive, she executed a full–on side kick.

Contact. The Eagle has landed.

Buffy set to work, slamming her fists in an alternating pattern as the thing grunted and began to make its signature whistle. Her hands were dripping with gunk.

Also, I am eating no more tapioca pudding.

"Look out!" Faith shouted suddenly.

Razor-sharp tentacles burst free from beneath the layers of goo and whipped at Buffy as she jumped out of range. In a fresh attack, she concentrated on using the flats of her feet, which were the most protected part of her. The leather upper of her boot flapped back and forth, smacking against her arch; the wound stung pretty badly, and Buffy took a moment to wonder if part of what was flapping was layers of her flesh, like thinly sliced pieces of pastrami on rye.

Oh, God, I am so grossing myself out.

The fog rolled and eddied from the furious motion of the tentacles, and then the blanket of gray was parted and Buffy saw Faith ramming the thing with a thick limb from a nearby Bishop pine.

The tower of gelatinous goo tumbled and rolled into a thicker section of fog. Shortly thereafter, there was another splash.

Faith whooped. Buffy saw Faith's big grin and heavily lined dark eyes hovering in the fog. She was beaming.

"Some workout, huh?" Faith asked in her south-Boston accent. She executed a side kick, followed by a roundhouse kick, directly into the thickest part of the fog. There was impact. "Looks like tonight I'm concentrating on my quads."

"Well, I should be concentrating on my French," Buffy said. "But hey, why freak my mom out with good grades at this point?"

Faith laughed. Then, without a second's warning, a tentacle shot past Buffy's right temple and slashed Faith on the cheek. The sharp, green length sliced her to the bone and blood spewed down her face in a shocking cascade of crimson.

"Faith!" Buffy cried.

With a grunt, the dark-haired Slayer clapped her hand across the wound and flattened on the ground as Buffy flung herself into the fog, located the blubbery mass, and grabbed hold. Hurtling backward, she hefted the creature straight up and over her head. She heard Faith rolling out of the way, and the creature landed with a wet, slurpy *fwap* on the sandy ground just inches from the edge of the cliff.

As Buffy sprang to her feet, Faith barreled into the monster and shoved. Buffy joined in. It was like pushing an enormous, multiarmed jelly roll. Its dozens of tentacles flailed for purchase, and then the thing disappeared over the edge.

"Geronimoooo!" Buffy shouted after it.

Thud. Splash.

"We're down to one," Buffy said, "unless they've whipped up some reinforcements in their secret goop lab and beamed them down from Planet Nimboo."

Blood gushing from her cheek, Faith nodded, "And that last one's mine, Captain Janeway."

"You sure?" Buffy asked, narrowing her eyes and wrinkling her nose as she observed Faith's awesome blood loss.

"Sure as I am that one of the SOBs broke the little bottle of Chanel Number Five in my jacket pocket."

"In your pocket?" Buffy echoed.

"Yeah, what? You can't smell it? I swear, I reek like a hooker."

"But I thought you said you didn't have any money," Buffy blurted.

"Duh," Faith retorted. She wriggled her fingers. "Five-finger discount, B. Try it sometime, when you aren't rich. Like, never, in your case."

Before Buffy had a chance to respond, Faith disappeared into the fog. Buffy realized her arch was bleeding more heavily, and she pressed her palm over it to stanch the flow.

Man, she shoplifted, Buffy thought, not loving that. *I was right there and I didn't see her do it.*

Meanwhile, Faith got down to business. Faith's grunts came from her gut; her fists pummeling the last creature in a harsh, lightning-fast, jackhammer rhythm.

Then the thing flashed past Buffy, arced over the cliff, and smacked against the rocks jutting from the sea. This one screamed; then it whimpered, and then either death or the ocean overcame it, and all Buffy could hear was her own breathing and Faith's semimaniacal laughing.

She is one weird chick, Buffy thought. The degree of intensity Faith brought to her slaying was blistering compared to Buffy's slam-bam get the job done, move on, go shopping. Shopping defined as actually paying for things. When Faith fought, it was all she did. She didn't worry, she didn't strategize, plan ahead—none of it. There was a sort of purity in her unvarnished lust for the kill.

Faith staggered up to Buffy. The fog swirled and

eddied with her movements, thinning into wispy membranes of moisture and light. Faith's clinging black top was blacker still, and clinging more because it was wet with blood cascading down her chin. Her black leather pants were none the worse for wear—unlike Buffy's boots—and she walked with the swagger that usually made goat-boy Xander's eyes pop out.

Buffy felt significantly more ordinary in a pair of dark gray pants, a maroon T-top, and a belted white vinyl jacket. And the ruined black boots, of course. Her hair was in a ponytail held in place by a black-and-gray scrunchy, and she wasn't wearing much makeup. A trace of glimmer on the cheeks from the mall. That and some lip gloss were her Slayer glam for the evening.

Good thing we haven't run into Angel, she thought, even though it wasn't, really. She'd been hoping to see him all evening. So far, no go.

"We rock, girlfriend!" Faith cried. "Jeez, one minute you're trying on lipstick and the next, we've got lip-smackin' red blood all over our mouths." As if to prove her point, she wiped some of the blood off of her face with the back of her hand. "Were those things wicked-ugly or what?"

"Or what," Buffy said, smiling faintly at Faith's exuberance. Faith was the one who lived for the battle. Buffy just wanted to live.

"Think there are any more?" Faith pressed the meat of her hand against her cheek. "Man, I hope I don't get a scar. Or maybe it would look cool there. What do you think, B?"

"I think we got them all," Buffy said. "And as for the scar, I'm thinking you might need stitches. Me, too. One of them got my foot."

"So, trip to the emergency room?" Faith suggested.

"The last med student who sewed us up was pretty sweet. Told me to be more careful when I was handling dangerous equipment." Her chuckle was lusty and she made eyes at Buffy. "And speaking of dangerous equipment, maybe we could get your undead boytoy to thread us the catgut."

"Faith, Angel is not my 'boytoy,' " Buffy said stiffly, limping along with as much dignity as limping would allow. "Or a med student. And he doesn't own any catgut." She hesitated. "I think."

"And I'm not sure he's really gotten over me trying to kill him," Faith added thoughtfully as she moved her shoulders and cracked her knuckles. "He might sew some of my stuff shut just for the hell of it."

The dark Slayer dabbed her face with her increasingly wet T-shirt. "You know what? I'm starving. If we go down to the E.R., we'll have to sit in the waiting room for five or six hours. The caf will be closed and we'll be forced to loiter around the vending machines. I am just not in the mood for candy bars and breath mints. Let's just bag a stapler and go for fries afterward."

Faith lit up, which was a freaky sight with the blood all over her face. "With lots of bacon bits and gooey cheese on 'em."

Buffy made a face that she hoped was currently less terrifying than Faith's. Sometimes when she got home, she was startled by the number of bruises and cuts she found on her body. Sure, rapid healing and all, but injuries still took their toll.

"Fries with bacon bits and gooey cheese. I'd almost forgotten to cross them off my list of food I will never eat again, thanks to Baffle buddies."

"With jalapeño chilis, too," Faith added, smirking. "You're such a lightweight, B. You'd never survive in

Boston. We eat weird crap stuffed into animal intestines and call it all kinds of fancy names. Like 'sausage.' "

"Faith, be realistic. You're covered in blood, and my boot's sticking to what remains of my foot. I'm not sure this is how I want to turn boys' heads at the mall tonight."

"So we go shopping first, and get us some fashions that don't scream 'we're so violent we belong on HBO.' You've got the momstercard, right?"

"For emergencies only," Buffy drawled, then sighed as she squished along in her destroyed footwear. *Brand new boots getting ruined by upside-down ice-cream-cone demons from hell constitutes an emergency, right?*

"Aw, shucks," Faith riffed.

She shrugged and kicked with her boot tip at a clump of ice plant stretched across her path. Buffy thought with sorrow of her snail homicide. The good news was that her foot still stung but the amount of blood gushing from it was slowing to the mere speed of whitewater rapids. Slayers truly did possess remarkable powers of healing.

Which we need, seeing as how often those of the bad try to kill us.

"Plus, mall's probably closed by now," Faith observed. "What about your house? Your mom's got good credit and a fully stocked first-aid kit. And a fridge. And, hey!" She snapped her fingers. "Last time I looked, there were frozen fries in the side compartment and a block of Velveeta in the dairy section."

"Oh, my God!" At the mention of her house, Buffy made a face and slapped her forehead. "Willow!"

"You totally forgot about your sleepover," Faith said. Buffy was surprised Faith knew about that. She also wondered if Faith was hurt that she hadn't invited her to spend the night with her and Will. In spite of the fact that the two Slayers spent so much time together, they didn't do much actual socializing except at the Bronze, at least so far. Faith was still pretty new in town, and she had no friends, no money, and no car.

Maybe she'll steal one, Buffy thought uncomfortably. *Or hot-wire an ATM.*

"About that," Buffy began.

"I never can stand to sleep at other people's houses," Faith said easily. "Waiting to use the john, worried you're waking up too early. Trying to find the coffee. I'm glad I've got my own place."

If you call a depressing room in a run-down motel a place, Buffy thought. Still, she was relieved that Faith had basically opted out of being included.

Will and I need some one-on-one time, she thought, *and to be honest, I need some away-from-Faith time.*

She pretty much wears me out.

"It's only eleven. That leaves you gals all night to stay up and dish," Faith continued. She shrugged and shook her head, smiling brightly at Buffy. "Don't worry, girlfriend! We just took down half a dozen monsters, Buffy. You think Willow's going to hold it against you that you're late on account of that?"

Buffy sighed. "I told her I'd be home early."

"So what's she gonna do to you? Break up with you?" Faith snickered. "She'll take one look at us and all will be forgiven and forgotten."

"Yeah, okay." Buffy limped on down the path. The fog was thinning, revealing the picturesque details it had hidden from view: a couple of empty beer bottles on the left side of the trail, some cigarette butts, and a squashed Diet Coke can. On her right, the sand stretched, a dull, moonlight yellow that met the foamy scallop of the incoming tide; then jet black darkness extended into the night horizon.

The moon hung low and weathered, like an old paper lantern, and the stars around it were the color of an old man's hands. Four silver points close together hovered for a moment; Buffy assumed they were airplane lights.

She watched them idly as Faith chattered about something funny that Xander had said, which reminded her of a boy she'd slept with, and Buffy listened with half her attention.

The lights didn't move. Then suddenly, one separated from the others, falling incredibly fast, and disappeared into the sea.

"Whoa," she blurted, interrupting Faith. "Did you see that?" She pointed to the sky.

The quartet of stars was no longer there.

"What?" Faith scanned the darkness.

"Shooting stars, I guess. Four of them, only first they just hung there. I thought they were airplane lights. Then one of them burned out or something." Buffy considered. "Gilesworthy, do you think?"

"No clue. My Watcher saw portents, like, everywhere." Faith was quiet for a moment, as if in respect for the dead.

Then she slid Buffy a sly glance. "Speaking of joy, did you make a wish?" When Buffy frowned, puzzled, she elaborated, "You're supposed to wish on a shooting star. I'm guessing with four, whatever you wish for you get quadrupled." She chuckled. "If you can stand that much happiness."

"I wasn't even thinking about Angel," Buffy said, then realized she'd betrayed her thoughts. Faith snorted and Buffy sniffed, retreating back to her posture of her limping dignity.

"Four, four, four boytoys in one," Faith chimed.

"Gross."

"Give it up, B. You'd love it." She wiggled her eyebrows. "Hey, girlfriend, don't knock it 'til you've tried it."

"Oh, like you have," Buffy said.

Faith kept grinning.

"Oh." Buffy couldn't help her shock.

"Hey, you gotta share the love, B."

"That's not love," Buffy said, sounding stuffy, even to herself. But it *wasn't* love.

"No. It's better," Faith retorted. She burst into laughter and ran down the path, her arms spread wide like a kid. *Like the kid she should still be. She sure works overtime to be Miss Trailer-park Trash. And I sure don't understand why.*

"I'm the fastest! I'm the best!" Faith chortled.

"Yeah, yeah," Buffy gruffed. "Dream on."

She limped behind, by the light of the wrinkled paper moon.

Chapter Three

See the White Eagle soaring aloft to the sky,
Wakening the broad welkin with his loud battle cry;
Then here's the White Eagle, full daring is he,
As he sails on his pinions o'er valley and sea.

—EDGAR ALLAN POE, *A Campaign Song*, 1844

Rupert Giles was not in his cups. His walk was steady and his senses were keen. He had taken one neat, one only; and a nice single malt at that, in the closest thing Sunnydale had to a pub.

Despite the excellence of the whiskey, however, the bar had been a bar, with throbbing music and furnishings of cold glass and sleek chrome; nothing homey or publike about it. Nor was it in any way conducive to conversation or camaraderie, the main attractions of a pub. Tonight he would have loved to talk—about ideas, and art, and whether or not he and Jenny Calendar should marry. But it had not been the proper place, nor the time. No one in the bar had cared two wits about oil paintings or marble statues.

And his Jenny was dead.

Stuffing his hands in his pockets, Giles walked the fog-choked streets of Sunnydale. It was Friday night, and he still had on his librarian tweeds. Upon occasion, his condo was too quiet for him. He was an Englishman in exile, the British Watcher currently charged with the care of not one, but two living American slayers.

He had been sent to Sunnydale two years before, in anticipation of the Slayer's relocation from Los Angeles. Merrick, her first Watcher, had been killed. Buffy Summers herself had been thrown out of Hemery, her L.A. high school, ostensibly for burning down the gymnasium.

Buffy had detested moving to Sunnydale as much as Giles had. At sixteen, it was rather a lot for any young girl to properly handle, much less a Slayer who had been inadequately prepared for her destiny.

The petite blonde was in no way a typical Slayer—she had friends, lived with her mother, and not to put too fine a point on it, had had no interest in being the Slayer whatsoever. She had never heard of slaying before she was chosen, and all she wanted was a normal teenage life centered around boys, shopping, and gossip.

When she and her mother moved to Sunnydale, she had thought she was free of the entire affair.

Alas, that was not to be. She was a Slayer, and would be until she died. Or so Giles assumed . . . now that there were two Slayers, it did make the future unpredictable. Technically, Buffy had died, which had called another Slayer—Kendra. Kendra had died, thus calling Faith. Now Faith was in Sunnydale, with Buffy and him, and who knew what that meant? The Watchers Council was still trying to puzzle it out.

Giles began to climb the hill and stopped halfway up. He turned around, surveying the horizon, his gaze sweeping the landscape below. The cool air was bracing.

A matrix of orderly city lights twinkled in the fog. Sunnydale seemed like such a pleasant place to live.

But looks are so deceiving.

"Oh, little town of Sunnydale, how you lie," he murmured. "So . . . innocuous. Unremarkable. But you're the mask the monster wears."

People walk their dogs here in Sunnydale, as if nothing's amiss. But you lie in wait, beneath a shroud of darkness spun of starless nights and death. Evil chokes your harbor and presses down hard on the gravestones of the dead and the restless. It sneaks into tombs and takes up residence among moldy bones and mildewed grave clothes.

You lie; you are the lie that things are as they should be. But the shadows devour them all—dogs, and cats, too, and high school students and toddlers. Vampires rule the night, rent apartments, and play in garage bands. Demons congregate at Willy's Alibi, trading information for shots of rather nasty gin.

You lie in wait. For my Slayer, Buffy, and the new one, Faith. I know you want them. Your voracious appetite and your evilness lust for their destruction. You can't wait to taste the souls of the Slayers.

I shall never let you have them.

A wind whistled sharply. Rupert Giles drew his houndstooth jacket around himself as the fog swirled around him, caressing his cheeks and clutching at his ankles; he could almost hear mocking laughter at his ear. As in London, ghosts lived in the fog of Sunnydale, and they could not be dispelled with one shot of single malt, neat, or a bouquet of roses on a carefully tended grave—Jenny's grave, his first stop this evening.

"You shall never have them," he said aloud.

The fog clung to him, and the wind laughed softly. He almost heard the words:

But I took Jenny. And her roses are already beginning to fade into moonlight.

"Jenny," Giles whispered.

Eyes welling, he glanced upward at the stars. Almost directly above him, an unusual cluster of four lights moved together as they crossed the sky. *Airplane lights,* he thought, *or helicopters.*

Or something else. He checked his watch; it was just about eleven. *I'll check my books, see if there's anything about autumnal star groupings.*

Then one of them flashed with ice-blue brilliance, plummeting toward the ocean.

A wind whipped up. Giles cocked his head as the sharp, bitter breeze slapped his cheeks. His hair was ruffled, his clothes tugged at. Dark gray clouds scudded across the sky, choking the moon.

To his right, storm clouds gathered; a bolt of lightning issued from the base of a thunderhead, a jagged electric connection that disappeared behind a ridge. It was the Sunnydale National Forest.

Like the fuse leading to a powder keg, a row of distant pines ignited, one after the other, washing the night sky with an orange glow. As Giles watched, more and more trees went up.

Giles stayed no longer. He hurried home to alert the fire department.

Books and stars, for the moment, forgotten.

Chapter Four

Willow bolted upright as loud voices startled her awake.

"Lucy?" she called softly.

Alone in the Summers living room, she put her hand to her forehead as if she could keep the rapidly dissolving fragments of what might have been a simple dream from dissipating altogether. *Did I dream about Lucy Hanover and some other Slayer? Were they trying to contact me?*

But it was no good; Buffy could remember her own dreams, but not Willow. She'd never been good at it, despite the fact that now that she hung out with Buffy, dreams had taken on a sense of importance. She slid off the couch and followed the noise into the kitchen. Buffy and Faith were there, Faith in some kind of "fear me, I wear black" getup and Buffy, very fashionable as always in white vinyl and otherwise dark colors.

I don't get why Cordelia rags on the way she dresses, Willow thought. *Just because Buffy doesn't kill vampires in designer clothes doesn't mean that she dresses . . . like me.*

Joyce was bustling around the girls. The two were extremely disheveled, both covered with blood and slime. Faith's cheek was bleeding badly, but except for bruises and scratches, Willow saw no major damage to Buffy.

Pushing her hair out of her eyes, Buffy hurried to Willow, saying, "I'm so sorry. We got cornered by these demons—well, actually, not cornered, but we had to fight and—"

"What happened?" Willow asked.

"It was the Baffles," Buffy told her breathlessly, laughing. "Will, they *do* look like ice cream cones."

"Did," Faith cut in, grinning. "We took 'em out." She gestured a one-two rock-em sock-em at the air.

"Oh, good!" Willow clapped her hands together. "You have to tell Giles. Well, in the morning, because it's really late."

"I know." Buffy grimaced, crossed over to the sink, and unrolled the kitchen towels. "I am so majorly sorry about the sleepover, Will. As usual, Sunnydale Video will make a mint off the movies I did not get to see. Is it my imagination, or do the forces of darkness seem to actually know when I rent vids, thus ensuring I waste my hard-earned money?"

She wrinkled her nose and glanced at her mother. "Big slip of the tongue there. My mom's hard-earned money."

Joyce, Willow noticed, was not smiling. She looked ashen, and she had been crying. Willow was even more confused. When had that happened? While she was asleep on the couch? Had she said something that had hurt Joyce's feelings, or frightened her?

Faith noticed, too. She blurted out, "Jeez, who died?"

Buffy fell silent and stared at her mother. All three girls waited anxiously. The problem with being one of Buffy's friends was that a lot of people did die, and some of them were people Willow knew and cared about.

"Mom?" Buffy demanded, in a frightened, pleading voice. "What's wrong, Mom?"

Willow watched Joyce Summers visibly calm herself down and pull herself together as she gently approached her daughter. Buffy's mother took her child's hands in hers and gazed into her eyes. Buffy paid attention now. Wordlessly, Willow kept watching. So did Faith.

If it was Oz or Xander, she would have told me right away, Willow reminded herself. *Or Cordelia. Or Giles.* She was panicking. *I've lived here all my life. I know so many people, despite being a social outcast and a computer geek.*

"Buffy, Irma Hernandez called," Joyce began. Her lower lip was trembling and her eyes began to well. She inhaled sharply.

"Mom," Buffy blurted, as if to keep her mom from continuing. "Mom, um . . ."

Mrs. Summers swallowed hard. "Oh, Buffy, Natalie was very sick. I didn't know. No one else knew. But she'd been in the hospital for a long time. And she . . . she died tonight, honey."

Silence fell, thick and suffocating. The kitchen clock ticked. Outside, a car backfired. A dog barked, and another answered.

Nobody I know. Willow's relief was overwhelming, but so was her guilt. By the stunned, blank look on Buffy's face, Natalie was someone very dear to her.

Awkwardly, Willow sat in one of the kitchen chairs. Faith, her legs crossed at the ankles, leaned against the dishwasher, wet paper towels pressed against her cheek. Blood was leaking into the wet clump, spreading like a rose. She looked more curious than anything else.

Buffy began to cry. The tears rolled down her cheeks and she moved away from her mother, her friends, everyone. She stood beside the sink, sobbing.

No one spoke. No one moved.

"Hey, we all gotta go sometime," Faith muttered. Still holding her wad of bloody paper towels, she turned abruptly and headed for the door. Before Willow realized what was happening, Faith was gone, leaving the kitchen door ajar.

Willow got out of her chair. She went to the door and looked out.

Spotlit by a neighbor's patio light, Faith was loping through the backyard and into the fog. Willow stood in the doorway as a chilly, misty night breeze swirled across her face and lifted her hair. Tears stung her cheeks.

What if the call had been about Faith? she thought. *Or Buffy? About if she was . . . if she . . .*

Unable to complete the thought, she shut the door and came back into the kitchen. Buffy and her mother had their arms around each other. They sobbed together for several minutes. Buffy's head was on her mother's shoulder and Joyce's arms were tight around her.

After a time, Joyce walked Buffy toward the living room. They shuffled along like two little old ladies.

Awkwardly, Willow followed behind. Mother and daughter curled up together on the couch and wept. Their mutual sorrow rose around them like a wall, and Willow kept her distance, respectful, and feeling out of place.

"Natalie's my best friend," Buffy sobbed. "My best friend in all the world. She's . . . she . . ."

"I know, honey," Joyce Summers murmured gently as she held her daughter. "She was a lovely girl. The nicest girl in the world. It's horrible that this happened."

For a time Willow stood, feeling entirely invisible. Then she went back into the kitchen and made herself a cup of tea because she didn't know what else to do.

She opened an art magazine on the kitchen table and stared at a shiny color photograph of some broken plates. Her heart was thudding.

Every time I think I'm used to all the death, it finds a new way to scare me, she thought. *Because I had a dream, which I don't remember, but here we are, with someone dead, someone the Slayer cared about, and that usually means it's more than just the dying. And the dying is plenty.*

In fact, it's way, way too much.

"Hey, Will," Buffy said, coming up behind her. Her eyes were swollen and her nose was red.

"You want some tea?" Willow asked her.

Buffy blew her nose on a piece of tissue and nodded. Willow got another cup out of the cabinet and put the kettle on. Buffy took lots of sugar, so she checked the bowl.

"She was a friend of mine back in L.A.," Buffy began. "We were on the squad together. Natalie was the captain."

Squad, Willow processed. *Captain. Cheerleading.*

Willow nodded. "At Hemery."

"Yeah." Buffy swallowed hard and looked lost, as if she had no idea what to do next. The kettle whistled, and Willow dropped a peppermint tea bag in the cup while Buffy, moved to action, took the lid off the sugar bowl and got a spoon out of the drawer.

"I didn't even know Nat was sick. She used to be my best friend, and I didn't even know she needed a liver transplant."

"Times change," Willow croaked. That sounded cold, and not for the world was she lacking in sympathy. "I mean, maybe she didn't want you to know. There wasn't much you could do to help her."

"I could have done something." Buffy heaped sugar in the tea and stirred it. "Given her a liver."

"You only have one," Willow said gently.

"Oh. Yeah. Kidneys, two. Lungs. You'd think I'd remember stuff like that, with all the ripped-open dead bodies I've seen." She gestured to her cup. "Besides, with all this sugar, she probably couldn't have used mine. If I wasn't using it, I mean."

Buffy carried the cup to the table. As she sat, she ran a hand through her hair and grimaced big-time, looking very miserable and forlorn as she picked up a paper napkin and wiped some of the goo and blood off herself. "I'm so gross."

"You look okay." When Buffy frowned skeptically at her, Willow shrugged and added, "On the scale of grossness, you're, well, actually, an eight or nine. Taking that into account . . . you look okay."

"She should have told me." Buffy's voice was thick with hurt as she wadded up the napkin. She put it beside her on the table and brought the tea cup to her lips. Making a quick face, she pushed back her chair and rocked back on the legs, reaching for the sugar bowl, very much not paying attention to anything she was doing. "Confided in me."

She looked at Willow. "I mean, am I wrong?"

Willow thought for a moment. "It's confusing when you feel helpless. When someone you care about is in danger, and all you can do is sit and worry, maybe it's better not to know what they're going through."

But I don't believe that.

"So maybe she was trying to spare you," Willow concluded.

"I guess. But I was her best friend." Buffy added the additional sugar, tasted, and put the sugar bowl on the kitchen table. She exhaled heavily. "I just hope . . ." She looked at Willow, stricken. "I hope she didn't suffer."

Willow said, with all her heart, "Me, too."

They sat for a while, staring at their cups. Willow's mind wandered to the many times Buffy had risked her life to save hers; to all the girl-gossiping, first about Xander and then Oz, and of course, Angel, to the cookies they'd baked and the monsters they'd killed. She felt small and mean to be even the tiniest bit jealous of a girl who had not shared any of that, and never would.

"Where'd Faith go?" Buffy asked suddenly. "Maybe I should have asked if she wanted to stay over with us."

Willow stifled a reaction. She had decided she didn't like Faith all that much. She wasn't sure the other Slayer was that good an influence on Buffy. Faith was really wild and extremely cynical about men. Plus, she'd dropped out of high school. In Willow's world, that was incomprehensibly wrong.

Ashamed, she swallowed down her discomfort and said, "I don't know what happened. She just took off."

"I'll go by her place tomorrow," Buffy said. She gave her friend a rueful smile. "Some sleepover, huh? I'm sorry, Will."

"Oh, that's okay," Willow assured her. "Friend of Slayer, you know." She pursed her lips together and smiled. "I'm good for the hard times."

"I know. Thanks." Buffy leaned her chin on her hand and stared back down at her tea. "It's just . . . I mean, I know people die. I see it all the time. But if she can die . . . " She trailed off, her eyes ticking toward Willow, as if to gauge if she was boring her or bothering her. Willow tried to convey her sympathy and willingness to listen, and Buffy sighed pensively.

"Miss Calendar was the first, really. I mean, you know, we've lost friends. There was Jesse, right when I got here. I didn't know him all that well, but you did. There've been others, too."

Willow ventured, "Angel."

Buffy nodded. "I thought I would die when I killed him." She looked hard at Willow. "I really thought I would. In a way, I did."

"I know," Willow replied.

Buffy moved her shoulders. "If I did, I mean for real, if I died, there would be another Slayer."

But there wouldn't be another Buffy, Willow thought. *Oh, please, Buffy, outlive me. Outlive all of us. You're the best we've got.*

Only, be real old when you do it, okay?

They sat together for a while. Willow said, "Did your mom go to bed?"

"Yeah. Don't know why. She won't sleep. When my parents split up, Irma was there for my mom. Really there." Buffy looked defeated. "This is the stuff I can't do anything about."

"Not beating anybody up about," Willow agreed. "But your mom and you have a bond over this. You're here to help each other with the grief."

"I suppose." She smiled sadly and said, "Go on to bed, Will. I'll be up in a little while."

Willow blinked. "No, it's okay. I'll stay here with you. In case you want to talk."

Buffy gave her a look. "You were starting to doze off."

"Nuh-uh." Willow blinked. "I'm wide-awake girl."

"Yes, you were. Your eyes were closing. I'll be up in a little bit." Buffy drank her tea. "I want to be alone. Do a little thinking."

Willow gave in, though her protective instincts clamored to stay by Buffy's side. "Okay. See you upstairs."

"Don't forget. You've got the bed. I'm on the air mattress," Buffy reminded her.

"And you've got Mr. Gordo," Willow replied. She took her tea with her, rose uncertainly, and looked at Buffy as she left the kitchen. The Slayer's eyes were unfocused. Her tea cup was cradled between her hands.

She's remembering a dear friend, Willow thought. *Someone who was her best friend, once.*

Like I am now.

She climbed the stairs, wishing Buffy would follow. But the Slayer had her own thinking to do, and Willow was very tired.

Angel stood in the shadows outside the Summers home and watched Buffy at the kitchen table. She was lost in grief, tears rolling down her cheeks. Yet the Slayer's fists were clenched, ready to take down the enemy if it dared show its face.

Silently Angel moved to the back door and stood, raising his hand to knock. When she saw him, he opened the door and crossed her threshold. After he had been cured, she had invited him back into her home.

And her life.

Buffy rose and moved to him. The tall, dark-haired vampire enfolded her in his arms, and Buffy wept soundlessly against his chest. His unbeating heart bled for her in this hour of darkness, no matter the reason. He was there for her, completely, no matter what she needed from him.

"Buffy, what's wrong?" he asked.

"My best friend. Oh, Angel, she died."

He was confused. "But Willow's here. I saw her go upstairs."

"Oh." She grimaced apologetically. "Natalie used to be my best friend back in L.A. She and I were so close. Back then, anyway."

She grew wistful, wandering back to earlier days, happier days. "We used to do everything together. Shop, skip gym."

I wonder if she was on the school steps the day Whistler took me to see Buffy, Angel thought. *One of those shallow young girls, obsessed with boys and makeup and being popular. The superficial kind of person I was when I was a living lad, back in Galway.*

Before I was turned.

"Before I became the Slayer," Buffy added. She laid her head back on his chest.

She didn't need to finish the sentence. In his own life, he had to leave so many people behind. He always thought he would get used to it, but he never had. He was glad his heart no longer worked. That way, it could never break.

Her voice dropped. "There was so much I couldn't tell her once Merrick and I started training. And the slayage."

"And then you had to move on."

Buffy looked up at him, anguish and hurt constricting her features. "No. She dumped me," she said bluntly. "She told me that best friends never keep secrets from each other, and if I couldn't tell her why I was acting so bizarre, then it meant I didn't trust her."

Angel thought, *Then she wasn't a very good friend, much less a best friend.* But he didn't give voice to his thoughts. Buffy needed a shoulder, not a lecture.

"Angel, why do people die?" she asked, clearly not expecting a reply.

Why do they live? That was the question he wanted answered.

No answer came; but sometimes he wondered if when he knew that, he would find peace. He had no idea why he lived; why he had been brought back from a hellish dimension and given back his soul. He wasn't even sure if he had the right to look for an explanation. After everything he'd done, every crime and sin he'd committed, he had no right to ask for anything.

Which was why he was so very, very grateful for the love Buffy freely gave him.

So he kept his silence. Instead of trying to comfort her with empty platitudes, he rocked the Slayer in his arms. She was smeared with something that reeked of demon, as well as the warm, passionate scent of her own blood. Her heart was beating quickly, the rhythm speeding up the longer he held her in his arms. Her muscles were supple and pliant; her stomach contracted as she moved past her grief and into desire.

For him.

Her lips grazed his chest. Her arms began to hold him rather than to be held by him. He couldn't help but be stirred; he would never forget their single night together. They could never have that again, but that knowledge did nothing to dampen his desire.

Then he felt her stiffen in his embrace, and he was sorry for the tension that always existed between them now. They could never be one again, or he would lose his soul; they both knew that, and accepted it, and yet the yearning was always there, on both their parts. He knew Buffy loved him, and he knew she wanted him.

"She was so young," Buffy continued, her voice hoarse and strained. Her powerful fingers gripped the folds of his black duster.

To me, you're all so young. And you, most of all, Buffy Summers. If you live to be a hundred, you'll die way too soon.

Quietly he held her, not speaking. He didn't know what he could say that could possibly make things better. Despite his many years, he had no profound wisdom about life and death that he could share with her.

Buffy seemed to sense that. After a time, she sighed and broke their embrace.

"My mom said something," she said. "She was talking to me about how Irma still had Nat's brother." She looked up at him. "How does that make it better?"

"Maybe she meant that Irma's not alone," Angel said. "She has someone to comfort her."

"Oh." Buffy looked troubled. "I thought she meant that if you have more than one kid, you can somehow automatically transfer all your love to one of them if you lose the other."

"No."

She took that in. Sometimes he forgot that the world was still very new to her, despite all the killing and struggle.

"You're not alone, Angel," she said suddenly,

sounding very wise as she gazed into his eyes. "You have me."

"Yes," he replied. "I know."

But it was, in many ways, a polite fiction between them. She could not be his; he knew that. And yet, in some ways, she would always be his.

Perhaps because he would always be hers.

Until my dying day.

Chapter Five

It was easier not to say anything.

So when the guy Faith was dancing with decided to get fresh, she kneed him without a second glance and left the floor as he groaned and dropped to the floor.

Her boot heels thumped on the sawdust-strewn floor as she walked to the scarred varnished table where he'd parked to buy her her fries, then asked her to dance. Legs wide apart, she stood in her tight black leather pants and the black sleeveless leather vest she had changed into, and finished off his beer. There was a bit of change on the table, couple quarters, a dime, a rash of pennies. She left it for the waitress, who deserved a lot more for working in a dump like this—and for needing to—and picked up his pack of cigs.

"Hey, hey, that's my last pack!" he half-shouted, half-pleaded, one arm flailing in her general direction.

He was doubled over and it was pretty clear by the expressions on the other pool-playin' beer-swillin' guys in the bar that no one was going over to help him. Faith's former groper was a young, cut biker, bandana and biker boots and a chain through his wallet, and no one else wanted to get near his bad self. His reputation had preceded him, north, south, east, and in the pool room, the minute he had walked through the door: *Bad news, worse temper, great right hook.*

It had been a rush to dance with a guy like that, daring everybody else to shake their booty straight at danger like she was. Plus he was still good-looking, had all his teeth, and some awesome tats.

"Last pack?" She tsk-tsked. "Then I guess you're quitting," she called over her shoulder.

The juke box was pounding out something fierce and sexy, the name of which escaped her. She sauntered toward the exit to a couple of hoots and appreciative grins from the guys the biker had terrorized during the night.

Also the bouncer, stocky dude with a goatee, who gave her an appreciative once-over and said, "You want a job?"

"Got one," she shot back, grinning at him. "The pay sucks, but there're some perks."

"Such as?" he drawled.

"I work alone and I got no one to answer to."

Back on the dance floor, Fred Astaire was still moaning as she left the dive known to some as the Fish Tank and to others as the cheapest place in town to numb yourself out. You wouldn't solve any problems at the ol' Fish Tank, but you wouldn't mind so much that you had them.

The Fish Tank afforded every man, woman, and child with a fake I.D. a cheap drunk; maybe afterward, your old man would still be cheating or your kids would still be ravin' on Ecstasy; maybe you still wouldn't have a job or a best friend or anybody who would fall apart if you died.

But you wouldn't care.

At least not as much as when you first walked in.

Stomping outside, she was surprised to discover that quite a storm had worked itself up—*same as me*—and it was windy and rainy and cold. And her without a jacket or an umbrella.

Who cares? I can take the elements. After all, I'm from New England.

Faith crumpled up the pack of cigarettes and tossed them into a crusted-over oil barrel she guessed might want to be a trash can. A disheveled shape lumbered out of the shadows and dove its arm into the can, rummaging for whatever treasure the black-clad maiden had just relinquished.

Peering through the rain, Faith hung a left into an alley that reeked of motor oil and tires. It was a short cut from the Tank to the main drag, which led to her home-not-so-sweet-home, the lovely Sunnydale Motel.

All that room, you'd think Buffy and her mom would ask me to stay over, too, she thought. *Not that I would want to. I've got better things to do than put up my hair in curlers and rag on about what sluts the cheerleaders are.*

She moved through the alley, taking her time despite the weather, keeping her eyes and ears open not because she was in a really bad part of the bad part of town, but because she was a Slayer, and that's what Slayers do. Her earlier trip of the evening home to change had been uneventful, except for dodging the night manager. She was behind on her rent. *No news there.* Funny thing about being a Slayer; you got hazardous duty without the hazardous duty pay. As a matter of fact, you didn't get paid at all.

And the dental plan bites. . . .

Ah, there it was, the pitter-patter of footsteps behind her. *With any luck, some action.*

Faith didn't break stride, but she listened hard.

Probably about ten feet away, probably either two regular people or one four-legged thing.

She grinned. She was all worked up from dancing with dangerboy and it would be nice to burn off all the calories from the two orders of fries with cheese she had cajoled him into buying.

B. and Hopalong probably went to bed hungry, she thought derisively. *Wouldn't have the strength to kick ass if they needed to. And man, I need to. I've got so much adrenaline coursing through me—*

The footsteps halted. There was a pause. Then someone—*or something*—took the rhythm up on the rooftops of the ramshackle buildings on Faith's right as the rains came a-tumblin' down.

The Slayer chuckled soundlessly and got ready to rumble.

Then a shape leaped down at her, hurtling toward her as it uttered an ear-piercing, inhuman shriek. Faith's reflexes went into high-gear, processing immediately that it was trying to scare her into going flat, as she had done during the Baffle attack. So she ran with it instead, facing it as it dove, fists out, thighs taut, and rammed into it with all her juice.

It was a lizard-thing, about ten feet long, black-scaled with a massive, elongated head and a matching tail. Between the two ends was a back with ridged diamond-shaped plates finished off with quills. As she flung it backward, the quills released, shooting off in the opposite direction, that is to say, straight at her. She dodged them. The quills rat-a-tatted the aluminum siding and pierced a few rotten boards.

Just then, something—a burning arrow, an explosive dart of the incendiary variety, a gout of flame— whizzed where she would have been if she'd hit the mud, missing her by a mile. But it caught her dive-bombing adversary in the back as it tumbled head over claws, igniting it. Its shrieks were painful to hear, but Faith ran toward it and gave it a cannonade of sharp, hard kicks just in case its spine hadn't shattered into a dozen pieces of jagged, lizardy bone.

Her assailants were two tall, über-skinny vampires wearing leather jackets, muscle shirts, and low-slung jeans. One of them carried the weapon that had just killed their pet velociraptor. They were fully vamped out, throwing out major 'tude vibes of *"hey, we bad, um, until the sun comes out"* as they moved to take her, one circling left, and the other one going for her right.

She didn't give Vampire #1 time to reload or re-energize or whatever. She put herself on turbo charge and just flew at him, no hesitation, no fear; Faith was the extremest of the extreme and that was aces with her.

She ran into him so hard that #1 was flung back hard, smashing into some rusty aluminum siding with the greatest of ease. He lost his weapon as he went down for the count.

Faith dove forward and caught the weapon on its way down. It looked like a combination of a crossbow and a rocket launcher, and her forefinger found the trigger like a match finds a can of gasoline.

Whoomp! Vamp #1 went up like a torch.

Vampire #2 growled as she whirled around and got him in her sights. He ducked down, then straightened, pulling something from his jacket. It was a very cool-looking battle-axe, and as he prepared to throw it at her, it began to glow with magickal green energy.

"Wow, awesome," she said admiringly.

The vamp, however, cried out and let go of it. It clattered to the ground, zizzing and glowing. He dropped to one knee to retrieve it, but Faith beat him to the punch—so to speak—by diving through the air and sliding through to home, directly into him.

He fell onto his skinny vamp butt while she picked the weapon up, gave it a look-see, and tapped the handle against the open palm of her left hand. The magickal energy coursed through her, making her tingle like some dorky preteen with a crush on Enrique Iglesias.

It looked very demonic, the blade joined to the handle by a leering, bearded head of brass or gold. The single blade had a strange curve to it, like a butterfly wing, and the handle was crosshatched into a leathery, skin-like design.

Giles will wet his pants when he sees this thing, she thought merrily.

"Nice wood," she said, grinning at him as he crabscrabbled backward, then stumbled to his feet. He could go left, he could go right, but he stood still as if he knew she'd waste him the minute he moved. "Should dust you just great."

The lean mean chomp machine did not look too happy about that.

"I'll tell you who sent us," he offered.

"Okay," Faith said, slapping the handle against her open palm. She wasn't too thrilled to be holding a magickal axe that someone had just tried to throw at her, especially since it was giving her what amounted to a mild electrical shock, but hey, Slayer machismo and all that. "I'm listening."

"Tervokian," he announced, like this would be a crushing blow to Faith's morale.

"Yeah?" Faith laughed heartily. "Good old Tervokian. South Boston's answer to Michael Corleone."

In Tervokian's dreams.

And if the Corleones had been really ugly and very stupid demons.

The vamp nodded and blinked his eyes, his gaze riveted on the axe.

"What did you do to rate this job?" she asked pleasantly. "Did you get caught trying to boost his Corolla?" She looked down at the axe. "So, what is this thing?"

How could a vampire pale? But he did. "I don't know."

"Uh-uh-uh," Faith said, crinkling her eyes and wrinkling her nose. "No lying."

"I don't know," he insisted, shaking his head. "Tervokian told us to use it on you. That's all I know. I swear it."

"You swear it?" She chuckled, amused. "On what, a stack of *Necronomicons?*" She cocked her head as she checked out her reflection in the blade of the axe. She didn't look so great, but hey, streetlight and all. And at least she cast a reflection.

"Why were you supposed to use it on me?"

He looked puzzled. "To kill you." As if in, *Du-uh.*

That makes sense. He tried to do it before, in Boston.

"That's all you've got for me?"

She advanced. He retreated slightly to the left since going backward was no longer an option—chain link—and they made a semicircle, so that he was moving in the direction of the body of the lizard thing. His good buddy Mr. Dustpile was of the past by then, blown away by the night breeze.

The vampire glanced anxiously over his shoulder. "He said the axe would take you out. Guaranteed. We just had to cut you with it. Draw some blood."

"And so that's why the James Bond weaponry?" she asked, her voice dripping with sarcasm.

"Just to slow you down." He held out his hands. "Hey, I'm not lying to you. I got no reason, now." He tried to laugh but he couldn't do it. "You know, dudes like me, we like to live same as the next guy."

"Bummer that you're a stinking vampire, then," she said, her voice growing cold. "In other words, already dead."

He looked very worried, which, given his situation, was the first intelligent thing he'd done. Spilling his guts—so to speak—had bought him nothing. Maybe there was honor among Klingons, but between Slayers and vampires? No freakin' way.

Maybe he was beginning to realize that when he said quickly, "Hey, come on. I've told you everything."

"Oh." She raised her eyebrows. "Then I guess it's time for you to die."

He turned and ran. She ran after him, axe in hand.

He was fast. She was faster.

Then the door to the Fish Tank opened and whapped her in the face. At her speed, she let go of the axe, which careened backward over her shoulder, flying into the alley; then the door broke off at the hinges and knocked over the drunk who had stumbled outside. Meanwhile, Faith ricocheted backward onto her butt.

She hopped back onto her feet and gave chase, but the vampire was long gone. She heard the squeal of brakes and figured that was him, getting the heck out of Dodge.

The drunk who'd gotten in her way rolled over and groaned up at her.

It was Johnny Bravo.

AKA, her biker boytoy.

"Thank you, thank you very much," she flung at him.

"Oh, God," the guy replied. "Not *you.*"

Faith whirled on her heel and stomped back into the alley to retrieve the axe.

It was gone.

She looked left, right, and wondered if whoever took it knew what it was for. For the next few minutes, she hunted for it, but no luck. She returned to square one plenty ticked off, and not loving a mystery.

She stormed back to the biker, whose nose was bleeding, and grabbed his arm, hoisting him to his feet.

"Get up. We're dancing some more," she told the guy.

"Can I have a cigarette first?" he pleaded, swaying like a corn stalk. He undid his bandana and soaked up his nose blood.

Faith barked, "No."

"Okay." He shuffled. "My nose hurts. I'm cold."

She winked. "Don't worry, baby. I'll make you steam."

Wide-eyed, he let her push him inside.

Once through the door, she scanned the place, giving off as much attitude as she felt like. *Yeah, like the vampire would be sitting there waiting for me; or some homeless guy was gonna have the axe in his lap, "You drop this, miss?"*

She dropped the dork on a bar stool, figuring he was too drunk to do her any good. *Plus, disgusting.* She snapped an order to the bartender, who went to work, and started surveying the catch in the Tank.

So many sharks. Way too many guppies.

Where have all the mermen gone?

Just then, a cute guy made a dash for her and said, "Wanna dance?"

After Angel left, Buffy made sure all the doors and windows were locked against the heavy rains and started upstairs. A crash of thunder and lightning made her pause on the step, wondering if, like the fog, the weather was somehow significant.

She unpeeled her extremely gross clothing and took a hot shower. She was yucky with goo from head to foot; she didn't know how Angel could stand to kiss her. Smiling faintly, she remembered a time when he'd asked her not to kiss him while he was vamped out, and she hadn't even noticed that he hadn't been wearing his human face.

Love's like that, I guess.

Buffy finished her shower and toweled off. She slipped into something fleecy and pink and padded into her room. Willow was asleep, all curled up, and Buffy settled in on the air mattress.

I'm not going to be able to sleep, she thought anxiously. *I'm going to think about Nat all night.*

In less than five minutes, the Slayer was asleep.

Wanna dance?

Mark Corvalis was having trouble concentrating on the burn. He kept thinking about a certain little hotpants he'd met at the Fish Tank a couple of hours before, name of Faith.

Sopping wet chick had sauntered in with some drunk with blood on his chin, dumped him, and looked around like she half-expected someone to try something funny—throw her on the pool table, ask her to star in a porno movie; Mark couldn't exactly figure out what— and she glared at every man who stared at her, not that you could blame them, and hey, way she was dressed, she was insisting on it. All she had on was a sleeveless black leather vest cut halfway down to her hipbones, hip-hugging black leather pants, and boots. Lots of makeup, streaked from the rain, true, but she was the kind of chick who'd look super-excellent without any. Long, dark hair and a native tattoo around her biceps completed her total biker-babe look.

After she unloaded her previous companion, she'd told the bartender to make her something to drink; the bartender seemed not only to know her, but to be genuinely afraid of her, and he served her right away, no questions asked. The pool balls clacked and the juke went on, almost like she told it to, and she perked right up at Joan Osborne's "St. Teresa" and started dancing by herself.

Mark seized the moment, got to her first, asked her to dance. She threw back her head and moved her shoulders as she led the way to the dance floor. The black leather was tight and she knew it; throwing a grin over her shoulder at him, she let him know she loved it that he couldn't keep his eyes off her. She slammed her beer down on some dude's table without asking for parking privileges and grabbed up her hair as she started to dance, moving like a pro, frankly. She smiled at him, her big brown eyes making all kinds of promises, such as, he was not gonna go to sleep alone tonight. Wake up alone, sure, maybe. But that was hours from now, and he wasn't looking to get married or anything.

"Corvalis, do you mind?" asked the captain.

Mark stirred. The section of fireline he was supposed to be watching was whipping up a little too high, a thick bloom of flames gathering momentum and threatening to jump the ditch he and the other Sunnydale firefighters had dug to contain the blaze on this end of the forest.

He shoveled some dirt on the fire to cool it down, frowning at what had happened next with Faith. Man, she'd made *him* burn. Danced with him all night, gave him these looks, let him buy her drinks. And then . . .

"See ya." She'd turned to go. Just like that. And if he recalled correctly, she was swigging his beer at the time.

Fairly drunk and incredibly horny, he grabbed her wrist.

With a flick of that wrist, she decked him. The guys in the bar hooted as she whirled on her heel and sashayed away, never turning back as he tried to get to his feet. Damn, that had hurt. His knee was still sore.

But he couldn't stop thinking about her.

Shaking his head, grinning, he shoveled some more dirt onto the fire. The flames were still too concentrated, so he worked on his section of the line for a while, shoveling, getting sweaty, thinking about how after they got the blaze under control and he was back off-duty—this was his night off, and he'd had the bad luck to get paged onto the job while he was still at the Tank—he might go down to the bar again and see if she was still there.

"Corvalis!" shouted the captain, and Mark jerked and looked up; then he cried out and tried to jump out of the way.

Not only had the fire grown, but a tongue of flame

about twenty feet high was arching upward and curling back down, headed straight for him. As he dodged to the right, the flame actually changed direction with him; he gave a shout of fear and lost his footing; he went down on his right elbow, which made a terrible grinding sound.

Then, in the middle of the flames, a figure appeared. Taller than a normal man, it was outlined in black flames, like a surreal silhouette. It seemed to hover in space, and its feet slid along on top of the tongues of fire.

It was completely wrapped in moldy, filthy strips of material. It was a *mummy*.

"What?" Mark cried.

"Get back, you idiot!" his captain shouted.

The mummy came straight at him. In one hand, it carried a box, the weirdest looking box Mark had ever seen, with skull designs and—*oh, my God, they're not designs, they're real!*—in the other hand, it held a carved axe.

He grunted in pain, holding up his left hand to ward off the fire. But it dove right at him, like an entity with a mind of its own; as he screamed, it hit him full force in the face.

He was not aware of pain, not at first; it was more like a strange, white-hot pressure. There was no sound, just a buffeting.

Then the awful pain rushed in, and he could hear his own voice screaming as if from very far away; he could feel that he was holding something in his left hand, which he couldn't see, but he was moving it very quickly.

Lie down, lie down, so they can smother it out, he told himself. But he couldn't stop thrashing and screaming. The world was on fire; everything was flames, except that they were black, not orange and red, not hot or cold; and he dimly understood that he was a human torch, and that he was going to die.

Because nothing hurt anymore; nothing. He couldn't see, couldn't hear, couldn't breathe.

All that was left was dying.

Chapter Six

The Slayer slept, and the Slayer dreamed:

Palms swayed in the hot, dry air. Winds blew the sands across the dune fields, pitting the trunks, scattering the few living creatures that could survive the hostile desert environment.

The air reeked of death, and the vultures that circled overhead mimicked the flight patterns of the buzzing flies.

The carcass was that of a girl; mummified by the heat, her body bore no distinguishing marks or characteristics. She could be any girl, or every girl; her skin the color of granite, her features shrunken. Her arms were crossed over her chest; in her brittle, clenched hands, she held four hand axes, two in her right hand, and two in her left.

The air shimmered with the wailing of invisible mourners as she lay alone beneath the sun, utterly desiccated. Winds rose and fell with the keening of women, a bass backbeat of male voices. Animals howled. Birds screeched.

Black smoke rose from the sands, thick and evil; then the dunes began to shake. The desert rumbled and shuddered; the winds gathered together like a single, killing breath and blasted the sands, hurtling the dunes one into another. They became concave, their humps thinning until they rose up, up, into the shapes of epic tidal waves, hovering at their crest, shimmying atop the wind as they promised to crash over the palms, and the dead girl.

Then all at once, the elements froze, in a static tableau of disaster. Earth. Air. Water. Fire.

Four identical earthen jars appeared at the dead girl's feet. They were covered with runic symbols and sealed with curses and waxed insignias: who opens these, invites total annihilation.

Inside one jar lay her heart. Inside another, her brain. The third contained her spinal column. The fourth, her earthly spirit, which was a shimmering rainbow.

There was a pool of water in the middle of a desert. There was something in the water.

As the waves hung and the sands hovered; as the earth stopped in midshake, a pool of water formed beneath the girl. It was bottomless; it was the bitter water of the River Styx, the river of death; it was the burning sea the dead suffered in; it was all the despair the drowning feel before their last bitter breath.

From the water, four gaunt figures swathed in strips of linen gauze rose straight up, unmoving, and perfectly dry. Without so much as glancing at her, they shouldered the body of the dead girl and began to glide across the desert. Their bandaged feet never touched the sand. Silent phantoms, eerily serene, they carried the girl away from the pool.

Then she began to tremble, and then to shudder. Like sticks rubbed together, she burst into flame. Her body cracked open like hunks of charred corn husks and water spilled out, splashing onto the sand, where it immediately evaporated.

The winds caught the fragments and hurled them up, higher, until they left the atmosphere to drift endlessly in cold, black space. Stars twinkled, and a voice said, Four stars, four.

There have to be four.

The four gaunt figures kept moving. There were no eyes behind their bandaged sockets. Unaware of their surroundings, they pressed forward. The sand beneath them was hot enough to melt glass. The howl of the wind was deafening, but there was no evidence of so much as a gentle breeze. The glassy dunes were undisturbed, even where the figures walked. Beneath the merciless sun, the sands rolled, waves of a forgotten ocean.

Strips of decayed fabric tightly encased the four, the cloth filthy and frayed, flies buzzing around it, and dozens of tattered ends fluttered in the blistering desert wind. Each figure was bandaged, head, neck, arms, and hands, but the torso and legs were draped with yards of mottled, webby gauze, deteriorated to paper-thinness in some parts, so that they resembled sagging sheets of cobwebs.

Each figure carried an object, its bandaged elbows at right angles. Long black fingernails protruded from each one's wrappings, fingers tightly clutching the object. They were boxes, horrible and revolting: made of dead faces, dead bones, dead skin.

There was a handprint on the lid of each one; as each lid was thrown back, winds roared out, blowing sand

and bandages into the air; an axe hurtled out of each and began slicing the sky into shards, which fell in ringing explosions, smashing to earth, to reveal a sphere, then spheres within spheres, then nothing, nothing at all.

The axes hacked and slashed, tumbling end over end over end over end, sharp and fatal. The sky was falling, the world was ending; and a voice shouted out, "The four!"

On the air mattress in her room, Buffy woke up, gasping. At the exact same moment, in Buffy's bed, Willow sat up and shouted, "India, come forth!"

Across town, another Slayer dreamed.

The bandages were on fire. The whole thing was on fire. The figure kept walking, a human torch; and it was carrying something. It was on fire, but it didn't miss a step, a beat—

—my heartbeat, Faith dreamed, *If it opens that thing, it's gonna stop my heartbeat—*

It had a box. There were faces of girls on it—Asian, black, deep brown and pinkish white—and they opened their mouths and screamed, many voices weaving into one. Faith covered her ears.

They kept screaming.

I know what's in it. In the warehouse, Tervokian—

Faith woke up fast, disoriented.

Damn, she thought, rubbing her aching head. She had a bad hangover. *What a wicked-bad dream. What about Tervokian? What was I dreaming about him for?*

She thought a moment. But her head hurt way too much for thinking.

Yawning, she saw the guy conked out next to her, the one she'd moved on to after Mark the Fireman had had to leave to go do his duty. Her current love interest—*ha ha*—was the Fish Tank's bouncer, and not bad in the bod department.

She took a look around at his ratty apartment with no windows and some very bad comic-book-type sketches of busty babes tacked on the walls, and thought, *Oh, well. At least this one had sheets on his bed.*

Maybe the next one will actually wash them now and then.

She got up and dressed quickly. As she headed for the door, she spotted a book lying next to a battered acoustic bass guitar.

There was something kind of poetic about the pairing of the guitar with the book, which was *The Collected Poems of George Gordon, Lord Byron.* She opened it up:

"So, we'll go no more a-roving
So late into the night,
Though the heart be still as loving,
And the moon be still as bright.

For the sword outwears its sheath,
And the soul wears out the breast,
And the heart must pause to breathe,
And love itself have rest.

Though the night was made for loving,
And the day returns too soon,
Yet we'll go no more a-roving
By the light of the moon."

It moved her.

So, big dreams, gets lost along the way . . .

Better dreams than mine, anyway . . .

Squatting, Faith strummed the guitar. It was horribly out of tune, and dust floated in clouds from the strings. He obviously hadn't played it in a long, long time.

"He's a freakin' bouncer, moron," she murmured to herself. "Not a rock star."

She tossed the book back onto the floor.

"Loser," she flung at him, and let herself out into the alley that was his front yard.

It was hours before dawn. Between the two-story buildings covered with unpainted aluminum siding, the rain had gotten worse. A strong wind was kicking pages of drenched newspapers and old magazines along the chain-link fence lining the loft structure where her white knight slumbered. It was cold for Sunnydale, especially Sunnydale in autumn. Faith wished she'd brought a jacket.

This is almost Boston-cold, she thought, frowning, as she rubbed her bare arms and walked along. She huffed, and her breath made a puff of mist in the icy rain. *Wrong. This is Boston-cold.*

The wind whistled, gusting, and the trash can to Faith's right slammed onto its side, releasing the pungent odor of coffee grounds and overripe fruit. A rat emerged, and the wind actually picked it up and skipped it along the gravelly ground like a stone on a river.

Faith had to brace herself in order not to be hustled along in like fashion. Her teeth chattered. Slayer or not, she was freezing. Her hair whipped around her head. The chain link clanged back and forth against its frame, and the trash can began to roll, slowly at first, then as quickly as a car, barreling along, likely to do some serious damage.

Faith ran after it, lunging forward with both hands to stop it. Something slammed into her butt and sent her sprawling over the can; instinctively, she tucked her head and turned her fall into a forward roll. The can rolled over her, causing pain but no serious damage, and coasted onward down the alley.

Gravel smacked the back of her neck and she slapped her hand against it as if she were squashing mosquitoes.

At the end of the block, she came across three kids a couple of years younger than she. One was a girl in a light black sweater, black belly pants, and Doc Martins. Her two guy friends had on T-shirts with Goth designs on them, and one was pulling a sweatshirt out of a backpack.

"Man, what's going on?" he asked Faith. "This is like the end of the world or something."

"There's a *Twilight Zone* about this," the girl chimed in. She pulled out a cigarette and a black plastic lighter. "The earth is moving away from the sun, and everyone is freezing to death." She flicked the lighter which, duh, did not ignite in the strong wind. "In the episode," she added, "not here. But I am pretty much freezing to death." She looked meaningfully at the guy who was getting out his sweatshirt.

He grinned as he slipped it on over his head. "Cool. The ep, I mean. The synchronicity with what's happening here."

"It's freaky weird," Faith said to the girl, who nodded as if to say *Yeah, but I'm used to freaky weird cuz I'm, like, so hip,* and cupped her hand around her lighter.

"I like it," the guy insisted, settling into his sweat-shirt, unaware of the daggers Tori Amos Junior was throwing his way.

Faith sighed, not because these folks were too strange—before she'd become a Slayer, she was like them, digging on stuff that carried with it the illusion of meaning something, plus self-centered—but because she had a hangover and wanted nothing more than a shower and her own bed—*and a toothbrush*—but hey, bad dreams and bad weather equaled an increased need to find Buffy and compare notes. Also, a trip to the G-man's apartment—Xander called the Watcher that, and Giles hated it—which wouldn't be all bad. The dude made good tea and he had a lot of sweaters.

I'll let 'em all wake up first, she decided.

"Okay, well, keep the keep," she said, giving them a head nod, because she knew from experience that people this tragically avant-garde did not wave buh-bye.

As she passed out of range, she heard the girl grouse, "Jeez, Alan, give me your sweatshirt, for God's sake. You pig."

Share that love.

Faith hurried on, eager to get out of the cold, when the lights went out.

Every streetlight along the street went black, and every neon sign and traffic signal and even lights that had been on in windows. It was pitch-black dark, and the moon was covered with rain clouds.

Wicked strange, Faith thought, as she hurried along.

Chapter Seven

Canetown Plantation, Jamaica

It's so windy tonight, Roger Zabuto thought, as the shutters on the old plantation house clattered and banged. He thought of the famous novel, *A High Wind in Jamaica,* and how it had ended in death for the main characters, pirates who had not committed the crimes for which they had been found guilty by a court of law. They'd committed others, though, and so their captain was content to be hanged, and his crew with him. Their sins led them to the gallows.

Mine lead me here.

He was drunk. Through the slats, the dark-haired man watched the waving cane fields. He thought of the Sargasso Sea, in the West Indies, famous for its murderous, thick miles of kelp beds, in which ships became entangled. Cursed and feared by sailors everywhere, the sea was a graveyard of hulks and men.

Like this hulk of a house.

Like me.

Despite the night—it was actually early morning—Roger Zabuto sat in the sweltering heat. He wore a loose white shirt and a pair of khaki trousers. On his feet were woven sandals. There was a single silver earring in his right ear. It was a black pearl, a gift from his cousin, Timothy, who was his only living relative. Timothy was an oceanographer who specialized in the Pacific Rim—California, Hawaii, Japan, Indonesia, Malaysia; the exotic places. Timothy was the last of the Zabuto male line, and not likely to pass the name along, as he was gay.

Maybe he'll adopt, Roger thought vaguely. *It's strange to think the Zabutos would ever die out.*

Strange to think that I'll die.

The cane fields rustled. Rats lived among the stalks of sugar; feral cats, too. In the old plantation days, Canetown had been the premier plantation on the island. The Zabutos had not been the original owners— that had been a white Brit, of course, named Jezruel Spaeth. Spaeth, a drunkard and an inveterate gambler, had lost the plantation to Roger's great-great-grandfather in a game of faro.

The plantation had thrived, despite the prejudice of the other plantation owners against a black man entering their ranks. But then Roger's father had sold most of the land, retaining only a few acres of cane. Roger devoted his life to training Kendra, and his cousin chose to become an oceanographer, and so the short-lived dynasty came to an end.

Maybe I'll start raising cane again.

He smiled grimly at his own weak pun and stared out the window. Lightning crashed in the lowering sky, and a sudden rain struck the earth like hammers.

In the black recesses of the ruined mansion, the madwoman, Mirielle LaSalle, shrieked and danced. As Roger sat in what had been the music room, he saw her dart across the passageway, her sleeveless white dress swirling. Her lush, black hair streamed behind, tangles of wild curls framing her chalk-white face. She was laughing now, spinning in a circle as she teetered down the hallway toward the nursery. Mirielle was his mad wraith, the residue of Kendra's battle with Baron Diable, the zombie king of the island.

Mirielle, one of the most beautiful women Roger had ever seen, had been targeted by the baron—also known as Simon Lafitte, a powerful businessman—to become the vessel for his mother's soul. The drums spoke of it for months, as moons waxed and waned. Mirielle begged the authorities for help, but they turned her away. The official reason given was the usual—the practice of voodoo, per se, was not a crime.

But Mirielle knew that no one wanted to help her because she was doomed. People from Kingston to Ocho Rios knew what happened to someone who crossed a voodoo master. Goats were not the only things left hanging in trees with their throats slit.

The desperate Mirielle went underground, hiding out in the jungle, depending on offerings of food left in obscure places by sympathetic people, most of them women.

Finally, she found Roger Zabuto, who served as Watcher to the Vampire Slayer, Kendra. Kendra was in America at the time, and Mirielle almost despaired of help. Roger hid Mirielle in his house.

But somehow Baron Diable discovered the whereabouts of his intended vessel. The moon was hidden that night, a night much like this one, and the vast, overgrown plantation fields Roger had inherited soon tangled the footfalls of scores, if not hundreds, of the walking dead.

Zombies stumbled through the thick, shadowed

night, mindless, speechless, soulless creatures that deadened the courage of Roger's security guards. Oh, a few of the advance phalanx of zombies were shot, but when the others shuffled implacably forward, trampling the corpses of their fallen comrades, it was too much for the guards.

They ran, leaving Roger to drag Mirielle through the house as fear overcame her and her madness began.

"Mon Dieu," she breathed, falling to her knees, "Roger, *s'il tu plaits,* kill me. Before they take me, make sure I'm dead."

But he could not. He had sworn to the Watchers Council of Britain that he would protect human life, and not shed human blood.

More importantly, he had begun to love her. She was warm and beautiful, clever and witty. His life as a Watcher had been like his Slayer's—isolated and lonely. Their mission was so sacred that all distractions were sacrificed—friends, family, company.

Now this beautiful woman was in his life. He couldn't bear the thought of ending that wonderful dream.

"Then give me a gun. Oh, my God, give me a knife!" she had shrieked, clawing at him in her terror. "I'll do it myself. I'll rip open my veins with my teeth!"

But it was too late. As he tried to find a place to hide her, the dead army of Baron Diable broke into the house. They never made a sound, never grunted, never sighed, never breathed. They simply walked.

In panic she bolted out the back door, sobbing and cursing his name as the zombies surrounded her. If it would have done any good, he would have run out to save her.

From his research, he knew there were elaborate rituals to perform before Mirielle's body was emptied of her spirit, and Tutuana's could invade it. He had perhaps two weeks, maybe three, before Mirielle would be lost forever. His hope was that Kendra would return in time to help him save her.

The drums celebrated the victory while Lafitte's mother, Tutuana, directed the brewing of the curare-based potion required for the transfer of her spirit into Mirielle's lithe body. It was complicated, and each step had to be completed perfectly. By the time it was finished, three of Baron Diable's most valued lieutenants lay dead, the consequence of their lack of attention to quality control: the potion had to be thrown out and re-created—under new management.

At last it was done. With great ceremony, in her finest robes and headdress, a necklace of rooster claws hanging down her chest, Tutuana drank her share of the potion. Mirielle's share was forced down her throat. It rendered them both catatonic.

In the rays of the full moon, Baron Diable, resplendent in black robes and a headdress of his own, oversaw the placing of Mirielle's body in a coffin layered with talismans and flowers, and sprinkled with the blood of dozens of offerings, both animal and human. The next step was to seal the lid and lower her into the earth.

The celebrants—many of them Simon Lafitte's well-heeled business colleagues and political cronies from around the world—toasted with champagne as the Baron's still-living followers sang and danced, leaping into and over fires and drinking the blood of yet more sacrifices. The zombies—hundreds of soul-dead men, women, and children—stared straight ahead, immobile, awaiting a simple command to stir them into a semblance of life.

The zombies were hideous, with mottled faces and slack musculature, lacking everything that distinguishes a person from a simple body. After a time, whatever animated them began to wear off, and their organs started to fail. They died slowly, on their feet—to the last, slaves of Baron Diable.

Some people claimed, however, that just before they finally stopped existing—they couldn't actually be said to die, not by then—their souls returned for the briefest of moments. It was the worst of all the horrible things which had befallen Baron Diable's victims, for in that moment they realized what had been done to them . . . and to remember everything Baron Diable had forced them to do: destroy, ruin, ravage, murder.

Mirielle was to be set apart: Baron Diable planned to rip her soul from her body at a different point in her transformation, and the physical process halted. Tutuana would take over the body, and animate it. It would not be truly living, but it would be more alive than dead. How vigorous it could be made to be would depend upon the force of Tutuana's will.

The voodoo priestess was as feared as her son. It was said she bathed in the blood of virgins to retain her beauty, which was still extraordinary, even at her advanced age and her poor health.

Kendra arrived home almost too late; Roger had filled her in when he picked her up from the airport. His hands shook with fear, both for Mirielle and for his Slayer.

"This is a deadly situation," he'd told Kendra.

And she had looked soberly at him and said, "Sir, they all are."

Roger had loved Kendra then, the way a Watcher should love a Slayer—as a samurai admires a fine sword, or a soldier relishes a precision sidearm. She was a well-honed weapon in the battle against the forces of darkness, and one he could take some credit in refining.

But in that moment—that dark midnight when she left to save Mirielle LaSalle—he had looked at Kendra's retreating form in the muggy heat and thought, *And what does that make her, but a zombie? Her every thought is for her calling. Her every action is to improve her killing techniques. She has no expectation of a normal life, nor of a natural lifespan.*

And what did I do to her? Roger Zabuto thought, as Mirielle danced mindlessly through his ruined mansion. He drank his rum and stared at the stormy cane fields, the vines and flowers dripping like raindrops over his field of vision.

I did nothing but prepare her for her destiny, he thought defensively. *Kendra was the Chosen One, and that was not my decision. She was called, and I was as well.*

Without me, she would have died much sooner.

But the insanity that was Mirielle LaSalle was a reminder that he had failed both of the women he cared for. Kendra had been quite young as a Slayer when her throat had been sliced open by the razor-sharp nails of Drusilla, a mad British vampire. Her attempt to save Mirielle had been one of her last major undertakings. It had been a terrible debacle, and he was certain that it had sapped her self-confidence. By the time she had left for America, he had already begun to mourn her.

The rescue of Mirielle was botched, and that was his fault. He hadn't done his homework. When Kendra fought her way across the field of zombies, dug her up, and plucked her out of the coffin, she should have had a means at hand to keep Mirielle's soul inside her body.

Mirielle's spirit left her body for two nights, while Roger worked to restore it. When he brought her back, something else crept inside her, and now she was quite insane.

Tutuana's soul was barred and forced to return to her own body. The great voodoo queen died a painful death soon after.

Her son's fury was uncontrollable. He killed a hundred and fifty innocent people by setting off a bomb in an open market. His grief was worse: he tortured animals, zombies, and living people, as if they could absorb his agony.

The rains poured down heavy and hot, and the wind was ferocious. Roger was drinking rum neat, and watching the gathering storm. He thought he heard footsteps.

He thought he heard death coming for him.

Or was it all the rum?

Maybe it's Simon Lafitte, he thought. *He's finally coming to get his revenge.*

I should call for help.

But his telephone was not working. Such was often the case on the ruined plantation.

I should get a cellular.

A presence startled him; it was Mirielle, who had somehow come upon him without his noticing. When he jerked, startled, she laughed. Her fingertips plucked at her gauzy dress. In the years he'd kept her safe—*imprisoned,* an interior voice reproved him—he'd bought all her clothes, her toiletries, and her food and drink.

He was fairly certain that somewhere beneath the

exterior craziness, she hated him for keeping her walled up alive.

"Do you like my dress?" she asked, twirling. "It was a present. From *her*."

He studied her face, not understanding, afraid to press her for details.

"She came from here. From our island. These are her roots," she confided. "She was a priestess, and they betrayed her. They sent her to him, to Taran. But she got even with *him*."

Does she speak of Tutuana? Does the old priestess live on after all, inside Mirielle?

With a broken sob, she began to dance again, bounding and dropping to the floor, springing back up. She whirled and whirled, arms outstretched, head back.

She staggered to an abrupt stop. "Roger," she said, out of breath from her frenzy, "the stars dropped out of the sky tonight."

"*Oui, mon amour,*" he said cautiously.

"I counted them. There were four." She waved her arms.

He regarded her with weary sympathy. "Were there?"

She nodded and touched her forehead. "The dead are speaking to me tonight, Roger. They are walking." She leaned forward. Her gaze was intense and filled with hatred. "They are saying, 'The Gatherer is coming.'"

Roger reached out a hand to steady her as she lurched to the right, grabbing his shoulder; she giggled, and the sound frightened him more than any of her pronouncements. She was filthy, and she stank, and she was the only human being on earth he had spoken to in three weeks. He had been desperately lonely, but he was too ashamed to go to town. The Watchers Council had invited him to London numerous times. He knew they were concerned about him, and they had a right to be. He was not handling the death of his Slayer well. Not well at all.

I should locate Christopher Bothwell, see how he's doing, he thought. *Last I heard, he'd become a beach bum in Southern California. Can't get over his Slayer's death, either.*

Mirielle rested her head in his lap. "Make the dead be quiet," she begged. "Tell them to hush and go away."

Roger stroked her hair and drank his rum, trying to figure out what the devil was going on. The cane fields waved like sailors' arms as the sea's new victims sank in the Sargasso Sea.

Life is a morass, he thought, *just too bloody much to contend with. We ought to initiate some sort of support group for Watchers who have lost their Slayers. It's rather criminal, actually, that we have nothing in place for this terrible situation. Of course, that's not at all British, is it, to wallow in one's sense of worthlessness? Best to keep a stiff upper lip, old man; best to show them the sterner stuff a good Watcher is made of.*

It's a wonder we haven't all gone completely mad.

He drank his rum and watched the cane wave at him. Roger watched the stormy fields, seeing shadows that shambled toward the house, seeing nothing at all; shadows of past lovers and friends, blurs of memories soaked in rum. He was astonishingly drunk.

And he and Mirielle were no longer alone. He sensed it before he really knew it; then slowly Roger turned his head, his lips parted at the strange image before him. He thought, *Am I so drunk I'm hallucinating?*

A tall figure swathed in strips of material glided two inches above the floor, oblivious of the obeisance

Mirielle paid as it floated toward Roger. The eerie figure was carrying a cube which appeared to be made of bits and pieces of human beings.

Twirling, Mirielle struck a pose, extending one foot in front of her body and draping her arms as if to display the creature like a prize package on a gameshow. In ringing, elated tones, she announced, "It's called a Wanderer, *mon vieux*. It's a messenger of the Gatherer and it's looking for a Slayer!"

The thing stood silently. If it looked like anything familiar, Roger would have called it a mummy. But it wasn't, really. It terrified him. *I thought I had given up on living. I thought I wouldn't care if I died.*

But I do care, very much. If it comes any closer, I'll start screaming. And I won't be able to stop, ever.

This is what happened to Mirielle. It was this kind of fear that made her insane.

Behind the figure and Mirielle, a man wearing a voodoo mask of painted wood posed on the threshold of the room in black, shimmering robes and a tall black headdress. Behind him, a throng of dark people with slack faces and hollow eyes stared straight ahead.

Zombies.

As he removed his mask and held it against his chest, the voodoo king of Jamaica, Simon Lafitte, strode grandly into the room. He regarded the mummy-like figure with great interest, circling it once, staring it up and down.

He looked at Roger. "You killed my mother viciously and cruelly. But something wonderful came of it. When my mother's soul was freed from her body, she went back into the past. She found the ancestress of ours who gave my family our power, and then my ancestress found me.

"Her name is Cecile Lafitte, and she is a powerful priestess of the Black Arts. She serves a dark god with her consort, and they seek to feed it Slayers, for which it has a most intense craving."

He stepped toward Roger. "We are looking for Slayers, old man. Can you tell us where we might find one? Or more?"

Roger fought very hard not to show his fear. "I'm no longer in contact with the Watchers Council," he said evenly. "When Kendra died, I retired. Now . . ." he indicated his tumbler of rum.

"You know many things about the Council. You wrote a diary. Which I have read." Lafitte's smile was wicked. "I have a friend on the Council. I know there are two Slayers, for example. Cecile's god will devour their souls."

"Then . . ." Roger murmured, ashamed at how his mind was racing ahead, trying to discern a way in which he might save himself; or at least, how he might cooperate sufficiently to be awarded a less painful death than the one Tutuana had endured. "Then why do you need me?"

I'm so weak, he thought, disappointed in himself. *I don't want to die at all.*

"This is a Wanderer," Baron Diable said, indicating the creature. "In point of fact, it is the Wanderer of the Earth. Did you know that Slayers can be divided into four elements? Kendra was of the Earth. Stolid and implacable. A worthy opponent."

"She was a Slayer," Roger said. His voice was strong, and he felt slightly more in command of himself. Perhaps remembering how fearless Kendra had been had inspired him.

"This poor creature has been searching for her for

years," Lafitte explained. "Its only reason for existing is to find the Slayer with whom it corresponds. Then it opens its little box, which you see, and takes out its axe, and hacks the Slayer to death."

Roger regarded the box in the thing's grasp. It seemed to be made of nothing but skulls and bones, and the top was glowing in the shape of a diamond. A bony handprint floated inside the diamond. As he watched, blue energy formed in a circle above it, and hovered chest-high.

"Here is the situation. Faith is a Slayer of Fire. And Buffy Summers is a Slayer of Air. My ancestress has been searching for the Axe of the Air, and happily, an associate of my Granddame Cecile claims to have it. But meanwhile, the Axe of Fire seems to have gone missing in Sunnydale."

Roger closed his eyes. He wondered if Faith, who had taken Kendra's place, was still alive.

"I can't help you," Roger said, growing cold.

Lafitte looked thoughtful. "I am in league with powerful magicians and sorcerers, and we're exploring all avenues to give the two living Slayers to Cecile Lafitte's god. It has a name, by the way. It is the Gatherer."

Mirielle clapped her hands. "She is speaking to me," she announced. "I hear you, Lady Cecile! You are beautiful!"

"I want you to get on the phone and call Rupert Giles," Lafitte said to Roger. "My Granddame Cecile says the portents indicate that the Slayers are ripe for harvesting. Sunnydale is being assaulted by disasters of fire and water, which means that the Wanderers of Fire and Water are homing in on the Slayers. If they have a storm, it will be that the Wanderer of Air has shown up. Our colleague will be able to arm it."

Baron Lafitte clapped his hands. The blue energy emanating from the box turned a brilliant blue-green. The sphere enlarged until it encompassed the entire box, and grew larger still to surround the draped figure.

Then it disappeared.

"The Wanderer of Earth should arrive in Sunnydale shortly," he announced.

He pulled a cell phone from the folds of his robe. "Call Rupert Giles. *Now.* Find out where the Axe of Fire has been taken."

Roger did not reach for the phone. Instead, he put his hands behind his back. He thought of Kendra, and though his eyes watered with fear, he clamped his mouth shut and began a litany: *For love of her courage, for love of her courage, for love of her courage . . .*

Lafitte snapped his fingers. The zombies walked forward. Roger Zabuto blinked, jerking visibly.

Among them shuffled Kendra's mother and Kendra's father.

"Ah, you recognize them," Lafitte crowed. "Perhaps someplace inside them is the desire to rip you apart because their daughter is dead. I know I would like to rip you apart because my mother is dead," the voodoo king hissed at him. "But if you'll call Giles, I'll kill you quickly. You have my word that I won't turn you into one of my creatures.

"If you call him now."

Roger tried to breathe. He couldn't make his chest move, and for a moment, he thought Lafitte had paralyzed him. Then the urge to inhale became overwhelming, and he realized it was sheer panic that kept him from drawing in oxygen.

The other man shrugged. "Take your time, Zabuto. Think it through. And while you do . . . " He took

Mirielle's hand. "I'll have this place searched. Perhaps you've started a new diary, or made some notes."

Roger ran for the window that looked out on the cane. He flung himself against the wooden blinds, was momentarily stunned, and hit them with his fists. Pummeling them, he began shouting for help. None would come, he knew. He and Mirielle lived alone on the plantation grounds.

When he had worn himself out, he turned back around to find Lafitte and the zombies moving toward him. The zombies were fanning into a semicircle, with Lafitte slightly in front of them. Mirielle stood beside him. Her eyes gleamed. Drool dripped from the corner of her mouth.

"You may begin," he said to the beautiful madwoman. He snapped his fingers and chanted in a language Roger did not understand.

Wearing a frightening grin, moving with the jerking awkwardness of a zombie, she reached into the bodice of her white dress. Her hand disappeared among the lace ruffles to her wrist. For a moment she paused; then slowly, she drew her hand upward. A thin line of red began to appear, then to darken and spread. She appeared to be unaware that she was cutting herself as she pulled a long, sharp knife from her dress. The blade dripped.

She advanced slowly on Roger. His heart bruised his rib cage. He swallowed, remembering her own terror as Lafitte invaded his house, searching for her: *Mon Dieu, my God, kill me, please.*

"I'm so sorry, Mirielle," he rasped.

Her eyes rolled back in her head. She swayed for a few seconds, speaking in the same language Lafitte had spoken. From inside his robe, Baron Diable produced a snake and held it up to Mirielle's ear. She laughed and continued to chant.

Then she opened her mouth wide; her tongue flicked out; it was black and forked, a serpent's tongue.

Mirielle closed her eyes. When she opened them again, they were reptilian, yellow and round, the pupils narrow, vertical slits. Her tongue flicked and she slowly trudged toward Roger, like a sleepwalker.

She lifted the knife above her head.

She said, "Know me. I am Cecile Lafitte. And I will give the Gatherer all the Slayers I can track down, living or dead."

"Can you be of any help to her?" Lafitte asked, with mock concern.

"No," Roger whispered. He crossed himself.

"Make the first cut, *ma belle,*" the Baron invited Mirielle. "You should have that pleasure."

Chapter Eight

"Well, that was pretty weird," Buffy said.

Willow took a breath and let it out slowly. "The fact that we had the same dream, or the fact that the dream itself was weird, and also that we had the dream that was weird?"

The moonlight spilled over Buffy's room, casting Willow's red hair with soft golden highlights that made her look almost like a different person. Buffy was beyond unnerved, and not just because she couldn't figure out what Willow had just asked her.

"What do you think the mummy guys stood for in our dream?" Buffy asked her. "And what about the clay jars?"

Willow blew her bangs out of her eyes. She was wearing an oversize Dingoes Ate My Baby T-shirt. She and Oz had only recently gotten back together, and Buffy figured Willow was being conscientious about showing how much she valued Oz's decision to trust her again.

"In ancient Egypt, when they mummified people, they took out the viscera and stored them separately, in canopic jars," Willow explained. At Buffy's blank expression, she added, "The guts."

Buffy grimaced. "Yum. Okay, Egypt theme. Are the axes Egyptian? What do you think they meant?"

"That we should live life because we never know when we will be chopped down by death, and time will stop for us?" Willow shrugged. "As a wild, um, stab?"

"Do not start with the stabbing jokes, Will." Buffy was seated cross-legged on the air mattress. "Also, you know, rainbows are not guts. One of the canopic jars had a rainbow in it."

"Symbolism," Willow suggested. "For um, optimism? It takes guts to be optimistic?"

"Or symbolism for rainbow sherbet ice cream?" Buffy asked. She gave Willow a questioning look.

"Absolutely," Willow answered. "It's gotta be the ice cream."

As one, they both stood. Willow stepped into her traveling scuffies and Buffy glanced around for her bathrobe, which she'd left over by the window.

"Before the weird dream we shared, I had another dream of my very own," Willow informed Buffy. "And I remember it," she said proudly.

Buffy looked interested.

"I saved Matthew Broderick from radiation poisoning."

Buffy flashed her a weak, lopsided grin. Her heart was still thundering, but the safety of reality was sinking in. No monsters here, no mummies. Just her very best friend.

"Was Matty grateful?"

Willow smiled in fond remembrance. "Extremely. So were our children."

"Your children?" Buffy drawled, amused.

"Twins," Willow said wistfully. "Redheaded girls."

Buffy glanced through the blinds, seeing nothing but the pine trees, the stars, and the streetlamp. A blue Chevy truck drove down the street. In the still night, a dog howled. Crickets scraped.

"You pick the strangest guys to dream about, Will," she said, reaching for the robe. "How come it's never someone current? Y'know, like Seth Green?"

"Plus we lived in Paris," Willow continued, belting her own robe. "Or maybe it was Hawaii. Anyway, gratitude was definitely involved. Chocolate, also."

"Nice dream."

"Yeah. And I remembered it," she repeated proudly. "Oh. And I had a dream on the couch, earlier tonight before you came home."

"Back in the good old hours, before I knew about Nat," Buffy murmured. She wandered back to the air mattress and picked up Mr. Gordo and played absently with his nose. "I like the Matthew Broderick dream better."

"Me, too," Willow said. "Less complicated plus, you know, smoochies and food."

"Smoochies, eh?" Buffy chuckled. "You didn't mention the smoochies."

"Hey, I'm entitled to some smoochie dreams," Willow insisted. "Just cuz, you know, Technicolor with Angel, doesn't mean the rest of us don't have fantasies. Which are dreams," she added hastily. "When I'm awake I am fantasy-free, and think only of Oz."

"Since . . . all the past has become more pastly, I don't dream as much about Angel," Buffy murmured. "Lots of my dreams are like knock-knock jokes, you know? After I get to the 'who's there' part, something of the bad's usually behind the door."

Willow nodded soberly. Then she gestured to the window and less-than full, yellow moon. "Sunday we were thinking of going to the beach to watch the grunion run. Oz is all done with the wolf-out for the month, so we're going to do lots of relaxy stuff. Wanna come? It should be major fun."

Buffy thought briefly back to a time when she, Natalie, and a bunch of kids from Hemery had gone down to Redondo Beach to watch the finger-long silvery fish wriggle through the wet sand, spawning their hearts out. That occasion had included a lot of laughing and a big bonfire, and Natalie's confession that after graduation she wanted to try out for the Lakers cheerleading squad.

Willow's hopeful smile became a bit uncertain. "Or do you have slayage with Faith on your calendar?"

"I think we killed all the Baffles, so it would seem some fun is in order." Buffy grinned. "Of the non-slayage variety, at least for me. Cuz you know, Faith thinks all that chop-socky is just a hoot."

Buffy's smile drooped. "Unless we have to go to L.A. Mom and me, I mean. They're having Natalie's service on Wednesday, but we might go up early."

Willow looked thoughtful, also faintly pleased. "That would be nice. People shouldn't be left alone when they're really going through something."

"Mrs. Hernandez still has Irma's brother Ernie," Buffy continued, examining Mr. Gordo. "So she won't be alone."

"That's true." Willow smoothed her T-shirt and pushed her hair out of her eyes. "She'll still have someone to fuss over. Remember when Mr. Gutierrez died, and we got Mrs. Gutierrez a puppy? That cheered her up."

Mr. Gutierrez had been one of the school's security guards. What Willow was avoiding saying, Buffy knew, was that Mr. Gutierrez had been vampirized on Faith's watch. Faith had not known that the vampires in Sunnydale could waltz into Sunnydale High whenever they wanted. There was a sign out front in Latin that welcomed anyone who sought knowledge. Loophole, but it counted.

She decided to change the subject. "Did you check out Faith's cheek? And can you say that three times fast? I wonder why she bolted out of my kitchen."

"Too crowded?" Willow asked.

"I think she figured I'd want to be alone with my family," Buffy said. "And she was right."

"Oh." Willow raised her eyebrows and her lips in her signature pleased expression. Buffy remembered the first few times she had tried to be friendly with Willow. The redheaded girl had been so used to being mistreated by popular girls that she hadn't honestly believed Buffy wanted to be friends. "So, grunion for sure."

"Grunions with onions," Buffy said. "Yeah. I'm most definitely in."

Willow smiled. "And thus we return to the subject of food, which means we still need the ice cream."

"We still need the ice cream," Buffy concurred.

They were quiet in the hall and on the stairs, which creaked anyway. Buffy led the way toward the kitchen, moving with caution once she realized that the light was on. She gestured to Willow to stay behind her. It would have signified a bit of overkill in just about anyone else's life, but to quote an old saying from the Slayer Handbook, just because you're paranoid doesn't mean they aren't after you.

"Oh, hi, honey. Willow," her mother said guiltily. A

carton of Ben & Jerry's was open on the counter, and Joyce had a bowl in front of her. A big spoon was raised halfway to her mouth.

"Got the nervous munchies too, huh?" Buffy said, coming into the kitchen. "Hope you didn't eat it all."

"I didn't," Joyce assured her. Then she added, "We had some Nutter Butters in the pantry."

"Mmm," Buffy said, headed there.

"Had," Joyce repeated.

"Oh."

Buffy changed course and walked to the cabinet. She got out a couple of bowls while Willow gathered the spoons. With the fancy scoop her mom had bought in a cooking shop in L.A., Buffy dug in, piling ice cream high in the bowls.

"Did you by chance have a dream?" Willow asked.

"No." She looked concerned. "Did I wake you two up? I called Irma back." She looked down at her bowl; her mouth clamped, a sign of distress. "Natalie asked to be cremated. Irma's not happy about that. The family's rather . . . traditional, I guess is the term. Catholics prefer to be buried."

She touched her forehead. "Irma told me that Natalie spent her last days planning her own service, just in case they couldn't get a donor."

"Oh," Willow commiserated. "Can you imagine what that must have been like?" Then she glanced at the two bowls in front of Buffy and said, "That's enough ice cream, Buffy. For all twenty-eight of us."

"Oh." Buffy had unknowingly created two leaning towers of Chubby Hubby. She gave them a couple pats to keep them upright; for good measure, she licked the ice cream scoop.

As she ran the scoop under the faucet, Willow put

the top on the nearly-empty container and returned it to the freezer. Willow's shoulders were hunched, a sure sign that Will had moved squarely into wiggins territory.

Buffy wondered if she could lure her back by assuring her that she, Buffy, had not planned her own funeral. Not even what colors she wanted.

Which, it being a funeral, would probably be basic black.

Frankly, she had always figured funerals were more for the living than the dead. *Unless, of course, you died from being bitten by a vampire, in which case you would be undead.* Having had a lot of experience with death, she wasn't exactly certain what happened to one once one died, especially if one were Chosen and all like that. But it didn't seem like anybody knew what their own funerals were like—*okay, zombies, maybe. And that's debatable because their brains are pretty much not there anymore. Or ghosts, they could know, unless they're stuck haunting where they were killed or can't leave the house or something.*

And maybe this is more complicated than I thought. Maybe I should plan my funeral.

Emphatically she shook her head. *As a Slayer, I can't afford to think about dying. Staying above-ground is the perfect shade for my amazing Technicolor dreamcoat, speaking of colors and what to wear.*

"What are you going to wear, honey?" Joyce asked her daughter.

Buffy gaped at her. "Huh?"

"To Natalie's service."

"I hadn't given it much thought," Buffy replied, smiling reassuringly at Willow. But Willow was already carrying the bowls to the table.

"Funerals. Who plans for them?" Buffy asked, seating herself.

"In many cultures, people prepare for their deaths all their lives," Willow said. "It's not at all unusual to plan a funeral service. Look at the ancient Egyptian pharaohs. Their pyramids took years and years to build."

"That's right." Joyce nodded. "I just read an article about mourning wear during the Civil War. They had large wardrobes of black gowns and special jewelry made out of the hair of the deceased. There were even quilts with tombstones on them, and when someone in the family died, their tombstone was moved to the center of the quilt graveyard."

"I think it's Indonesia where the widow has to sit with the body for something like three years," Willow continued. "The village has to construct an entire village for her husband's ghost to inhabit."

Suddenly I'm feeling like a slacker, Buffy thought. She dug into her ice cream.

Buffy's mother looked thoughtful. "I think that's somewhere else in Southeast Asia. But you could be right."

"Will there be cake?" Buffy blurted. "At the reception?"

"Buffy," her mother said reprovingly, "how can you ask such a thing?"

"But . . . " Buffy protested. *Clothes okay topic, food not.* "I'll wear something black," she said decisively.

"And not too revealing, all right, dear?" Joyce asked.

"I don't suppose you'll sit shiva," Willow ventured. "We sit with the body, you know. Only, not for three years."

"It's a lovely custom," Joyce replied. "I'm sure it

gives the bereaved a lot of comfort, to have friends and family gathered around."

"It's supposed to, anyway." Willow made a face. "It's actually a little bothersome."

"What do you wear?" Buffy asked.

Willow took a thoughtful bite of ice cream. "Something conservative. Dark-colored."

"Not too revealing," Buffy added authoritatively.

"Never." Willow wore her earnest face. "Some of my relatives are Orthodox. They wouldn't even wear short sleeves to a funeral."

"Then it would be a bad deal to have someone die in Reseda in July," Buffy mumbled.

"Also?" Willow continued. "We don't embalm people."

"Ewww." Buffy looked first at her friend and then her mother. "How come we can talk about that stuff, and not cake?"

Despite staying up until almost dawn, Willow woke early. She tried to get dressed quietly and leave the Summers home, but Buffy caught her and herded her back inside. "What are you doing?" she asked like a stern mom. "We'll drive you home."

"It's no big deal, Buffy," Willow said. "It's really early and I don't have to be at the bat mitzvah for hours yet. So I have plenty of time to walk it."

Buffy was not pleased.

"Willow, no way. Besides, Mom will want to cook you some pancakes because you always tell her how good everything is and I'm an ungrateful wretch who wolfs them down, belches, and then retires to the couch to watch the big game with my hand in my pants."

"I've never said you were ungrateful," Joyce said, coming down the hall in her bathrobe. She was smoothing down her hair, which was in serious bed-head mode. Even when Mrs. Summers was disheveled, Willow thought she was one of the most beautiful women she'd ever seen in real life.

"But you have said I wolf them down," Buffy countered.

"Maybe once I said that." She looked at Willow. "The problem with daughters is that they hold a grudge."

Buffy turned to Willow. "The problem with moms is that they never forget anything."

Buffy and her mother started bickering gently, nothing worth paying attention to. Willow was relieved that the heavy sorrow of last night had not followed them into the sunshine.

After the breakfast dishes were done, Buffy, Willow, and Mrs. Summers dressed and trundled into the SUV. Chatting about this and that—Joyce about the art gallery, Buffy about getting some new boots—they headed out for Willow's house. Willow sat up front with Buffy's mom, watching the familiar scenery while Buffy begged her mother to change the radio station from easy listening to something "from this century, and also, from the Earth planet."

"Neil Diamond is still trendy," Joyce countered.

"Oh, Mom, please. At least turn it down. It's humiliating," Buffy whined. She was leaning from the backseat into the rearview mirror, putting on some lipstick.

"Will, this is your color. Most definitely," she said, smacking her lips and examining them.

Willow gave her a look. Buffy was always trying to get her to "accentuate her beauty." Which was her nice way of encouraging her to visit a makeup counter more often than once every two years or so.

"I think Willow looks charming the way she is," Joyce said. "Fresh and natural." She smiled at Willow, who smiled back. "When I was your age, we either wore tons of makeup or none at all. There wasn't much in between."

"Just try it," Buffy insisted, tapping her on the shoulder. "If you don't like it, we'll give it to the poor."

"Okay." Willow reached for the lipstick, but Buffy let go before she had it. It tumbled down the front of Willow's pink sweater and thence between her feet to the floor of the car. "Whoops. I'll get it."

"Sorry, Will," Buffy said. "I'm all butterfingers. I missed a perfectly good kill last night, too, I am so mortified to say."

"You be careful, honey," Joyce said quietly. "Wow, it's getting foggy all of a sudden."

"Mom, you know I always am," Buffy replied.

Willow unbuckled her seat belt and bent over, snaking between the console and her knees. The floor mat was black and that made it hard to see anything. She fished around with her fingers.

"Where is it?" she muttered. "I don't see it anywhere. Buffy, did it roll back there?"

"Mom, look out!" Buffy shouted.

That was the last thing Willow heard before the crash.

The Book of Twos

Prologue

In the Desert of the Arabias, A.D. 1200

Sallah ibn Rashad understood now why he had not been buried up to his neck in sand and left to die. It was a far worse punishment to be sent to this forsaken burrow of a town, and made to act as physician for the repugnant human refuse who inhabited it.

The city walls had long since fallen into disrepair. The local pasha, son of a son of a son who had proven himself a bold and merciless conqueror, was a dissolute man who cared for nothing more than his hookah and his harem. Through the broken-down streets of my lord's "kingdom"—a warren of filthy mud hovels, populated by degenerates, thieves, and low, common women—talk of King Suleiman's assassination was rife. But that was all it was, mere talk. No one wanted to bother with the murder of such an ineffectual prince. He did no good, but he committed no ill.

"Let sleeping dogs lie," the people said.

They came to ibn Rashad for toothaches and labor pains, and open sores that an occasional washing would have prevented. They stank and they had no teeth. They had precious few brains, and their entire economy was built on graft and corruption: remove bribery, and there would be little commerce at all.

Sallah ibn Rashad wanted to thank Allah for sparing his miserable life, but misery kept him silent. He had been banished from the now-distant Court of the Great Suleiman because of his interest in magick. Though the sultan surrounded himself with astrologers and diviners, Sallah was not of the proper caste to toss bones and read bloody entrails. If the jealous magicians of the court had known he could conjure the dead and speak to demons, they would have murdered him while he slept. But that much, at least, had remained a secret.

Now, as he waited for the next miserable patient, in what surely was the town's most magnificent home, but was to him tangible proof of his downfall, he thought of the young maiden who had betrayed him. Ceceli was her name; a veritable *houri,* a dewy young thing presented to him by a grateful landowner named Taran. Sallah had cured him of gout, and the man had paid him in gold and jewels, and Ceceli, his most prized possession.

"She is from another land," Taran had explained. "One I've never heard of. But the people there are a lovely brown color, and her hair is a heavenly mass of curls, and her blood is hot."

Perhaps for the landowner, she had been thus. When Sallah approached her, she wept bitterly and begged him to leave her alone.

He had never been so insulted in his life—and by a woman!—and he informed her that he would have her whipped and sent back to Taran, who would hear of how she had disgraced him.

"I have no doubt that he will cast you into a pit and let you starve," he added.

Awaiting the next caravan back to the landowner's

vast estates, Sallah grew careless. He conjured Hilmesh, a demon, a brilliant, if evil, creature with whom he enjoyed a game of chance of an evening. Ceceli saw Hilmesh, stole evidence of ibn Rashad's work in the Arts, and packed them into the saddlebags of the lead camel when the caravan finally arrived.

When he put her in the palanquin, he thought she seemed eager to leave, which was odd, since once the caravan reached their destination, she would certainly be put to death.

However, once she revealed his conjuring, first to Taran and then to King Suleiman himself, she was rewarded with her freedom, an estate, and a handsome bridegroom of aristocratic breeding. It was he, Sallah ibn Rashad, who then awaited execution!

But the insufferable girl came forward one more time, and begged the sultan to exile him to a faraway land, where his magick could be put to good use. Without guile, she told ibn Rashad she had interceded on his behalf because he had not forced her when she begged him to stay away.

"For this kindness, I have begged my sovereign for your life," she explained, filled with her self-importance.

"You honor me," ibn Rashad had replied. He kept his hands in the sleeves of his thickly embroidered robes so as not to lunge at her and strangle her to death, right on the spot.

And now she had her slaves, and her palace, and her status while he lived no better than a beggar.

I will have revenge, he thought. *I will repay her one day, and she will die screaming.*

As he walked into his private office, arrayed in robes he once would not have clothed a slave in, his weathered, dull manservant wafted a censor of fragrant smoke at him in preparation for the arrival of his next patient. The smoke cleansed; it also perfumed. But nothing could really obliterate the stench of the disgusting wretches who contaminated his walls.

"Well?" ibn Rashad said to his man, who was very old and very grateful to have a floor to sleep on and scraps from his lord's table to eat. He had come with the house, and the only reason Sallah had retained him was that he had a beautiful granddaughter who came to visit now and then.

"Your Honor, your next patient has come from a great distance. He travels with a retinue and at least one concubine, to keep him warm on these cold desert nights." The old man leered.

Despite his elation—*finally, I will once again entertain a person of quality!*—ibn Rashad felt queasy at the notion of this toothless fool in the throes of carnal ecstasy.

"Why did you not inform me of this sooner?" he demanded of the creature. "This house is hardly prepared to welcome a man of means and taste!"

The man pressed his tremulous hands together and *salaamed.* "I apologize most abjectly. Who knew that the winds of Allah would blow such a fortunate into the path of Your Honor?"

He had a point. *Still.* "Make haste. Where he is? Prepare something to eat. Something decent." Again, his senses were assaulted by the mere thought of his serving man touching food, but these were the circumstances under which he now lived, and he must make the best of them.

If I ever see that woman again, by Allah, I will gut her.

The doddering ancient bowed low. "Honored and

esteemed master, his servant sent ahead a runner. That one tells me that his master is near death, and has struggled to stay alive only in hopes of help from you."

"I see." Ibn Rashad was amazed, and profoundly curious. *Who could this man be?*

Just then, the heavy velvet and silken hangings parted from the mosaic archway.

It was Taran. Though ibn Rashad had last seen him only three years before, the landowner had aged horribly. The middle-aged man was now an old man indeed, bent with infirmity. He tottered forward and leaned against one of the intricately decorated columns.

"Sallah ibn Rashad," he wheezed, making an attempt at a *salaam.* "One hundred thousand apologies for this intrusion. But I am quite ill, and you cured me once."

Ibn Rashad frowned at the swaying heap of fine velvet robes. "You have the temerity to come to me for help, when you nearly caused my death?"

The man's hands trembled. "Prolong my life, and I will give you all I have." At that, he clapped his hands; they were so thin and brittle that ibn Rashad half-expected them to snap off his wrists.

A woman stepped forward, her luxurious veils completely concealing her appearance; from the crown of her head to the curves of her golden sandals, she was concealed. Gauzes and delicate gold tissue hid even her eyes. But sensuality radiated from her, and ibn Rashad was speechless by the attraction he felt for a female he could not even see.

"This one has kept me alive, with elixirs and potions handed down in her family. But she has done all she can. She begged me to come to you, in order that you may restore me. If you succeed, I will extol your virtues to Great Suleiman, may he reign forever in

mercy and compassion, and give you all my lands and
my place in the Court."

He nodded to the woman, who reached up her hands
and pulled down her veils. It was Ceceli, more beautiful and desirable than ever before. He thought to himself, *How could I have condemned her to death? How
could I have sent her away?* He was mesmerized by
her; fascinated. He could barely think as he surveyed
her modestly covered form. When she had come to him
the first time, she had been dressed for pleasure, and he
knew what lay beneath those wifely robes.

"Her young husband died soon after their wedding,"
Taran filled in. "She is unprotected, and she offers herself in marriage to you if you will help me. As her lord
and master, you will be doubly welcomed in our homeland."

Ceceli lowered her head, then looked up at ibn
Rashad through her kohl-rimmed eyes. He swam in a
thick pool of heat. Perspiration broke across his brow.

"Is this true?" he asked her.

She dipped her head. "If you already have one or
more wife, I will gladly take my place beneath her in
status," she said meekly.

"She betrayed me," ibn Rashad pointed out to Taran.

"In order to save her own life," Taran replied.

Then the landowner began to cough. Soon the spasms
racked his body, and Ceceli guided him to a carved
ebony bench, upon which he sat very slowly and
painfully. Light shown down upon his face from a brass
lantern whose sides were cut into geometric shapes.
Taran's features were lost in wrinkles and the skin hung
down in slack jowls on either side of his mouth. If he
could see, it was but poorly. His eyes were milky.

Ibn Rashad examined him, using percussion against

he man's bony chest. What he heard there confirmed
his initial diagnosis, as well as the man's prognosis:
death, within days, if not hours. Ibn Rashad was bitterly
disappointed, but he avoided the urge to lie. There was
nothing to be gained from it.

"You have the consuming disease, and you are going
to die very, very soon. I cannot cure you."

"Of course, great physician," the man rasped, without a trace of irony. "That much I know. My hope is
that you can prolong my life."

Ibn Rashad was confused. "That is up to the
mercy of Allah, may His Name be revered throughout the ages." He *salaamed.*

"I ask only that you give me time enough to travel to
the Pool of the One Who Gathers and Preserves," Taran
continued.

Frowning, ibn Rashad pulled on his beard. He had
no idea what Taran was talking about. He looked to Ceceli for an explanation.

"We have heard of it at Court," she said. "It is an
oasis of healing deep in the desert." Her gaze was
steady, but she leaned forward, as if willing him to ac-
knowledge the truth of her statement. "Do you not
know of it?"

"No," he said frankly.

She looked markedly shocked, even disappointed.

Taran frowned at her. "Foolish, useless woman," he
snapped. "You told me he would know!"

Clearly flustered, she moved her hands. "I thought I
understood . . . I must have misheard . . . " She looked
to ibn Rashad, and again, he was fired by her beauty.
He would do anything to help her.

"Great one," he said to Taran, "I pray you, come
into my home and rest. You have traveled far. Let me

consult with this woman, and with my books, and see what I might deduce."

Taran had slumped. He looked half-dead. Listlessly he waved a hand and said, "Oh, very well."

"We must make good use of our time," Ceceli said to ibn Rashad. Her eyes grazed him, and her lips turned up in a secretive smile. Ibn Rashad reeled.

"I shall do what I can, but I, unlike the God of Everything, can not perform miracles."

So Taran was put to bed, barely in his right mind; he muttered something about needing his potion and Ceceli set about at once mixing powders and pouring them into a glass of mint tea. He drank it down and fell into a deep slumber.

Ibn Rashad reached for the glass, wishing to examine the contents. She held it out toward him, but it slipped from her delicate fingers and shattered on the tiled floor.

"Ah! A thousand apologies," she murmured.

"No matter." He took her hand. "You may tell me the ingredients."

As her master slumbered, she unfastened one hook, and all of her robes fell to the ground, revealing her form by the light of brass lanterns.

"Later," she whispered huskily.

And he had her, this wild tiger of a woman, in whom all the passions of Paradise dervished and simmered. Skilled lover that he was, he made her sigh and cry and hold him, weeping his name, cherishing his presence. The delight he took in her arms was unbelievable. Never, ever in his life, had he been pleasured as with Ceceli.

The stars glittered through the wooden window shades as he lay drained and exhausted beside her in his great bed. His eyes were half-open, and he barely registered her movements as she climbed down from the bed and walked to the window. She opened the shade and peered out across the desert.

"Where I come from, I was a queen," she said to him, her gaze steady on the stars. "A priestess."

"How did you come to our lands?" he asked her.

"As a captive. A prisoner of war." Her voice was low, angry. "I was gotten rid of."

A *political coup,* he thought. "It is just as well," he told her, admiring the length of her warm brown back, her long black hair cascading over her shoulders and swaying over the center of her back. "Women should not be compelled to govern. It's most unfair to put that kind of burden on them; they are not created for such things."

He looked at her exquisite form, then cast an eye at the stars. Puzzled, he stared at their configuration; he knew the constellations as he knew his own name.

These stars are not in their right places, he thought fuzzily, as they drifted through the still, warm night. One by one, they took up new positions, until they were almost an angled line descending toward a place on the horizon. *There is something quite amiss with the universe.*

"The stars . . . " He was very, very tired. "They're moving."

"They always move," she said brusquely.

"They're wrong."

As he dozed off, he heard her laugh deep in her throat. He was certain that he heard her say, "You are a fool."

But in the morning, when he questioned her, she told him sweetly that she, too, had gazed at the stars, and found nothing out of place with them. She insisted he must have dreamed the entire episode. Also, that she had spoken at all, she must have said, "We must find the Pool."

In the morning, ibn Rashad checked on his patient, who seemed somewhat improved. He was surprised; he had half-expected the man to be dead. He was more interested than ever in learning what Ceceli had given him.

She shrugged. "Herbs that grow in the palace gardens," she said simply. "My cook selects them and grinds them into powder."

She handed him a small glass box filled with what appeared to be common sand. He was bewildered and intrigued. But this interesting oddity would have to wait until his patient had been either restored or lay dead.

"He is well enough to travel," Ceceli decreed. "We should leave today."

If no other reason than to remind her that he was the physician, not she, ibn Rashad snapped, "He is not. A journey would kill him. He needs to recuperate from his journey here."

That night, Ceceli was a wanton, a veritable harlot, and as ibn Rashad lay gasping on his back, she slipped from the bed and crouched beside a beautifully carved wooden box he had not noticed before. He had no idea how it had come to be in his bedroom.

He sat up, watching her. She smiled and took off the lid with great ceremony. Then she reached in, first with one hand, then the other, and held up a one-bladed axe.

It was clearly ceremonial, and not made for actual combat: the handle was exquisitely wrought, showing the head of a demon. Ibn Rashad was taken aback; it resembled his demonic gaming partner Hilmesh to great degree. He looked at Ceceli to see if she was aware of that fact, but her smile remained the same as before.

From the opened windows, starlight hit the axe and sent vivid, glowing rainbows across the whitewashed walls of the bedroom. They swirled and eddied, and he knew magick emanated from the weapon. As he observed the rainbows, one transformed into the image of fire, flickering in space high above his head; a second whirled and dervished—fierce winds; a third showed him rain, a most uncommon sight. Then the fourth gathered up his bed and lifted it from the carpeted floor; it shook the massive bed violently, until ibn Rashad was forced to shout, "Stop it!"

At once, she put the axe away.

She said to him, "There are four of these axes, Your Honor. They came from the Pool."

Though the bed had stopped shaking, he still trembled. But he would be loathe to let a woman see him behaving in a cowardly way, so he cleared his throat and said, "Let me see the other three."

She looked very apologetic. "I only have the one."

"How did you come by it?" he demanded.

"It was a gift." She looked at him without guile, but something in her expression truly frightened him. "The one who gave it to me, told me of the other three. But he could not locate them. He did not know where they were."

It was her husband, he thought. *After he had done many things for her, proven his love, she killed him.*

He had no idea how he knew such a thing, but the images came cleanly and vividly to him. He saw her conjuring, saw her pouring over forbidden texts of the Black Arts; saw her husband in a trance, performing unspeakable acts at her command. Their exquisite home was guarded by men she had killed, then made to rise as mindless slaves. She had made the stars move; she had killed every woman in his harem with a wave of her hand.

Her homeland was an island, and there she had raised the dead and made them walk; her reign had been one of terror and debauchery. They had attacked her encampment as she slept, killing all her followers; and gagged her, and bound her, and thrust her into a tiny boat, sending it far out to sea.

But she had survived. Slavers had seen her boat, taken her aboard. In her weakened condition, she was no match for them, for their lusts, and their cruelties.

Then and there, she had vowed never to submit to any person, man or woman, again. On the entire race of mankind, she would take her revenge.

Now she said to ibn Rashad, in a voice low with menace, "I'm letting you see what I have done, and who I am. The veils are down, my lord, and this is what you've let into your life. You will take us to the Pool, or I will kill you."

"W—why do you need me?" he asked.

She sneered at him. "Now your voice is filled with humility as you address me, a mere woman. You don't need to know why I need you. You have only to obey, or die."

Their caravan left the next morning. She was properly veiled and rode in a closed palanquin. It must have been like an oven inside. Taran the landowner seemed more improved, and when ibn Rashad made mention of it near the palanquin, she chuckled with great humor.

She's been poisoning him, he guessed, riding glumly

along on his camel. *She arranged everything in order to come back to me. But why?*

When she came veiled to his tent that night, she murmured to him, as she climbed onto the satin pillows and took the hookah from his mouth, "You were so proud and boastful before. Why this unnatural cowardice? Do you not see that you are a wise and mighty magick-user? I saw you conjure the demon, and I was afraid. But after my marriage, my husband confided certain magicks to me. He taught me all he knew."

Her laugh was evil. "I knew a few other things as well, from my old life, before I was driven away. I told you I was a queen, and I was. The queen of the walking dead." She stretched languorously on his pillows, smoking his pipe, enjoying his mixture of terror and fascination as he listened to her. "How my enemies feared me."

"But you took my things, informed on me . . ." he reminded her.

"I took your things in order to investigate your magick use," she told him. "I myself wished to conjure Hilmesh. But Taran found everything, and so to save my skin, I pretended that I had planned to tell him of your conjuring."

"And did you?" he asked.

"Did I . . . ?"

"Conjure Hilmesh?"

She stretched languorously. "Oh, yes. Hilmesh was mine."

He noted the use of the past tense, and fell silent. He was terrified of her.

Five long days and nights they dragged through the desert. On the sixth night, something changed in the air. Ibn Rashad was certain he heard a sort of humming sound, very like that made by blind, tongueless eunuchs chorusing a lullaby for Great Suleiman's many baby sons. The night was swollen, the moon round and glowing with promise.

"Look," Ceceli whispered, taking ibn Rashad's hand.

Together, without bodyguards or witnesses, they walked a short distance from their encampment, night shrouding them. The moonlight shifted accommodatingly with their footsteps, illuminating the sand.

Palm trees drooped over a black, glassy surface, and Ceceli caught her breath. She gave his hand a squeeze and picked up her pace. He had trouble keeping up with her, but he was afraid to fall behind.

The sand directly in front of them began to shift and move. Ibn Rashad jumped back as something beneath the surface began to wriggle violently, sand running down either side of what looked like long tubes of gray. His mind went back to the violent shaking of his bed as the ground shuddered and shook.

As he moved away, the heads of enormous cobras popped through the surface, one by one by one, gazing at the two of them. Rising from a base of coils, they stood at least as tall as ibn Rashad himself. Their eyes glowed a malevolent crimson, and their tongues flickered menacingly. Their hoods were broad and enormous.

Laughing beneath her breath, Ceceli gave ibn Rashad a little push forward. He stifled a cry in his throat, and she laughed like a brazen whore.

"Don't you have magick to protect you, great physician?" she asked.

His eyes were riveted on the serpents. There were at least twenty of them. He had treated many patients for cobra bite. Not one of them had survived.

And their deaths were terrible to behold.

Then, as he watched, she uttered words and moved her hands in circles. The glowing eyes of the creatures grew brighter, yet their bobbing slowed. Their tongues stopped flickering. They were not precisely motionless, but they were clearly under her thrall.

"Step forward," she commanded him.

He remained where he was. She glared at him and pointed her fingers at him. "Step forward," she said again, her voice dripping with menace.

Sweating with fear, he shuffled one foot toward the serpents. Their eyes shifted and gleamed.

"Good. Another step."

He ran through the maze of gently swaying monsters; her delighted laughter ran over the cold desert as he stumbled, fell, ran on, zigzagging past all the snakes. He was gasping, panting with fear; and he was so frightened he was afraid his heart would give out.

He didn't know how he succeeded in reaching the other side of their territory; his run was blind, and his only thought, as he passed each one, was to pass the next.

Now he was standing beside an oasis pool, which was surrounded by what looked to be small round stones, and Ceceli was beside him, imperious and serene.

"You see what it is like to be at someone's mercy," she said to him. "Can you imagine how I felt when you tried to violate me?"

"But . . . but I'm a man," he replied. He was honestly perplexed. "I am created to rule over you."

Her mouth drew in a small line. She was exotic, foreign, and beautiful. Even now, he could barely keep from approaching her and attempting to take her into his arms.

"And so, you remain unchanged from everything

that has happened to you, my lord cobra," she said. "What a terrible pity." She shrugged. "No matter. We are here now."

"I-I have no understanding of why you came to me," he said. "Why didn't you simply persuade Taran to caravan to this place?"

She moved her shoulders. "Some of life must remain a mystery, perhaps, so that we never tire of living." Then she indicated the pool. "This is the place," she said. "We are here."

He could sense her excitement, and turned his attention, as she had, to the waters.

The moon shifted above them, casting sickly yellow beams over the smooth stones surrounding the pool. Three or four deep, they circled the pool, which was at least ten times as long as he.

The hair on the back of his head rose and his face prickled. They were not stones. They were skulls—of animals, and birds, and of human beings.

"Sacrifices," she told him. "There is a tribe nearby— there *was* a tribe nearby—which worshipped this place. They gave this pool what it wants. Now it hungers for more."

She looked at him, and he tried to keep his fear from overruling his reason. Had she brought him here to kill him?

She laughed again. "Taran," she said. "I will give them Taran."

"B—but his promise upon a cure. His lands," he blurted.

"I will make it all come to me upon his death. And I will give you everything he had." She came up to him, rubbing herself against him, inflaming him. "Everything. Only swear your loyalty to me."

What choice did he have? And so he did; and the next hours were spent in a nightmare from which he couldn't awaken: at her signal, the cobras slithered to the encampment and sentenced the caravan riders to agonizing, protracted deaths. Only Taran was spared, and Ceceli compelled ibn Rashad to tie him up like an animal for slaughter and drag him toward the pool.

Ibn Rashad stood in a stupor as Ceceli prepared for a ritual. From the tent she had shared with Taran, she brought the box which contained the magickal axe; also, many vials of potions and herbs, and oil lamps. All this she carried as if they weighed very little.

She set them down at the pool's edge. Ibn Rashad gazed at the water as she knelt and began to perform a long, complicated incantation. As with the stones that were not stones but skulls, eventually he realized that the water was not water, but something very thick, like mud. It reeked, and as the woman's voice rose and fell, the pool gave off an even more revolting stench. Then the surface moved, very slightly, and ibn Rashad tried to tell her that something was inside it.

But she knows that, he thought. *She is praying to it even as I stand here, inert and helpless.*

The night wore on. He was forced to stand beside her, though he swayed with fatigue. She held him captive with strong magicks, forced him to watch as the thing in the pool expanded, then contracted, like the side of a great, slumbering beast. The air above it thickened and swirled, becoming after a time, a great, white mist such as he had never seen. It was as though phantoms moved inside it as it churned and roiled.

At one point, he thought he heard a sharp cry, but then the sound faded in his ears. He didn't know if he was asleep or dreaming.

At the blackest hour of the night she said to him, "It is time."

He knew exactly what she wanted him to do, and he couldn't stop himself from doing it. He turned to the rasping landowner, who was more dead than alive, and lifted him in his arms. The man's eyes rolled and his face was very hot.

He won't live much longer anyway, he told himself, as he carried him to the edge of the pool.

"Throw him in." Her voice was hard and eager, and ibn Rashad felt a terrible wave of guilt and despair. Yes, he had conjured; and yes, he had been proud. But he had never been evil. Allah would never forgive his murder of another man.

"Spare him," he blurted, fighting against his enchantment.

She gaped at him. He could feel his will returning to himself. Somehow, the Lord of All had allowed him to break her hold over him.

"Spare him," he commanded her.

"We will gain more power than you can imagine," she said. "I have prepared his body for months for this moment. The fools who sacrificed their own were primitives. Savages. Taran is cultivated. And he carries within himself a wonderful demon, who is my servant in all things. Hilmesh."

He gaped at her. "The demon is the thing that is killing him."

"And you thought he had the consuming disease." Her voice dripped with contempt.

"The creature will absorb Hilmesh, and he will bind its power to me. And then you and I will explore the depths of the unknown."

Her tone was tantalizing, but he could tell that she

was frightened. He felt a sense of triumph as he crossed his arms over his chest and concentrated all his energies on defying her.

"You will obey me," she insisted. Her voice shook with rage. "You will obey me, or you will die."

Steadfast, he glared at her. She said words in a strange language, but he refused to be intimidated. The smell and the fog thickened and grew, and began to envelop him. He tried to hold his breath, but the mist came inside him with his breath.

There was a longing; there was a starvation. There was lack of focus; there was promise. Ibn Rashad found himself picturing an angry child who has been denied a favorite toy—the frustration, the sense of entitlement, the rage. The overriding emotion of need.

It wanted him.

It wanted *him.*

Offered an alternative, the creature in the pit preferred him, ibn Rashad, to a demon encased inside a dying man.

Alerted, he exhaled as hard as he could, trying to cleanse his body of the mist. He staggered left, then right; he was shrouded in the whiteness, and could no longer see which way he was going.

Then she shouted, "You fool!" and he fell.

Into the thickness, into the foul paste; it dragged him in and then it cradled him, and rolled over him. It completely enveloped him, even over his face. The pain was tremendous; it was unspeakable.

It is killing me, he thought.

As he suffered in agony, stars grew brilliant, and close; he saw them as eyes in the dark face of the universe; the sun was an immense heartbeat. The moon glistened, a tear of victory. Islands shook; huge mountains exploded, shooting boiling rocks into the air. The wind blew away every sand in every desert; fires raged throughout all the cities.

The pool in which he lay grew, and drowned the sun, the moon, the stars, everything.

He writhed in his travail; every part of him burned and sizzled; no torture invented could have been worse. Yet it continued, ceaselessly, and ibn Rashad wished only to die.

In that single moment, when he released his will, the pain stopped.

When Sallah ibn Rashad stepped from the pool, it was dawn. Completely clean, in his dry, clean robes, he was ibn Rashad the Physician in form only. He had been transformed. In some magickal way, he had become the eyes and ears of the One Who Gathered. He was its willing and obedient servant.

Taran the landowner lay dead at his feet, the demon apparently with it; and the viperess, Ceceli, had wisely fled into the desert, taking with her all the camels of their caravan.

Ibn Rashad smiled cruelly as he surveyed the dead bodies of their guards and servants, already baking in the sun. Vultures wheeled overhead. The smell rivaled that of his new master.

"It doesn't matter where you go, woman," he promised Ceceli. "I will keep you alive until I find you. And then I will make you pay."

Chapter One

Sunnydale

Holly Johnson was very hungry. From her place behind the rocks piled against the water's edge, she watched two fishermen as they unfolded lawn chairs a few feet away. They had just carried a whole bunch of stuff out onto the Sunnydale Municipal Pier and now they started getting more things out of boxes and paper sacks and coolers. One of the men was an old guy wearing a denim jacket and jeans, and the other wore a stuffed down jacket and a pair of baggy pants like Holly's grandpa's.

The sea gulls wheeled and cawed; the water lapped the rocks. A sign to her right said, NO *something-something* BEVERAGES. PETS MUST BE ON LEASHES. Salt coated her face and her fingernails were broken and torn. There was a hole in her brown corduroy pants, her matching brown sweater was ripped, and her red T-shirt was stinky.

The men had some food with them. Holly could smell it. She was so hungry she was shaky. She wanted very badly to take back running away, but she wasn't sure what would happen if she turned herself in. She was eight years old and her next-door neighbor, Gigi Hazelin, had explained to her that her mom was never going to get another husband because of her. That was what had happened to Gigi's mom, and everybody knew Gigi's mom was a real mess.

"They have us kids and then our fathers leave them, and then other men don't want them, either," Gigi had explained. "They only want ladies who don't have kids."

That had made perfect sense to Holly, and since she loved her mother more than anything in the world, she had run away the morning after Mr. Cho, from her mom's work, had come over for the third night in a row to have dinner.

Just like always, Holly had gone to bed when her mom told her to. But then she remembered she had forgotten to tell her about her spelling test—her mom had helped her study for it, and Holly had gotten one hundred percent—and Holly went down the hall toward the living room to give her the good news.

She stopped in the dooway, suddenly uncertain if she should go any further. From where she stood, she could see her mom and Mr. Cho, but they couldn't see her. They were watching *X-Files* and sitting very close to each other on the couch. Holly got distracted; she loved that show, but she wasn't allowed to watch it because it gave her nightmares.

Then Mr. Cho picked up a glass of wine and took a sip, and asked her mom, "What about your little girl?"

And Holly's mom's voice got all funny and she said, "You know she comes first, Ben."

He said, "Of course. I wouldn't have it any other way. That's why I love you so."

They were both quiet for a while, and Holly got

cared. She was afraid to make a sound. She watched more of the *X-Files* but then Scully got lost in a forest, which was scary; so Holly turned her attention to the glass swans on their fireplace mantel. The swans were filled with colored water—they had a green one, a pink one, and a purple one—and her mom had arranged them on a glass lake with flowers around them. They were beautiful, just like Mom.

Holly's eyes filled with tears, and when the two adults started to stand up with their arms around each other, she ran back down the hall and climbed into her bed.

Her mother called, "Holl-holl?" but she didn't answer. She curled up with her face to the wall, pretending to be asleep.

After a while, she was asleep.

In the morning, she had told Gigi all about it. Gigi sighed, shaking her head, and said, "It's gonna happen. He'll leave her because of you and she'll start drinking."

"My mom's not like that," Holly insisted.

Gigi looked at her; her eyes glistened and her mouth trembled, and she had bad breath. Gigi always had bad breath. She didn't brush her teeth because her mom didn't care if all her teeth fell out. She said, "Mine wasn't like that, either, until it happened."

"He said he loves her because I'm first," Holly informed her. But her heart was pounding and she felt a little sick.

"That's just TV talk." Holly's best friend waved her hand and they continued their walk to school. Gigi was skinny and her clothes were too big. The waist part of her dress hung around her hips and the rest of it was

long enough to trip on. Holly's mom said that Gigi
should be in foster care, "with that mother. She's a real
mess."

"That's the stuff they tell each other because they
think they should say it," Gigi continued. "But they
don't mean it."

"They don't?" Holly felt even sicker. It had never
occurred to her that her mother would ever lie to anyone. "Then why do they say it?"

"Because Jesus is listening," Gigi answered authoritatively. She was Catholic, and she went to Sunday
school. "They don't want to get in trouble with him. So
they say all the stuff they think he wants to hear."

Holly bit her lower lip and twisted her hands together. She didn't want her mom to get in trouble with
Jesus. She didn't want her to start drinking. She didn't
want her to start dressing Holly in funny clothes and
sleeping all day.

So now Holly watched the fishermen opening up
bags from Happy Burger, her stomach rumbling. The
man who looked like her grandfather picked up a plaid
Thermos and unscrewed the top, then poured coffee
into a small red plastic cup. The other man started sipping from a Happy Burger cup and they both laughed
about something to do with battery acid.

Holly didn't know how long she had been gone from
her house. She was tired and dirty and most of the time
she was hungry. She slept all kinds of places at night,
and she was a little surprised that the police hadn't
caught her and thrown her in jail by now. No one
seemed to be looking for her.

Mom's glad I'm gone, she thought. That made her
even more afraid to take back running away. Maybe her
mom had already married Mr. Cho, and if Holly came

back now, Mr. Cho would divorce her mother, just like Daddy had.

The men settled back, fussing with their fishing poles, then casting them in the water. One of them picked up a radio and set it on his lap. He pressed a button and on came the sound. It was a news report.

". . . fire still raging out of control. At least seven more deaths have been reported, and numerous casualties have been taken from the firelines and are being transported to Sunnydale Medical Center for emergency treatment. City officials are considering calling on the Governor for aid. In other news, local band Dingoes Ate My Baby triumphed at the Battle of the Bands held at Crestwood College last night. The group's lead singer, Devon MacLeish, said—"

The man changed the station. Soon the air filled with a song Holly didn't know. It was slow and dreamy. The words were something like, "But I know we'll meet again, some sunny—"

Then the man shouted, "I got a big one!"

He grabbed the pole with both hands. The other man caught the radio as it began to tumble from his lap. He got excited, too, and started yelling at the other guy to reel it in, then to let the line slacken, then to do this, then that.

Holly crept forward, watching eagerly. Both the men wrestled with the pole, yelling and whooping. The pole itself was curving so hard Holly was sure it was going to break in two.

Fog was gathering beneath the pier, slightly obscuring Holly's vision. It came rolling on the tops of the waves, thick as the stuffing in their couch at home.

Waves slapped the rocks, much harder than just a few seconds before. Spray leaped into the air and dappled her with droplets of sea water. The next wave rolled in much harder, bringing more fog, and the next splashed her with a bucketful of icy cold ocean.

"Hey," she protested; then swiveled her head toward the two fishermen to see if they had heard her.

But they were busy themselves. The waves were crashing up against the pylons that held up the pier. It was as if the ocean was a bowl somebody was shaking back and forth. Fog was rising in big gobs all around them.

Holly ran backwards to dodge the next high wave as it slammed the breakwater, but she wasn't fast enough. It not only drenched her, but knocked her hard onto her caboose.

The men were shouting in the mist. As they pulled back their hands and raised them over their heads, their fishing poles dove into the water. Water crashed down, really hard, throwing the man who looked like her grandfather onto his back.

Holly crawled away as fast as she could, wave after wave knocking her to the sand, then trying with all its might to pull her back out to sea. Fog chased her; and it smelled horrible. It smelled like dead things. It was so awful that Holly had to stop to throw up.

Then she got to her feet and crab-scrabbled away from the breakwater and toward the gravel parking lot.

Other people came running, some out of a little coffee shop a ways down the jetty. The fog swirled around them and the waves roared like wild animals. A couple with a little teeny wiener dog waved and yelled at the men on the pier, and Holly scampered between a white car and a black minivan.

The man of the couple pulled out a cell phone and started bellowing into it. The lady picked up the dog and hurried out of the ocean's reach, toward the parking lot. Holly made herself smaller.

The waves were huge now, arcing over the pier where the two men had flattened themselves against the wood, screaming and yelling.

Then, as Holly stared, the pylons gave way, and the entire pier crashed into the stormy water. It didn't go all at once, but cracked into bits like the *Titanic*. Big posts smacked into the hills and valleys and other pieces, like the decking, ripped apart and floated for a few seconds before they sank from view.

The fog covered the scene; Holly saw no sign of the two fishermen.

What she did see rooted her to the spot:

As the waves rose and collided with each other; as the sky darkened from the immense towers of water and the fog; as people scurried away like ants, something came out of the water.

It appeared in the center of a wave, dripping wet. It was man-shaped, and its feet did not touch the water. It kind of flew through the fog, kind of glided, and it was moving toward the breakwater.

Moving toward her.

The closer it got, the more fog it cleared out of its path, and the better she saw it: it was a *mummy*. It was just like something out of the *X-Files*, wrapped in bandages that were dripping wet.

In its hands, it carried a box.

Its feet made no sound as it approached the graveled lot; seawater and kelp rushed up beneath and around its bandages and caught Holly up to her knees as she crouched. There was a stream of warmth, and she realized she had wet herself. That was the least of her worries.

It was coming closer.

It was coming for her.

It began to open the box. Holly saw its fingernails, long and black, and covered with fungus. They protruded from the wrappings. That was the only part of its body that she could actually see.

It reached its hand into the box.

It pulled out something shiny. Holly squinted.

An axe.

It raised the axe above its head.

Holly ran. She ran faster than she had ever believed she could run. She did not look back.

Beneath the roaring sound of the ocean, she thought she heard a plaintive yipping, like that of a little dog.

Holly burst into tears and ran faster.

The fog-laden waters chased her for miles, it seemed, and by the time she reached dry ground, she was so exhausted she couldn't move, couldn't even keep her eyes open.

If that mummy gets me, I'm dead.

But she was so tired, she couldn't do a single thing about it.

"Mom," she whispered, as the fog crept over her and covered her. "Mommy, find me."

Chapter Two

San Francisco

In the ultra-chic Pacific Heights district of San Francisco, Kevin Harris's mother put down the letter from her sister-in-law and sighed. Seated at her new "shabby chic" writing desk, she picked up the school photo of Alexander, her nephew in Sunnydale, and regarded it.

"What's that?" Kevin asked, leaning over her shoulder. "Oh. The dork."

"Your cousin is not a dork." She slipped the photo back in the envelope decorated with children with over-sized eyes, the latest misspelled, rambling letter from Sunnydale.

"Okay, the loser," Kevin said. He was eating s'mores for breakfast. If she said anything about it, he'd remind her that he was on the football team and coach wanted him to bulk up. She smiled faintly. Kevin was a typical teenager; slept all weekend and ate like a fiend, but still he didn't put on any flab. She envied him.

"He doesn't want to, like, come visit or anything, does he?"

"Be nice," she admonished. *But he's right. Alexander is a dork and a loser.*

They're not like us, she thought, only slightly ashamed for being smug as she looked around her beautiful, professionally decorated living room. The entire house had recently been completely redone, in greens and golds that flowed from one room to the next. The kitchen, too, fully equipped with a fantastic Sub-Zero refrigerator and a state-of-the-art gas range from Denmark. Her son was a straight-A student and her husband pulled down more in a month than Alexander's parents both made in a year.

We are doing so fantastic.

Kevin gave her a kiss on the cheek and hustled off to practice. She smiled at the retreating figure of her son—*He's looking thin; growing like a weed*—and put the letter in one of the cubby holes on the desktop. *I'll have to answer it.*

But that meant she would have to pretend she cared about Alexander's family, which she patently did not. They were an embarrassment. She'd been at their house one Christmas—and one only—and it was an experience she hoped never to repeat.

She pushed away from her writing desk and arranged her hair. She had a standing ten o'clock appointment with Miguel, and then a lunch with her husband in the city, and then a meeting with the local board of the Make-a-Wish Foundation. They wanted to approach her about participating in a fundraiser.

Checking her watch, she raised her brows slightly. She'd have to get going if she wasn't going to be late for Miguel. If she was late for him, then she'd be late for lunch, and then for the meeting—a full domino effect.

She closed up her desk and made sure she had her keys. She was out the door and into the Mercedes before she realized she had left her cell phone beside her bed, on the charger.

For a split-second she debated about going back inside to retrieve it, then decided she didn't really need it. Miguel would let her use the phone if she needed to make any calls, and her husband always carried his cell in his briefcase.

Besides, not being reachable for a few hours would be a delicious guilty pleasure.

So she pulled out of the driveway and went on her merry way.

That was how, when she showed up *(on time!)* for lunch down in the financial district, she had not heard any of what had happened to her son at football practice.

"His upper arm snapped," her husband told her outside the restaurant. He had been waiting for her, pacing in the parking lot in his dark gray suit, cell phone in hand. "Then he told the doctor he's been having some pain in his joints."

"He never told me that," she said quickly. "Never."

Kevin's father looked stricken. "And with the weight loss, and the fatigue . . ."

A horrible chill ran through her. "It's not what you're thinking. My son does not have cancer."

He said gently, "They took some X-rays."

She shook her head, slowly at first, then faster. "Not Kevin."

"They want to do a biopsy. As soon as possible."

"Not my son!" she screamed. She hit his chest. Then she burst into tears as he enfolded her in his arms and cradled her.

"We'll find answers," he promised her. "We'll do whatever it takes."

I have connections, she thought. Her mind went into high gear.

She grabbed his phone.

Sunnydale

I must be dead, Willow thought wonderingly.

Below her, the operating room was filled with whirring machines and pieces of white cloth. There were drapes of white everywhere, and an enormous, circular light gleaming down on a body. The body lay beneath a vast, tentlike expanse of pieces of white on an operating table, and the heads bent over it hid the face. But Willow knew that body was hers.

I look like I'm in a shroud, she thought. *Oh, yeah. Accident. We hit somebody. Did they die? Am I dead?*

Where are my parents? Where's Oz?

Don't I get to say goodbye?

"No, no, no," said one of the figures bending over her body. Willow couldn't make out any of the details; the figure was hidden from her view by blurs of green.

Scrubs, she guessed.

Someone said, "We should call it. We're going to need this table. I hear we're getting some more firemen."

Someone else grunted. "I hate burn victims."

"Plastic surgeons are probably upstairs drinking champagne," someone else said. "Fat bastards. They should try practicing *real* medicine sometime."

Another voice chimed in, "Is Corvalis still alive? I used to hang out with his older brother in high school. He was a nice kid."

"Barely," came in the answer. "Someone should be kind. If I was in that much pain . . ."

There was a moment of silence.

"She's gone," said a different voice.

"I'm not leaving," said the figure. "She's going to make it. Come on, Willow. Come on, dear."

"Doctor Fleming, we really should call it," said one of the other figures. "There's no activity."

Willow blinked, feeling sad.

Oz is going to miss me . . .

Then the world turned very bright, as if she were staring directly into the big, circular light. She couldn't blink, so she tried to raise her hand to cover her eyes. But nothing came between her and the light.

I don't think I have arms, she thought, bemused. *But then I must not have eyes. So why does the light bother me?*

The light grew more intense; it was a shimmering, brilliant white that filled her field of vision. It stretched across her horizon; she had the sensation that it was solid, and that if she could touch it, it would be very, very pleasant.

The whiteness faded, and grew dull; it flattened into a matte nickel color. There was nothing but grayness the color and consistency of fog. Again she tried to reach out a hand to touch it, but there was nothing to touch.

Panic rose along with her disorientation. She looked down and saw nothing below.

Not even my own feet. Nothing.

She heard weeping, and then shadowy blurs began to form around her. They were indistinct flashes of darkness against the dull twilight.

Then a face appeared, its features contorted and grotesque. She saw a disembodied hand. A stream of gray hair matted with dust and cobwebs.

Half of a skull.

The perfectly formed arm of an infant.

Help, Willow whispered. But no sound came out. She heard herself inside her head, but not with her ears. She listened for her heartbeat, but instead heard the flatline of a heart monitor.

More weeping.

Then a slow, sad moan trailed across her, touching her in some palpable way. It was almost subaudible, a whispery keening that made her shudder as it caressed her, then seeped inside her, penetrating her with a coldness that permeated her being.

Whatever my being is.

Oh, God, I'm already a ghost. I'm a dead ghost person.

For a moment, panic overwhelmed her. *I really am dead!*

Her hand flashed before her, but only briefly. It moved toward her face—*if I have a face*—but disappeared almost as soon as she realized what it was.

Come back. Be my hand again. I want to be Willow again.

Forever.

She was cold, so very cold. She bowed under the weight, sinking deep down into a quicksand, or a morass, of nothing.

No, don't let me die, she begged. *Buffy, where are you?*

There were still no actual words, only her inner thoughts. No one to hear her plea, unless they could read her mind.

Shapes darted around her; something icy darted right through her. The gray haze revolved around her, or maybe it remained perfectly still. She was unbelievably dizzy; it was like being seasick. Dimly, she remembered once telling Buffy how she had gone out on a boat with her adorable boy cousin Moshe from New Jersey and wound up barfing over the side half the day.

Barfing in a wine-dark sea, a wine-dark sea, she thought, not recognizing the reference, but knowing it was from something she had read.

If I'm really dead, do we get to read books?

And is this all I'm gonna get of my life flashing before my eyes, barfing in front of Moshe?

A face popped in front of her, its gaze level and unblinking. It had a mouth, and it inhaled sharply. Then it smiled and said, "Hello, little witch."

Willow blinked. The face stretched and became transparent; then she blinked again several times and the features became more formed. Willow brightened, relieved to see—at last—an old friend.

"You're Lucy, aren't you?" she asked brightly. "It's really, really good to see you. In all senses of the word. Seeing, as with actual eyes," she added. "Eyes, good, too."

The figure of the dead Slayer, Lucy Hanover, vibrated in the gray, like a cheesy hologram. It was like a stuttering, and then the vibrating stopped.

"Hello," Lucy said. "Yes, it is I. I'm both sad and relieved to find you on these roads, Willow."

Lucy Hanover the Vampire Slayer had died during America's Civil War, and she was dressed for the occasion. She wore a high-necked, formfitting black silk dress with a large, puffy bustle. Lucy's hair was pulled back in a becoming bun, and dangling earrings of jet hung from her ear lobes. She had the palest skin Willow had ever seen, including Angel's. She was literally whiter than a sheet.

Willow finally understood.

"I'm on the Ghost Roads," she said.

Lucy's smile was reassuring and kind, and she reached out a hand as she nodded. "Don't be afraid."

"You mean, don't be afraid because I'm here, or because you're dead, or because I'm, um, dead?" Willow queried uneasily.

"All three, but I meant, because you're dead," Lucy said gently.

Willow was sick with dread. "I really am? It's not a dream?"

Nodding, Lucy clasped her hands in front of herself and sighed. "I'm so sorry, Willow, but you really are."

Willow sagged. "Darn." She made a little face. "No offense."

Lucy said, "None taken, I'm sure. I was no more delighted to find myself here than you are now."

Nervous, Willow began to spill, blurting, "You know, okay, death issues because I'm a teenager, but I really thought I'd live a really long time. I guess everyone does, huh? I mean, thinks they'll live a long time?"

"Even Slayers," Lucy murmured. She held out her hand. "This is a pocket of quiet, but the dead are restless. They're frightened. You remember how it was before, when you were trying to save Xander?"

Willow did. She and Cordelia had traveled the Ghost Roads last summer to save Xander's life. But the ghosts who had traveled there were frightened, and tried to block their way. Also, to force them to leave Xander behind, because he was dead.

"We brought him back to life," Willow said hopefully. "Are you here to tell me how to save myself? Like, dunk myself in a magick cauldron or something?"

Lucy shook her head. "It's too late to bring you back

in that way. Your friend Xander had a stronger life spark than you do."

Willow found that somehow very embarrassing, as if not having a strong life spark was her own personal failing. *So call me an overachiever.*

She said, "What about all the modern medicine? Are they doing C.P.R.? Or maybe the thing with the paddles, like on *E.R.*, where Dr. Green yells 'clear' and everybody lifts up their hands and they zap me and I go back—"

"Willow, I don't know about those things. For the moment, my dear, you are truly dead," Lucy said.

"Oh." Willow was still, taking that in. Then over the unchanging landscape, she heard rustles and tears, sighs and whispers.

"Oblivion," someone said breathily.

Then Lucy took her hand, and Willow saw that she, too had a hand again. It was almost, but not quite, as white as Lucy's.

"Your life is draining out of you," Lucy said, as if she'd read Willow's mind.

"Then I'm not quite dead," Willow replied.

"I pray—and the dead *do* pray—that they will bring you back to your living world." She reached out a hand, and Willow took it. It was ice cold. "But for now, walk with me, Willow. Buffy and Faith are going to need your help."

They did walk, and as the gray merged into more gray on the vast, flat horizon, Willow lost track of spatial distances—if there were any there, on the Ghost Roads—and how much time had elapsed. She knew there was only a short span of time where shocking a person's heart was any use, because if there was no oxygen to the brain, everything else shut down in rapid order.

Lucy looked around. "There's a great evil moving through the living world, young Wicca. Do you know what the Gatherer is?"

There was a momentary flicker of light; someone breathing; Willow heard a heartbeat—

And then she was positive she heard someone calling her name from very far away.

"Have you been listening?" Lucy asked, startling her.

Willow jerked. She was dizzy and unfocused, as if she'd fallen asleep, and she flushed.

"I drifted off," she confessed. "I've very sorry. I didn't mean to."

"You must have gone back. But it wasn't for very long, or I would have noticed," Lucy told her, as Willow began to get excited.

"I was resuscitated!" Willow said.

"But it didn't last." Lucy's voice was kind but firm. "Please, Willow, I need your attention while I have it."

"I'm sorry," Willow said unhappily. "But I don't feel like I belong here. And if they're working on me, well—"

She half-opened her eyes. The blazing white made her shy away, squinting, until two large blue eyes blocked the beam. Below the eyes stretched a mask of white paper.

"She's back," said the figure. The blue eyes crinkled above the strip of white.

There was a chorus of cheers in the operating room.

Then: "No, damn it! Stay here, Willow! Stay with us!"

Willow knew she had let go again, and she began to feel guilty about her inability to either stay alive or stay dead.

Then after a moment, she returned to the Ghost Roads. This time she knew it, and didn't wig.

Which, this time, may be a good idea.

Lucy wasn't there, but a lot of other people were.

The dead were in a wild panic, threatening to run right over her. They slammed into her, knocking her over, swarming around her like stampeding cattle. Their mouths were contorted into terrified shrieks. They jostled one another and shattered into fragments, to be ground under the heels of the next panicked phantom.

Oh, yeah, Willow thought, remembering her previous travels on the Ghost Roads. *Brittle. One sock and they're dead meat.*

So to speak.

"It's here!" a white-faced wraith screamed directly into Willow's face. Its hands wrapped around her shoulders and shook her, hard. It was so terrified that it was trying to crawl up Willow's body, scrambling in fright and complete panic. Then it let go of her and ran shrieking around her, arms thrown above its head as if it were on fire.

Willow cried out as a semitransparent child rushed up to her next, its face a hole filled with screaming. Sobbing, it clung to her, and in its fright, began to pummel her chest. Willow blocked its blows with her wrists, struggling to push it away.

"Stop it, stop!" she shouted.

"Mama! Mama!" the child screamed. "Mama!"

The child kept batting at her. Willow tried again to push it away, her fist accidentally catching the child in the chest.

It shattered into shards of brittle bone that clattered against the gray, as if it had hit a solid wall. Willow stared in shock and remorse.

"Sorry," she murmured.

The panic level rose, until Willow could no longer distinguish the blur of white around her. Then she realized it was like fog, rolling in, a thick, rolling mist that blanketed everything. And it *smelled*.

A fleeing skeleton swiped at her, its bony fingertips just missing her cheek. Willow ducked, crying out, and covered her head in a defensive posture.

Something slammed against her back, knocking her forward onto her knees. As the offender—another phantom—dashed on, Willow looked over her shoulder just in time to see a blanket of fog unrolling toward her. *Not liking that.*

She pushed her hands and feet against the road—which was solid—and sprang sideways out of the way. Inside the fog, there was a blur. As the mists shifted and curled, the blur became a figure wrapped in bandages. Though its face was covered, it appeared to look straight at her.

It came toward her. Then a box appeared in its arms, and it slowly lifted the lid.

She kept well away from it, backing up to stay out of range.

"Lucy?" she cried, looking around for the dead Slayer. "Help would be good!"

Willow woke up.

For a second dizziness roiled over her and she thought, *I'm at Xander's, watching some dorky horror movie.*

No. I'm at Six Flags Magic Mountain. I'm on the Viper roller coaster.

Lights flashed overhead, bright, not, bright, not, and

omething was rattling and banging and there was creaming everywhere.

She opened her eyes. She was strapped on a gurney, nd people in masks were racing her down a corridor. Lights overhead flickered and strobed.

"My head," she moaned. It throbbed with pain. "My head."

"My God, she's back again!" someone said. "Get er back in surgery!"

The gurney she was on bobbled down a hallway. Rattle, rattle, rattle. Willow's eyes began to close.

Then she heard, "Willow!"

She couldn't speak again, but she thought tears were liding down her temples.

"Willow, damn it, stay with us!"

"It must have honed in on me," Lucy said, as the two aced hand-in-hand along the Ghost Roads. "Don't go nywhere on these roads without me, all right? It's so asy to get lost on the paths. So many twists and turns. Try to concentrate on me if you have to leave and then come back again like that."

"Sorry."

The phantoms were in full retreat around them, hrieking and screaming. White and gray raged around hem, crackling and rumbling like weighty summer torms. Brighter lights flickered and flashed, explosions on a distant, nonexistent horizon.

The fog rushed over Willow and Lucy like a net again. Something close behind them was breathing down Willow's neck; she felt its shadow, and its panting breath stank like rotten things.

"Lucy . . ." Willow said.

Lucy nodded. "It's a Wanderer, Willow. It's following us because of me, not you. I'm a Slayer. We have to find a way to tell Buffy and Faith that the Wanderers are coming to Sunnydale."

Willow said, "The what?"

"The Wanderers. They're hunting for Slayers, for the Gatherer. It wants them. It needs Slayers, Willow. It craves them."

"Like nicotine?" Willow asked.

Then Lucy shrank to the size of a needle. Willow realized that she herself was floating up into the air, leaving the dead Slayer behind.

Lucy reached up for her. "You have to tell Buffy, Willow. Don't forget—"

Willow opened her eyes.

A man in scrubs was straddling her, his mouth over hers. She felt her breath pour into his mouth. His eyes flew open, and he sat up.

"She's breathing!" he shouted.

"B—bu," Willow tried. "Buff . . ."

"Don't talk," said the man. A clear plastic oxygen mask came down over her face. "Don't say a word. Just breathe in, honey. C'mon, Willow, stay a while."

Chapter Three

Okay, Oz thought, as he rushed into the waiting room of the Sunnydale Medical Center. *This is the part where I wake up.*

Only, he knew better. Going to Sunnydale Medical Center to check on one of his friends—*or worst, of all, my Willow*—was his least favorite but most common form of déjà vu.

He had seen Willow in the hospital before. He had already faced the possibility of losing her, to heart-break, yes, and to death as well.

So why does it feel so horrible and new?

His heart was pounding as he pushed open the door to the waiting room. The plastic chairs were the same. So were the out-of-date wooden coffee tables crammed between the couches. The TV was turned on to some talk show, just like always. There was the fish tank with the neon tetras and the zebra fish swimming around.

He saw Buffy and her mom, and no one else, even though there were other people in the room.

"Oz, thank God!" Buffy cried when she saw him.

She ran to him and took his hand. There were stitches at her hairline, just to the right of center.

"Hey." He gave her a nod as he searched her face, looking for something, anything, to tell him how Willow was. The skin around her stitches was puffy and red. There was a bruise on her right cheek. But except for that, all he saw was a frightened young woman with swollen eyes, who looked like she'd just lost her best friend.

And does that cliché suck.

"Hello, Oz," said Mrs. Summers. Her right arm was in a sling. She had a Styrofoam coffee cup in her left hand. It was full. She looked down as if she'd just realized she was holding it and set it down on the nearest dark veneer tabletop, which was littered with out-of-date golfing magazines. Then she held her hand against her chest in an awkward position, as if she didn't know what to do with it.

All this Oz saw, with a strange, dizzying clarity. *It really is a dream,* he thought. *A nightmare.*

He thought he might lose it when Buffy started to unravel. But the Slayer got hold of herself and said, "Oz, she's hurt."

"What happened?" They'd told him on the phone, something about a car accident, but he couldn't pull any of it together.

"I didn't see him at first," Joyce said anxiously, looking at her daughter. "There was this sudden fog. And then, this figure. A-a tall man. He just appeared in the middle of the street. From out of nowhere."

Oz ticked his attention to Buffy, who moved her shoulders in a gesture of helplessness and apology.

"We were talking about makeup and I gave her my

lipstick, but I dropped it. And then Mom hit something, a car—"

"It wasn't a car," Joyce insisted. "It was a man. A white man, like a silhouette."

"It was too foggy to see," Buffy conceded. She turned to Oz. "All this fog rushed in, like a fire—"

Oz ran his fingers through his hair. Dropping his arms to his sides, he said, "Where is she?"

"In surgery. We've been waiting to hear from the surgeon," Joyce said.

He couldn't speak; he swiveled his head at Buffy, who took a deep breath.

"Her back's messed up. And there's pressure on her brain, Oz," she said carefully. "They're . . . they're trying to fix it. The pressure, I mean. It's like shaken baby syndrome, they said."

"You were looking for *lipstick?*" Oz shouted, slamming his fist down on the table. The coffee sloshed over the edge of the cup.

Everyone took a beat to register his uncharacteristic outburst. Everything inside him wanted to break something, throw back his head in a howl and—

I'm not the wolf, he reminded himself. *Wolf inside, sure, but just three nights a month. Otherwise, I'm just a regular, normal guy.*

Whose girlfriend is having brain surgery.

"I was driving, Oz. Not Buffy. Good Lord, no, not Buffy." Buffy's mom laid a hand on his shoulder. "I was paying good attention. The man just appeared out of nowhere."

Oz wheeled around and strode out of the waiting room. Buffy followed him. He stopped in the hall, looked left, right, and saw a middle-aged woman dressed in a pink smock with a name tag seated behind a semicircular console. She held a phone against her shoulder and typed on a computer keyboard.

"Mr. Tullus, your wife's in Room 413, maternity," she said cheerily into the phone. "She's still in labor. If you hurry, you might make it. But be sure to drive carefully."

Smiling, she hung up.

Oz leaned into her face and said hoarsely, "Willow Rosenberg." He looked at Buffy. "Where are her parents?"

"In the chapel." At Oz's confused scowl, Buffy added, "With their rabbi."

"R-O-S-E-N-B-E-R-G. Here she is," the woman said, typing. Her name tag read GRACE BECK. "Oh," her cheery smile faded. "I'm afraid she's still in surgery. It's estimated to be another two hours, at least."

Oz broke out in a fresh sweat.

Grace Beck fanned her hand and gestured for him to stay calm. "Just because it's taking a long time doesn't mean things are going badly," she told him. "Spine and head injuries are both tricky. Sometimes it takes a while for the surgeon to make sure all the factors have been taken into account."

Footsteps clattered up behind Oz. He and Buffy turned, to see a disheveled Xander, shirt unbuttoned and untucked, dashing toward them.

"Guys," he said.

Oz said nothing.

"Where is she?" Xander asked. "What's happening?"

"She's in surgery," Buffy said. "Brain surgery." She burst into tears.

"Oh, God." Xander paled and put his arms around

Buffy. He held her for a moment. "How's your mom?"

Buffy pulled herself back together. "Just a little banged up. The . . . something . . . hit Willow's side of our car."

"The something," Xander said carefully.

Buffy looked up at him and nodded. "Looking like a something's involved."

"Kids, there's not much more I can tell you. The surgeon will come to the waiting room," the pink lady informed them gently. She smiled at Oz. "Ms. Rosenberg's doctor is an excellent physician. In fact, Dr. Fleming cared for my husband before he passed away."

Passed away? As in, died?

Oz reeled. Buffy took his arm and said, "C'mon."

He didn't remember going back to the waiting room. Or Buffy getting him a can of Coke from the machine. Or the Rosenbergs showing up. He kind of came to with Mr. Rosenberg lighting into him before the man realized that Joyce Summers, and not his daughter's musician boyfriend, had been driving the car at the time of the accident.

Mrs. Rosenberg was involved in some surrealistic scene of her own, talking on her cell phone about getting some people to handle her classes for the rest of the day. What was so bizarre was the fact that she seemed more uptight about finding substitute lecturers than that her daughter might be dying on an operating table.

She never does have time for Willow, Oz thought bitterly, thinking back to so many times Willow had hoped that one of her many achievements would elicit some response—any response—from her mother.

Xander paced up and down, never sitting. It wasn't so very long ago that Xander had moved in on Will, when Spike had imprisoned them both in the Factory.

Guy could have had her any time he wanted, until she finally got tired of waiting. Then he decided he couldn't live without her.

And I'm being petty. Cuz I'm scared.

"And of course, Cordelia hasn't seen fit to show," Xander snapped. He gestured to the clock. It was almost noon. "I suppose she's got cheerleading practice or a bikini wax or something far more important than Willow."

"Hi, Cordelia," Buffy said loudly.

Oz turned. Cordelia was standing at the entrance to the waiting room with her mother, who was a beautiful, older version of her daughter. Cordelia looked pale and wan, and she was pressing her fingers into the crook of her elbow.

"Hi, Buffy," Cordelia said pointedly. "Oz." Ignoring Xander, she walked into the room. "How's she doing?"

"We don't know," Buffy replied.

Joyce added, "She's having an operation. It's taking a long time. It's brain surgery."

Cordelia sighed. "Brains. They're so . . . whatever." She turned to her mother. "Thanks. I'll call you."

"Sure, honey." Her mother air-kissed her, turned, and left.

Cordelia walked into the room. "Hi, Mr. Rosenberg. Mrs. Rosenberg."

"Hi, Carmela," Mrs. Rosenberg said to Cordelia. She was not so good with the names; she usually called Buffy "Bunny."

Willow's mother put her phone back to her ear. "It's me again, LaTonah," she said. "The sub will need an overhead projector. They should have one in the lecture hall but just in case, would you check it for me? Thanks." She disconnected and looked at her husband.

"That's the last time I ever agree to do a Saturday lecture."

Xander grimly watched as Cordelia sat down and fished through the magazines. "Golf?" she said with disgust.

"Yeah. Some old dude swiped all their copies of *Vogue*," Xander snapped. "I'm sure if they'd realized you were planning on gracing us with your presence, they'd have restocked the waiting room."

"Oh, Xander," she snapped, rubbing her forehead. "Just shut up." To Oz, she said, "How long has she been in there?"

"Oh, only half the day," Xander cut in, before Oz had a chance to answer. He gestured to her. "Giving you ample time for grooming prior to your grand entrance. And may I say, you're a little light on the blush? Your look's just a tad bit too pale."

"For your information, I've been in the hospital lab for the last forty-five minutes," Cordelia said icily.

"Got sent to the wrong place, huh?" Xander flung at her. "Or did they have a better class of anxious friends and relatives?"

"I was in there giving blood. In Willow's name. In case she has to have a transfusion." Cordelia glared at him.

Xander was obviously stunned. He opened and closed his mouth like a fish. Blinked. Then he said, "Oh. That was a good idea."

Cordelia scanned the group. "Am I the only one who thought of it?"

Cordelia pursed her lips into a thin line. Then she picked up another slick golf magazine and flipped it open. She lowered her head as if she were reading every single word.

Buffy came over to her. "That was really nice of you," she said sincerely.

Cordelia shifted. "Do you mind? You're standing in my light. I'm reading."

"I know," Buffy murmured, moving away. She said to her mom, "I'm going to the bathroom." Joyce nodded as if she barely heard her.

Buffy walked to the restroom and splashed water on her face. *First Natalie, now Willow.*

But this is not about me. These are people I love, but no one is deliberately taking them from me.

She caught her breath and looked at her reflection. *So not a pretty sight. One minute you're there, and the next . . .*

The next you're dead, or a vampire.

She turned off the tap just as the door slammed open and a nurse poked her head in.

She yelled at Buffy, "Do you work here?"

Buffy shook her head.

"Damn it." The woman looked grim. "We have tons of incoming. Burns from the fires. And now a damn tidal wave."

Brushing back her hair with one hand, the woman went back into the hall, leaving Buffy to puzzle out her words.

Tidal wave? In Sunnydale?

Then the air filled with the sound of sirens. They rose and fell, screaming and wailing, like falling bombs or airplanes. Buffy ran into the hall just as her mother and Xander ran out of the waiting room, and the trio headed for the foyer.

The pink lady was half-standing, punching buttons, asking people to hold; with her other hand, she was scribbling something on a notepad.

"What's going on?" Buffy asked; and as often happened, the air of authority in her voice got the woman to tell her.

"It's—it's just unreal," Grace Beck told her. "There's been a tidal wave on Sunnydale Beach. Drowning victims. People hit with debris. And the fire's gotten worse."

Buffy wheeled around and headed down the corridor to the woman's right, which led to the emergency room. Buffy knew the floor plan of Sunnydale Medical. She figured she'd spent more time there than anywhere else, except for the library at school, on account of it being Slayer Central. The medical center was usually Aftermath Central.

"Miss, get out of the way," shouted a voice as she rounded a corner.

There was a parade of gurneys headed her way, personnel grouped around them, wheeling along IV's and crash carts. The wheels clattered and squealed as the doctors and nurses raced the wounded and injured along. Every single person's scrubs were covered with blood, and an undercurrent of groaning filled in the bottom-most layer of sound.

"What happened? What's going on?" Buffy demanded, but this time, no one answered her. She tried to flatten herself out of the way, realized the futility of that, and ran back to the juncture of hallways. Gurney after gurney flew past her. An old lady was writhing; Buffy covered her mouth as a burned man lay inert. A man cried out, "Kipper! Kipper!" and another man shouted, "My son! Find my son!"

Then a woman of about thirty-five glanced over at Buffy; her face bruised and cut. She said, "It was a mummy. In the fog."

"It was wrapped in bandages?" Buffy asked. "All wrapped up like, um, frozen fish, only not in paper?"

The woman groaned and nodded.

"Miss, are you family?" a man in teal scrubs asked as he trotted up beside the woman's gurney.

Buffy nodded. "Yes." She looked at the nurse. "What's wrong with her?"

"Deep gash to the back of her right leg," the nurse said. "Shock. Do you want to give blood? She's had two units already."

"This mummy . . ." Buffy said to the woman, but she had fallen unconscious.

Just then, a steel-haired woman in a white lab coat ran up to the gurney and said, "Okay, nurse, what've we got?"

They moved into medical-speak and Buffy moved off. She jogged down to another gurney, this one a girl she recognized from math class. The left side of her face was bandaged and her left arm was in a sling.

"Did you see a mummy?" Buffy asked without pre-amble.

"What?" the girl asked. "Who are you?"

"Miss?" the man in the teal scrubs called to Buffy. "Let us do our job here?"

"Okay, okay," Buffy murmured, backing off.

She hurried back to the foyer, where her mother and Xander were waiting.

"It's a zoo," she reported. "People talking about mummies." Her mom was stricken. "I'm thinking your car accident guy."

"Oh, yay," Xander groused. "Time for another thrilling episode of as the world turns wacky."

As they talked, the lobby swarmed with new arrivals, some in wheelchairs, others limping with the assistance of whoever brought them in. Sound bounced off the walls: babies shrieking, tears and shouts; people yelling for help, rudely insisting on it the way some people do when they're frightened to death. The hysteria level was rising to fever pitch, and a few of the injured were shutting down, staggering in a daze, or slipping off to a corner just to sit.

The air was thick with the mingled scents of sweat, blood and dirt. The coffee cart beside the entrance wafted mocha java and fresh pastries; Buffy caught heavy perfumes. A man in a cowboy hat pushed past her; he was way heavy on the Old Spice.

"My downstairs is completely flooded," an elderly woman said to Joyce. She had on a brassy red wig and way too much nonmatching orange lipstick, and her raincoat was sopping wet. "I have three thousand dollars in inventory, covered with mud." She touched Joyce's cheek appraisingly. "You should call me sometime for a complimentary facial."

Beyond the double glass doors and large windows, cars were stacked like jets waiting to taxi out of Los Angeles International Airport. Red and blue emergency lights flashed; sirens blatted and blared.

"This isn't looking right," Buffy said. "Even by Sunnydale standards, this is way more bad karma than we should be having on a Saturday."

"And I second that duh." Xander was not being sarcastic, only observant. He said to Buffy, "I'm thinking Giles."

"Me, too." Buffy hesitated and looked upward. Somewhere above them on another floor, Willow was in surgery, or not, and Buffy wished that X-ray vision had come with the Slayer package. *No such luck.*

"Willow's in good hands," Joyce said, touching Buffy's shoulder. "There's nothing you can do for her here, honey."

"Okay." Buffy looked unhappy. "It's just . . ." *Natalie died. That was bad. But if Willow died, I couldn't handle it. And that won't keep it from happening. The universe really doesn't care how much pain any of us can stand.*

"I'll call you at Mr. Giles's place the minute we have news," Joyce promised her.

Still Buffy hesitated. Xander said, "I've got wheels today, Buffy. I'll drive you over."

"I'll call him," Buffy decided finally. "I'll ask him if he knows what's the what and if he says I have to go see him, I will."

Joyce looked as if she were about to say something. Then she pursed her lips and nodded.

Buffy found a bank of pay phones. Standing beside a man with tears rolling down his cheeks as he spoke in Spanish into a receiver, Buffy put in some change in the next phone over and dialed Giles's condo.

"Buffy. Good," he said, as if they'd been in the middle of a conversation. "I've been reading some astrology texts and I believe that we're about to begin a phase called 'the Illumination.' I want you to—"

"Who's India?" she cut in. "Not like the country, but In-*dee*-ah. Because Willow dreamed about her, and everything's falling to pieces around here."

There was a pause on the other end of the line. Her heart skipped a beat. Or three.

He knows.

He knows who she is.

"She dreamed about her?" Giles asked.

"And she's in the hospital now, with a hurt back. Also, a bad brain."

"What?"

"Willow. In the hospital. There was a terrible accident. And a lot of people are having them, too." She was speaking too fast, but she couldn't slow down. "My mom said she saw someone, like a mummy, and it was like my dream, but also, other people are seeing it. Willow stayed over, and when she woke up, she said, 'India.' Which is different from what I dreamed, but that's the only part that was different." She paused. "Except for Matthew Broderick."

"You're certain Willow said 'India' when she woke up?" Giles asked carefully.

Buffy swallowed. "Also, 'come forth.' That wigs you why?"

"Buffy, come to my home. This is important. I can't tell you about it over the phone."

"But . . ." She glanced over her shoulder. Her mother saw her and waved.

"Buffy. Do this. We clearly have a lot to discuss. In fact, gather the group. We need to have a meeting."

Buffy sighed. Giles was her Watcher. Not that that meant she did everything he told her to do. But he did hold a little more sway than, say, a teacher assigning homework.

Or a pink lady telling her it would be hours before they heard anything about Willow's condition.

"Okay, Giles. On our way," she said, then quickly added, "I haven't seen Faith yet today."

"She's been to see me already. And what she had to tell me makes me even more concerned about the situation as you've described it."

Xander walked up to her. She looked at him grimly and said, "Wheels are good. We also need Cordelia and Oz."

"Then avengers, assemble." Xander nodded. "We live to ride."

Chapter Four

As they ran hand in hand, Willow looked around at the gray, and then at Lucy, and said, "No offense, but I was kind of hoping I wouldn't be coming back here."

"Willow, listen," Lucy said, speaking in a rush as she pulled Willow along. So far, they had outdistanced the mummy guy, but Lucy didn't want to take any chances, and Willow was all for no-chance-taking. "I'm going to take you to see India."

"India?" Willow asked anxiously. "That's good, with the breaking free. And we're going to see her cuz she's . . . who?"

Lucy cocked her head, a fairly impressive feat when one is barreling along in the land of the dead. "Buffy's never told you?"

"Told me . . . ?" Willow was not too happy with the direction of the conversation. She had had enough surprises. *Dying, for one. Big on the surprise list.* "Not with the telling about India, no."

"Oh. I see. Perhaps it was too painful for her. Or she was afraid to upset you." Lucy stopped running and faced the way they had come. "I think it's gone. Maybe it left the Ghost Roads."

"Good?" Willow guessed.

Lucy sighed. "Good for us, bad for Faith and Buffy. The Wanderers are created to track down Slayers, Willow. To kill them."

"Oh. Then I'm glad it didn't do that, Lucy. Kill you. Cuz you know . . ." She trailed off, totally confused.

Lucy was gazing someplace Willow could not go. Her jaw was clamped, her chin slightly raised, her eyes glittering with anger. Her fists balled, making the muscles and veins on the backs of her hands prominent. There was no mistaking Slayer moxie, and Lucy was oozing with it.

"A Wanderer did kill me," she said simply. She looked at Willow. "Didn't you know that, either?"

"Um," Willow said.

"Let me tell you who India is," Lucy said.

Excerpt From the Diary of India Cohen

June 29, 1993

> *Dear Diary,*
> *We landed in Japan tonight. We got to Narita Airport, and then we had to take a bus for two hours to get to Tokyo. Then we had to go further south to our city, which is called Yokosuka. I'm dead.*
>
> *I can't believe how hot it is. I'm sweating like crazy. We're billeted in the nurses' quarters while they get our house ready. Their air conditioning is laughable and we're trying to survive with some*

fans in our rooms. They're also burning mosquito coils, which stink way bad and as far as I can tell, are not killing any mosquitoes. Or else there are so many of them that they manage to get around the coils and bite me anyway.

I'm writing instead of sleeping because Mom and Daddy had a huge fight about ten minutes ago. I don't know what it was about, but Mom is already out the door. She took the car and the driver. Daddy sounded really upset but he hasn't said a word to me so far. He never does. Am I just being a melodramatic fifteen-year-old when I say sometimes I feel like an orphan? And is this what getting married is going to be like? Cuz I am thinking, "Pass!"

I'm all in knots. I'm so tired and hot and I'm already homesick. Who would ever guess I would miss anything about South Carolina? I miss Munchkin so much. I know Gramma will take good care of her up in Green Bay, and I know Daddy warned me when I brought her home that we might get transferred overseas, but I couldn't leave her in that box in front of the Piggly Wiggly when all her brothers and sisters had already found good homes.

I think this whole "runt of the litter" thing is a bunch of you-know-what, anyway. That may be because I'm so short. Munchy's little for a Samoyed, but nobody can keep up with Munchkin, not even the football players at school, and the only way I could make sure she got enough exercise was letting her run while I rode my bike. She could do ten miles, easy.

*She wouldn't do well in this heat, though.
Daddy has a point there. A big, fluffy dog like her
shouldn't be put through this. As I'm writing this,
the paper is actually limp from my sweat. My pen
is running on the damp page and my arm is all
slick. Yuck.*

*I wish I had pushed harder to stay in Green
Bay with Gramma, too. Mom and Daddy said no
but they usually say no to anything I ask the first
time around. Then later they give in. I wish I
knew what they fought about tonight. I hope it
wasn't me. I don't know why it would be about
me—I haven't said or done anything wrong—but
what else do they have to fight about?*

*Daddy is the captain of one of the biggest
ships in the Seventh Fleet and Mom used to be
one of the most famous actresses in Asia, definitely the most famous in the Philippines. She is
still way beautiful.*

*She keeps asking me how a lady like her could
have a jock like me for a kid. But she doesn't actually say "jock." I'm not sure she knows what jock
means. She just goes on about how I don't wear
makeup and I wear my hair just in a boring ponytail, and when am I going to stop playing sports
with boys and start thinking about my appearance?*

*I do think about my appearance. I'm fashion-
able without being all overboard about it, wearing
jeans and T's, and so do lots of girls who aren't
succumbing to fashion victimhood. Jeanne
Schaumberg's mom said she wished Jeanne was
more into sports and less into boys. Most of the
other girls' moms say stuff like that. So why can't*

*my mom be happy that I'm doing well at some-
thing, even if I'm not the prom queen or whatever?*

*Daddy just came in and told me that he's sorry if
the fight upset me. He didn't ask me if I heard it. I'll
bet half the base heard it. Stuff like this is bad for his
career. Mom knows that, but I guess she doesn't
care. Sometimes I feel like it's Dad and me in one
family, and her and me in another. It doesn't seem
like we synch up well when it's all three of us.*

Hold on . . .

*Oh, my God. I can't believe this. This is too,
too, too weird. Am I on drugs and don't know it?
Check it out—*

*Daddy came back in and asked me if I wanted
anything before he went to bed. He looked really
lost. I almost started crying but he looked like he
would cry if I did, so I held it in. He said something about Mom missing her career, and I said,
"Why can't she have her career?" and he said
some stuff about he'll be going to sea a lot and
who would take care of me?*

*So I said, "Hey, Daddy, I am fifteen, you know.
And I'll be sixteen before school starts." And this
set him off; he did start to cry so I was really
freaked out and also I was kind of mad at him,
even though I still don't really understand why.
Almost like he was asking me to solve this problem for him. Does that make any sense?*

*If it does, good. Cuz what happened next does
not make any sense.*

*He wiped his eyes and said he was sorry and
went out the door. I decided to take a walk, because maybe it would be cooler outdoors and besides, I needed to walk off the tension.*

So I went outside and there was this amazingly cute guy standing across the street. He had black, black hair and big, big, big green eyes. He was smoking a cigarette. And when he saw me, he looked kind of startled and said, "India?" And he pronounced it correctly. (Nobody ever gets it right the first time. In-DEE-a. I always tell people, "NOT like the country," but they still don't get it.)

When your dad is a commanding officer of a ship, you learn early on how to deal with people you don't know, but who know you. Plus, famous mother. So I said, "Yeah?"

He replied, "I'm your Watcher."

I was freaked out, cuz what does that mean, that he's my stalker?

I said, "Really. How about that?"

And he looked at me like I should know what that means. So then he said, "It's happened. You've been called. "You're the Chosen One."

He put his hand on my shoulder. I didn't give him another chance. I decked him. He landed on his butt and his cigarette went flying.

I stamped out his cigarette and said, "I'm getting my father right now."

He looked up at me and made kind of this "Wait, wait" hand gesture, and said, "Don't you know about your destiny?"

I shouted, "Daddy!" and there was a commotion over at the nurses' quarters and the guy ran off. By the time my dad showed, my "watcher" was long gone.

So I told him what happened, and gave him a description, and he called the Shore Patrol. Now they're looking for the guy, and Daddy told me

*that I did the right thing in defending myself first
and asking questions later, cuz you never know.
Never know what? That some people are kind of
psycho? Not news here!*

*But I do feel like I overreacted. Maybe that's
because he was so amazingly cute. He's probably
at least twenty. He was wearing shorts and an
Annapolis T-shirt and he looked way hot.*

*My mom just came back and my dad told her
about what happened and now she's yelling at
him and telling him that Americans bring vio-
lence with them wherever they go, and he's saying, "Oh, yeah? Anybody tell Ferdinand and
Imelda about that?"*

*He means Ferdinand and Imelda Marcos. Fer-
dinand Marcos was the dictator of the Philippines but he's dead now. The Marcoses helped my
mom with her career and now they've been declared of the bad, and that embarrasses my dad.*

*Anyway, that's old news. The new news is that
they haven't found the guy and I'm kind of sorry I
didn't wait to ask more questions, no matter what
my dad says.*

*The strange thing is, I'm not really scared. I
almost feel like I know what this is about.*

*I feel wired. I feel like something is gonna hap-
pen. Something very big.*

Sunnydale

Amanda Johnson stood by the window of the Carey
Quinn Cho Law Offices, where she worked, and gazed
down in horror at the mess that was the Main Street of
Sunnydale.

Floodwaters had overwhelmed the storm drains, and the rushing river had spilled over the curbs, sloshing beneath the doorways of all the street-level stores. Trash cans sailed along, and now and then a scattered flotilla of floating garbage, cardboard boxes, even a bicycle. She'd heard that the first two rows of the Sun Cinema were underwater, and it was fairly easy to believe that that was more than just a rumor.

Tears rolled down her cheeks as she stood with a fresh bundle of flyers from Sunnydale Copy Center under her arm. They were fluorescent green, and hard to miss. But an eight-year-old girl was hard to miss, and nobody had seen her daughter, Holly in three days.

When Ben came up behind her and put his arms on her shoulders, Amanda shut her eyes tight to keep herself from losing it.

"I'm sure she's safe," he said soothingly. "I'm sure of it, Mandy."

"How can you be sure? You're not even a parent!" she yelled at him, trying to move away. But he wouldn't let her go; he held her more tightly, as if he were waiting, and she did not disappoint. She burst into heavy, wrenching sobs, lowering her head in abject misery to stare at the flood, seeing not boxes but her daughter lying helpless somewhere, whimpering and cold, and crying for her mother.

"She ran away because of you," she added bitterly, and she was immediately ashamed. "Oh, Ben, God, I'm dying. I'm just dying."

"We will find her," he promised. "And you and I will get married, and she'll be the happiest girl in the world." He paused. "Even if I have to bribe her to be a flower girl with Barbies and *X-Files* tapes."

She couldn't smile, couldn't register the fact that he

had just proposed. Somewhere out there, her baby was in trouble. She could feel it deep inside the marrow of her bones; in every cell. She pressed her abdomen, remembering the first flutter of life that had been Holly. The pain of her birth, and the joy of seeing that screaming, red face up close for the very first time.

I will die if she dies, she knew; and the thought was oddly comforting. *I won't have to go on without her.*

"She's my life," Amanda whispered. "Ben, she is my entire life."

There was silence behind her. She wished she could care that she had just wounded him.

But she couldn't care. She could do nothing but will Holly to be alive.

San Francisco

With a cool, dry, steady hand, Kevin Harris's mother dialed the number for the Harrises of Sunnydale. She was on a pay phone in the hospital corridor, having been chastened by a nurse for using her cell phone inside Kevin's room. Something about the monitors; something about rules. Something about Kevin having bone cancer, and the most likely donors being blood relatives.

She didn't care who she had to ask, what she had to do; she didn't have the slightest bit of hesitation about getting whatever she needed to save her son. She would give a potential donor anything, do anything, if there was a match. She would beg, plead, bribe, cheat, steal, kill to get everybody to submit to testing. There was nothing she would not do.

Nothing.

That realization brought with it a kind of elation. She felt oddly empowered.

The connection was made; the phone on the other end rang. Someone picked it up; there was a pause, and then a strange noise, as if someone had dropped the receiver. Someone swearing. A woman.

It had to be Alexander's mother.

"Hi," she said, not cheerily. Purposefully.

I will do anything.

Holly was slogging through the rushing water as fast as she could. There was so much of it, and it was so deep; and just now, a dead rat had floated past her waist, but she kept the scream inside herself, because fog was gathering behind her.

Thickening and swirling and eddying, like dry ice in the haunted house at the school carnival last year; she had always been fascinated by dry ice. Before he had left them, her father had explained how it was made, and how it kept things very, very cold. Holly had decided then and there to become a scientist. And a ballerina.

She didn't know where she was; there were two-story brick buildings on either side of the river, which had once been the street. Some of the windows in the buildings were broken or completely missing; the roofs were rusty and some of the raingutters had pulled away. They canted over at strange angles, giving the structures a weak, unhappy look, like they were old men bent over, fumbling for their glasses.

Grandpa, she thought, but she didn't cry. She had to pay attention, keep ahead of the fog, because something bad was in it. She could feel it following her, coming after her. Her feet kept slipping from the bottom of the river—which was the center of the street—and she bobbed around the stalled cars, all deserted, and covered her mouth when her foot kicked something that gave way, and felt gooey.

The fog swirled on either side of her, like the arms of their rocking chair at home; she still liked to cuddle up and listen to stories at night. She thought about *The Runaway Bunny,* and how the mommy bunny always found the runaway bunny by changing into things like sailboats and kites. The book had kind of creeped her out, cuz the mommy seemed scary, but now she wished her own mother was in the fog behind her, and not anything else.

She also hoped Gigi was right about Jesus listening to everything everybody said, because right now she was saying, "Jesus, tell my mom where I am. Tell her to come get me."

The fog slid down in front of her face, like something curling in slow motion, and she darted to the left with a little cry. The fog clung to her, moving around her.

Something touched her. She screamed and turned around.

The mummy was directly behind her. What had touched her was its box.

Its box that had faces of screaming girls, and skulls, and it was made of bones and skin and it was opening; the mummy was opening it—

The fog whirled around them both, Holly and the mummy, faster, faster, like they were inside a washing machine. Faster and thicker, becoming a cone; and Holly realized the fog was coming out of the box. It whooshed and blew and rushed; it was wind, with fog in it. It circled around her, moving more rapidly, until she was staggering through the water with it, spinning around and around, and screaming.

Then the mummy reached in its box and she knew it was going to pull out an axe, just like the other one had. Or maybe this was the same one. She didn't know.

But the mummy stopped, frozen, with its hand in the box. The winds dervished around both it and Holly. It stared straight ahead, like a robot that had been turned off, and Holly took off. She fought the wind and the water and she started screaming, and screaming, and screaming, and she didn't stop screaming until someone grabbed her and dragged her out of the river.

And dragged her into a doorway and held her tight; and said, "Come with me."

Holly had no idea who spoke; she was so frightened that she couldn't even see a thing. She could barely feel the hand wrapped tightly around her forearm. The person was pulling her along too fast, so fast she was half-dragged through the water, but Holly didn't care. It wasn't the mummy, so it was someone better; and that was as far as she could think.

They sloshed this way and that way and then they went up some stairs, and then there was a door opening and the person in front of her yelled, "Giles!"

Next thing she knew, Holly was in somebody's house. And a dark-haired boy and a kind-of old man were sitting on a couch surrounded by books. They both looked at her, and she looked at them, and she said, strangely calm, "There was a mummy, but he didn't have his axe, I think. The first one did. The first one . . . the first one came at me . . . and I . . . and I . . ."

They stared at her, and then each other.

The person who had saved her knelt in front of her. She was a very pretty girl with blonde hair and blue-green eyes, and Holly felt a moment of confusion, as if she had met her before and she should know her name and everything.

"I'm Buffy. You're safe. What's your name?" the girl asked kindly.

"Holly," Holly confided. Then she collapsed into the girl's arms. "I want my mommy!" she shrieked. "I want my mommy *now!*"

Chapter Five

Watchers Council Headquarters, London

It was late afternoon in London. The rebuilt headquarters of the Watchers Council were as unremarkable as they had been when William the Bloody and the demon Skrymer had destroyed the original in 1940.

Select members of the Watchers Council, a handful of whom had survived that horrible bloodbath, gathered to mourn one of their own. Though he had officially retired from service, Roger Zabuto had kept in touch with many of his old friends. He'd been to Eton with a number of the men seated at the long conference table.

Black bunting was draped over the crown molding at the juncture of wall and ceiling. Each Watcher wore a black armband, and everyone present was dressed from tip to toe in ebony. Black was the color of grief, the color of failure; it represented the unsatisfiable maw of death, who ground men's bones to make bread that never sustained. Death could not get from the vanquished what it wanted, and so it demanded more, and more . . . and more.

And the Council gave it more, and more . . . and more. Today, it had given Death Roger Zabuto.

There was only one woman present. A tall and stately woman in an expensive black suit, she had been Roger's lover when he'd first become a Watcher. Her name was Neema Mfune-Hayes.

It was widely known that Neema had been on the short list for assignment to Kendra, and that she had deeply resented Roger's selection over her. She had gone so far as to file an official complaint, but like much of Council business, it came to nothing.

Shortly thereafter, she withdrew her name from active status and devoted herself to research. Her particular specialty was hunting down lost Watcher's Diaries, in some cases translating or transcribing them, or extracting as much text as she could, from books burned hastily in fireplaces or buried to prevent discovery. The forces of darkness were quite eager to learn all they could about Slayers, always had been, and always would be.

As a result of her efforts, Neema probably knew more collectively about Slayers than any other person in the room. The consequence of that, of course, was that she was a highly sought-after prize. There had been numerous attempts to kidnap her, and even more to bribe her. Demons could be a practical lot.

As with the male Watchers, a Waterford snifter of Napoleon brandy sat before Neema on the highly polished table. A fire crackled pleasantly in the hearth, but it was not enough to dispel the chill in the ancient stone room. Beyond the high wall which blocked most of the frail English sunlight, the traffic of London swirled and raced, cabs circling in the roundabouts like dogs chasing their tails.

So much normality, Neema thought sadly, *yet Roger is dead. How the world does go on.*

How we must go on, as well.

Her throat was clamped shut with unspent grief. Though she had married another—also a Watcher—she had never stopped loving Roger Zabuto. *In fact, until this moment*, she thought, *I assumed that somehow we would finish our lives together. That he would miss me too much, and my choice would be so simple.* . . .

"To Roger," Lord Anthony Yorke said gravely, lifting his glass. He was the most senior member of the Council among them—trotted out, Neema assumed, to indicate the high regard in which Roger had been held.

The others followed suit. "To Roger," everyone chorused, and sipped their brandy with one motion.

Sir Anthony looked steadily at Neema. He was her confidante; he had known of her deep and abiding love for Roger. Now she could see the sympathy etched on his features. She was profoundly grateful; more often, the upper echelons heartily disapproved of any sort of strong feelings between Watchers, or between Watcher and Slayer, for that matter. Somehow, he excused Neema her weakness.

The Watchers sipped in silence, as was the custom, each remembering Roger and the part he played in their constant, unending struggle against evil. Theirs was a difficult calling, theirs, a lonely way to live.

There were two vacant seats at the table. One, of course, was for Roger. And one was in honor of Rupert Giles, the current Watcher of the two American Slayers. Kendra had been called because Buffy Summers had died, albeit briefly. Kendra's death had called Faith to service. So the lineage had been both preserved and altered, and there had been innumerable discussions about the propriety—if such a word could be used—about having two Slayers at the same time.

Whatever the case, Giles was at present in charge of both of them, and such a thing had never happened before.

"It is a sorry business all around," Lord Yorke said, as he set down his snifter. "Slayer and Watcher, both gone. A double loss for our side."

"Amen," Neema said.

"I'm worried that something similar may happen to Rupert Giles," Lord Yorke continued. "As you know, he's extremely vulnerable at the moment, as the Watcher of both the Slayers. I have it in mind to fly over and see how he is. As some of you may know, we have had a number of mental breakdowns in the past when Watchers have outlived their charges, and it might do well to check in on them at more regular intervals."

"But it's a rather normal state of affairs, is it not?" another of the Council said casually. "The girls rarely live beyond their mid-twenties."

"I think it would be a lovely idea to visit Mr. Giles," Neema said. "He cared about Roger a great deal."

"Then I shall leave as soon as possible on the Council private jet," Lord Yorke said. "Unless there are any serious objections?"

No one spoke. It would have been quite disrespectful of anyone to voice any, once such a highly placed member had spoken.

Sunnydale

"Okay," Cordelia said to the group as they settled in their usual spots in Giles's living room. The Watcher was in the kitchen, making another pot of tea. Much with the tea-drinking. "We have fires. We have floods. We have wind. Apocalypse much?"

"We don't have earth," Giles said thoughtfully. "At least, I don't think we do."

"Lacking in earth, to my thinking," Xander concurred. "Since the water is covering it up a bit more than usual."

"And mummies," Holly Johnson whispered.

Wearing one of Giles's sweatshirts as a long dress, the little girl was anxiously pacing, waiting for her mother, who was on her way. Cordelia had driven Joyce Summers home, then shown, and did not look too happy to be there. Xander was busy with the books, and Oz had elected to stay at the hospital, and promised to call as soon as he had some news.

Faith was of the absent, having dropped by to tell Giles about her dreams and then boogied on to damper pastures.

Meanwhile, Buffy was so very glad she'd gone outside to see what the heck was going on with the wind. She had seen no mummy thing, but she had seen a lot of fog and a terrified child racing in the opposite direction. *Slayer to the rescue, and bonus points for finding Holly Johnson.*

"So, meanwhile," Buffy said, "India." Giles hesitated. Buffy frowned at him. "Giles, you said you had her diary."

He cleared his throat and said, "I suggest we wait a bit." To the girl, he said, "Holly? Would you care for more tea?"

She was trembling. Buffy could practically see the fear coming off her in waves. Gently the Slayer took her hand and led her to the sofa, made a face at Xander to get him to move, and eased the little girl into a sitting position. Holly almost bolted back off the couch, as if she were afraid to stay in one place, but Buffy knelt before her and gave her a smile.

"I need to ask you some more questions," she said. "While we wait for your mom, okay?"

Holly's thin shoulders slumped and she nodded as if she really didn't care anymore. Buffy knew that look. She had seen it on more faces than she cared to admit: it was defeat. It was the look that came over someone's face when they had had enough.

"Never mind." Buffy picked up Holly's tea cup and handed it to her. "We'll just wait for your mother to come."

She heard rapid footfalls and said, "That's probably her now."

But the door crashed open and Faith dove over the transom, shouting, "B! Front and center!"

"Why?" Buffy yelled, but didn't hesitate to run to her fellow Slayer's side.

They dashed outside, Faith sailing into a bank of unbelievably thick fog. She said, "There's something in here, and it tried to nail my butt! It followed me all the way over here."

"It's probably a mummy," Buffy said. "Maybe it caught my scent when I saved Holly."

"Whatever. I just wanna kill it."

Buffy started swinging, on the off chance that she might make contact. Then she slammed her fist into something as hard as iron. The jarring impact made her bones vibrate and her teeth rattle. She swung again, before whatever it was had a chance to put distance between them. Executing a flawless sidekick, she used the momentum to deliver a whipkick as she switched standing legs. Then a swift uppercut. Whatever it was . . . did not budge an inch.

"I got it, I got it," Buffy said, "but it's not going anywhere."

"Okay," Faith said. "Me, too. I can feel it."

They both went into pummeling mode. Buffy said, "Can you see anything? Is it a mummy?"

"Doesn't feel like one. It feels like a Sherman tank," Faith said.

"What is it?" Giles called from the doorway. Buffy glanced at him, took in the fact that Xander had joined him.

"Don't let the fog inside," Buffy advised. She doubled up for another punch and flew forward, impelled by her own momentum. She continued to sail through the air; her target had moved.

"Where is it?" she cried to Faith.

"I don't know. I think it's gone."

"Let's get inside," Buffy said.

Both Slayers hightailed it back into the house, narrowly missing Giles and Xander as they backed into Giles's apartment. Faith, at Buffy's heels, slammed the door and flicked the locks. Then she took a couple of giant steps away from the door, assuming a clean, steady fight stance, and Buffy did the same.

They waited for a few moments. Nothing happened.

"Huh," Faith grunted.

When the doorbell rang, Buffy nearly put her fist through the door.

"Holly?" a woman called.

"Mommy!"

The little girl raced to the door. Buffy stood in front of her and said, "Hold on a sec." She nodded at Faith, who unlocked the door, got ready to rumble just in case, and opened it.

A woman who resembled the little girl ran into the room. She was followed by a man whose smile lit up the apartment. Distracted, Buffy nevertheless scoped out the courtyard. There was nothing there, not even a wisp of fog. She traded glances with Faith, who had joined her.

"Holly, Holly," the woman cried, falling to her knees and enfolding the child. They clung to each other, sobbing, while the man stood by.

Then the little girl looked up at the man and blurted, "Please don't make my mommy drink."

"What?" the man said, then wiped his eyes and came to the mother and daughter and tentatively gave the little girl a quick hug.

The reunion continued. Faith rolled her eyes at Buffy and ambled into the kitchen, where the tea kettle was screaming. Giles joined them, rescuing the screaming kettle, while Faith smoothed back her dripping hair and said, "Well, that's a happy ending, eh, blondie?"

"What was in the fog?" Buffy asked her. "Did you see anything?"

"No clue. But it was following me, or something." She grimaced at her wet leather clothes. "It's a bitch when this stuff dries on you," she said. "It's like wearing a corset."

Giles was doing all the tea things he did, fussing with the bags, sugar, and milk. Everything went on a tray, always did, even if it was just him and Buffy and a couple of mugs. At the moment, Buffy found comfort in the ritual, and put her hand on the jamb as she watched him go for it.

Then she said, "Okay, Giles. They're too busy to listen to us. Spill. India."

"Oh." Faith brightened as she picked up a sugar cube and licked it. "The chick who came before you." She wrinkled her nose. "Hell of a way to die, huh?"

Buffy stared at her. She was thunderstruck. "My . . ."

"Your predecessor, Buffy." Giles's voice was soft. "The girl whose death called you to your destiny as the Slayer."

The phone rang. Giles touched Buffy's shoulder and said, "I'll be right back, Buffy. That may be news about Willow."

"Yes," she said blankly. Then, processing, more urgently, "Yes."

Giles picked up the phone. Buffy watched him, aware of how hard her heart was beating. *India. The Slayer before me. And I never even asked him her name.*

"Giles here," her Watcher said. "Yes?"

Faith popped the sugar cube in her mouth and crunched.

Was she strong? Was she a good fighter? How did she die?

Giles paled. He reached for something to hold onto as he breathed, "Oh, my God. How? When did it happen?"

Buffy's stomach lurched. "Giles?" she called. "Is it Willow?"

He had the presence of mind to shake his head, then hold out a hand as if to fend off more questions. Slowly, he sat, as Holly, her mother, and her father left the apartment in a happy chorus of farewells.

"Wait, it might not be safe," Faith said, but no one was listening. She started to head for the door just as Giles hung up the phone.

"Buffy," he said, looking at her through the breakfast bar cutout in the wall. "That was a contact of mine in Jamaica. Mr. Zabuto . . ."

"Kendra's Watcher," Faith filled in, coming into the living room.

Giles turned his back to both Slayers. Tensions spanned across his shoulders and his spine was ramrod straight. He looked off to the side, the way he sometimes did when he simply couldn't handle saying something directly to Buffy's face.

"He's been killed."

"What?" Buffy was shocked. "As in . . . ?"

"Brutally murdered. His belongings have been ransacked, as if the murderers were looking for something."

"Money?" Faith asked.

"Doubtful." Giles exhaled. "Roger was not a wealthy man. The mansion in which he lived had fallen into disrepair. Dire neglect. One assumes they were searching for something else."

"Like what?" Xander asked.

"Give me a moment, please," Giles said. "Alone." Slowly sitting on the chair opposite the sofa, he hung his head in his hands.

Faith, Xander, and Cordelia tiptoed into the kitchen, joining Buffy near the refrigerator. Cordelia looked at the others and snapped, "It's always death with you people."

"Yeah," Buffy breathed, watching Giles. Hurting for him. And somehow, missing Kendra more than ever. It was as if that now that her Watcher was dead, she was even more gone. Buffy didn't know how to explain it, but she felt it.

It's always death with us people. So much death.

Chapter Six

San Diego, California

In her lovely rented mansion in the rich San Diego neighborhood of Point Loma, Cecile Lafitte threw the bones, read them, and gathered them up again with her blood red nails. The signs were not all there, but the majority of factors pointed to a good resolution. Translation: Despite the fact that things were not perfect in Sunnydale, she should continue to move her pawns. Two living Slayers lay within the grasp of the Gatherer, and it wanted them. Desperately.

Rich rewards would come to the one who delivered them up to the insatiable god.

She threw the bones again, came up with the exact same answer, and dropped them into a skull on the black varnished table. The planks of the table had been cut from the coffin of Tutuana Lafitte, her wily descendant. Clever woman that she was, she had nearly succeeded in achieving immortality. In her attempt, she had reconnected Cecile with her bloodline, and of that, she was very grateful.

Cecile picked up her phone and punched in the familiar North Carolina number. She tapped her nails and waited expectantly; Cameron usually picked it up on the first ring. He did not disappoint.

Her smile was in her voice as she said, "It is time, *mon amour.* It is the correct moment to transport our master."

"Everything is ready?" he asked eagerly. After all this time, Cameron had not lost his Southern accent.

"Almost everything," she replied. "There are still a few loose ends, but I have confidence that they will be resolved in time." She tapped one of her lovely manicured nails against the vellum pages of *Le Livre des Quatres. The Book of Fours.* She reminded herself that without Cameron, her plans would have been much more difficult to accomplish. When she assumed her rightful place in the new world, she would remember his past services to her.

She took a moment to reminisce. With victory so close, it was time to reflect on all that had been accomplished.

After she had fled, as "Ceceli," from ibn Rashad, she had languished in a small desert village, cowering from his wrath, until she realized that she was not aging. Nor was he hunting her. Either he had lost track of her, or lost interest in her. Either way, she was not about to waste her valuable time pondering this fortuitous event.

So she continued her studies of the Pool, gleaning all she could of its origin and creation; and to her delight, she made friends with a local sorcerer, who taught her about scrying stones. They were like tiny windows through which one could see across vast distances, even across time. She learned, also, that ibn Rashad was said to dwell in the city of Jerusalem, and that he was worshipped there as a god.

It took her years, but at last a confederate agreed to

infiltrate ibn Rashad's fortress, deposit a stone, and then, hopefully, escape. In return, Ceceli showered him with pleasures of every sort, including her own, promising him much, much more upon his return.

But he never did return.

However, he managed to do as he promised before the desert took him: the stone was in place, in ibn Rashad's privy chamber, where the sorcerer communed with his god. The One Who Gathers and Preserves, which he now called the Gatherer, lived in an elaborate pit, and ibn Rashad merged in some way with it by thrusting his hands into its hideous, rank form. That this was both excruciating and sublime was clear from the expressions on his face and the sounds he uttered; but even better, he maintained a private diary of his experiences with the Gatherer. With her scrying stone, Ceceli read every word he wrote—and made herself a copy of his book. It was she, not he, who eventually called it *The Book of Fours*.

It was she, not he; nor the next man who had served the Gatherer; nor the next, who had eventually realized that four was the crucial number in every magickal equation having to do with the Gatherer.

But I get ahead of myself, she thought, running her fingers along the text which she herself had written, years before.

Fifty years after she had taken ibn Rashad to the pool, rumors circulated regarding ibn Rashad's depravity. The kings of Europe were determined to take Jerusalem, "saving" it for Christianity. With Christian armies on the march, she knew she must go soon to ibn Rashad, and challenge him for control of the Gatherer.

But fate had intervened, and she had been forced to wait.

Which turned out to be a very good thing, she thought. *It saved me so much traveling.*

With a smile on her face, she picked up the phone again.

"Kit?" she asked, when the connection was made. "It's I, Cecile. Would you be interested in a session tonight? I can feel the vibrations. I'm certain we shall reach your friend on the other side this time. What did you say her name was? India?"

Boston

"Okay, Willy, thanks for the update," Tervokian said into the receiver. He scratched one of his horns, a nervous habit, and popped the brown scale in his mouth. Serrated teeth ground the keratin to bits. That was a nervous habit, too, and he'd tried everything to break himself of it. "You'll be getting your usual retainer in the mail."

He hung up without saying goodbye to Willy the Snitch, the barkeep of Willy's Alibi Room, where all the demons in Sunnydale went to drink. Willy didn't care about manners. He cared about cash. And for a nice, crisp fifty, he had told Tervokian some lousy news.

Though he'd kept it light and easy during the conversation, Tervokian was angry enough to rip the phone from the wall of his dark, comforting lair, but he was also cheap enough to know how much it would cost to replace it. The wall, that was. Phones, he got for free, on account of he and his boys stole them.

Hey, fun was where you found it.

Fun was not pissing off a big cheese like Cecile Lafitte, no way, no how. But according to Willy, his vampire bounty hunters had failed, and failed big.

Faith the Vampire Slayer was still alive and very much kicking, and his boys had lost the magickal axe he was supposed to give Cecile.

Marone, as they said in the North End.

He held his breath and counted to a big number while his *capo,* the vampire Kenny the Fang, stood beside him, idly going through a box of old handguns, flicking them open, spinning barrels, checking triggers.

Tervokian plopped down in his recliner and buried his head in his hands. "So, Kenny, Miss Faith Big-shot Slayer not only dusted my employees, but she took the friggin' axe right out of their hands."

"That is bad, boss," Kenny told him, admiring several weapons, as if trying to decide which one was best. He pointed at an imaginary target across the room and made a ka-pow sound beneath his breath. "It makes us look like idiots. Screw-ups. It's humiliating."

"Beyond humiliating," Tervokian agreed.

Kenny said, "So, lemme guess. The Slayer took the axe to her Watcher. That British guy with the fancy-schmancy accent. And Cecile knows we've lost possession of the Axe."

There's always a little ray of sunshine, Tervokian thought. *That's what Mamma always used to say.*

"Willy don't think so, Kenny. On account of the Master's followers are still waiting for it. They're hanging around his place, getting nervous. I asked Willy to check it out for us."

"So they don't know our assassins were in town?"

"Doesn't look like it," Tervokian said. *How many times do I have to remind myself not to let it get personal? Man, am I in trouble.*

"They don't know we were there, and Madame Cecile

still thinks we're delivering the axe to San Diego even as we speak."

"So sending them to Sunnydale first to get rid of Faith . . . not our best idea?"

Tervokian was angry. He did not like his underlings questioning his judgment. Which, in this case, was fair. Everybody in the universe had wanted that axe—the Master's people in Sunnydale, and Cecile Lafitte down in San Diego. They were going to pay handsomely for it—if the Master rose, Tervokian was gonna sit at his right hand. If Cecile got it first, she was gonna make Tervokian the next Servant. He couldn't lose. So what did he do?

Decide to use it on Faith first, make sure she got taken out no matter who ended up with it.

He was such a freakin' idiot. No wonder he'd never gotten South Boston like he wanted.

"We gotta find that axe before someone finds out we lost it, boss. Asap," Kenny informed him. "If they hear we don't got it, they'll probably kill us both."

Tervokian flared. "As long as we're the only two who know, it's a secret, right?"

"Right," Kenny said smugly.

Wrong, Tervokian thought to himself.

The demon picked up a gun and pretended to admire it while he pressed open the hidey-hole built into the surface of his desk. He popped it open as he kept his eyes on the gun, gauging what kind of ammo it took.

"How long they got to try to bring the Master back?" Kenny asked. "Is there, like, an expiration date on their offer?"

"We're supposed to give it to them by the Night of the Stars, which is in two or three days." Tervokian kept his face a mask. He didn't mention that Cecile had a similar time window.

Seemed the beautiful broad was in league with an entity called the Gatherer. This Gatherer required a Servant, who acted as its figurehead and got to use its massive power as long as the Servant agreed to be loyal to the Gatherer and let it live vicariously through him. That was okay with Tervokian; he didn't mind subletting his experiences if the price was right. The current Servant was Cameron Duvalier, and the Gatherer was no longer pleased with their relationship, on account of Cameron pretty much having gone completely nuts.

So . . . there was a job opening. Cecile did not want said opening for herself because she was already the Gatherer's consort. Tervokian grinned at the word. What she was, was the Gatherer's babe. And the way the Gatherer got to "experience" its babe was through the Servant "experiencing" its babe.

Guess ol' Cam ain't measuring up, he thought smugly. *Guess I do.*

Anyway, his audition was to give Cecile the magickal axe he'd tried to kill Faith with once before, back here in Bean Town.

He'd gotten the weapon from a fence who was very vague about where *he'd* gotten it, but that somebody had promised him that it was a Slayer-killer, guaranteed. The first time, Faith had gotten away before he'd had a chance to use it on her—the box it came in had started on fire or something, and the entire warehouse they'd imprisoned Faith in had burned down.

So . . . still not tested in combat, but hey, taking Faith out was only part of his current scheme.

This time, Tervokian had played a couple of additional

angles, figuring to lend the axe to the Master's followers before he gave it over permanently to Cecile. A sort
of a little side deal. All they wanted to do with it was
chop Buffy Summers up into little pieces, sprinkling
her blood on the Master's bones. That was supposed to
bring him back from the dead.

Then they'd give it back and he'd give it to Cecile, a
little used, but hey, she hadn't made any stipulations
and he'd made no exclusive-use promises. So, he'd end
up buddies with the risen Master—if their ritual
worked—and with all that power the Gatherer was
gonna let him have, he'd get to hack Faith to death, too,
if his bounty hunters failed, which they had. Plus, he'd
have a woman so gorgeous she'd make you scale faster
than a shedding fungus demon.

So why did I have to try to take out Faith? he asked
himself. *Why couldn't I just be patient?*

*And, say, speaking of local double-dealing demons
with questionable loyalties . . .*

"Hey, Kenny," Tervokian said.

Kenny looked up from the gun he was playing with.
"Yeah, boss?"

Tervokian shot him. Kenny looked stunned, and then
he died.

"Putz," Tervokian said. "Only way to keep a secret is
never to share it with anybody, not even your own
mother." Now, nobody else knew he had lost the axe.

He picked up the phone and punched in a number.

"Cecile," Tervokian said smoothly. "Hi. It's me."

"How are things in Boston, *chérie?*" she asked
sweetly. "How is the axe?"

*Can I fake her out until I find that damn thing
again?* "So far, so good."

"Listen, my darling," she continued. "I have cast the

runes and it is time. You must bring your axe to me."

"Okay. Man, I can't wait to see Faith get it. Or that other Slayer," he said with false joviality.

"That axe will not kill Faith," she said again.

"Impossible. I had it tested myself," Tervokian said, sweating. "I used it on Faith back in Boston . . ." *and it didn't kill her then, either.*

"Not to worry. It will kill Buffy Summers."

"Oh," he said, confused.

"There are four Axes," she explained. "One for each of the four Elements. Your axe can only kill a Slayer of the Air, and that is Buffy Summers. But Faith is a Slayer of Fire."

"Uh-huh." He was a little nervous that she was telling him all this. In the movies, when one of your fellow villains told you the details of their schemes, you usually winded up dead.

"But Buffy is a good kill, so bring it to me now, please? And by the way . . ." She lowered her voice. "Cameron is on his way as well. He thinks his status is unchanged." Her voice grew deep and husky. "But the Gatherer wants a new Servant, *mon amour.* Someone clever. Like you."

"Hey, I'm on the plane." He laughed nervously. "Well, not really, but I will be soon as I make my reservation."

"That makes me so happy," she told him. "I cannot wait. Our plans cannot fail, once we are working side by side."

Tervokian hung up.

Oh, man, am I screwed, he thought.

He glared over at Kenny, who might be the lucky one after all, him having a nice, easy death and all.

*   *   *

"So, Tervokian threatened Faith in Boston," Giles said. "But not with an axe such as either of you described from your dreams."

Faith, remaining with the others at Casa de Rupert, was wearing Giles's bathrobe, which Buffy found rather weird. But she didn't say anything, because she herself had on his sweats. Her clothes were in the dryer, while Faith's leather was carefully blocked down with phone books and some dishes. Meanwhile, Xander was upstairs taking a shower, and Cordelia was taking a nap on Giles's loft bed. It was getting dark, and still no definitive word on Willow. Only that Oz was with her, and she was in the ICU, and her parents were acting like nothing major was going on.

Talk about denial.

"He got me in this warehouse," Faith reminisced. "And then there was this demon, and . . . *wait.*" She nodded, replaying memories in her head. "They had me chained up, but there was something in a corner. It was really dark, but it was a block or something." She looked at Buffy. "Could have been a box. A very gross box."

Buffy nodded. "That's what I dreamed about. Not the kind you put a Christmas sweater in. More of an Ed Gein special."

"Bones and skin," Faith filled in. "Very disturbing, in a sort of arty way."

Buffy wrinkled her nose. "Let's leave it at disturbing. Very disturbing. The first mummy that was threatening the little girl had one, according to her. The one that walked out of the water. The second one had a box."

"Could it have contained an axe such as the one you dreamed about?" Giles asked. "Because I'm thinking about Roger, and he said something about axes once. Though in what context I can't recall." He sat back and sipped his tea. "His diary should arrive tomorrow morning. That may shed some light on things."

Buffy swallowed and said, "What about India? Did she have an axe encounter of the closest kind?"

The extreme look on Giles's face was answer enough. For a moment, Buffy thought he had had a heart attack. "I do know she was hacked to death in some way," he said finally, taking off his glasses and polishing them.

"Oh. Yay," Cordelia said from the loft.

"I thought you were asleep," Giles called up to her.

"Heart pounding too hard to sleep," she said. "Somehow, I find it difficult to drift off while listening to conversations about evisceration."

"We haven't used that word once," Buffy shot back.

"Oh, sorry. 'Hacked.' One of *my* favorite synonyms, anyway."

Faith grinned at Buffy and chuckled silently as she slung one leg over the arm of the sofa. Then she leaned forward on her knee, back to business, and said, "So, you calling India's Watcher? See what he has to say?"

Giles nodded. "I was going to wait until you were gone," he confessed looking up through his lashes at Buffy. "Thought it might be difficult for—"

"Me. You're right." Buffy got to her feet and tried to put her hands in the pockets of his sweatpants, but the pockets were too low. So, she fastened her hands on her hips; as she heard the shower door open, she called, "C'mon, Xander. We've gotta patrol."

"Naked?" he said. "In that case, I'll be right there."

"Oh, please," Cordelia said. "Then all the monsters will run away and Buffy will have nothing to hack."

"Can't hack the full Xander experience, eh?" Xander riffed.

"Do. Not. Go. There," the dark-haired Queen of Pain retorted.

Faith unslung her leg and got to her feet, "I think I'll go over to the Fish Tank, see if anyone has seen my stolen axe."

Just then there was a soft rap at the front door. Buffy brightened; she'd know that knock anywhere.

Angel.

Giles let him in, nodding brusquely. They still weren't all that buddy-buddy, which was not to bag on Giles. Angel had tortured Buffy's Watcher for hours when he'd reverted to Angelus, and just for the fun of it.

His duster swirled around him as he came into the room. He went to Buffy, took her hands, kissed her gently. His dark eyes serious and concerned, he asked, "How's Willow?" and Buffy made a helpless shrug. She'd called over and spoken to someone who was too busy to be the slightest bit polite or interested in helping.

"The doctors don't say much. Mumble, mumble."

"Giles. Faith," Angel said, by way of greeting. Faith shifted her weight to one hip, looking far sexier in the oversized bathrobe than Buffy did in the sweats.

"Hi," Cordelia called from the loft.

"Hi," Xander chimed in, mimicking her.

Angel looked puzzled. He mouthed at Buffy, *Are they back together?*

She shook her head.

"And speaking of crazy, the whole town's about to riot." Angel walked to the window and peered out. "The water's still rising and the fires are moving toward downtown. Wind's carrying the flames." He looked at them. "What've you guys got? Find anything out?"

"We have the three mummies of the Apocalypse," Xander said, peering over the loft railing. He had a towel around his waist and another across his shoulders. Water droplets clung to his black hair. "Or else it's an Earth, Wind, and Fire reunion tour."

"Except we don't think we have any earth thing," Buffy filled in. "Just the other stuff. Air, fire, and water."

"So, no reunion, but we could give rides on a steam locomotive," Xander added helpfully.

"Three of the four arcane elements." Angel looked at Giles. "Something big is brewing."

"Angel, you have such a way with words," Faith drawled. "Heard anything about axes?"

"As in, hunting? For dismemberment? Skinning? Ritualistic?" Angel asked.

"As in, mummies carrying them around," Buffy elaborated. "Slicing people with them. Or causing tidal waves with them. We aren't sure what they're for."

"Faith had possession . . . briefly . . . of a rather intricate ceremonial axe," Giles told the vampire. "Apparently, the vampires who brought it to Sunnydale were confident that one nick of it would kill her."

"But I'm nick-free," Faith crowed. "Score one for the Slayer side."

Angel frowned at her. "Where'd you get that big cut?"

Faith touched her cheek, where the cut was healing nicely, but still pretty impressive. "We fought these other things that came out of some fog," she said. "They didn't have weapons. They *were* weapons."

"And yet," Buffy said. "Baffles. Fog. Mummies. Fog."

"There was a little girl just here who saw one of

them up close," Giles continued. "Holly Johnson. And she said it was surrounded by fog."

"The missing girl?" Angel queried.

"I saved her. The mummies seemed to like her a lot. Why her?" Buffy frowned. "What's the draw?"

"Maybe she's got something to do with arcane elements," Giles suggested. "We're the clay of Adam, some such thing."

"Hey, excuse me, clay here, too." Xander nodded. "From the top of my clay head to the tips of my clay feet."

"You said it, not us," Cordelia zinged tiredly.

"Would you just get up and do something?" Xander flung at her. "Like move?"

"Oh, God, don't start all that up again. We're not dating any more, you know."

They started bickering. Angel said, "Let me go look around. I'll check the Alibi, see if I can shake anything out of Willy."

Faith raised her finger. "Tervokian wants control of South Boston. That's why he tried to take me out back home." She thought a moment. "I was fighting off some of his vamps and they got me cornered in a warehouse. They chained me up but they put something inside the door and lifted up the lid before they locked me in.

"The whole thing went up in flames. I thought they set the warehouse on fire. But maybe the fire was inside the box, and when they opened it, it ignited the place."

"Catastrophe in a box. Like takeout. I like it," Xander said, coming down the stairs. He had on his clothes, which Giles had dried for him.

Faith continued. "I got out and I ran like hell. The warehouse burned up, and I figured that was the end of

that. But he followed me all the way to Sunnydale."
She shook her head. "Still using vamps to do his dirty
work, too."

"So why bother?" Buffy asked. "I mean, if you're
here, and he's in Boston, which also has South Boston,
why track you down?"

Faith looked taken aback, as if the question hadn't
occurred to her. Maybe she was used to demons with a
grudge following her all over the country. "Got a point,
B. But I don't have an answer."

She got to her feet. "I'll be at the Tank." Then she
looked down at herself. "But not in Giles's bathrobe."
She flashed a lopsided grin at the Watcher. "Nice ter-
rycloth, Giles. You like the quality stuff."

"And I'll go to Willy's," Angel said, heading for the
door.

"Xander and I will patrol," Buffy announced.

From the loft, Xander said, "Oh, yay."

"I'll stay here and keep Giles company," Cordelia
said, "and also, if people need rides, I'll be here."

"We could use a ride," Xander said.

"People who aren't here and need to be somewhere
else other than here," Cordelia added.

Buffy leaned forward and put her hand on Giles's.
"I'm so sorry about Mr. Zabuto," she murmured. "I
didn't know you stayed in touch with him."

He pushed up his glasses. "Actually, I've had many
conversations with him. I didn't mention it to you," he
said quickly, "because, frankly, I didn't want you to think
about the fact that Kendra had died. I tried to find out
everything I could about her. What her weaknesses were.
What battles she walked away from. How she trained."

"Why?" Buffy asked, puzzled.

"I need to learn everything I can to keep you alive."

He hesitated. "I've often thought of calling Kit Both-well, but I never have. It was just too close to home."

"I understand." She cleared her throat. "I won't stay, if it will make you uncomfortable."

"Perhaps, when we aren't quite so . . . distracted, you and I might go down for a visit with him. He lives in San Diego."

She wrinkled her forehead. "You know where he lives?"

He nodded. "Not his precise location. Only that he's down there. And that he's not handled the death of his Slay . . . of India very well."

Buffy made a face. "He knew the job was dangerous when he took it. So did she."

"It doesn't matter, Buffy. Hearts don't just turn on and off." He looked both weary and affectionately put out with her. "People are not interchangeable, though the Council would like us to think they are. One Slayer dies, another chosen . . . but it's a lot more complicated than that. Human beings, with human feelings, are involved."

So I would be missed? she thought. *Or after a while, would I just be one of the long line of Slayers, somebody you can talk about in the old Watchers' Home when you don't have any teeth left?*

Am I going to matter? Is my life going to matter?

Is my death going to matter?

Giles said, "You'll both need coats." He went to his hall closet and opened it. "I've got a nice London Fog and this all-weather jacket." He pulled them out.

"Jacket," Buffy told him. "Xander can look like the James Bond wannabe."

"I beg your pardon," Giles said. "This is nothing like what James Bond wears."

"Pierce Brosnan had that very coat in *GQ*," Buffy informed him, and Giles looked pleased.

"Really?" he said, admiring it. He held it out. "It does have style, doesn't it."

Xander came over and said, "We blowin' this pop stand?"

Buffy grinned at him. "You got it." She smiled at Giles. "Later."

"Take care." His voice was soft, wistful.

Buffy looked at him, really looked at him, at the crow's feet along his eyes, the creases in his forehead. There was more gray in his hair now than there had been a year ago.

Does he wonder about his life having meaning? Does he worry about dying?

"Don't get killed," Cordelia said.

"We'll do our best," Buffy replied.

"Buffy, do be careful."

She looked at him. "I never asked you. About . . . her." Her throat caught. "God, am I just the most superficial person who ever lived or what?"

Giles's smile was sympathetic and reassuring. "It's a documented fact that most Slayers never ask about the one whose death called them to service, Buffy. I wasn't at all surprised that you didn't ask me about her. To be frank, I didn't want to discuss it, either. It's distressingly . . ."

"Close to home," Buffy finished.

He closed his eyes and nodded, walking them to the door. As he opened it, heavy winds ripped it from his grasp and slammed it back on the hinges, nearly breaking it off. Rain was tumbling into the courtyard like a waterfall.

"Yikes," Xander said. "Not a good day for hang gliding."

"Or walking," Buffy muttered.

Giles brought them umbrellas and Buffy found herself wishing for a desk job—maybe she could become Buffy the Computer Virus Slayer except, okay, knowledge of computers; or Buffy the Data Input Entry Mistake Finder except, okay, boring.

Slaying it is, then.

"To Oz?" she asked Xander.

"Or Atlantis?" Xander said. "Or a really nice, warm room? Oh, wait, we were just in one."

Giles said, "I'll have tea and hot water bottles ready."

"You're all heart," Xander replied.

He and Buffy opened their umbrellas and together, they breached the gale.

Chapter Seven

San Diego

It was very stupid of him to have a go again, and he knew it. But the thought, the hope, was like a terribly addictive drug. And Christopher Bothwell could no longer stop himself.

Dressed in a robe of midnight blue spangled with kabalistic symbols, Kit stood in the center of his living room in the Ocean Beach section of San Diego. His female consort stood at his side also robed. Her magickal name was Cecile, and he'd met her at a Wicca singles group three weeks ago. By day, she was temping at a law firm; by night, she danced naked around bonfires on the beach and claimed to be able to speak to the dead.

She had warm, cocoa-colored skin and brilliant red hair, but he suspected that she dyed it because it was the traditional hair color of those imbued with magickal abilities. Her affectations concerned him—*methinks she doth protest too much*—but on the other hand, she had managed a number of spells. Thus far her most notable accomplishment was that she had lit all the candles in the room with the power of her voice alone; for another, she had seen—or claimed to have seen—the ghost of Kit's uncle, who had recently died. Of course, there were innumerable ways to fabricate such a story.

"Abracadabra," she intoned, her eyes closed.

"One," he replied.

They had ingested powerful hypnotic drugs together, herbals that he had ground according to ritual with his mortar and pestle. Simple paraffin candles provided the only source of illumination, in a protective circle which he, as the male, was to protect. The female was there to actually perform the rituals. Most magick traditions were matriarchal, a fact he had learned in his Watcher's training.

His tiny, cheap flat reeked of smoke, lavender, and incense. In another neighborhood, perhaps, the neighbors would complain, but Ocean Beach was the last bastion of hippiedom, replete with graying surfers, wrinkled flower children, and wizened, middle-aged folk who worked for nonprofit organizations to protect the rights of animals and legalize various drugs. If they worked at all.

The raggedy drapes were tightly shut against the front window, but they could not drown out the twang of the truly hideous country and western music Kit's neighbor across the common listened to night and day—especially night, all night, every single wretched night.

On a metal folding card table, herbal tea was steeping in the pot his mother had purchased for him in Cambridge, to celebrate the day he had graduated from University. The china pot was shaped like a wise old owl, wearing the cap and gown of a scholar. Two mismatched cups were placed beside it. One, he had pilfered from his job at Kinko's, where he managed the special orders desk. Once upon a time, he had owned a splendid coffee service of Royal Doulton bone china; he had sold almost everything of value in his quest to connect with India.

If it would have helped to sell his soul, he would have done that as well.

Cecile took his hand. Her hands were small and always warm. "I feel a presence," she murmured.

He concentrated hard, constricting his face into a grimace as he strained to become receptive to whatever vibration or influence Cecile was sensing. As usual, he felt nothing.

He had begun to wonder if she ever felt anything during these sessions, or if these sensations of hers were her way of coming on to him. This was their fourth attempt at contacting India. Last time, Cecile had mentioned that in her coven, they performed most rituals "skyclad," which was the pagan term for naked. She'd also suggested that sexual magick was the most potent form of conjuring in existence.

He was not a naïve person. He knew that charlatans abounded in the pursuit of the Arts. But he also knew that magick was very real, having devoted his life since the death of India to exploring the mystical realms. He himself had been elevated to high priest status in the coven he had recently left, though he'd never mentioned that fact to Cecile. He respected his Witches' vow of silence, in the same way that he had honored the oath he had taken upon becoming a Watcher.

Magick had worked for him in the past. Since India's death, he had most definitely felt her presence, twice. Once he had been reading, and once sobbing over a silly photograph of the two of them in Spain. And on each occasion, he had dreamed of her that night. Lovely dreams, they'd been. If all he ever managed from his magick was to have another dream of India, the efforts and expenditure would be worth it.

I never knew I loved her, until she sacrificed herself to save me. Oh, my India . . . my lovely girl . . .

"Abracadabra, abracadabra," Cecile chanted.

"Two," he replied.

Then he gasped.

He *did* feel something.

Cecile squeezed his hand. "Don't open your eyes," she whispered. "Stand perfectly still."

There. Something brushed his lips very gently; it took a conscious act of will not to squint one eye open to see if it was Cecile.

In the kitchen, Mariposa, India's little dog, barked sharply. Then the pup growled and scratched at the closed kitchen door.

"Who is here?" Cecile whispered.

Kit's heart pounded. Tears welled at the corners of his eyes. It was a terrible temptation to open his eyes, but he resisted. There were rules, and he followed them, even if they did make it more likely that he was simply being played for a fool by a woman who fancied him.

"Who is here?" she asked again, her voice firm, in command.

Please, India, Kit thought. *I don't want to disturb your rest. I only want to know that you're all right.*

Suddenly, the room grew warm and fragrant; the scent of oranges filled the room and he smelled wistfully, remembering Spain. *Spain was where I came to care for her so very much; dear God, if for one moment I could see her, tell her what a great Slayer she had been; thank her, tell her that I did love her, only never realized it . . .*

"*Alors, mon vieux,* do you see her?" Cecile whispered. Her voice was filled with excitement.

In the distant landscape of his mind's eye, a figure shimmered like an angel.

India?

Watchers Council Headquarters (rebuilt), Great Russell Street, London

Micaela Tomassi dreamed.

In her dreams, she sat on the lap of her adoptive father, the handsome old Italian, as they watched the fieldworker harvesting the grapes. She smelled cinnamon in the air, and rosemary, and closed her eyes. The scents of her life were heavy and thick. The colors of her childhood were Merlot and burgundy, apricot and burnt sienna.

On her tongue, sugared almonds delighted her taste buds and made her eager for the homemade nougats in the monkeypod bowl at her father's elbow. She reached for them excitedly and—

—opened her eyes to the gray fluorescent light, and the gray stone, of her dismal cell inside the prison of the Watchers Council.

The meeting rooms were on other floors, true; and many Watchers and operatives passed hours within their walls, discussing the progress of the eternal war against evil. Perhaps they never wondered about the other places they never went; perhaps they knew that those who were found guilty of crimes against the Council were housed beneath the first floor, condemned to pass years surrounded in a fog of colorless, lifeless monotony. Many would do anything to end such an existence, and some had managed to kill themselves while in captivity.

There was something Micaela could do to end it. The temptation was there. To be able to look at colors again, and eat food that tasted; to smell flowers; to lie in a real bed and pull the covers up. To drink wine.

To make love—

Rupert, she mouthed, and tears sprang to her eyes. Did he know what had become of her? Did he care? Had he protested, or had he acquiesced to her sentence, believing it to be exactly what she deserved for obeying her father, the evil sorcerer, Fulcanelli?

She got up from her cot and walked to the bars. Holding onto them, she stared at the gray wall six feet away.

Because of her magickal abilities, she had been ordered to fulfill her sentence of ten long, excruciating years in solitary confinement. If that wasn't purgatory, she didn't know what was.

Just as she closed her eyes and lay back down on her cot, she heard the familiar footsteps. She clenched her teeth and her fists, fearful and feeling more alone than she had in her entire life.

It was the man who had asked her to call him Tony. She knew full well who he was—Lord Anthony Yorke, one of the most highly placed members of the Council. And if he didn't realize that she knew that, he was a bigger fool than she'd imagined. Stupid men were far more dangerous than cunning ones. With an intelligent man, one could match wits. But stupid men were unpredictable because they didn't think reasonably and logically. Hence, it was more difficult to plan strategy against them.

The aristocrat, a tall, middle-aged man of slight build, with luxuriant gray hair and a trim goatee, was not only a Council member; he was also a traitor. Many other Council members and operatives had come privately to Micaela's cell, hoping to bribe her into goosing their pursuit of private personal gain—wealth, success in business or in love, even a promotion within the Council hierarchy. Others had threatened her life if she didn't give them what they wanted.

All of them, she had managed to deflect with what amounted to a few parlor tricks, when compared with the powerful magicks she had at her disposal. Her adoptive father had taught her much that, over time, she had forgotten. But with nothing else to do as the days, and weeks, and months dragged by, she had begun to remember a great number of things she had previously suppressed. Perhaps it was the proximity to other magick users—operatives and allies of the Council—or perhaps it was the unceasing sense of danger she felt herself to be in. Whatever had called forth her forgotten knowledge, Lord Yorke had sensed it.

A minor magician himself, he knew powerful magick when he was in its presence. He admired and respected it.

And he wanted it.

"Signorina Micaela," he said pleasantly as he walked into her view. "How are you? Enjoying the view?"

She glared at him, remaining silent.

He was holding a piece of very old-looking parchment. She tried to see what was on it, but it was at a bad angle. Or else her eyesight was beginning to go. With very little to focus on, she found herself seeing double on occasion.

He looked down at the parchment, then turned it around and pressed it with his palm against the bars of her cell. "Does this look familiar?"

It was a drawing of a battle axe. The handle was

more of a scepter. The ram-like horns of a bearded demon curled around the top of the blade, whose shape reminded Micaela of the sensuous arabesque forms of ancient Middle Eastern art.

She shrugged. "It's beautiful, but I've never seen it before."

"There are four of these," he said. "They were made as a set." He smiled provocatively, and her stomach turned. "My colleagues—the ones you've refused to help—are searching for one of them. My own finder's spell, alas, is not working. If you'll work on recovering it, I will get you out of here."

Her answering smile was as cold as her heart was dead. "Do you know how many people have made offers like that? I'll be freed if I'll find the Gem of Amarra; or if I'll open the portal to Xanadu; or if I will make contact with Lucifer himself—"

"But you know that I can free you. And I promise you, I shall."

The temptation was there, that much she could not deny. Lord Yorke had a sense of honor, as despicable as he was. She remembered how she had been pampered and loved by Fulcanelli, one of the most evil beings who ever walked the Earth. He had treated her like a princess.

But Fulcanelli also tried to kill me.

The lines between good and evil were, at best, a foggy gray.

The Watchers Council were, by nature, a very serious group. Their vows included words such as "Guardians of Eternity," "unceasing vigilance," and "unswerving loyalty." Quentin Travers had once said, "Being a Watcher is like guarding the door to your child's nursery while wild animals roam the halls of your home." Thoughts such as those moved one to seriousness. Laugh, and you might get eaten.

It was, in many ways, a disheartening, thankless task. All personal hopes and ambitions were subordinate to the calling. Marriage was, at best, difficult. Friendships withered. One couldn't hope for a career that demanded too much, and as a result, many Watchers were severely overqualified for their "day jobs," which could be stultifying as well as financially unrewarding.

The sacrifices were bad enough; worse was the realization that one was only a cog in a much larger machine. Watchers lived, Watchers died, and still the ferocious beast growled and slathered in the passageway. Look away for a moment, and it might spring. Die, and the burden was passed on to someone else who could not, dare not blink.

Faced with such circumstances, the notion of "morale" was set aside. It didn't matter how Watchers felt about their situation. They had a job to do and they had better jolly well do it. Turn traitor, and you were dealt with.

Seriously.

In Neema Mfune-Hayes' opinion, the prison in which Micaela Tomassi spent her days and nights was positively medieval. Amnesty International would certainly have protested the conditions she was forced to endure, had they been aware of her situation. Her cell was cramped, barely long enough for her canvas cot, and the stone floor was always wet and cold. The stone walls wept moisture. There was no ventilation, and the sole source of light was from a bare bulb hanging in the passageway beyond the heavy metal door.

Neema knew that Rupert Giles had spoken on

Micaela's behalf, documenting her many acts of self-lessness in the battle against her one-time adoptive father, Fulcanelli. She had risked her life to help the Slayer and her friends protect the heir of the Gatekeeper, young Jacques Regnier.

Neema wondered what they would have done to her if Giles had not made his report.

She had no official business with the Council prisoner; she had only wanted to speak to the woman because she provided a connection, however tenuous, with Roger. Neema couldn't let him go, not yet; she had no one to grieve with, and she assumed another woman would understand the depth of her grief.

Now Roger's former lover stood in the passageway, facing the doorway, listening in horror to Tony, her confidante, attempting to force Micaela into helping him with some secret plot.

She withdrew into the shadows, holding her breath.

"I find your sense of morality most puzzling," he said. "But I can adapt. Here is further inducement for you. If you don't help me find that axe, I shall kill Rupert Giles the moment I set foot in Sunnydale."

"No," Micaela breathed. "Not if it's used against the Slayers."

"It will be. Slayers die; it's what they do. Watchers often live to a ripe old age."

Neema's skin felt tight; she was prickling with anxiety. *Don't do it,* she begged Micaela. *Whatever it is, don't betray the Slayers.*

"I need to prepare," Micaela said, and Neema pitied her for her weak attempt to buy time.

"No, you don't. Do it now, Micaela, or Giles will die."

Soon green light shone from the cell, and Neema

knew Micaela was performing the spell. After a time, Lord Yorke said, "Hello, that's most intriguing. So all four of the axes are in Sunnydale. I wonder why Cecile told me that Tervokian had the other one in Boston. . . ." He broke off. "Right. Hold on, then." There was a moment, then: "Cecile, *ma vie,* yes, it's Tony. Hang on, here's a shock: they're in Sunnydale. All of them. Yes, I know that's what Tervokian said, but he must be lying. I just had a finder's spell done and I've no reason to disbelieve the result. Yes, well, you'd better discuss that with him, eh?"

Neema heard the sound of something snapping closed; the cell phone he'd been using must have been state of the art, to work at this depth.

"Well, she found that rather shocking, I must say," Lord Yorke drawled. "I wonder how shocking she would find it if she realized I know who and what she is, and what she intends to do."

"What are you talking about?" Micaela asked carefully.

"Have you ever heard of Cecile Lafitte? No? How remiss of Fulcanelli. She is a sorceress of awesome ability. I believe she is over eight hundred years old. She's enticed me into working with her in her attempt to empower her god, the Gatherer, so that it can rule this dimension."

Neema listened hard. Micaela said derisively, "Oh, Tony, there have been so many attempts to rule this dimension. Even my foster father failed."

"Cecile will fail, too," he replied, chortling. "You see, she's playing a number of us against ourselves. She's promised each one of us that we will be the Fourth Servant. The Fourth will be the acolyte of the risen Gatherer. Let's see, there's Simon Lafitte, who is her descendant; and the demon Tervokian, who keeps insisting that all he wants is control of South Boston. Then there's Cameron Duvalier, the Third and current Servant, who has no idea she wants to replace him. And then, there's me."

"Ah," Micaela said. "Of course. You."

"I'm the only one who realizes what she's up to. I'm going to beat her at her own game. That's why we're going to Sunnydale. When I rendezvous with her there, I'll kill her."

There was a pause. *Keep going,* Neema mentally prodded.

"Have you ever heard of the *Book of Fours?* No? Well, Roger Zabuto had some fragments of it in his diary. I have no idea how he got them. But they actually tell how to kill 'Ceceli,' as she called herself."

"How?" Micaela asked him.

He chuckled. "You'll see. A promise is a promise, luv, and it's time to leave."

"What?" Micaela asked faintly.

"You're coming with me, of course," he said simply. "How else did you think you'd be leaving here?"

"You bastard," Micaela said. There was the sound of a slap.

Neema inhaled sharply, afraid for her. There was a pause. For one heart-stopping instant, she thought Lord Yorke had heard her. But nothing happened, and she exhaled as slowly and silently as possible. Her heart would surely give her away. It was pounding so hard she was afraid she was going to have a heart attack.

"You're not going to free me," Micaela said slowly. "Ever."

"No. Of course not. But I will make you my queen, Micaela. You'll be happy."

Micaela made some kind of noise. There were rustling noises, and Micaela's muffled groan of protest.

"You're so beautiful," the man breathed. "I can't wait until we're alone in a beautiful setting, where I can make love to you properly."

"Are you positive we're alone now?" she asked him.

"There's no need for you to be afraid, Micaela," he said, sounding bemused.

"Oh, but, Tony, there's plenty of need." Micaela's voice was hard and cruel.

Without warning, the hall lit up with bright blue light. A harsh, hot force wrapped around Neema's body. There was a muffled shout, and then nothing.

Neema looked around the corner, to find Micaela Tomassi bent over the body of Lord Yorke. She whirled around. In her hand, she held some fragments of ancient-looking paper.

The small blonde blinked at Neema. She said quickly, "I know who you are, Ms. Mfune-Hayes. I know you heard. These are the pieces of the *Book of Fours.* Help me. We have to stop this."

"But—"

"We have to get out of here. We have to help. Get me out of here. I have no one else I can trust."

"But the Council—"

Micaela looked hard at the other woman. "Roger Zabuto was tortured to death at the orders of Tony and his co-conspirators. These same people are trying to kill Faith and Buffy. And perhaps Giles as well."

Micaela took a breath. "If not for them, then for Roger."

Neema's eyes glistened. "All right," she said. "Come on. There's another way out."

Chapter Eight

Sunnydale

James Asakawa, president of the Sunnydale High School International Relations Club, loved France Tranh more than he would have thought one human being could love another. He couldn't look at her enough, couldn't listen to her voice enough, couldn't be around her enough.

"Will you get away from me, you psycho?" she screamed at him, as she half walked, half ran to her car.

The Sunnydale Mall was being evacuated. Most of the kids James knew from the Game Players of Titan, the mall comic-book and game store, were extremely ticked about being told to leave. But James had lived half his life in Japan, and he knew a hurricane when he was in one. This was not some "hokey little storm," as some of the guys were saying.

"France, I don't have a ride home," he said, loping alongside her. The rain and the wind were fierce; the storm blew them both so hard that they bumped into the cars lined up in the parking spaces. "My dad was supposed to pick me when the mall closed. That's in two hours. I can't stay here."

"That's not my problem," she snapped. She whirled around to stare him down. "You scare me. You're always following me."

"I-I love you," he insisted, as the rain smacked him hard enough to leave bruises.

She was holding her hair out of her eyes with both hands. Soaked to the bone, she was thinner than James had realized. So slender. So beautiful. She would blow away in all the wind and rain, just like a tender leaf. . . .

"Then leave me alone."

"Give me a ride," he pleaded. "Look."

The queues for the city buses were as long as the lines for the good rides at Disneyland. People were yelling and pushing as two buses pulled up. No one got out, and they were both full. The mall lights were still on but security guards were signalling everyone that the shopping center was closed.

France rolled her eyes. "All right. But if you act weird, I'm throwing you out of the car."

"Thanks." He caught up with her, crossing his arms over his chest and shivering as she unlocked the car with the remote. She gestured for him to go around to the passenger side and he did, realizing he was getting so freaked out he wasn't thinking straight.

Man, my one chance to be alone with her in a car, and I'm too terrified to do anything about it, he thought.

Both of them had just slipped inside when the ground began to shake. Then it undulated, just like someone flicking a sheet prior to making a bed. The asphalt rolled and then began to crack, as huge, jutting sections of earth shot through, then broke the asphalt apart.

France screamed and turned on the engine. She put

the pedal to the metal and threw the car in reverse. There was a thud that James didn't even want to think about, and then she slammed it into drive.

She got about two feet before she crashed into another car, the impact throwing her forward, over the steering wheel. James had buckled his seat belt; she had not.

Then the car burst into flames. James shouted, unfastened his seat belt, and got out. The top of France's head had shattered the windshield, but lucky for her, it had not penetrated the thick glass. She was groaning, which was a good sign, because that meant she was still alive.

"I'll get you," he yelled to her, crossing to her side of the car.

He was just about to open her door when a familiar-looking, grubby man shoved him out of the way and yanked open the door. The man grabbed France around the waist and threw her to the ground.

"It's the aliens!" the man shouted. "I seen 'em. I seen 'em all!"

Shortly thereafter, a chain of explosions tore through the mall, and the Robinson's-May shot skyhigh into the air.

Perfume counter and all.

The man ran crazily off into the night. He pulled something from his pocket and waved it over his head.

"I'm armed!" he shouted. "I'm Carlos New Mexico and I got me an axe! Don't abduct me!"

He ran on, grateful to his bones that that sweet little brown-haired girl from the Fish Tank had dropped her weapon when she'd dusted those two aliens.

Through the wind, and the rain, and past the fires, Carlos ran, until he drew near to Willy's Alibi Room. Willy was okay with him; sometimes he let Carlos have a pickeled egg for free and he'd let him sleep in the basement if he didn't have anywhere else to go.

He was just about to go inside and ask for that pickeled egg, when a really tall man grabbed him by the collar and said, "Where did you get that?"

Before Carlos could answer, the man snatched the axe away from him.

"Hey," Carlos protested. But faster than you could say "New Mexico," the really tall man turned into an alien and broke Carlos's neck.

Good Lord, are we having another earthquake? Giles thought, as every single item in his home rattled and shook. Some of his *feng shui* crystals smacked into each other, clanging like wind chimes. An old Sumerian tablet jittered off the book shelf and crashed to the floor.

Well, that completes our set of the arcane elements, then: earth, air, fire, water.

Sighing, he picked up the phone and hit redial. It was apalling that no one at the Council of Watchers was answering the phone. *I could understand it if we were headquartered in Paris,* he thought. *The French are always on strike—garbage men, railway workers, phone operators—but good Lord, we are British.*

"Ah, yes," someone finally said. "Hello?"

"Is this the Watchers Council?" Giles asked indignantly.

"Who is speaking, please?"

"Oh, for heaven's sake. I'm Rupert Giles. I—"

"Oh, Mr. Giles, I'm so frightfully sorry," the speaker cut in. "We're rather in the midst of a situation here, I'm afraid."

"Situation? What sort of situation?" Giles demanded, frowning. "No one's answered my calls for the past hour, at least; hold on, it's been two, and—"

"Sir, Lord Yorke has been killed. He was coming to see you, sir. A prisoner escaped; we assume she meant to take him hostage."

Giles was stunned. "What? Tony Yorke's been murdered?"

"It was Miss Tomassi done it, sir," the speaker said, reverting in his distress to what appeared to be his native accent, which was Cockney. "Disappeared, she 'as."

"Micaela?" He sat down slowly. "What . . . ?" He scratched his forehead, trying to digest the information. *Impossible.*

"Thank you," he said; then, "Wait. I need Christopher Bothwell's phone number. It's urgent."

"Sir . . ."

"I need it *now.*"

"Very well. I'm not authorized, but I'll find the correct person and ring you back, sir."

"Oh, very well," Giles said, sighing.

He put down the phone and tried to do some research. *Meteorological Magick* came to hand, and it was tedious going for the next half-hour or so. He had just plowed through a discussion of N. Richard Nash's play, *The Rainmaker,* when the phone rang.

"Sir, it's Thomas Andrews," said a voice new to him. "George Salisbury forwarded your request on to me. I'm authorized to give you Christopher Bothwell's home phone number."

"Thank you ever so much," Giles said, exhaling.

He wrote down the number, rang off from London, and stared at it for a moment, suddenly reluctant to dial it. *What does one say? How does one commiserate, sympathize?*

Sorry your girl died?

Frightfully glad mine hasn't?

Summoning his backbone, he punched in the number. It rang a number of times, during which Giles tried to remember what he could of the history of India Cohen. *One would have assumed I'd have memorized it,* he thought, ashamed of himself.

"Bothwell," slurred a British voice.

"Rupert Giles here," Giles said.

There was a moment of silence. "Yes. How may I help you?" Christopher Bothwell asked politely.

He's drunk, Giles thought. *Well, it is rather late at night . . .*

"We've got a bit of trouble up here," Giles said. "And it appears that your Miss Cohen figures into it in some way." That didn't sound quite right, but he let it go.

There was another pause. "India? How?"

"A friend of the Slayer's dreamed about her, for one thing."

"A friend? She has friends? How extraordinary."

Giles reddened slightly. "She's rather an unorthodox girl, for a Slayer. Has friends."

"I see." Another pause. "Well, what did she dream, this friend?"

Giles adjusted his glasses. "I'm not sure, exactly," he admitted. "The friend is in hospital at the moment. We're also concerned about some axes. Now, I understand that Miss Cohen . . . that she . . ."

"She was killed with an axe," Christopher Bothwell said.

"I am so sorry," Giles murmured. "I know this must be difficult."

When next the other Watcher spoke, his voice was muffled, as if the man was struggling for composure. "You say that this friend dreamed of India, or got her name, or something."

There was another long pause before he spoke again. "I suppose I ought to tell you that I've been using magicks to attempt contact with her. And I believe I have succeeded. I think I was in contact with her just a short while ago, in fact."

"I beg your pardon?" Giles was taken aback.

"To a small degree. Look here. I'm in San Diego. You're, what? Bit up the coast? It might be a good thing if I came up."

Giles nodded, then realized that of course the man couldn't see him.

"Yes. That would be good indeed. But we've got rotten weather here. Quite, ah, apocalyptic."

"I'm a sorcerer of some small skill," Bothwell announced. "I should be able to maneuver, don't you think?"

"If you say so," Giles ventured.

"But first I, uh, need to . . ." Bothwell sighed. "I'm pissed. Drunk as a skunk, as the Americans say. I suppose you can tell."

"I am British," Giles teased gently. "We do like our ale."

"Far too well. I'll sober up and get on the road. Expect me by morning, won't you? I'll need some directions. And your address and number, of course."

"Good." Giles glanced at his watch. "I'll try to have both the Slayers here."

"I beg your pardon? Did you say *Slayers?*"

"Oh. Yes. There are two of them at present."

"How extraordinary," Bothwell said again. "I had no idea."

"It was rather a surprise all around." Giles smiled ruefully. "Caught the Council off guard, I can tell you."

"Would have liked to have seen their faces."

The two Watchers chuckled together. Then Giles gave him his address, phone number, and basic directions to Sunnydale.

"Right, then. I'll come 'round directly," Bothwell said.

They clicked off.

Giles looked at the phone for a moment, then went back to his book.

The hospital corridor rattled again and Oz calmly walked under the transom of the nearest door. The quakes had almost become commonplace now, and everyone was remarking about how glad they were that the hospital, so far, had not sustained any major structural damage. News of what had happened at the Sunnydale Mall traveled fast.

More wounded poured into the desperately overcrowded hospital. Despite the torrential rains, the fires were spreading all over town. What with the additional burn victims, car accidents, and people injured during the quakes, the Sunnydale Medical Center was like a field hospital during a war.

Oz was getting himself some more coffee, and some tea for Willow's mother, which was not the most pleasant thing to do. He had to walk down the corridor past the burn unit to the vending machines, and the burn unit was bad news.

Oz tried to keep his gaze centered straight ahead; there was always that ghoulish temptation to peek into one of the rooms, but he avoided that as best he could. The injuries were horrible; worse still was the amount of pain the burn patients endured.

Fishing in his pants for some change, he paused, just long enough to hear a man talking in the room off to his left.

The man said, "We've got the freakin' thing at the station, Mark. I don't know how it could have cut you, though. It was on the ground."

There was murmuring, and groaning, and Oz couldn't help but glance at the name on the room sign. CORVALIS, MARK.

The door was open. Despite his best intentions, his gaze ticked to the interior of the room. The opaque white curtain was pulled, concealing the person inside the bed, but Oz had a good view of the man's visitor, who was seated in a chair at the foot of the hospital bed, his profile to the door. He was a fireman, still in his yellow coveralls, his face covered with soot.

"I'll be back, buddy," he said, and started to walk out. He saw Oz, and shook his head. He gestured for Oz to follow him back into the hall.

"Not looking good," he told Oz. "He's more upset about losing his hand than the burns. But the burns are what're gonna kill him."

Oz took that in. He realized the man assumed Oz knew Mark Corvalis, but Oz didn't correct that impression. He just let the man talk.

"Way I figure it, someone stole it from the museum, something like that. Just Mark's luck to fall on it. A freak thing, you know?" He ran his hand through his dirty hair. "We're firefighters, we half-expect we'll get burned someday. But falling on some weird-looking axe, cutting off your hand . . ." He started crying again.

"He fell on an axe?" Oz repeated, very puzzled.

"Satanic-looking thing. Very creepy. Looks valuable. We've got it down at the station. Captain wants to see it before we try to find the owner. Maybe give it to the police first."

Oz nodded. He was not unsympathetic, but he was weary of hearing about accidents. It was all he'd heard about all day. The world had taken on a surrealistic tone for him; he'd been inside the hospital for so long, it was hard to believe there was anything more to the universe than Willow's bed in the intensive care unit, the nurses' station, the bathroom, and the vending machines.

"Tell him I had to go on home, will you?" the man continued. He shook his head. "I just can't handle it."

"Sure," Oz told him.

The man hurried away. Oz continued on his way and got the drinks, then headed back for the waiting room. Willow's mother had fallen asleep on the dark brown couch. Her cell phone was cradled in her hand like some people might hold a picture of a loved one. Mr. Rosenberg had left earlier to check on things at home.

Oz left Mrs. Rosenberg alone and looked in on Willow in her room. She was alone for the moment, because her roommate had died about three hours ago. They'd taken the body out, but no one had been brought in to take the extra bed.

They had partially shaved her head. Oz's features softened as he gazed at her; he thought she looked rather elfin. There was an IV in the vein on the back of her hand and another in the crook of her elbow on her other arm. They said she was going to be okay, probably some back problems later in life, but that was it.

Oz put down the cups of hot liquid and pulled up a chair beside her bed. He cleared his throat and very softly sang.

"'Wise men say, only fools rush in . . .' "

He couldn't continue. His throat was dry. As he sat beside her, he swayed; he didn't think he had ever been more stressed or drained in his entire life.

This is the one thing the Slayer can't protect her from, he thought. *And I can't, either. But I'd give up more than my hand if I could be in that bed instead of her.*

"Hey." Faith was standing in the doorway, arms folded. She was sopping wet. She gestured to the styrofoam cups and he shrugged; she came in and took the tea and sipped it. "How's she doing?"

He shrugged again. She nodded as if he'd said something profound and smoothed her hair away from her face.

"It's wicked out there." She grinned. "Dusted a couple of vamps, though. Weather doesn't seem to bother 'em much."

He wondered what she was doing at the hospital. He picked up his coffee and drank. Faith came farther into the room and stared down at Willow.

"Her hair will grow back," she said, as if that would comfort Oz in the least.

"So anyway, I'm out there freezing my butt off and I went to the Fish Tank to see if I could find out what happened to my axe, and I got zip, so I screwed around for a while and then I came in here to get warm," she said, holding the tea in both hands.

Oz thought a moment. "Axe. Some guy down the hall got cut by a strange-looking axe."

Faith's eyes widened. "Kidding, right? Axes are our big thing tonight. Wow. Where did it happen?"

He shook his head. "The axe is at the fire station."

"Awesome!" she cried. "I'll go get it." She set down the tea and gave him a wave.

"Hey, be careful," he warned her.

"Careful's for wimps."

"Wimps live to tell the tale."

"Wimps never live." She winked at him and left the room.

Chapter Nine

There were miles of tunnels beneath the surface of Sunnydale, for which there was no truly practical reason, but it made being a vampire less inconvenient than it otherwise would be in sunny Southern California. Traveling from one end of town in the middle of the day posed little difficulty to those for whom sunlight—like crosses, garlic, and holy water—was not a factor in living large.

Or living at all.

It also made reconnaisance a hell of a lot easier. In fact, there was actually an entry tunnel that led right into the basement of Willy's Alibi Room. It had been used during Prohibition to smuggle liquor.

The joint had been a hangout for bikers, pikers, and demons for a long time. Willy's Alibi, Sunnydale, was a pushpin on the maps of hellmouth habitues everywhere. Angel had actually once seen a tourist brochure for demons in Willy's office, labeling Sunnydale "the anti-Sedona of the demon travel wonderland."

The basement smelled of age, dirt, stone, and booze.

In the days of Prohibition, when alcohol had been illegal, Sunnydale had been a major center for underground trade in bootleg liquor. Even now, the cavernous walls were lined with rum-soaked packing crates and bullet holes. Occasionally, Angel would kick an antique ammo casing out of his way with his boot tip.

He strode through the room and entered the pitch-black corridor. Anyone who had business in Willy's basement knew the total absence of light lasted for only a couple seconds, as one moved swiftly from the bottom of the steps and into the first-floor storeroom, which was illuminated with not one, but two, incandescent forty-watt bulbs hanging naked from cords wound around a makeshift catwalk of sawhorses and ladders. When it came to obeying state safety regulations, Willy was not one to spare expense.

When it came to trying to sue Willy for injuries incurred on his property, one found out that Willy himself had declared bankruptcy, and the bar was listed as being owned by a nameless, faceless group called The Death Dealers. So, not much suing occurred.

In fact, none.

From the storeroom, where Willy kept what he optimistically liked to call "the good stuff;" Angel crept into Willy's office. The side wall of the office was shared by the bar.

Most of the time when Willy went to get the good stuff, it was to eavesdrop on a particularly interesting conversation. On that side wall, he had drilled a peephole, which was covered by his copy of the swimsuit calendar of *Cable Sports International*. He didn't have cable in the bar and never would, but he got the calendar for free. His customers had never caught on that he spied on them, which was incredibly stupid of them, but

Willy's clientele did not reside anywhere near the high end of the bell curve.

On the other hand, Angel knew that as soon as he walked into Willy's, everyone would zip up their mouths—those whose faces came equipped with mouths, anyway, and those who had faces—and throw away the keys. Demons suspected of selling information to the renegade vampire were generally found in the alley behind Willy's, beaten to a pulp and left to ferment with the rest of the bar's garbage.

Of course, many of the ones administering said beatings had provided Angel with information in the past, and would eagerly do so in the future, if the price was right. Usually, Angel could make the price right. It didn't take much money to buy someone when they were low-rent to start with.

Angel removed the calendar—Willy didn't know that he knew about the peephole—and scanned the bar.

Demons, demons, demons. And many of them were vampires Angel didn't recognize.

Some good ol' boy from a nether dimension was wearing a black cowboy hat and a duster. He was green and scaly, and Angel thought he looked like a cheesy monster from an old scary movie. Clint Eastwood from the lower forty of hell. The cowboy was holding forth over a glass of beer while several demons were grouped around, listening and drinking.

"... so the Ono-movi demon's daughter pouts and says, 'If you loved me, you'd buy me a nice diamond ring," the good ol' boy continued, mimicking the falsetto of a female. "And the Fungus demon says, "Baby, that's all the money I got, and I hadda roll a Fyrall demon to get that. So she says to me, 'Where's the Fyrall? I hear they've got a cream filling in the middle.' "

The bar rippled with laughter. Angel found it in himself to pity Willy, surrounded by cretins day and night. Then Willy stepped into Angel's field of vision in front of the peephole, and the man was laughing as hard as his customers. Angel withdrew his pity. Willy was in his right place and time, after all.

"I gotta get some more Old Reliable," Willy announced, throwing down the rag he'd been running along the varnished wood bar and bustling out of Angel's sight.

Angel put the calendar back, strolled to the threshold of the office, and waited for Willy there.

Willy's nose came half an inch short of colliding with Angel's chest. He stopped on a dime, looked up, and said, in an extremely loud voice, "Hey, Angel. What a surprise! How you doing?"

Angel stepped back into the office. Willy hesitated, obviously nervous. Around Angel, he was often nervous. Around Angel, he had cause to be.

"Come in," Angel said, leaning up against Willy's cheap old desk. It was littered with pieces of paper, receipts, phone numbers written on matchbooks, and a paperback called: *Bliss: Writing to Find Your True Self,* by Katherine Ramsland, Ph.D.

"Why are you here? I ain't got nothing," Willy whispered, running his hands through his oily hair. Angel suppressed a shudder. Willy had never left the greasy look behind, and the cheeseball insisted that his barber had assured him it was back. That gave Willy a nice excuse to really grease up.

"Just thought I'd drop by," Angel said. He and Buffy—and now Faith—did that on occasion. They'd shake the tree, see what kind of worm-infested apples dropped. "What's with all the fangs?"

Willy blinked, incredulous. "Hey, man, have you been outside?" He laughed nervously. "Nobody wants to be out on a night like tonight. On account of Disasters Are Us." He chuckled at his own feeble joke.

Angel just kept looking at him.

The barman closed his eyes and nodded. "Oh, of course. That's why you're here. Slayer sent you. Hey, nobody's said squat about doing spells to mess with the weather. I swear that, man."

"Who are all the vampires in your bar?" Angel asked impatiently.

"Them? Heh-heh. No idea." He shrugged and moved his hands, went to rake his fingers through his hair, but must have seen something on Angel's face—such as extreme revulsion—that stopped him. Willy was one of those guys who looked, acted, and, no doubt, felt guilty even when all he was doing was taking up space on the planet.

Pursing his lips, Angel narrowed his eyes and gave Willy the full-on stare treatment. "Don't screw with me, Willy. I'm not in the mood."

The smarmy barman took a couple of steps backward and lifted his hands, palms facing Angel. "I can see that, Angel. I certainly can. Please, no cause for anger, you know?"

Angel kept staring. He'd learned that it didn't take all that much to make Willy cave.

A few more seconds ought to do it. . . .

"All right, all right," Willy said, and hesitated. Without shirting his gaze from Willy's face, Angel pulled a twenty-dollar bill from the wallet in his pocket. Willy's theatrical surprise and pleasure at such an offering was almost comical. But not quite.

"I heard some demons talking, okay?" he said uneasily.

His gaze kept fluttering to the bill in Angel's hand like a bee about to pollinate a totally gorgeous rhododendron. "They were talking about some demon in Boston. *Boston*, you know." He bobbed his head left and right. "I'm figuring he's after the new Slayer."

"Boston." He stared Willy down. Willy's soul—if he had one left—was easily purchased, or at least rented, by the highest bidder. But he was also a coward, and he hated to be hurt.

And Angel knew how to hurt people.

It was frightening how easy it had been to learn.

And awful at how impossible it was to forget.

"Um, well also, there were these two vamps came into town a couple of nights ago, said they were sent by this demon. Um, I think his name was Tervokian. Gonna take her out with some axe or something," Willy said in a rush. He held out the twenty. "That information's on the house, Angel. Keep your money."

"And of course you weren't going to mention that to Buffy, Faith, or me," Angel said icily.

Willy frowned and touched his own chest. "You cut me to the quick, Angel. Ha-ha, get it? Axe? Of course I was gonna come tell you. I just ain't had the opportunity to get away from this crowd."

"You got a phone?" Angel asked.

"It's out. On account of the storm. Honest. You can try it." He gestured to his incredibly messy desk. Then he swiveled his head in its direction and caught his breath.

Angel followed his line of sight. He saw nothing out of the ordinary besides the extraordinary chaos of a man who truly had no sense of organization, and no ability to think past the present moment, which usually centered around making a quick, dishonest buck.

With a glance at Willy, who had quickly ticked his gaze back to Angel, he crossed to the desk. He stared down at the papers and matchbooks, pens, and a well-thumbed edition of *What Color Is Your Parachute?*

Willy hurried up beside him and said, "Ain't nothin' there, Angel. Honest."

Angel looked over at Willy, who was staring directly at a strip of yellow-lined notebook paper near the center of the desk. Angel tentatively moved toward it. Willy visibly tensed. Angel snatched it up.

"Don't be mad," Willy blurted.

Angel ignored him. He was reading the scribbling on the piece of paper. It read: *Carlos New Mexico, axe?*

"Oh, that. See, nobody's seen the vamps since but that crazy old man, he's been talking about axes and stuff." He looked nervous, and made with the hair again. Angel's stomach churned. He was sincerely glad he had no need to eat anything in the near future. Willy's grooming habits were ruining his appetite, even for fresh, warm blood.

"I was gonna let you know," Willy sniveled. "I figured you already knew everything, so—"

"Something wrong, Willy?" one of the demons called. Willy swallowed hard.

"Please, Angel. They find you in here with me, I am so dead."

Angel gritted his fangs. He said under his voice, "If someone brings that axe in, you let me know."

Willy's dark Italian-style eyes got big and round. "Of course. Of course." His voice dropped to a whisper. "All the demons in town come here. I hear a lot of things. You know I've told you about a lot of things."

"You nearly got me killed, too," Angel said, whirling back around, his patience completely gone.

"The first time Kendra came to Sunnydale, you were going to let me fry in the sun."

"That was a misunderstanding," Willy prevaricated. He was looking a little pasty. "I didn't realize how, um, vital you were to the community back then. C'mon, Angel. Give me a chance. I'm a good guy now."

Angel shook his head. He might be a vampire cursed to endure centuries of remorse for all the evil he had brought into the world, but at least he wasn't Willy. The fates had not been that cruel.

"All you have to do is prove it, Willy."

"You got it, babe. I mean, Angel." Willy smiled brightly. He had very bad teeth.

Disgusted, Angel left the office and headed for the tunnels.

Once below, he heard thunder rumbling. Almost immediately, the storm drains began sluicing foul water into the sewer tunnel in which he was traveling. The water flashed to ankle-height, and as he swore under his breath, he had a brief flash of the chase scene in the sewer from *Les Miserables*. He'd read it in the original French, and had wondered at the time about Victor Hugo's accuracy at getting every single inch of French sewer correct. Some vampires claimed the writer had been one of them, but Angel figured that to be an urban legend.

He sloshed to the nearest ladder and climbed up to the semicircular deluge that indicated a manhole cover.

Not a problem.

For a normal human being, the cover would have been quite heavy. There was something on top of it that was weighing it down.

For Angel, however, it was an unexpected factor he took into account before he slid it out of his way.

Rain slammed down on his head and shoulders with the force of a fire hose. He clung to the ladder, regrouping, and fought against the torrent as he climbed out.

He tried to stand. The wind was like a jet engine. His duster flapped behind him like a pair of wings, and it was a major struggle to stand upright.

Then he saw what had caused the extra weight on top of the cover.

It was a man, and the storm was rolling him down the street like an empty trash can. Angel ran after him, staggering against the force, ducking as a wooden door whipped past him, Frisbeelike. A streetlight on a pole crashed inches from his feet, bringing down electric lines that snapped and sizzled. Sparks flew everywhere.

He dodged the live wires, not because they could kill him but because getting hurt would slow him down. The man, still rolling, flipped up over the curb and rammed into the corner of a building at the waist, where his upper half bent backward at a sharp, spine-snapping angle.

Angel finally got to him, not at all surprised to find him dead. But he was disappointed at the man's identity: he was Carlos New Mexico.

He gathered the old homeless man up in his arms and pressed himself as closely as he could to the wall to keep free from the wind shear. At the first alley, he fell into the shelter of the close walls. He began to feel through the dead man's pockets.

An old woman in a man's filthy overcoat was huddled beneath a set of concrete stairs leading down to a basement. She was holding two kittens against her chest, and her face was covered with grime. She smelled of cheap alcohol, and fear.

"It's the end of the world," she told Angel.

He figured she was right.

After Angel left, Willy started acting even more nervous than usual. He knew he was doing it, but he didn't
know how to stop. He kept washing the counter over and
over, like somebody with that obsessive-compulsive
thing that made you do everything in threes or whatever. The only thing he was obsessed about was staying
alive, and the compulsion to make a little money, well,
hell, he was a red-blooded American and that was in
his genes.

So after he started humming a little too loudly, a
couple of out-of-town vampires looked at some other
out-of-town vampires, and a couple of vampires who'd
been around since before the Slayer moved to Sunnydale. They gave Vampire #1 a nod, and he walked over
to Willy and grabbed the front of his shirt, hauled him
so they were nose to nose, and then vamped out. His
glowing eyes lasered directly into Willy's, and he made
a mental note to put Depends on his grocery shopping
list.

"What is wrong with you?" the vampire demanded.

"Nothing," Willy squeaked.

Vampire #1 was joined by several others, who just
stared at Willy as they let their vampire features take
over their human faces.

"Um, I'm having trouble breathing," Willy said.

"Get used to it." The vampire pulled tighter.

"He was gone too long, getting the 'good stuff,' "
one of the vampires said, air-quoting the last.

"It's hard to reach. I'm short," Willy offered.

"Wanna be shorter?" Vampire #1 asked.

"Um, you guys with the ritual to bring back the

Master? You might want to speed it up a little." Willy tried so very hard to smile. "I think the um, cops know about it."

"The cops," Vampire #1 said, glancing at the others. "Are your cops a problem around here?"

"Not usually," said one of the previously silent vampires. "In fact, you might argue that they turn their heads the other way more often than not."

"Or bury them in the sand," said a third. "They know what's good for them. And what's bad."

All the vampires chuckled with not so much bad as evil humor.

"Please," Willy said. "I gotta live here, okay? I'm just saying, bump it up. Um, if at all possible."

They looked at each other. "Those two bounty hunters of Tervokian's should have showed up with the axe by now," one of them said. He glared at the barman. "You know anything about that?"

"No. I swear," Willy said. He sighed. "Okay, I shouldn't tell you this, okay? I'm dead if he finds out. Angel came by, asking about the axe, too."

The vampires looked very unhappy.

"How come that bastard always finds out about everything?" said Previously Silent. "You told him, didn't you? He knows we're gunning for the Slayer."

"Gonna carve her up and bring the Master back with her blood," #1 gloated.

"If we ever find the axe."

The door to the bar opened and a really tall vampire stood dripping wet in a long raincoat. He was vamped, and he was smiling.

He stuck his hand in the pocket of his coat and said, "Check it out."

He had the axe.

Willy's inquisitioners laughed and cheered. Then they got back to the business of making life hard for Willy.

"You told Angel what we're planning," #1 insisted.

"I didn't. You people always talk too much. And too loudly," he added.

"We are not people," one of them huffed.

"I'm sorry, Mr. Demon," Willy groveled. "But anyways, he came to my office recently because, um, he wanted to know . . . something else. Anyway, it was an entirely different subject. But then you guys started muttering about the ritual and raising the Master and all that stuff and he knows about it, and I didn't tell him nothin'. "

One of the good things about bad guys was that they were always suspicious of each other. So even though the next five minutes of Willy's life revolved around each of them protesting that they had not said one single word about the ritual to raise the Master. But the more they protested, the more positive each of them became that someone among them had spilled the beans.

"So, I'm thinking, hurry it up or just forget it," Willy concluded.

Everybody got into grumble mode at that suggestion. Then Previously Silent said, "Let's move to plan B."

"Plan B being the plan to not do it?" Willy suggested.

"The plan to kill you if you don't shut up," Vampire #1 shot back. He turned to the others. "Let's get her now, before Angel tells her what we're doing. We'll split up into search parties and get moving through the tunnels. And on the surface, too, if the weather holds."

To Willy, he said, "Go get us a round of O-neg. On the house."

"Hey," Willy protested, then thought the better of pissing these guys off when they were already fairly pissed off to begin with. "Okay. My pleasure."

He hurried back to the office, to the fridge where he kept the really, really good stuff.

The stuff that would keep these guys from ripping his throat open, hopefully.

"Wow," Cordelia murmured, and that was an understatement.

The town of Sunnydale was aflame, whole blocks blazing despite the hurricane that was yanking palm trees straight out of the ground and sending billboards sailing like guillotine blades, topping off power line poles. The streets here, on higher ground than Main Street, were anything but dark, although most of the power was out: firelight flashed on the crowd of people intent upon breaking every single unbroken window in every single building.

On the lower streets, the water had risen to the level of car windows, and stalled vehicles had been abandoned long before now. The force of the water was beginning to move them, and Giles figured more damage would be inflicted once they built up momentum.

Giles rather regretted the need to get to the school library, where he had additional books on weather-related portents and signs. He'd exhausted his research materials at his apartment.

"This is so bad for my skin," she bellowed, since they could only be understood by yelling at each other. "All this stress, you know? I've had more emotional trauma on the drive over here than I was planning on having in my entire life. And you know what happens? Your skin ages. Before you know it, dermabrasion won't work. I'll have to go the Botox route. Then it's only a matter of time before real surgical lifting."

"It's rather amazing, the lengths you're willing to go to to help us save the world," Giles shouted.

"Thanks." She gestured to the school. "Well, it's still here, thus proving there is no God after all."

She jerked to a stop and they both jumped out, racing as fast as they could to the main entrance. Giles had a key and he let them inside. When the door slammed behind them, Cordelia let out a whoop.

"Thank the Lord," she said.

"That would be the one that doesn't exist," Giles replied.

They hurried into the library and Giles went into his office to check his voice mail. There was no word from Buffy or Xander, which concerned him.

Where can they be? he wondered. *Is she all right?*

"Okay, so books?" Cordelia asked.

"Books."

It was, for the moment, the best he had to offer.

Chapter Ten

The mummy was coming straight for Buffy.

The hurricane is good for something, Buffy thought. *Blows the fog away. We finally have a perfect view of the enemy, and it looks just like what I dreamed about.*

She and Xander had been following some vamps sneaking around in the Shady Rest Cemetery. Got 'em dusted, and then Xander had turned around and let out a yell.

And there it was, gliding above the ground between SONIA BUCHANAN REST IN PEACE JAN. 2, 1907–FEB. 17, 1953 and LLOYD BUTTNER U.S. ARMY 1912–1989.

It was carrying one of the boxes.

"Buffy, don't go near it," Xander cautioned. "It's after you."

"I can handle it. Get out of here."

"This is no time for heroics, Buffy." He feinted a punch at the mummy—well out of the creature's reach.

"Xander, I'm the Slayer. My time for heroics is 24/7." She ran up to the mummy and executed a sharp kick to its midsection. It was pushed slightly backward by the force; otherwise, it hung in the air, unaffected.

Buffy went to work on it, punching-bag style. She pummeled it, kicked it, smacked it, doubled her fists and got brutal.

Nothing.

As she stopped, trying to figure out what to do next, it glided toward her. Then it reached its hand inside the box.

"This is wiggin' me," Xander said. "Let's go."

It brought out the axe.

It raised the axe above its head.

It froze.

Buffy and Xander both said, "Huh" at the exact same time. Then Buffy sidled up to the thing and stood on tiptoe to peer into the box.

"Buff, watch it," Xander pleaded.

She couldn't see anything. It was pitch black.

But she could hear something. Something awful: the screams of girls in mindless agony. The cries echoed against the sides of the box, then faded.

Then stopped.

Buffy felt sick at heart, as if her soul had been stripped of something precious and vital. The despair in the voices seeped into her, making her cold and tired. She was threaded through with a terrible sense of loss.

"Not liking this," Xander said firmly.

"Okay. We'll go," Buffy agreed, her voice weak.

And we can't get away from that thing fast enough.

"Damn it," Faith muttered, from the shelter of her newly stolen umbrella.

The National Guard had come to town.

The Sunnydale Fire Station was surrounded by green trucks of every shape and size, and men and women in drab uniforms barked at each other in the storm like feisty German shepherds. Faith could only go so far in comprehending the allure some people had for the commando lifestyle. Weapons, maybe, and the authority to use them. But otherwise, it struck her as a lot of strutting around without getting much done.

Thing was, they were also preventing her from getting much done. If one of the axes was actually inside the fire station, it was going to be pretty hard to waltz in and snag it. Lifting a bottle of perfume at a department store or snagging an umbrella that had rolled down the street was one thing—okay, two—but locating and squirreling away a very fancy axe was quite another.

Then Faith remembered hearing about the wacky hijinx that had ensued when Xander got turned into a soldier two years before. If anybody in the Scooby Corps could do the soldier-boy swagger, it'd be him.

Nodding to herself, she slipped away.

The only thing the pilot of the Watchers Council jet knew was that he should expect two passengers. Two had come aboard, and soon he had filed his flight plan and taken off for America.

Micaela cast a warding spell and said, "Perhaps I'll manage to decipher these pages before one of Tony's confederates figures out what we've done."

Belted in across from Micaela, the Watcher smoothed her skirt and moved her neck in a slow circle. The strain was telling on her. And yet she remained quite elegant, and kind, and Micaela was sorry the woman had become involved in this situation. People were going to die.

Neema pursed her lips. "How long were you going to be incarcerated by the Council?"

"Years." Micaela threaded her hands together. "I knew it was only a matter of time before one of them cornered me. At first I dared to hope that Lord Yorke was a good man, trying to do something noble. He lied very convincingly." She moved her hands. "That's not quite true. I wanted to believe his lies. I didn't want to have to make any more moral choices."

"We seem to have more than our share of rotten apples," Neema said, concerned.

Micaela silently agreed. If someone as high up as Anthony Yorke could do so much harm undetected, there was no telling what else might be going on within the Council walls . . . and beyond them. There were Watchers and operatives all over the world, and they were often incommunicado with the rest of the organization for months. It was a system with a potential for great misuse. Unfortunately, the snafu with William the Bloody during the 1940s had convinced many members of the Council that the less centralized and formal their structure was, the more likely that they would never be rendered so vulnerable again.

Micaela said to her, "It's the power. There's so much of it. If evil is strong, good has to become stronger. There's a relentless escalation."

"Very true," Neema agreed. "I've read so many Watcher's diaries. Not all of them withstood the temptation to send their Slayer out on a mission for purely personal reasons. And when you add magick use into the mix . . ." She moved her shoulders in a gesture of helplessness.

Micaela nodded. "Many people never stop to consider that each spell, each magickal 'event,' if you will, costs some kind of energy. Sometimes it's simply the expenditure of physical energy. Other times, a minor bit of karmic pollution. Other times, it's a piece of one's soul.

"There are always repercussions. Consequences. But since it's magick, even seasoned spellcasters forget that there's always a cost."

Neema took that in. Then she ducked her head to look out the small window. She jerked, startled.

"The fog's building," she said worriedly.

Micaela flashed her a small, proud smile. "I'm creating it. It's laced with magickal barriers, to make it harder to detect us." She closed her eyes and intoned, "'Clearly I see, but it touches me not.' Don't worry. Our pilot will have good visibility. He won't even realize what I've done."

Neema glanced away.

"I can't quite forgive you for helping Lord Yorke. I know you didn't do much, but . . ."

Micaela's sigh was world-weary. "I can't quite forgive myself. Fulcanelli taught me to be a survivor, above all else. But I would like to depart this life with some sense that my good deeds outweighed my bad."

Neema looked at her, studying her face. Micaela was used to life as a chameleon-like person, able to convince people of her sincerity when it suited her. Truth be told, it made for a lonely existence.

But in her statement, she was utterly sincere. She wanted to die a good person.

Wanted that very much.

Buffy called Giles's apartment to fill him in on her and Xander's recent exploits and discovered that he'd recorded a phone announcement directing everyone to convene at the school library, where he and Cordelia would be researching.

"Oh, I'll bet she's loving the books," Xander said, grinning at Buffy as they headed on over. "She only put up with all that stuff so she could be with me, you know."

Buffy gave him a sly glance. "And now that you two have broken up, she does it because . . . ?"

"She wants me back." His expression dared her to make fun of him, and then he laughed wryly and said, "Women. Can't live with 'em, can't change 'em all into ferrets."

"Xander, that's gross," she said.

He made another face. "Didn't mean it the way it sounded."

"Good. And changing the subject . . . arms dealer convention?"

Their school campus was overrun with National Guardsmen and vehicles. Jeeps and trucks were parked all over the grass; soldiers in raingear were marching beneath the shelter of the second-story overhang in the quad. It was as if the entire population of Sunnydale had driven up outside and parked their cars, trucks, and armored tanks wherever they felt like it.

Buffy and Xander managed to slip inside the main building. They headed for the library; there was so much activity that the floor was shaking as if they were having another earthquake.

They entered their usual meeting place to find Giles and Cordelia surrounded by stacks of books. Also, to find the floor surrounded by stacks of books. There had been some earthquake damage to the walls—long, deep cracks and chunks of chipped-off stucco.

"Good," Giles said. "Everyone's trickling in. Faith's on her way. She wanted you especially, Xander."

"Doesn't everybody?" he piped.

Both Cordelia and Buffy stared at him.

"Don't answer that," he said, wincing.

"I've heard from Oz as well," Giles said. "Willow's doing well. Also, he mentioned that an axe was said to be at the fire—"

A bulbous, semihuman head poked into the library, and its grin was fascinating in its special revolting way.

It was Principal Snyder, the principal most people loved to hate.

As opposed to poor Principal Flutie, Buffy thought, *the principal some people loved to eat.*

"Mr. Giles, there you are," Snyder said, in his smarmiest "Oh, yay, I got bad news for you" voice. "And Miss Summers and our own Cordelia Chase, who is obviously turning into quite the delinquent herself."

Just then, Angel walked up behind Snyder. Snyder gave a shout of surprise and said, "And who might you be?"

"We saved him from all that stuff outside," Cordelia said quickly. Everyone looked at her. "Well, he saved us. Me. Saving was involved," she amended. "And hey, excuse me, but I am not a delinquent. I don't hang out with these people."

"I suppose looks can be deceiving," Snyder said nastily. To Giles, he continued, "I'm sure you'll be just delighted to know that we're going to finally get some use out of this library."

"Oh?" Giles asked, peering over the tops of his glasses.

"The Red Cross is setting up an emergency shelter in the gym. I invited the nurses to bunk in here."

"Oooh, nurses," Xander blurted. Everyone looked at him sharply. "O-kay, sexist private notion, which is frowned upon by the current administration's thought

police. Nurses can be men. Ugly men." He smiled a
Principal Snyder. "Better?"

"Get a haircut," Snyder snapped. His head disappeared back behind the swinging double doors.

"Ja, mein Führer," Xander muttered.

"This is great," Buffy muttered also. "Giles, we're ir
the middle of fighting a big evil. What are we going tc
do with civilians around?"

"We won't even be able to discuss the exciting read
ing you two have been doing," Xander added.

"Hey, we could use a code," Cordelia piped. "You
know, like when Buffy left town because she killec
Angel and she couldn't face being such a loser? For ex
ample, Xander could be Night-hawk, again."

Xander was moderately flattered. Buffy chucklec
slightly. Cordelia had totally grooved on the Nighthawl
thing.

"Only you'll have to be something else now, like
Chickenhawk," Cordelia said scathingly. She looked pas
him to Giles. "And when we want to say 'vampire,' we
could say, um, 'surfer.'" She blinked at her own bril
liance.

"As in, 'The surfer sucked all that chick's bloo(
while shootin' the curl?'" Xander asked pointedly.

"Hey. Let's use some vampire-friendly language,"
Buffy said, indicating Angel.

"Sorry, Angel," Cordelia said to Angel. To Xander
"Of course not. 'Blood' will be in code, too. 'The
surfer . . . waxed his board.'"

"That sounds vaguely obscene. Not even vaguely, a;
a matter of fact," Giles observed.

"I like it." Xander rubbed her hands together. "And
we could use the term 'mustache wax' for—"

"We're not using a code," Giles announced. "We'l

have to think of something else in order to work efficiently, despite our lack of privacy. And—and we should make things nice for the nurses. It's a wonderful thing they're doing, being here. Except for the, ah, bothering-us part."

He started picking up dusty volumes of demon lore. Also, candy wrappers and empty Coke cans.

Not two seconds later, the library's doors swung open, and Snyder marched in, leading half a dozen women in jeans and jackets into what, for three years, had been pretty much exclusive Slayer Territory.

"And here we are," Snyder said, loving the discomfort. He noticed the disarray the earthquake had caused.

"You young people, make yourselves useful and clean this place up." He sighed. "Kids today. In my day, an earthquake was an opportunity to demonstrate good citizenship."

"Of course, the Hawaiian Island chain was forming back then," Xander muttered.

"I'll leave you all to get acquainted." Snyder turned to go, then wheeled around. "Just what are you all doing in here, anyway?"

"Cramming," Buffy piped up. She fumbled, adding, "For various tests."

"I think I'll go back to school," one of the nurses drawled as she glanced at Angel. She had red hair pulled back in a French braid and green eyes that just had to be colored contact lenses. She was good in the jeans department.

And also the slutty smile department, Buffy thought, narrowing her eyes and moving closer to Angel.

"We sought refuge," Cordelia said. She looked at the others. "And cramming. Refuge and cramming." She nodded vigorously.

"Principal Snyder?" boomed a deep male voice.

The doors opened and a tall, broad-shouldered man in cammies and a helmet looked down from his chiseled large soldier heights at the pointy-toothed little rodent man. "My men would like to inspect the earthquake damage, sir."

"Of course." Snyder smiled triumphantly at Giles. "I'll put you in charge of the library detail, Mr. Giles. That's how bad things are around here."

He left.

"I'm for dropping out of school and enlisting," Cordelia said. She touched her hair, which bordered on Bride of Frankensteinian, and unknowingly transferred some soot from her chin and smeared it down the entire side of her face.

Giles smiled grimly at the redheaded nurse and held out his hand. "I'm Rupert Giles, the school librarian. I'm sure I speak for our entire town when I say thank you for coming. We're in rather bad straits here."

"Yeah. Monica Hamilton here. What the hell is going on?" she asked, ignoring Giles and swiveling her head toward Angel.

"Hell," Cordelia said simply. "Hell is happening. Because we live on a hellmou—"

Giles snapped his fingers at her and she shrugged as if to say that divulging classified information was not of the dire.

"Okay. I'm picking up books," she grumped

"Anything to keep you quiet, Miss Loose Lips," Xander whispered to her.

She gave him an imperious glare. "I wouldn't talk about my lips if I were you, Drool Boy."

"Atmospheric disturbances," Giles said authoritatively. "I believe they've been pinpointed as the cause of all this wind and rain. The fires, well, you know Southern California. All the dry brush. So much dry vegetation could be set off by something fairly minor. A cigarette tossed from a truck, for example. And earthquakes ... simple movements of the earth's crust."

"Or the end of the world," Xander pitched in.

One of the other nurses, a chubby, short blonde, said to Buffy, "I haven't ever seen anything like this. And you wouldn't believe some of the disaster sites I've been to."

"I can't imagine," Buffy drawled.

The nurse held up a huge book with *Vampyre* written across the front. "Do they actually let you guys check things like this out? I thought with all the political correctness these days, this would be *verboten.*"

"Oh. That, uh," Giles said, as Buffy looked to him for help. "Special collections. We have a fine ... fantasy collection. Um. Yes. If you please. That book is very dangerous." He caught himself. "I mean, old."

"He means old," Buffy echoed, wide-eyed and innocent. *At least, I think I look wide-eyed and innocent. Or maybe I look guilty as sin. Which leads me to an interesting thought: How can sin be guilty? Can you say "guilty as sloth? Guilty as envy?"*

Buffy snapped out of her reverie. "I'll just put that book away in the weapons ... collections." She grabbed the book out of the nurse's hands. "And also, the collections that are special are there."

"Mr. Giles, we'll have cots for ourselves," Monica said briskly. "We'll be happy to get some extras for you and your students." She looked at Angel. "The atmospheric disturbances are getting worse. You'll all probably have to stay here through the night."

Buffy looked at Angel. Angel looked at Buffy.

Two hearts, with just one thought:

Uh-oh.

It was almost dawn. In a puffy down bag, Buffy lay awake. Her lips were still tingling, and had tingled for what seemed like hours and hours, a timeless, sweet dream that had everything to do with Angel and nothing to do with walking fabric dummies.

Angel had crept to her side, taking advantage of everyone's deep, exhausted slumber, and murmured, "Buffy, I'm going to the boiler room. Fewer questions that way."

"Or more," Buffy pointed out, wanting very much for him to stay with her.

He shrugged. "My guess is that either the Red Cross or the National Guard will have a lot of equipment to unload." At her questioning look, he added, "From their trucks. Parked outside. In the sun."

"Ah." She flashed him a brief smile. "Some people will do anything to get out of a little manual labor. Even turn into vampires."

"It's not a dodge I recommend," he said.

Then he bent over her bag and gathered her up in his arms, kissing her deeply and tenderly. A powerful thrill formed at the base of her spine and fanned outward and upward, making her catch her breath. His lips were gentle and probing, and Buffy closed her eyes, willing herself not to want him so much. So incredibly much.

She slid her arms around his neck and heard his soft groan against the hollow of her ear. He lingered at her jawline, nuzzling her neck, and a frisson of fear mixed with the wanting, making it all the more irresistible. Slayers thrived on danger.

Vampires lived for the hunt, and the kill.

Most vampires, Buffy amended. Her heart was thundering. *Every single one of them, except for Angel.*

"Buffy," he murmured softly, spanning his hands across her back. He trailed a fingertip down her nose and across her mouth. She caught it and held it between her teeth, looking up at him languidly. His eyes widened slightly in response, and he kissed her again, more deeply this time.

She wanted him to keep going. She wanted . . .

. . . *all the things we can't ever have,* she thought, clinging to him. *Oh, Angel, Angel, I want you.*

So bite me now and—

Firmly, Angel moved away. He touched her eyebrow, cupped her cheek. With a steady, intense gaze, he got up and moved away, his footfalls soundless on the library floor.

After he left, she heard Xander chuckle.

"Shut up, Xand," Buffy said pleasantly.

Then she slept.

In San Diego, Christopher Bothwell slumped at his kitchen table and drank the coffee Cecile had made for him. Apparently he'd passed out on the couch during the ritual, and he had a hell of a hangover, though he could have sworn he'd only shared a couple glasses of wine with her during the course of the evening. She'd stayed over—he'd picked her up and she hadn't wanted to call a cab, as the distance from his home in Ocean Beach and hers, in Lakeside, made it outrageously expensive.

He said, "I'm terribly embarrassed about all this. You know, we Brits generally boast that we could hold our liquor better than Australians."

She had changed her attire after the ritual; now she was wearing yesterday's pair of jeans and black turtleneck sweater. A turban of vivid colors was wound around her hair, a modified and much less Marge Simpson–like version of the headdresses favored by Erykah Badu. With Mariposa on her lap, she drank her own cup of coffee. She was reading *The San Diego Union-Tribune*.

She had the most elegant and classic bone structure, putting him in mind of India, whose mother was a beautiful and famous Philippine actress.

"It's no problem," she said. "I've been known to tie one on myself now and then." She put down the newspaper and smiled. "My temp job ended yesterday. I've been scheduled for a new assignment on Monday, but if I give them forty-eight hours' notice, I can cancel it. Would you like me to come with you to Sunnyvale?"

"Sunnydale," he corrected. He was flattered. "That's very kind of you, really. But this friend—"

"The sick one," she cut in helpfully.

"Yes. The sick one." He hated lying to her. She was a splendid girl, really. Yet he couldn't exactly bring her along on Watcher business. It would be extremely awkward; he and Rupert Giles needed to speak privately, and the Slayers shouldn't be shouldered with the burden of discussing confidential Council matters with a complete stranger in close proximity. And Sunnydale wasn't precisely the kind of town where one could find diversions for a companion while one went about one's business.

"Actually," he continued, "we haven't seen each other in quite a long time, and we've got a bit of, ah, emotional baggage to sort out. We had a row, if you must know." He made himself blush, which, he was embarrassed to admit, he could do on command. "It's frightfully dreary."

"Oh." She raised her brows. "Then of course . . . I didn't mean to intrude."

He loved her accent. And her sweetness.

"It was very kind of you to offer. I hope I haven't offended you."

"*Mais non.* We all have our secrets." Her eyes glittered and she tilted her head as if daring him to reveal his.

"Ah." He made a face. "I have offended you."

"Not in the least." She raised her coffee cup to her lips and peered at him over the rim. "I shall be eager to see you again."

"I, as well." Relieved, he smiled at her, and she smiled back.

"Right, then. I ought to pack. Throw a few things in an overnight bag."

"May I do anything to help?"

"Damn. The dog," he said, as Mariposa licked Cecile's hand. Back in England, he wouldn't have hesitated to bring the little dog with him. But he didn't know what he was getting into in the home town of the reigning Slayer. He cherished the dog; he had promised India he would take care of her forever and always.

"Perhaps I could watch her for you," she suggested. Brightening, she looked around. "I could stay here and house sit for you, or I can take her back to my place."

"That's extremely generous." He meant it. But he was hesitant to take her up on her offer. For one thing, he didn't know her all that well. For another, he didn't want to presume, but the thought of Mariposa staying in a stranger's home, where they might not be as careful about shutting doors before she could scoot outside and run away, was not at all appealing.

"I'd be happy to stay here," she said.

"Who'll watch your apartment? If you stay here, I mean?" Kit asked her.

Her smile was warm as she replied, "I have a roommate. It would be nice to have my own place for a few days."

"Ah." He felt a bit disingenuous; she was obviously interested in him, and he had no intention of moving forward in any kind of more serious relationship.

"It would be no trouble. *Vraiment.*" She gave the dog a pat. "We'll get along just fine, Mariposa and I. I feel as if I already know your little puppy dog."

The dog yipped with delight and settled onto her lap like the most entitled of spoiled, fat Persian cats.

"Very well, then." He scooted back his chair. "It's quite kind of you, Cecile."

"*Pas de tout.* Not at all." She gave the dog an affectionate scratching behind the ears. "It is I who should be thanking you."

The French, he thought, amused. *So flowery and gallant.*

Then he went to pack, giving his bedroom a quick look-'round to see if there were any telltale signs of his secret life as a Watcher. He was generally conscientious about it, not so much for fear that a friend or acquaintance would notice something, but because the crime rate in this part of San Diego was rather high. If someone broke in, he wanted them stealing items that were uninteresting and unremarkable. Nothing, at any rate, that would pique one's curiosity about him in the least.

He heard her in the kitchen, and realized that it was past noon and he hadn't offered her anything to eat. He was quite flummoxed; he didn't recall anything about ending the ritual. He himself had ground the herbals for the rite, and they had never interacted so strongly with alcohol before. Certainly, he'd gotten a buzz on other occasions, but nothing like what had happened last night.

So, did I actually see India? he wondered. He would need to discuss the evening with Cecile without revealing too much information.

But if I saw her . . . if I can speak with her, tell her that I love her, that she is, and was, cherished . . .

Perhaps then, both of us shall find peace.

The television went on and he set to packing his bag. When he was finished, he discovered that she had made them each a ham sandwich. She was eating hers on his sofa in front of the television. When he came into the room, she looked up at him and said, "Look at this."

On the screen, a woman dressed in a rain slicker and holding an umbrella stood before a harbor in the throes of massive tides. Large, angry waves slammed against the stone breakwater behind her as she spoke. Rain soaked her. Lightning flashed.

"The coastal town of Sunnydale is being slammed with alarmingly high tides, which local oceanographers are at a loss to explain. In addition, the fire which began in Sunnydale National Forest is now raging out of control and consuming huge sections of the historic downtown area. Additional firefighters are on call to be flown in, but the town is reeling under weather conditions too bad to allow planes into the air space."

He frowned. "Giles didn't say anything about any of that."

"Giles?" she repeated.

"My friend." He frowned at the images on the

screen: a restaurant whose windows had been shattered by the encroaching sea. Towering pine trees glowing with flame.

"I'd better go now," he said, "before there's no town to go to. I'll drive you home so you can get some things."

"No need," she said. "I called my roommate while you were packing. Cameron has to come out to this area later to do some errands. He's going to have someone follow him out with my car."

"Oh, that's far too inconvenient," he protested. He was mildly relieved to discover that her roommate was a man. However, she was not referring to him as "my boyfriend," which indicated, at least to Kit, that she was unattached.

"*Non, non.*" She waved her hand at the TV. "As soon as I saw this, I called him. It's no problem, and it would be better if you got on the road as fast as possible."

"Indeed. I wouldn't want to miss the tidal wave," he quipped.

Putting down her plate, she got up off the couch and walked him to the door, almost as if this were her home, not his. The dog skittered toward him and Cecile scooped her up, nuzzling her under the chin.

"Please drive carefully," she said. "And if you could give me a number where I might be able to contact you . . ."

"Of course." There was a small phone table next to the front door; Kit pulled out Giles's phone number from his pocket and copied it onto the scratch pad beside the phone. He thought a moment and said, "If you have trouble with the phone lines, here's his address. I'll find out if he has a pager, a cell, something like that, and call you with that as well."

She tapped the paper, then smiled at him. "I'm resourceful. I'll be fine. *Merci.*"

He hesitated. "Before I go, I need to ask you. What happened last night? Did we contact . . . someone?"

She shrugged. "I couldn't tell. There was a presence, and you spoke, but then you said you were dizzy and had to lie down. Pretty soon you were asleep, so I watched TV."

"I see. Well." He smiled at her. "Thanks again for this. It's awfully kind."

She tapped his chest once, very lightly. "You do remember the promise you made to me, do you not?"

He flushed for real this time. "I must tell you honestly, I don't."

She grinned at him. "I'll still hold you to it, Kit Bothwell."

"Well." He gave her a very polite smile. "Good-bye then."

"Good journey. Good driving."

She brushed his cheek with her lips, and to his surprise, it rather burned him. Then suddenly, a vivid memory rushed in:

Oh, my God. I made love to her last night. He was thoroughly mortified. *I didn't even remember it until just now. And it was fantastic.*

He stared at her. "Cecile, I . . ."

She put her fingertip against his lips. "Ah, you remember a little," she said. She tapped his chest again. "You'll remember everything soon. Including your promise."

Her laugh was like smoke. "Cameron Duvalier is the Servant now, Kit. But you could become the Servant, if you help me."

"What—?"

"*Allez*," she urged. "You'll remember. Soon."

Oz shouted for the nurse as Willow walked with
Lucy on the Ghost Roads. Lucy said, "You can't stay
here, Willow, and I can't come up this time. The two
others must be the ones. They're ready, but you'll need
help with the transference. And you'll need another
volunteer."

Willow said, "I'll get it done."

Lucy took Willow's hand. "This may be the last time
we ever see each other. I don't know what is to come,
Willow, but I'm glad to have known you." She smiled.
"You'll make a good Slayer."

"Thank you," Willow said softly. Then she let herself float up, up, waving goodbye to Lucy.

She opened her eyes, to find Oz holding her hand.

She said, "Hi. Get Giles. Get everybody over here.
We gotta get cracking with the plan."

Suddenly the room began to shake. Oz said, "Don't
be scared. It's been doing that."

The room shook harder.

"Okay," Willow said uncertainly.

"Oh, and Giles has India Cohen's diary with some
stuff Roger Zabuto sent him."

And harder.

The Book of Threes

Prologue

The Duvalier Plantation, December 1860

Rather than call his own father out, Cameron left the Christmas party.

I hate him. I hate his smugness, and his stupidity. I hate him for laughing at me in front of all our guests.

Tears of fury ran down his cheeks as he crossed the vast lawns of Oakhaven, the glitter and merriment receding behind him; the violins grew muted, overshadowed by the hooting of an owl, which echoed through the rows upon rows of oaks. Dark-skinned carriage footmen chatted with housemaids in their primitive languages and broken English; horse tack jingled.

Cameron's dress boots made powdery sounds as he stomped through the snow. Since he'd been dancing inside his own home, he wore neither overcoat nor hat, and his breath was steam as he half walked, half ran toward the icehouse. No one at that party had the faintest notion what was to come. War was more than fancy uniforms and white chargers, maidens waving farewell from balconies, and wives and mothers weeping sentimental tears. They all thought a conflict would last a couple of weeks at most, and then the chastened North would leave Southerners alone to live their lives as they chose. After all, America was all about freedom, wasn't that correct?

"Fools," he muttered, confused how he, at seventeen, understood better than any of his elders what quicksand they were standing in. Not only did his father and younger brothers not fear the notion of a war between the states, they welcomed one, as an opportunity to take a stand for individual liberty, and to be covered in glory and honor for their courage.

The icehouse was one of the many outbuildings on the Duvalier lands. Oakhaven, like all plantations, was a vast enterprise, which the Northerners—with their filthy factories and mills, forcing young children and innocent young ladies into servitude much worse than anything the slaves down South endured—did not seem to understand. The folks at the party reckoned that once the North understood that, they would leave them in peace.

Cameron charged into the icehouse, which was deserted at this late hour. After sundown, the punches and buffet dishes were served hot, as was his mother's custom, designed to ward off the chill of the snowy evening, There were no slaves heaving large blocks of ice over their shoulders with tongs, nobody making new blocks with the unexpected coming of the winter snow.

He crossed the darkened room, which was dimly illuminated by moonlight, found and opened the door to the basement, and climbed down the stairs.

A thin ray of light from several small rectangular windows lit up the place. In summer, all windows were covered with black shades. The towers of ice blocks were covered with straw and salt; it was colder than the air upstairs, and it smelled a bit. As to be expected.

He pulled the keys to the sanctuary, as he had termed it, from his tight trousers, and glanced surreptitiously over his shoulder as he crept to the false brick wall he had laid himself. Realizing he should have brought a lantern, he relied on his familiarity with his own handiwork to locate the single loose brick which concealed the lock. There was a keyhole there, and he always draped a bit of straw across it to make sure no one had tried the door. He felt for the telltale straw and found it undisturbed. All was in order. No one had discovered his secret.

With another glance around, he inserted the key until the lock caught. Slowly he opened the door, took a breath and squeezed into the space behind it, his boot on the top rung of the wooden ladder. It made him nervous to be there in the dark.

He pulled the door shut again, making sure the lock was still open so that he could make a quick exit if it became necessary. His hand was shaking; after all this time, he was still afraid. Quickly and silently, he descended the wooden ladder.

This was his special place. He had detected the cavern beneath the house and there had fashioned his own private quarters. Despite being a young man of privilege on a vast plantation, he rarely had a chance to be alone. For a young man like Cameron, being alone was absolutely necessary.

It was here that the Dark Ones had first begun speaking to him, at first in whispers in his head, then later as clear, distinct voices. He had discovered that they could communicate with him best down here, in the same place he had begun drinking alone and reading scandalous literature.

They made him prove his mettle: first it was frogs,

then birds, and small animals. Though it was rough going at first, he learned to detach so that he could do a good job and passed every test. Then they urged him to human sacrifice, and he did a fine job of it, if he did say so himself. The slaves had set up a howl about the missing girl, and it didn't die down until one of their own was found guilty of the crime and hanged.

After that, Cameron was more careful.

Blessings poured in upon him for his diligence. His older brother Edward died, making Cameron the next heir to the Duvalier estate. The doctor who had taken Cameron's parents aside after a dinner party to discuss his "grave concerns" about their son's "personality" had suffered a terrible accident on his way home. His horse's saddle came uncinched and the man had been thrown to his death.

After that, Cameron became more careful still. He never permitted so much as a hint of his interior thoughts and plans to seep through an exterior of charm and affability. Though it proved exhausting, he behaved as if he were the most ordinary of men.

In return, the Dark Ones had proven to be even more generous. Slowly and painstakingly, they had introduced him to their world of the Black Arts. They guided him in his reading, showed him where to find herbs, dirt from a grave, cobwebs, and dead things. *How to make a hand of glory from a dead man.*

Their bond with him was as strong as true love. Their pact was made to teach him everything, if he would continue to worship them and feed them. In the years since that first appearance, on a frosty autumn midnight when all he had had a mind to do was drink some moonshine his daddy's valet, Lucius, had acquired for him, and look at pictures of gals in their underthings, the Dark Ones had given him all that they had promised, and more.

In return, he had no other gods before them, and he kept them well fed.

Very well fed.

Even now, a young girl's body lay all blue and white atop a solid block of ice. If he recalled correctly, her name was Tess, and her parents wouldn't mind the loss of a mouth to feed. When she'd slapped his face for trying to take liberties, he realized he had been tempted by her beauty because the Dark Ones wanted her.

So he'd beaten her to death, and when darkness had fallen, lowered her down the wooden ladder with a rope around her ankles. He'd learned the hard way that bringing them down by their necks made a bad mess if their heads popped off.

In the four years of his apprenticeship, he reckoned he had killed at least fifty females in the practice of his art. Most had been slaves. People had figured a lot of those runaways had disappeared in the swamps, or made it to freedom. Now and then, he took a poor, hardscrabble sharecropper's girl like this one, or one of the tarts down in town. He prayed Tess was their type. He had a boon to request, the biggest one he'd every asked for, and he knew only the best, most delectable sacrifices would keep his masters happy.

The single lantern Cameron had lit earlier in the evening was still going, hidden behind an old wooden crate. Dots of mud across the straw-covered earthen floor indicated that his masters had inspected the sacrifice. Cameron had never actually seen them consume one of the chosen, but by morning, the ice would be melted and the carcass would be gone.

Now he knelt by the dead girl, set down the lantern, and lowered his head in an attitude of prayer.

"My Masters," he said reverently. "Long have I served you. And y'all have provided for my every need. But now I ask something not for myself, but for my beloved homeland. Do not let us go to war. Save the South from bloodshed.

"I will do anything that you ask."

He closed his eyes and waited for their voices. After a time, he nearly despaired. Their silence was an agony down to the roots of his being.

Then the whispering began inside his head; soon it fanned the air around him, as his gods took form in his own time and place.

Tell us, they said. *Tell us some of the things you will do to please us.*

"I will kill many, many sacrifices," he assured them. "I will torture them."

Tell us how you will torture them. Tell us everything you will do.

"All right, then," he answered, warming to the topic. He sat back on his bottom and crossed his legs Indian style. This was permitted. "First, I'll pick out some gal who's so beautiful she can't be real."

Choose the best. The chosen must be perfect in every way, to merit our notice.

"Yes, my Masters. Yes, of course," he said eagerly. He began to perspire at the thought. His hands were warm and clammy. "The most beautiful and perfect."

Each like a bright star. And then you will terrorize and mutilate her.

"I'll just cozy up to each one and pretend I want her. Y'all know how I do it." He laughed harshly. "I swear they must realize I'm not sincere, all the struggling they do. And the insults." He rolled his eyes.

Of course. If they knew you meant it, they would want you. You are handsome beyond compare, sophisticated, witty, and gallant.

"Thank you," he said. He tried to sound modest, but it was true. And the foolish, stupid women who didn't appreciate it deserved to die. Not that he did anything out of malice or revenge; no, no, it was to please the Dark Ones.

For a long time, he prayed beside the lantern. He knelt alone in the dark, head bowed until it ached; and as the time passed, he heard a rustling in the straw that made the hairs on the back of his neck stand straight up.

They're coming out. At last, I'll see them.

He waited. And waited. Finally his curiosity got the better of him and he squinted one eye open.

At seventeen, Cameron was handsome, with dark red hair and sorrel-colored eyes, a replica of his momma down to the scattering of freckles across the bridge of his nose.

"I swear, Judeena, there's not a drop of Duvalier blood in that boy's likeness," his father had once drawled, and his mother had paled.

"Of course he's a Duvalier," she'd blurted.

Shortly after that, his daddy had started creeping down to the slave shacks late of an evening. There was a lovely woman there named Cecile, and Cameron figured her for someone special, because she was always smiling. When she looked at him, she actually winked at him.

Now, eyes were winking at him just like Cecile did.

Hundreds of eyes, tiny and red.

Rats covered the body.

We are pleased, said the Dark Lords.

Cameron fervently balled his fists and held them against his chest. His heart swelled with gratitude.

"Then save the South. Don't let us go to war," he begged.

It shall be done.

There will be no war.

As long as you keep feeding us.

"Of course," Cameron promised, as tears of relief slid down his face.

The best. The most beautiful.

"They're yours. I swear it."

In return, we need you to renew your loyalty. Burn those who would harm us, who would defeat us in our purpose.

"Burn . . ." Cameron said slowly.

Then a rat scampered toward him and knocked into the lantern at his side.

Knocked it over.

It cracked open and perfumed oil spilled out, igniting as it trickled onto the straw, until a trail of flame began to grow like some mythic, exquisite creature—a glowworm, a magickal insect.

Burn our enemies.

Cameron's eyes glazed as the flames grew higher. The rats capered and danced, shrieking with delight; their eyes glowing red as hellfire. As he stared into the flames, he saw the unfolding of his destiny, all at once. Of the South's destiny, and the glory of the Dark Ones, hallelujah, amen.

Start the fire tonight inside the house, when they're

all sleeping, they advised. *Make sure your daddy goes up like a torch. He, of all of them, must die.*

He laughed at you.

"Yes," he said, awed by their brilliance, their clarity of purpose. Why hadn't he thought of it on his own?

We understand one another, then. You are ours, always ours. We will always care for you. As long as you obey every command we give you.

"As long as I obey."

Feeling dizzy with anticipation, he got first to his knees, and then to his feet. The ankle-high flames from the lantern shifted as he staggered toward the ladder. Slowly he climbed upward, coughing in the intense smoke as it followed his every movement. *I am their eyes. I am their ears.*

His heart thudded in his chest as he made it up to the main floor of the ice house. There was no sign of fire up here; it was all taking place below, in his private sanctuary. The melting ice would probably put it out, and no one would ever know the momentous events that had occurred there.

Except me. I'm their acolyte. I'm the only one they can communicate with.

I'm unique. Special.

He left the icehouse and lurched through the snow, remembering a time long ago when his daddy had shouted, "He's no son of mine! He's a devil!" and he understood perfectly why the Dark Ones now demanded his father's death. Because his daddy was right. Cameron Duvalier was not his son. He was the child of the Dark Ones, and no more loyal son had ever lived.

Exaltation welled in his heart and he balled his fists again, resolute and fearless. His mind was fevered, imagining flames dancing along each carpet, clinging to each drapery. The oil paintings of his ancestors igniting all in a row; his grandmother, in her wheelchair.

His mewling baby sister in her crib.

Before this night was out, the mansion would lie in ruins, and he, and he alone, would carry the name of Duvalier.

He smiled as he shambled forward, his gaze taking in the huge, wooden house, festooned with garlands of holly and ivy.

"Nero fiddled while Rome burned," he murmured. "These fools will dance in the fires of hell."

A movement among the snowy hedges along the walkway to the house caught his eye; it was the dark-skinned Cecile, magnificent in a crimson velvet cloak over her shoulders. Her throat was long and her face, a study in symmetry. She had a small, thin nose, and her eyes were shaped like those of a cat.

It had never occurred to him before how pretty she was. Unlike his father, he had not taken any woman to be his paramour, neither free woman nor slave, but he be damned if his daddy's gal wasn't quite the thing.

Cecile would be fine food for the gods.

Her hair, usually caught up in a turban, tumbled in a waterfall of black curls down her back; and she turned her head and smiled at him as if she had expected to see him.

"*Bon soir,* young master," she said. Her accented voice was sleek with tones of warm nights and drumbeats, promises and secrets.

"Evenin', Cecile." He made as if to tip his hat, which of course he would retrieve tonight before the fire took it. After all, his mother had given him that hat, and he loved her dearly.

He would miss his mother. He would ache for certain members of the family with longing and mourn their passing.

Alas. It can't be helped.

"Hold on, gal. I'll walk with you," he said, his eyes shining eagerly.

She raised her chin slightly, the corners of her mouth raised upward, as if she was trying not to smile. He knew she must be thrilled that he would deign to escort her, a slave, and with him so dressed up and hair slicked back. When he caught up with her, she moved on, her gait stately, like she figured she was really something.

"Mighty fine cloak," he observed.

"It was a gift." She shifted the luxurious fabric over her shoulders. "From an admirer."

They both knew who. "Generous man."

"Oui." She grinned at him. "He gives me many presents."

"Does he. Any man would want to make you happy, he sees you in that cloak," he drawled.

They locked gazes. Hers was penetrating and almost frightening; he was a little chilled but he kept smiling at her. She wanted him, all right. It was always so easy to tell.

"I know," she said. Her voice was as smooth as velvet, as soft as the newly falling snow.

Chapter One

Flying to California

Cameron leaned his head against the small, thick pane of glass. In the hold of the private plane, the Gatherer sloshed in its pit. Cameron was its faithful Servant, and according to Cecile, the hour of triumph was at hand. Once the Gatherer consumed both living Slayers, it would rise and walk, as it had yearned to do . . . and Cameron would reign over the human survivors of the glorious new empire with his loving bride, Cecile, at his side.

Finally, a victory over the North. A true victory. His mind cast back . . .

In the haunted mists of Confederate dead . . .

. . . a creature walked. It had no mind, and it had no soul. It had no life, and it had no heart.

Human-shaped, yet knowing nothing of humanity, or mercy, or evil, it was draped in tattered pieces of white cloth, concealing it from anyone unlucky enough to cross its path. The ancient, gauzy fabric swirled around it in a strange, delayed motion like rising smoke. A single piece covered its head like a child's First Communion veil, shorter in the front and reaching to its shoulder blades—

if, indeed, it was made of flesh and bones. Its bandaged feet never touched the ground; as it crossed a puddle, the surface jittered with tension, if not precisely mass or weight.

The spirits in the graves beneath its form remained therefore, undisturbed, except for the anguish that clung to them: the South had fallen, and they had died for nothing. Terrible wounds had killed them; terrible wounds kept them earthbound. All that remained of them was desperate regret. Failure and nature together rotted their corpses, and their heads were thrown back, mouths grimaced open, in a rictus wail of disbelief.

We lost.

The Civil War has ended, and we lost.

All of them had lost. Hundreds of them, thousands; a hundred boneyards, thousands of gray bones in gray uniforms. So many boys and men; they had figured each of them was special; each of them thought, *I'm the one that won't die. It will never happen to* me."

They would be spared, because of their sweethearts, or their mothers, or the good deeds they had done; because they were the only child or the only son or the one who was going to take over the plantation or the family farm. Because they were special, death would not take them. It would take the next soldier over; the point man; the officer who waved his sword over his head.

But death took them all. It made no distinctions. As the Bible says, "The rain falls on the just and the unjust."

Eternity had no favorites.

That was the damnation of it: All they had been was fodder. White boys dying. They had marched. Across fields of fire, they marched. Cannonballs slammed into them and they marched. The Union soldiers shot at them, and they marched.

Johnny fell, and Beau, marching behind him, stepped over his body to fire off a shot; Beau fell, and Hunter took up the slack in the ranks, aiming, firing, crumpling to the blood-soaked earth.

Death is the great equalizer. All men die. There's nobody spared.

And it's nothing special to God or the Devil. Makes no never mind. And once you're dead, you lose everything you ever thought made you different. Up in heaven, the angels are all the same, floating around and singing; and Ol' Scratch's imps are, too, prancing around and doing mischief. A sea of white, a sea of red.

Just like on the Earthly battlefield.

Mine eyes have seen no glory.

Just a terrible realization: The graveyards are full of "indispensable" men.

And Cameron, dressed in a fine black suit, spread forth his hands as he stared at the futility this graveyard represented, whispered: "This will never happen to me."

The collected sighs of phantom rebels rose in a mist to taunt him. The voice of his father, a religious man, warbled in his brain: *Why seek ye the living among the dead?*

Lucy Hanover would not have so much as an unmarked grave. She would be nothing, once he was done with her.

Savoring that notion, he closed his eyes and held his arms forward. Blue light danced on his skin, then coalesced, forming a sphere that permeated the sky, and the gravestones, and the earth. The sphere hummed and glowed, growing, and the man tipped back his head.

In his outstretched hands, a bizarre box appeared.
Made of skin—very special skin, Slayer skin—bones
formed the frame. Slayer skulls, ribs, hands. A handprint stretched across the top.

It was heavy, and it was lethal, and if things went as
planned, it, or any of the other four Elements, would
use it to kill the Slayer.

A slow evil smile traveled over his face.

He pointed at the figure and said, "Of the Four, you
are Water. The floodwaters will rise and take this ac-
cursed town, and I don't give a damn if my family's
plantation is destroyed along with it. Find her and kill
her."

There are bonds of all sorts in this world and the
others; the creature spoke no English, and it had no
mind to think with. But it knew what its creator
wanted.

It glided forward and stood. Its veiled face seemed
to regard him, taking his measure, although he told
himself that that made no sense.

*But what if it can? What if it finds me lacking, just
like my own daddy did?*

For a moment, the magician faltered, frightened out
of his wits by what he had conjured from the blackest
parts of worlds yet unknown to him, and to every other
sorcerer living or dead. Cecile had inspired him to it,
and then stood back to see if he could. Some sane portion of his brain urged him to stop now, before it was
too late.

But I can't, he thought. *I'm already in too deep.
Over my head, in fact.*

*And others have died in shallower waters than these.
Slayers, too.*

He said to the Wanderer, "Find her. Kill her. Wash

her flesh from her bones and bring her carcass back to me. I am the Servant, and our Master requires it."

To his horror, the figure nodded thoughtfully, as if it understood every single word.

And the beautiful Cecile glided to his side and said, "Cameron, you are a wonderful Servant. The Gatherer is pleased."

And he preened a little for his woman and said, "That's good, honey. That's real good."

Now Cameron rode in the plane, and as they got closer to their destination, he thought, *storms, earthquakes, fires.*

Looks like everything's just fine.

He sat back, smiling.

Life's good.

Then he got a call on the plane's air phone:

"Change in plans, *mon amour,*" Cecile said. "Come to San Diego, *oui?*"

Chapter Two

After Angel left, Buffy dreamed:

The Dark Ones had lied.

The war was raging, and the Yankees were on their way. Sherman was burning everything in his path, stealing the food out of the mouths of little children and doing worse to their mothers.

The South was dying.

Dressed in his Confederate finery, the redheaded, sunburned man whipped his horse as he made his way through the ruined plantation fields of his family's plantation. The slaves had run off, some to their martyrdom as cannon fodder, put in the first ranks of the Union army to shield the white soldier boys of the North. Others had succumbed to disease, or starvation.

There were no Duvaliers alive, save Cameron. His family's beautiful house was an abomination, all the loveliness and grace burned away clear to the foundation. The fault of the lying, thieving Dark Ones. The Dark Ones had also poisoned the well, then set fire to the fields. The exquisite oaks that had lined the drive to the house were charred, but they lived.

But there was very little else left alive at Oakhaven.

Only my hatred, he thought, putting the spurs to his horse. *And I've got enough of that inside me to put the entire North to the flame. I had me a Union boy right here, I'd burn him to death with one look of my eye.*

He leaped out of the saddle—no one to take his horse's reins—and walked to the lovely but modest one-story house he had built on the grounds near the abandoned slave huts.

"Cecile!" he shouted. "Cecile!"

"Now, Buffy, pay attention," said the woman standing next to Buffy. *"Here is the secret: She wrote this book in the Arabias. And then she lured the Second Servant to Jerusalem."*

Cecile appeared, fresh and dewy in one of his mother's silk gowns, on the threshold of the airy, wood-and-brick structure. It was furnished with the lovely things they had rescued the night Cameron had burned his family to death. Though many of his neighbors had offered to help him rebuild, he had instead requested they put their time and money into outfitting one of the many fine Southern regiments they'd shipped off to war.

That had been Cecile's suggestion, designed to avert an inquiry. Her strategy had worked. By February of the new year, everyone was distracted with the creation of the Confederate States of America, and the sole surviving Duvalier was left to sift through the ashes.

"Who are you? Why are you showing me these things?"

"I am Mirielle. You don't know me. But know this: part of my soul was left outside my body after Roger

restored me. That is why I went so crazy. The good part
was left to float like a butterfly through time and space.
This is that part, helping you. Tipping the scales."

Cecile greeted him with a kiss and brought him inside,
to their parlor. They still kept a few house servants, but
the grand days were gone. He was grateful to Cecile for
sticking by him. Granted, he had given her her freedom,
but that didn't seem to mean much anymore, not with the
way things were going in the war.

"Cameron, *mon amour*," she said breathlessly. She
wore the delighted smile that was the sole joy of his
miserable life. Her dark eyes flashed, and she nearly
pirouetted as she pulled him into the house. "Something wonderful has happened."

She lifted up a thick, grimy book. Half the cover was
burned away, but the other half was made of leather
and studded with jewels. He didn't know how to read
the strange script on the cover, but it was written in
gold.

As she watched, he flipped through the pages. It was
almost like a memory book, with chunks of writings
bound together with silk cords and other things.
Though the cover had been burned, the pages were vir-
tually untouched.

"It is *Le Livre des Quatres*," she explained. Her eyes
glittered. "Can you believe it?"

"Ah. French," he said, somewhat embarrassed as he
ran his fingers along the embossed cover. "I don't
speak French."

"It's written in many ancient languages," she told
him. "It's a journal of a legacy." She closed her hand
over his. "The paper is magickal and cannot be burned.
That is how I know it is the real book. My book."

A vague chill ran down his back. She had never

encouraged him to burn down the house, had she? It had been the Dark Ones. Always them.

"Where did you find it?" he asked neutrally.

"In the forest." She smiled at him, all innocence. "I was looking for herbs and I had this sense . . ." She moved her hands in the air. "I put down my basket and I dug with my bare hands."

He studied the cover. There was no trace of dirt or mud on it, only ashes.

There was no dirt on her hands or under her nails.

"Come. I will show you." She wrapped both her hands around one of his and pulled him along. Cameron carried the weighty book against his chest, like a preacher carrying the Bible to his pulpit.

The forest had encroached upon the tumble-down walls that had once guarded the perimeter of the proud Duvalier lands. Like old men's beards, vines and parasitic mosses hung down from the brick and mortar, sprouting from the cracks.

The woods themselves were thick with pines and lush, loamy undergrowth. Cameron's boots sank in the damp soil, but Cecile's dainty slippers barely touched ground.

Cameron was startled to realize that night had fallen. He looked through the ragged sleeves of the branches to observe the moon.

The underbrush was alive with scents and sounds, subdued by the cloak of night. They descended into a gully. The trees grew even more closely together. Trailing vines dotted with white and purple blossoms hung over the branches like wash lines. Something hung from them. Cameron recoiled; they were the heads of dozens of small forest animals and birds in various stages of decomposition.

Between two trees hung a woven straw mat decorated with human handprints in a dark-colored stain.

"Come in," said a voice.

Cameron followed Cecile as she pulled the straw mat aside.

A half-naked man squatted beside a campfire, stirring a pot of a noxious substance that boiled and popped. The smell took Cameron back to the many nights he had spent in the ice house, praying over his sacrifices until the Dark Ones came to claim them. His heart lurched with sudden recognition:

This man is a Dark One.

His eyes were incredibly light against his skin, which had been weathered and tanned by a merciless sun. He said to Cameron, "Cecile Lafitte has brought you to me, and I honor her in all things." He spoke with a strange, lilting accent such as some of the slaves had, but he was a white man. With gnarled fingers, he spooned some of the drink into a beaten metal cup, and handed it to Cameron.

Cameron blinked. "I didn't realize you had a last name," he said to Cecile.

She and the Dark One began to laugh. Cameron's grip tightened around the cup. He didn't know what was so funny, but he knew they were laughing at him. Their laughter moved around him in a spiral, and he fought to keep his balance. The forest seemed to press in on him, then retract, like a huge, breathing entity. He clutched the book tightly, as if it were something that could protect him from harm; somewhere deep inside his mind, he thought, *I'll be damned. I'm crazy as a loon. I'm crazy as they come.*

Then that thought faded as Cecile came to him and put her arms around him, kissing him full on the lips.

Her eyes gazed into his own and he calmed. When she put her hands on the book and gave it a gentle tug, he let her take it from him.

She handed the book to the Dark One, who caressed the cover with a loving hand.

"She has a name that never dies," the Dark One said. "Don't you know who she is?"

"She is . . . she was our slave," he stammered, perplexed.

"More the other way around," the Dark One replied, laughing heartily. "She is the Baroness Lafitte, the Queen of the Voudoun, back in our own land. I'm her descendant, Simon Lafitte. She's going to make me the new Servant."

Cameron hunched his shoulders. "That's my place," he protested.

"Buffy," said the woman, "she is playing them all. This apparition, this Dark One, is Simon Lafitte, the voodoo shaman who killed Roger Zabuto. He is part of your dream. Tervokian, Lord Yorke—though he's out of the running, obviously—and one other—are all in line to assume the role of Servant. She has promised each one that he will be the new Servant. She will betray Cameron very soon. Remember these things."

"Am I on the Ghost Roads?" Buffy asked. "Is this a trick?"

"Hush," the woman admonished her, pressing her finger against her lips.

"Who are you? Why are you showing me these things?"

"I am Mirielle. You don't know me. But know this: part of my soul was left outside my body after Roger restored me. That is why I went so crazy. The good part was left to float like a butterfly through time and space.

This is that part, helping you. Tipping the scales."

Cecile wrapped herself around Cameron, kissing him again, and again, and again.

"No one will ever take your place, Cameron," she whispered. "No one."

The forest whirled around him; against his bare skin dark leaves and moist earth pressed like a second skin; snowy frost and the scents of smoke and pine needles filled his lungs.

"Is it not wonderful? Will you help me serve the Gatherer?" she asked him. "The Gatherer will make everything even more wonderful, *mon amour.*"

"Yes," he moaned, barely able to focus on what she was saying. He was burning with passion; words and thoughts were nothing to him as he lost himself in his desire for her. "Whatever you want."

"You have said it, Cameron Duvalier," she whispered. "I hold you to your promise, on forfeit of your soul."

When he awoke, he was lying in their bed, Cecile in one of her lacy nightgowns beside him. The sunbeams caught the sparkle of the gilt mirror on the far side of the room, making it glint like flame.

He stretched and yawned, then looked over at the lovely, dusky woman who dreamed beside him, an innocent smile on her lips, one hand curled beneath her chin, as infants sometimes sleep.

It was all a dream, he thought, vastly relieved. He was amused; he chuckled as he put his feet into his slippers.

He stood.

Froze.

The book lay on a round brass table beside the bed. The cover was not printed in a strange wavy script, but in plain English, and it said, *The Book of Fours.* The pages within were also in English. All of them. Every single one. Stunned, he sat on the floor and pulled the book onto his lap, and began to read.

Buffy looked over his shoulder:

And dreamed of Sallah ibn Rashad, who was the first Servant. And of Chretien de Troyes, a French knight, who was the second Servant:

The Diary of Chretien de Troyes, Knight
The New World, 1629

I have at last escaped, and now will finish my story.

I was prisoner and Servant of the Gatherer for almost four hundred years, and I bitterly regret the vainglory of my youth, when I joined the Crusade of my sovereign, King Louis IX of France. We knights rode with splendid retinues to Jerusalem, bent upon freeing the Holy City of rule by the infidel Muslims.

At that time, we had heard the legend of a miraculous healing substance which had been brought to the city by a man named Sallah ibn Rashad. He was said to be at least two hundred years old himself, and the leader of a strange cult of people, who called themselves the Gathered.

They worshipped the healing substance, and, some claimed, willingly sacrificed themselves to it rather than allow natural death to take them. Ibn Rashad, it was also said, had brought the substance to Jerusalem and built a splendid temple to house it. The substance itself—which was a living creature—dwelled inside a carved stone pit on a dais in the center of the enormous stone edifice.

Arrogant young warrior that I was, I demanded to be shown this man and his miracle. My command was promptly obeyed—although, I was later to learn, ibn Rashad had already divined my arrival.

For ibn Rashad was the Servant of the Gatherer, as this substance was named. He was quite proud of this fact, and sought to demonstrate his especial position by the performance of many astonishing feats of magick. He levitated not only himself, but all within the temple; he cast a light upon the cavernous walls and revealed to me many things which were to come. With a flick of his wrist, he created beings to serve me in all ways as I might care to be reverenced.

This continued for seven days and seven nights, at which point I was both exhausted and awed beyond my powers to describe. Then the Servant, ibn Rashad, informed me that his master wished me to transport both him and the Gatherer to France. When I dared to question the reason for this, he became quite angry. He plucked from a hideous crate one of four hand axes, and threatened to cut off my head if I did not agree to help him.

I believed that a plot was afoot to deal poorly with the peoples of the lands of Christ and His Father, and so I refused.

Ibn Rashad became further enraged. So angry was he that blood burst from the corners of his eyes and gushed down his face. The hand axe, he smote upon the marble floors of the temple, much as Moses had done when faced with the recalcitrance of Pharaoh.

For another seven days and nights he threatened me. He was mad with fury. It seems that my acquiescence had been foretold, and I was not behaving as predicted. The more I refused, the more frenzied became his manner. He performed terrible rites of magick, the like of which I dare not describe, lest all hope of Heaven be lost to me.

I resolved to escape. It was clear to me that I had been entrapped by a mad magician. Ibn Rashad was an evil sorcerer who derived his power from the thing inside the pit. I prayed for deliverance, and resolved to become a monk if I was set free.

That night, an angel visited me. Barely more than a child, she came in the clothing of the women of Jerusalem, a lovely blue cloak wrapped about her features. She spoke to me in the local dialect, which I could partially understand. She informed me that her name was Shagrat al-Durr, and that she was the Slayer. She had been sent by her superior, or Watcher, to dispose of the Gatherer and his minion, and in that undertaking, had learned of my imprisonment.

She gave me an exquisitely forged scimitar to use as my defense. She herself carried a very short spear of wood.

We crept through the temple for perhaps an hour or more, but did not escape detection. The Servant's guards found us. We fought hard and well, killing many of them, but we were severely outnumbered.

We were taken and thrown into cells, and there was I most direly tortured.

Then I was to witness the execution of the young girl, the Slayer, who had fought more bravely than many of the knights under the French king.

Bound and gagged, the Servant's guards carried her up the stairs of the dais, as ibn Rashad chanted in a language I did not know.

Summarily, she was thrown into the pit, and I shortly thereafter.

What happened next is a blur to me. I seemed to burst apart with astonishing force. Each tiny piece shattered and exploded, becoming smaller pieces, and smaller still, each one shooting away from the others like stars in the heavens.

I was aware, and yet not aware, of what was happening. My thoughts scattered. I raced past stars and the spinning world; I saw the tears of the Virgin Mother spilling across the black void.

Through icy nothingness I soared, and then plummeted into the inferno; I prayed out to Christ the King to save me, and then I was reformed into a new creature. But alas, I was not a creature of the God I have striven always to worship.

I was become a demon.

Ibn Rashad had been freed of the curse of servitude, and I stood now in his stead:

I became the Servant.

I do not know if I was mad, or if evil. . . .

". . . *consumed me,*" Buffy murmured. Still reading over his shoulder.

*   *   *

But the Gatherer had transcended its original being upon devouring Shagrat al-Durr, and my new Master demanded more of her kind.

More Slayers, as the Gatherer called them.

And I provided. For now, I was part of the great creation that was the Gatherer, as was Sallah ibn Rashad before me. I absorbed his knowledge and his memories. I was now a formidable magician, capable of great evil.

Through the years, my powers exceeded ibn Rashad's in all ways, as did my cunning. I learned all I could of Slayers. I devised strategies to lure them to us. By the count of my damned head, I gave at least six young Slayers to my Master. Despite their allies—which I have come to know as the Watcher's Council—they were Gathered.

I myself, was freed however, by—

"Buffy," Giles said.

She bolted upright in her sleeping bag.

So did Faith, who must have crept in during the night.

"Giles, I've been dreaming," Buffy said. "I have to tell you all of it before I forget."

At that moment, the library phone rang. Xander took it.

When he was finished, he looked at the group. The nurses, stirred by the call, were all looking at him.

"Willow's awake," he said. "She wants Buffy and Faith to go with Giles to his condo. India Cohen's diary is there. They're supposed to read it and then go to the hospital. Something about the Ghost Roads. And Slayers."

Giles pushed up his glasses. "Her diary? At my place?"

Xander shrugged. "She says Roger Zabuto sent you some stuff."

Giles frowned. "Some weapons information I'd requested."

"Oz took the phone from her. She's wiped out," Xander said.

"Let's check it out," Faith said, crawling out of her sleeping bag. Buffy nodded and did the same.

The Red Cross nurse said, "What are you people talking about?"

"Nothing," everyone chorused.

That was when the earthquakes started in earnest.

Chapter Three

San Diego was a great town, and Cameron was just as happy to land there as Sunnydale. He didn't know the reason for the change in plan, but he didn't mind. Cecile was on top of everything, just like usual.

The plane landed smooth as glass, and Cecile was there to greet him. The Servant of the Gatherer dressed to pass: no one needed to know that he was in league with a god, and himself over a hundred and fifty years old. He had stopped aging at forty, but that was scarcely important. In his black jeans, black turtleneck, and cowboy boots, he sat like a king on a makeshift throne in Cecile's rented digs. It was of human bones and skins, just like his more permanent one back home, and he sat kinda like Conan the Barbarian and frowned down at that damn lyin' Yankee demon, Tervokian.

Cecile had the dog, Mariposa, with her, and she was watching every move of the Watcher, Christopher Bothwell, with a scrying stone, as he fought traffic, weather, and governmental bureaucracy to get into Sunnydale. The roads were closed, and she was amusing herself by watching him employ magick to get past the roadblock, which was manned by members of the National Guard.

All their pigeons were converging for the Great Moment. The Gatherer itself lay in a pit that Cameron loaded onto a pallet and wheeled to Cecile's Mercedes, and it was hungry for Slayers. Cameron and Cecile had promised it not one, but two, and then the Gatherer would have so much power that it would rise from its pit and walk the earth, and make him and his lady gods.

At last. We have worked so hard.

He smiled lovingly at Cecile, who was ravishing in the black jeans and turtleneck she'd worn to Bothwell's apartment. Watching her scrying stone like a TV set, she chuckled at the frustrations of the Watcher nitwit. *He'll get through,* Cameron knew. *If he needs a boost, she'll give it to him.*

Good ol' Christopher Bothwell was pretty much the magickal equivalent of a walking time bomb at the moment. He had no recollection of the dark magicks Cecile had worked on him, but it would all come clear at just the right time.

Meanwhile, Tervokian.

Poor, nervous Tervokian.

The demon was truly a ghastly looking fellow. In all the time the Servant had dealt with the forces of evil, he had never ceased to be amazed at the variety of horrors this dimension—and others—disgorged. Tervokian's head was multihorned, and his teeth were serrated. The cracked gray-and-brown covering of his body—one couldn't sensibly call it skin—was scarred and baggy, as if the wear and tear it had gone through was beginning to break it down so badly that it had lost its resilience.

The Servant had brought Tervokian here not so

much against his will, but without a proper invitation—
in other words, he had transported Tervokian here without warning, and right off his airplane. The blue sphere
around Tervokian wobbled as he surveyed his surroundings.

The altar, where Cameron's current victim lay
spread-eagled and half-dead, had been specially carved
by demons from another dimension, as tribute to the
Servant. The girl herself was nothing special, just a little chickie he'd picked up on the way from the landing
strip.

"Why have you brought me here?" Tervokian demanded, all puffed up, head like a shrimp. He was trying hard to look like a big shot unused to being treated
like a bumbling idiot, but the Servant could see his
claws trembling.

Cameron played absently with the gold earring in
his left earlobe and tsk-tsked at the misshapen creature.

"We're just debriefing everybody involved in the
plan," Cameron soothed. "You're here because you
have a personal stake in the demise of Faith and Buffy
Summers, oh, and also since your boys lost the axe you
had charge of. I just thought you should have a front-
row seat as the others weigh in with their contributions
and possible failures."

Tervokian's attention ticked to Cecile. Cameron
noted it, wondering if the savvy demon was trying to
figure out which one of them was more likely to spare
his life.

"We all make mistakes," Cecile assured the creature.
That puffed up ol' shrimp-head again, and the demon
stuck out his gut and looped his fingers through his belt
loops in the kind of good-ol'-boy Southern sheriff posture Cameron had always detested.

"Since we haven't had any lasting ill effects from your ineptitude, tell me what you think you should receive for your efforts," Cameron urged.

Cameron assumed Tervokian was thanking his lucky stars to be alive, but the big goofball just couldn't leave well enough alone. "South Boston?" he asked softly.

The Servant leaned back on his throne and crossed his legs. "See, that's the thing that I find so hard to grasp. You're so unambitious."

Tervokian looked startled.

"South Boston," Cameron said. "That's it?"

"I know my limits," Tervokian replied. "I can't control more than South Boston. There's some vampires who've got Cambridge, and I don't want to piss 'em off. My kind's been running South Boston since Tammany Hall, and I just want to keep it in the family."

Cameron scratched his chin and rested his cheek on his hand. If he set his elbow just so, he could position it directly in the eye socket of one of his first sacrifices. *The fun never quite goes away, but there's something special about the early days that's hard to recapture.*

"Huh." Cameron shrugged and glanced over at Cecile, who beamed at him. "Like I said, that kinda thinkin' is foreign to me. But then, I come from strong plantation stock. If the Yankees hadn't interfered, we'd have been running things from Florida to Vermont by now."

Tervokian shrugged. "What can I say? I'm an urban guy. I don't need a lot of territory. Just a lot of marks living in it."

The Servant recrossed his legs. Tervokian was squirming. That was good. It was always best to keep one's inferiors off kilter.

"You lost the axe that will kill Buffy and feed her to

my Master," Cameron said, his tone becoming deadly.

"You gotta give me another chance," Tervokian blurted, holding out his arms. "Please."

The Servant blinked. "I 'gotta'? Friend, I don't 'gotta' do anything." He smiled. "I'm the Servant."

"Sorry. I didn't mean to sound rude," Tervokian said, sucking it up. He was quaking.

Good. Cuz any minute now, this old boy is gonna be dead.

"We share a common goal," the Servant observed. "You want Faith dead so that you can control the Boston area without looking over your shoulder. I want her dead to feed the Gatherer. And I want Buffy dead for the same reason. But she must die by the axe you lost or my god can't absorb her correctly."

"Let me talk to some people," Tervokian offered. "See what I can do to grease the wheels in Sunnydale, see if I can locate the axe. I have friends there. Owe me a couple favors."

The Servant wondered if this moron had any friends anywhere.

One of Cameron's strategies throughout his long existence was to hire a lot of help and give 'em each one specific task to accomplish. That way, he wasn't overly dependent on anybody. If they didn't get Faith, hey, they could try for Buffy. One was good, two were better, but if he didn't feed the Gatherer soon, he, Cameron Duvalier, was likely going to be on the hot seat. *But this opportunity may never come our way again,* Cameron thought. *Two living Slayers within our grasp. I get it all done right, then my Master rises from his pit, and Cecile and me, we get to rule this li'l ol' planet.*

Then I'll make the North pay for what they did. Glory hallelujah, I'll make 'em pay.

"All right, then, Tervokian," Cameron said graciously. "I'm going to give you one more chance."

"Thank you." The ugly thing wiped his forehead with a hankie.

Changing his tone yet again, the Servant said casually, "As long as you're here, would you care to have a go at torturing my sacrifice before I return you to your plane?"

Tervokian bowed. "You're too kind."

The Servant led the way to the makeshift altar. He and Cecile had unloaded the Gatherer out of Cameron's plane. The Gatherer's pit was a distance away, its dwelling place resembling nothing more than an abandoned fishpond, something like that. The average visitor to the Servant's lair—if such existed—would not realize that a living god existed in such simple confines.

On the altar, the sacrifice groaned as the Servant and Tervokian approached. She wasn't yet dead, but she was in terrible agony. The Servant had learned that intense pain transcended the physical realm and became an emotion, far surpassing all the others in its potential for power.

Grief was a strong emotion. So was rage. But give pain a name and it would be Mr. Best. As far as he was concerned, pain fed the machinery that turned the wheels of destiny.

Pain turbo-charged all courses of action. It was the man, as they said in these times. These wonderful times, filled with debauchery and hatred and people willing to do all manner of things to each other, not for the cause of right, but out of sheer malice and boredom.

It was a wonderful age.

"What is your pleasure, Tervokian, knives or nutpicks

or what-all? Button hooks?" He indicated three roll-around cocktail carts pushed in a corner. He walked over to the nearest one, a nice teak number from the Hammacher-Schlemmer catalog, on which were arranged a number of exotic devices he'd had made up after seeing Cronenberg's *Dead Ringers,* a disturbing film about twin brother gynecologists. "I've packed me a vast array of every little knick-knack you can think of, and then some," he said pleasantly.

Unbeknownst to Tervokian, Cameron was sizing him up, trying to figure out which torture device would lay the demon out with the least amount of hoopla. Tervokian might be kinda dumb, but he was big.

"Oh, I don't know," Tervokian said. "What do you suggest?"

Before Cameron had a chance to reply, Tervokian whirled around, grabbed him around the waist, and smashed his forehead against the side of the altar.

Blood gushed from the Servant's forehead and, by gum, he saw stars. But he drew back his hand and delivered a bright blue fireball that exploded with a crackling flash and ignited Tervokian like a cord of firewood.

Tervokian laughed as the flames rose along his covering. His clothes burned away and he stood naked. He said, "You don't know much about my kind, do you? Fire's an aphrodisiac to us."

"Cecile! A little help, *ma chere!*" Cameron shouted.

From the lower shelf of the cocktail cart, Cameron grabbed a chainsaw and pulled the cord. It roared to life, and he advanced, just like Leatherface at the big showdown.

The flames died down. Tervokian was no longer laughing. He turned and started retreating, unknowingly drawing close to the pit.

Yessssssssss, the Gatherer whispered.

Cameron waved the chainsaw at the demon, who stumbled backward, glancing over his shoulder.

"What is that, a well?" he shouted at Cameron.

Cameron didn't answer. He just kept thrusting the chainsaw at the demon.

"Better keep a move on," he suggested, "or you're gonna start losing parts of yourself that you may miss on future social occasions."

Yessssssssss.

"What's down there?" Tervokian cried, sounding really frightened now. He tried to grab at the chainsaw, maybe figured that for a dumb idea, and stumbled. "I'm not going in there!"

"Oh, I wouldn't be so sure about that." Cameron waved the saw at him.

"Nor would I, *mon amour,*" said a voice behind Cameron.

Cameron didn't really have a chance to register what was happening before Cecile waved her hands. A sphere of green energy emanated from her palms and smacked into Cameron, her beloved. The force of the impact forced the chainsaw from his grasp; and Cameron, the Servant of the Gatherer, teetered on the edge of the pit for a heartstopping five seconds before gravity got the best of him and he fell, screaming.

Tervokian and Cecile hurried to the side and stared in revolted fascination. Cameron lay screaming and sizzling on an enormous, puddinglike mass all black and bumpy. Smoke rose from his body and he writhed wildly, giving forth an odor not unlike the stench of burning tires.

"I am Cameron," the Servant said, with bulging eyes. "I am Cameron."

Tervokian winked at him. "Not for long, old son," the demon said, mocking his accent. "Looks like y'all are going to get et all up."

"You, I'll get you. Cecile, you bitch!" Cameron shouted. "How could you do this to me?"

"I'm sorry." She blew him a kiss. "You've outstayed your welcome."

"When I'm with the Gatherer, I'll kill you."

Something popped and Cameron shrieked so loudly the sound echoed off the walls. Tervokian figured it for the back of the Servant's head. If he understood the Gatherer's mode of existence, it was now absorbing all the knowledge and personality of Cameron. But Cecile had explained that the Fourth Servant would be the one to fully commune with the entity that was the Gatherer. Whoever was the Fourth Servant would have the full power of the Gatherer at his disposal, not the other way around.

Then the Servant's body deflated and began to be pulled into the blob, arms and legs trailing in like popped balloons. Within seconds, the entire carcass had been sucked into the Gatherer's mucky form.

Tervokian smiled at Cecile. He knelt at her feet and said, "I did it."

She put her arms around his neck and beamed at him. "You were *magnifique.* Now, I think it's time for you and me to go to Sunnydale ourselves."

"Really?" He beamed. "Um, about the axe . . ."

"Don't have a care," she said. "I knew you had lost control of it. I handled it." She chucked him under the chin. "We all make little mistakes. Look at me. I chose

Cameron to be the Third Servant, and he was a terrible choice. So crazy." She made a circle with her finger, pointing it toward her head.

"Huh." Tervokian shuffled his feet.

"We'll need to put the Gatherer in the trailer," she said. "There is no way I will fly my god in a plane in that weather. I need a few minutes to prepare everything." She handed him Mariposa. "Watch my dog. Don't eat her."

He looked surprised but pleased to be holding her pet. "She's a cute little thing."

The dog licked his scaly face.

Chapter Four

The sun was up, and Angel was down.

In the tunnels, collapsing by the yard because of the earthquake, and back in Willy's basement.

Willy found him on the stairs and looked stricken. "Angel, so glad you're here," he said, obviously lying.

Angel kept silent, following up the rest of the stairs. Willy stood aside while Angel moved the cable calendar. He put his face up against the peephole while Willy stood behind him, fidgeting.

The bar was packed, and a tall, dark-skinned vampire was conducting some kind of meeting. He stood beside the varnished bar with a marker in his hand. An easel held a white board with the words, OUR BELOVED MASTER, CECILE LAFITTE, CAMERON DUVALIER, TERVOKIAN, SLAYERS DIE! scrawled on it.

"So, next," the vampire said, "Tervokian's assassins were killed. But good news, brothers. It looks like the axe we took from Carlos New Mexico is the thing we need to kill Buffy Summers."

"And we need to kill Buffy to bring the Master back,

right?" asked a skinny vampire who looked like he hadn't had a decent feed in decades.

"Right," said the dark-skinned vampire. "You got it, baby."

The skinny vampire nodded. "Righteous."

Then Willy knocked over something behind Angel in the office, and everybody scattered.

"Willy, you're in trouble," Angel growled as he vamped out.

Angel thundered into the bar room. He grabbed a pool stick off the table, cracked it over his knee, and took out a female with a sharp jab to her chest. He caught the dark-skinned male with a really vicious heel to the groin. When the vamp doubled over, he grabbed it by the belt loops of its jeans, thwapped it on its back, then pulled its knees back from their fetal position against its chest, kind of like opening a hot dog bun. As soon as enough surface area was exposed, he staked the sucker.

Another vamp jumped him; Angel registered its presence while he started pummeling a vampire directly in front of him. The backrider was getting in some powerful blows to Angel's head, but the punching bag was standing up to a lot of abuse. In fact, it was almost—but not quite—giving as good as it got.

Angel headbutted it, sending the vamp on his back sailing, and the other one staggering back just in time to collide with the other vampire as it cleared Angel's head.

Another vampire crashed a chair over Angel's head. Angel grabbed the chair and broke off one of the chair's legs, whipped around, and staked the vamp with it. Then he leaped onto the bar to get a bird's-eye view of the action, discovering in the process that the vampires had conscripted a couple of other species of demon in their bid to raise the Master. Which made sense: part of the Master's previous campaign platform had been to open up the Hellmouth and let the creepy-crawlies out.

From his vantage point, Angel peered around the bar, to find Willy there, cradling his head in his arms.

"Hi," Angel said cheerily.

"You've killed me, Angel. These guys are gonna kick my butt from here to Santa Monica once they realize I let you in."

"Gimme your baseball bat," Angel said. "I know you've got one."

Willy obeyed.

Angel cracked the bat against the bar to give himself a jagged, somewhat pointed end. A barroom brawl whipped up, vamp vs. vamp, Angel doing a grand dustorama, with Willy covering his head and moaning about insurance and death.

Then the room began to shudder, rock and roll. Some of the vampires freaked out, but most of them got very excited.

"The Master! The Master!" the skinny vampire one cheered. "He's on his way!"

That was a fairly logical assumption, seeing as an earthquake had trapped the Master in the sunken church he'd made his lair, and an earthquake had freed him. He didn't know if these clowns knew it, but earthquakes had also presaged Buffy's untimely death at least once before.

"Axe, axe, who's got the axe?" he said to himself.

Then he got back to looking for it.

* * *

The Red Cross nurses obviously detected that the gang was using their great secret Scooby code, even if they couldn't directly translate it. They were polite about it; actually, they didn't seem all that interested in it, and they filed out quietly after they dug their little bars of soap and washcloths out of their backpacks.

"Bye," Cordelia said, waving to them. "See you later."

"We'll have breakfast set up in the gym," Monica told them. "Please come join us."

"Hello, partially hydrogenated vegetable oil and heaps o' sugar." When Giles looked at him in puzzlement, Xander said, "That's code for 'donuts.'"

"Oh, I see." Giles paused. "Do you suppose they'll have jellies?"

"I've got my fingers crossed for fat-free muffins," Cordelia chimed in.

"I was just thinking to myself the other day that I haven't had a decent maple bar in the last, oh, say four or five potentially fatal crises I've participated in. Which reminds me," Xander continued, looking to Giles. "Are we going to be able to list Scooby Gang as one of the extracurriculars in the yearbook? Or get little pins or something?"

"Pins would be nice," Cordelia said.

Giles just rode them out, like a wave beneath his surfboard of adulthood, and finally said, "Everyone, eat as much breakfast pastry as you can possibly stand, and then Buffy and Faith will accompany me to the condo."

"Sure." Faith rubbed her hands together and joined Buffy as she headed for the library's double doors.

"Oh, and Buffy?" Giles said, raising a finger. "Do see if they have any jellies, will you?"

"Second choice sprinkles?" Buffy asked. At his nod, she smiled and left the library.

The school corridors were clogged with people—hurt people, scared people, and people who were there to help those people. Buffy was not loving having to see the vast numbers of small children who were in tears; it made her more determined to do something about what was happening, and now she was sorry she'd been such a pain about going to Giles's to check on the diary.

"B.," Faith set, as they walked into the crowded gym. "I had a wicked-weird dream."

"Me, too. Voodoo stuff?"

Faith nodded. "There was this chick, and she was explaining to me about how much the Gatherer loves to devour Slayers. Gives it, like a turbo charge. My words." Faith smiled crookedly. "I can't exactly remember how she put it."

"Maybe 'scrumpdiddlyumptious?' " Buffy suggested.

"Had to be." Faith chuckled. "We're like a sugar rush, or something."

"Huh. If it tries to eat me, I'll give it some major cavities. Say, Xander," Buffy called. "I had a funny saying for you. 'The Hellmouth's bad breath.' Get it?"

Xander frowned, exhaled against his palm, and checked it. "I do not."

"Oh . . . forget it," Buffy drawled. She looked at Faith. "It's pretty clever, don't you think?"

"Oh, yeah," Faith said. "I'm in stitches." She touched her cheek. "How's it looking?"

"Truth?" Buffy asked. Faith nodded. "Like stitches might have been a good idea."

Canetown Plantation, Jamaica, 1998

Kendra moved from her Watcher's plantation house into the thick overgrowth. The midnight sky ringed the moon with clouds; the air sweated, releasing the fragrance of night-blooming jasmine and frangipani from its pores. Kendra had rubbed her skin with a protective unguent Mr. Zabuto had concocted from an ancient native spell stick; around her neck she wore a mojo bag, to keep the night's evil away from her.

"Viens, vite," he had said to her in French, as he did upon occasion. Even after being raised by him since childhood, she didn't know what his native language was, English, French, or Swahili. But she understood, and nodded once.

He made the sign of the cross above her—he was a religious man—and she walked out of the house and into the jungle. Birds *coo-cooruu-coo'*ed; the lush growth rustled and shivered with movement. Kendra was alert and unafraid. Determination surged through her. Muscle and sinew, she was the Slayer. Her long-awaited destiny had been fulfilled: she had been chosen.

Because of the death of another, Kendra thought, and that was the very last thought she allowed herself on that subject. Slayers who thought about dying, did so.

Parting the growth before her, she moved soundlessly. For a time the jungle was still, craning its ears to detect her movements. Then its heartbeat began to pulse through the ground. Shimmering ferns jittered. A drop of moisture, clinging to a vine, formed an elongated arc and dripped onto Kendra's forearm.

The heartbeat grew louder.

Drums.

Kendra set her jaw. She made circles with her shoulders and flexed her wrists. It was time to stay loose and ready for action. Precision timing and quick reflexes were part of her weapons cache.

As was the blow gun she pulled from the bodice of her sleeveless leather top. Moving swiftly, vigilant and attuned to the language of the drums, she inserted a poison dart into the hand-carved pipe. The needle-sharp tip was dipped in *curare,* the same paralyzing compound Baron Diable injected into his victims. They would lie unable to move in their coffins, anticipating the horrifying moment they would be buried alive. Resurrected, they would be dead—in spirit, mind and body—alive only in the ability to move, and to obey.

Kendra would rather go to hell than live such an existence. Mr. Zabuto had explained to her that suicide was not an option for a Slayer; there was no honor in it and it would upset the balance of things to come. But Kendra was sorely tempted to disobey, rather than fall into the clutches of Monsieur Lafitte.

If all goes well, I won't have to worry about that, Kendra reminded herself. *And it will only go well if I pay attention to what I'm doing.*

In the moist, tropical night, crickets and frogs scraped and sang. Birds furled their crests. Somewhere nearby, water splashed. Kendra paid attention to it all, but allowed nothing to disturb her concentration.

The Chosen One guided herself toward the encampment of the Devil Baron by the light of the gauzy moon, veiled and mysterious, what Mr. Zabuto called "an occult moon." Monkeys cackled in the distance.

The pace of the drums increased; the timbre deepened, like gods tossing waves against the shore. They thrummed through the tree trunks and the feet and teeth of the Slayer.

The forest transformed.

Palms drooped, burdened by the sounds. The forest thrashed and protested, and changed, no longer a friend to the Slayer, but an adversary that sought to block her path. Vines trailed across her feet; branches scratched her chest.

Birds swooped on her as if to take a nip.

She stayed calm. She was used to the hostile vibrations that emanated from black magicks. As a new Slayer, she had a lot to remember, a lot to learn, and a lot to prove. Around the earthly world, powerful followers of the dark forces were waiting for the results of her first few battles as the reigning Slayer. If she failed tonight, yet survived, they would be on her like locusts.

If she died, they would rejoice and thank their evil deities.

Now the wind picked up as she crept within the vicinity of the camp. Flashes of firelight and vivid color swept past her field of vision, obscured by the intermittent waving of ferns.

Kendra crouched, and peered through the foliage.

Wearing traditional African-inspired dress, the baron's people were dancing around a bonfire. Their shoulders jerked and shook; their hips swiveled lasciviously. All of them were barefoot and the women had wrapped turbans in parrot hues around their heads.

Bare-chested men leaped through tongues of flame—not over the tall height of the inner flames, which roared over ten feet if not more—and whooped as they put out the smoldering portions of their khaki-colored trousers.

Kendra edged closer.

Behind the bonfire stood a hut with a darkened doorway. Mr. Zabuto had explained that Mirielle would probably be inside the hut, restrained, if not drugged. If Kendra could execute a surprise attack and get her out of there, so much the better. But she had a few other chances to save the woman before it was too late.

The drumming increased in rhythm and vibration, until Kendra sensed the pulsations through her body, through her veins themselves. That was a form of sympathetic magick, Mr. Zabuto had explained. If she ignored it, it would eventually go away.

The rhythm sped faster, faster. Her heart raced and perspiration poured down her face. To her right, a boa constrictor stretched its coils around the trunk of a mango tree, as if reminding Kendra that the night held many dangers, both natural and unnatural.

The throng rippled, and a cheer rose up.

Something swayed in the doorway of the hut. The dark silhouette of a woman in a full, lacy gown with full, curly hair tumbling down to her shoulders appeared.

Mirielle, Kendra thought. *My target.*

Suddenly, the drums picked up. Everyone shouted once, loudly, and a looming shape rose up behind the woman. It wore a huge, glowing mask. It was painted purple, green, and white, the distortion of a man's features primitive and sophisticated. Its eyes were misshapen and its mouth, a maw. Knives planted inside the mouth caught the firelight and threw rainbow glints on the bark and leaves of the surrounding trees.

Then the masked figure raised its hands to the sky and chanted in a language Kendra didn't know. Lightning flashed and thunder roared; the dancers lifted their hands as well.

Rain poured down, the droplets sizzling in the flames. Steam rose, but the fire kept burning. Dancers began throwing things into it, things which struggled and squealed, and screamed.

The dark-haired woman was Mirielle. She looked drugged.

Or dead already.

The faces of the people were horrifying as Mirielle was led forward. The masked figure bent toward her and chanted, and she collapsed in his arms.

He ululated in the back of his throat.

Then he turned and looked straight at Kendra, laughing with utter contempt.

Then something went wrong, said the ghost of Kendra to Buffy, who was dreaming again. *The Baron was inside me for a moment; inside my soul, inside my spirit. He polluted me. I didn't know it at the time. Time stopped for me while he made a nest inside my being, like a rat.*

If Drusilla had not killed me, eventually his evil would have grown inside my soul, and I would have gone to him. I would have served him.

The vampire woman freed me, only I didn't know it at the time.

But Baron Diable knew.

He was furious that his plans had been thwarted. He could do nothing against the vampire woman, as she was protected by her lover, Spike. But he can still do things to you, Buffy.

Beware of him. Of them all. They will try to trick you, Buffy. They'll set you against each other. They'll put a snake in the garden.

Then Kendra stepped away from Buffy, with a very sad expression on her face.

Willow stood quietly in her hospital gown. She said, "Buffy, I'm so sorry. I'm not going to make it after all."

Buffy gaped at her. *"Willow?"*

Chapter Five

Buffy had dozed off, so Faith took India Cohen's diary off the blonde's lap and read it for a while.

I really like this India chick, she thought. *She had a pair on her.*

Faith settled in.

August 20, 1993

> *I stopped writing things down because I finally realized that it could endanger my parents. My mother has been home for a couple of days, but it looks like she's going back to Manila to star in a movie.*
>
> *I have pieced some things together: I don't think I'm my father's daughter—I mean, that he's not my birth father or however you say it. I think it was someone else, in the Philippines. Someone the Marcoses knew about. I think Mom married my dad because my real father couldn't or wouldn't marry her. That seems*

incredibly old-fashioned, but I think that's what happened. I don't know for sure.

I think Kit does know. For a while I wondered if he was my father, but he's too young.

It would be cool if he was, because I feel like I have no one in the world but him. I feel incredibly alone. I used to think all teenagers felt this way, especially Navy brats, but being the Slayer makes it worse.

Kit talks to me about all kinds of things. I can tell he's lonely, too. He can't ever let anyone know who he really is. He spends all day talking with a fake accent, which he drops around me. I'm the only person he can be himself around.

I know he's an only child, and his mother (his "mum"!) died when he was around my age. Another thing we have in common—absent mothers. His favorite color is blue. Mine, too. And he's an Aquarius, same as me. Isn't that kewl?

He's not that much older than I am. Not when you take into account that I have had to mature very fast.

We have been training, and I have sort of a rep around the base now. I work out with the sailors and everyone gets a kick out of "the captain's tomboy," as they call me. I usually run with them in the mornings and sometimes I do their workouts on the perimeter of the field near the Naval hospital. I have a nickname, which is "Tuffie," and my dad is very amused by the whole thing. My mother doesn't like it at all.

Meanwhile, I'm writing because I'm too excited just to keep this in—we kicked a lot of butt today!

Kit and I went to Oshima Island—it's this island you can ferry out to, where American P.O.W.s were kept in World War II. Inside the mountain, the Japanese dug tunnels, and inside the tunnels, they made cells. They're covered over with mushrooms and moss now, and very gross.

But a vampire clan had moved in, and Kit wanted to exterminate them before they decided to take the ferry over to the main island (we live on Honshu, which is the most populated island in Japan).

So we went over this morning, and snuck into the tunnels (they're condemned) hoping that they were all sacked out. Vampires don't have to sleep during the daytime, but that's when they usually do sleep, because they can't go out in daylight or they burst into flames.

But remember, the tunnels are inside the mountain, so they are protected from the sun, and it was a pretty scary situation. We were tiptoeing down a slimey path, and Kit was explaining to me that these vampires are particularly brutal and dangerous. I said, "As opposed to the nice ones?" and we both chuckled. That was cool; I like it when I make him laugh.

I was incredibly nervous because he said it was time for me to start slaying on my own. He said he'd be there as backup, but he's supposed to be a Watcher, not a Slayer. I said, "Wanna trade jobs?"

Anyway, we tried to make as little noise as possible, with our backs together. He was staring into the tunnel, and I was staring the way we had come, so we looked like Siamese twins as we crept along. I was beginning to wonder if we were ever going to turn on our flashlights. The farther in we went, the darker it got. Vampires can see in the dark. Major disadvantage.

Before we went in, I suggested seeding the entrances to the tunnels with holy water and wafers. Kit was very proud of me for thinking of that, but he said the tunnels had too many hidden passages and we would never be able to find all the entrances and exits. If we put out traps, they would know we were onto them, and they might retaliate by putting the hurt on the islanders big time. (A few people still live on Oshima Island. That's how we got wind of the vamps in the first place—locals talking about bites, deaths, etc.)

Anyway, something made a noise and I jumped like twenty feet in the air. It turned out to be a rat. Just as I was registering that this was a false alarm, a whole bunch of vamps jumped out of the shadows and surrounded us. There must have been at least ten of them.

I was terrified, but I tried to keep my cool. We both had crosses out and were holding the vamps at bay. I flicked on my flashlight. Kit's came on seconds later.

They weren't pretty. Their features were vaguely Asiatic, and they had long Chinese-style mustaches. They were wearing robes so tattered and old they were falling apart.

And talk about stinking. Yuck.

I said to Kit, "There're too many."

He said, "That doesn't matter."

They rushed us. I figured we were going to die and I muttered "Good luck" to the next Slayer.

But as soon as they started attacking, I just kind of went into a trance. I was kicking and punching and whacking on them and they were grunting and fighting back, but they were getting nowhere. Everything was a blur of blackness and light, because somehow both Kit and I had hold of our flashlights and neither of us let go.

Then Kit started going nuts with the karate, and in less than a minute, he had staked his first kill. I could tell the vampires weren't prepared for the dusting, which made me think they'd been isolated for a long time. Or that maybe Japan has been Slayerless.

I had my stake out, too, and I lunged at the vamp across from me—it was extremely tall, maybe even seven feet—but I missed him. He laughed and hissed at me, and said something in a foreign language.

Kit said, "They're Korean. They have a queen," and I didn't say anything. I didn't even spare the time to be impressed that he could understand Korean and fight at the same time. I wasn't sure I was actually fighting. I didn't have a strategy. I was working with what was in front of me, going blow by blow. I had no clue how I had survived so far, and no idea how to keep my lucky streak going.

When you see a fight in the movies or on TV, you have to remember that's it's all been planned out in advance by the stunt team. We were not stunt people. We were real people. The fight was really happening, and the vampires were really trying to kill us.

Sometimes I had to remind myself to pay

attention, because it was unreal after a while. I was hitting and punching and I couldn't keep track of what was who. I heard another dusting, but I couldn't remember how many vampires had surrounded us. I could barely even remember my own name. That sounds hokey, but it was true. If you've never been that afraid, I envy you.

(Who am I writing to? Just myself. And I was there!)

We were still totally surrounded. Kit had dusted two vamps and all I could do was not get killed. That pissed me off and it was like suddenly, someone was guiding me, because I was making good moves that were bringing about some decent results—i.e., damaging vamps.

I grabbed the one in front of me by the wrists, then yanked hard and grabbed its forearms. I gave it a headbutt supreme and while it was reeling, I whipped my stake out of my jeans and slammed it directly into its heart.

That sucker screamed and poofed into dust right before my eyes. I couldn't help my whoop of triumph.

Kit cried, "Huzzah!" just like a real honest-to-goodness regular guy at a Renaissance fair.

I didn't have time to enjoy the moment, though, because another vampire took the place of the one I'd killed. I lunged forward, landing on one knee, and rammed my stake into it with an uppercut. It exploded, too.

Pow! Pow! Pow! I was like some super chick in a comic book. I was loving how powerful I was.

I am the Slayer!

We just kept going, and going, and I was getting

awfully tired. I had no idea how Kit was holding up, but he was still on his feet.

Then suddenly the vamps backed away, looking past our heads. They bobbed their heads and lowered their eyes, humble in their rotten silk robes and long, drooping mustaches. There were five left.

Kit said, "Oh, great."

I asked, "What?" But I didn't look away from the five vamps. One of the first things you learn in Vampire Slayer Academy is that you never look away from your adversary. Ever.

"Her Majesty has arrived," he replied.

It took me a minute to figure out what he was talking about. Oh, yeah. They had a queen.

I still didn't turn. I said, "What do you want me to do?"

"I'm not sure."

His voice was shaky. I wanted like anything to look, but then we might have five vampires on our tails at the same time that we had something worthy of "Oh, great" attacking us from the front.

Here is the weird part—like none of this has been weird—but right then, I realized I was hungrier than I had ever been in my entire life. I was so hungry that I would have eaten just about anything someone put in front of me, including peas, which I absolutely detest so much that even writing down the word makes me gag.

It was pretty much a passing thought because hey, survival, but I told myself that if I got us out of this, I would go to the commissary and buy myself an entire half-gallon of mint chocolate chip ice cream.

I said to Kit, "Count of three, you turn around and take on the five vamps behind us. I'll fight the queen. Don't argue."

I counted. When he turned around, I did a backflip over him—no lie!—and landed about one foot away from this incredibly startling thing, in like, this robe, with incredibly long, talonlike fingernails. When she smiled, her fangs glistened.

She said something in Korean—I figured—and while she was going on and on, I just kind of lost my patience. I can't explain it any other way. I rammed into her and knocked her over.

We went for it, a kind of bitchfight with extra cheese, and she was bashing the heck out of me and I was starting to feel very outclassed.

But then I thought, Hey, I've killed at least two vampires tonight! I just kept pummeling and trying every way I could think of to beat her back far enough to get a stake into her.

Then all of a sudden, she yelled something in Korean or whatever and all the vampires ran away! She whirled her cape around and went into a cavern.

I shouted after her, "Wimp!"

But Kit grabbed my wrist and said, "For God's sake, India, come on."

We ran like fools. We ran so fast I thought we were gonna start flying. I dropped my flashlight and Kit yelled, "No!" I left it there and we kept going.

We got outside, where the daylight was dying, and he said, "She told them to forget about fighting us in there and find a way to cut us off from the main island. She said that now that they've been discovered, they should go for it.

"She didn't know you were the Slayer. She's never heard of the Slayer. They were here long before World War II, hiding out."

He went on for a while about their history, but I wasn't too interested in hearing about it. I was so tired my bones were trembling. I could barely keep my eyes open. And he's going on about some Manchurian dynasty or I don't know what, with vases and stuff. He was all fired up and I wanted to ask him politely to shut up, but I was too tired even for that.

We got on the ferry and kept a watch, but no vamps showed their faces. Maybe they were holding on to the outside of the hull. We didn't see them when we landed, and we hung out for a while.

He drove me back to the base, and we parked about thirty feet from my new house. We live on a sloping hill with other homes for captains and admirals and their families. We have a Japanese house maid, a gardener, and a sewing lady who comes once a week. She used to make the most amazing dresses for Mom, but I'll bet she's wondering if she's still got a job.

Kit said, "You did it. You dusted vampires tonight." He looked very proud of me, but I could tell he was frustrated that we didn't finish off the clan.

I apologized, and then I got pretty emotional. He asked me what was wrong and I said, "It's never going to be over, is it? I'm going to do this until I die."

He went into all this stuff about my great destiny

and how I'm making a difference in the fate of humanity, blah blah blah, and I said that all I want from now on is to do sports and be left alone.

I told him, "When my mom goes back to the Philippines, I'm going with her."

He said I couldn't, that I had to stay and fight. The thing that hurt was that I realized he wouldn't miss me. He never said anything about not wanting me to go, only that I couldn't go because of my duty.

I told him to go to hell and I ran home.

I was crying for like an hour before my father came in my room. I told him I wanted to go with Mom and he acted really uncomfortable until I finally got it: Mom doesn't want me to go with her.

He didn't say it, but when I guessed it, his face admitted the truth. I fell apart. She doesn't want me and Kit doesn't care anything about me except that I'm learning how to kill vampires.

My dad said he had come to tell me he had to go down to the ship and he would probably have to stay there overnight. So I was going to be home all alone.

He asked me some questions, like, had someone hurt my feelings? But he wasn't very good at it. I told him I didn't feel good but I had taken some ibuprofen. That seemed to be enough for him to feel okay about leaving me.

It was too much for one night. I had finally killed some vampires but so what? There's more of them and there will always be more of them. My mom is leaving us, basically, and I can't go with her.

*Kit doesn't care about me, either. He probably
has a girl friend back in England.*

I hate being the Slayer.

"Well, damn," Faith said, "I can't take it anymore.
What a whiner."

She shut the book and put it down.

The floor trembled. She said casually, "Giles, another earthquake."

"Right." He sounded as unimpressed as she was.

Then Buffy woke up and said, "Hold onto something! Quick!"

The entire condo started rocking, tilting up and
down. The walls buckled, the floor cracked apart and
jutted up in large sections, like pieces of ice. The ceiling lobbed huge chunks of itself to the floor. Glassware
shattered. The tiles on Giles's stairway popped off, and
the bannister collapsed.

"It's the big one," Faith cried.

The floor was rippling and shaking; everything was
ripping apart and being flung around the room. Giles's
desk overturned, then slammed against the opposite
wall.

It was insane, it was crazy, it was Nature at her most
pissed off.

"Willow!" Buffy shouted. "Willow, tell Kendra to
run!"

"What?" Faith said.

Then up from a fissure in the floor, a swathed head
jutted upward. A torso followed, then arms. It was
holding a box. It rose into the air as the apartment shattered and split apart around it.

As the condo blew to pieces with the force of an explosion, a second covered head appeared.

Then the second story ceiling collapsed, trapping Buffy, Faith, and Giles in mounds of rubble.

Faith grunted and started swearing.

Buffy struggled, horrified, as both creatures pulled out axes and started gliding straight for Giles, who was pinned.

And who stared helplessly back at them.

The Book of Fours

Prologue

Kit just brought over my weapons trunk, and here's my diary. I'd forgotten all about it. I was keeping it so well hidden that I hid it from myself.

We've just moved to Spain. I think I'm going to love it here. My mother has made her move back to Manila fairly permanent. We all pretend she's so busy with her career that it makes more sense for her to be there rather than here. But it hurts. I'm alone a lot. Since I'm older, my dad's not as worried about me. Sometimes I wonder if he knows about Kit being my Watcher.

True to his word, Kit has managed to follow me from Japan to Italy to here. I don't know how he does it. He says the amount we move is "remarkable," and he has actually wondered if my dad's ship is performing covert operations.

As for Kit, my love for him has grown since we began working together. Sometimes I think my heart will burst from loving him so much. He's so handsome, and kind, and brave. There's a light in his eyes that takes my breath away. I'm certain that he knows, and that he loves me, too. We don't talk about it, but I'm positive of it.

Hold on . . .

A little while ago, Kit came to pick me up to go to a flamenco club. My dad had to go down to the ship, so I was home alone, and no questions asked.

The club is outside Rota, which is where the U.S. Naval Hospital is located. I love all the whitewashed buildings around here. They have tile roofs and the weather is mild. I could smell the sea—my whole life, I've smelled the sea—and there are orange groves and tomato fields everywhere.

We got to Cantina de los Gitanos, a popular hangout with white walls and wood-beamed ceilings, and the tables were jammed. It was smoky and everyone was drinking. The flamenco dancers were just getting started—it was eleven!—and Kit and I jammed up against the crowd.

At exactly the same time, we both had a feeling, and we both turned our heads to the left. About three people over, we saw a vampire couple. He was tall, with white-blond hair, wearing a black coat and black T-shirt and leather pants. She was all dolled up in a flamenco gown with a comb and black-lace mantilla. She was waving her fingers and stamping her feet, and there was something incredibly . . . demented about her.

The blond vampire guy turned and looked straight at me. He looked startled. Then he winked at me and hustled her out of there.

She was whining and smacking him. Then he

whispered something to her and she stared at me. She grinned and twirled in a circle, making the most bizarre growling noises.

Kit and I followed after them as best we could, but our way was deliberately barred by a bunch of Spaniards. Cigarettes, dark, flashing eyes, the Spanish guitar music—it was like some kind of movie (again with the James Bond!)

We turned around and made it through the cantina, just in time to see the blond vampire trying to get the female into a low-slung black car. When she saw me she started jiggling all over. Then she fell to the ground and pointed at me, shrieking and laughing.

She said, "The Gatherer wants you, poor lit'l thing! It will eat you all up!"

The pale blond man said, "Shut up, Dru! Cecile will have our heads!"

I don't know what she's talking about, but it was freaky.

So Kit said he'd research it. Then he suggested we go home, which was a drag.

Except that when we got home, he walked me to the door and kissed my cheek.

This was the first actual kiss between us. I think he's realizing I'm practically all grown up. We're in so much danger all the time that I want to seize the moment. I want to make love with Kit when I turn eighteen. I want to marry him. Will that get us in trouble with the Watchers Council?

Chapter One

"Giles!" Buffy shouted, as she wrapped her hands around the enormous chunk of ceiling on top of her and began to heft it off herself. The rain was falling so heavily that she had to contend with the pressure from it as well.

"Yes?" he bellowed, grunting as he pushed at the rubble that had trapped him and held him to the floor.

"Just, um . . ." She succeeded in freeing herself and scrambled toward him. "Y'know, don't die," she added lamely.

The creatures continued to move in the same direction, but they appeared to be completely disinterested in Giles. Also, in Buffy. And Faith.

"Check it out," Faith shouted, as the three watched in silence.

They glided slightly above Giles' head, and kept going.

"Yo?" Faith called to them. "Guys?"

Buffy glared at her. "You don't need to encourage them, Faith," she hissed.

Faith chuckled. "What, you afraid they're going to think I'm forward or something?"

She got to serious work pushing pieces of wood and stucco off herself, then got to her feet and assisted Buffy with Giles. Working against the wind and the rain, they uncovered the Watcher's arms and legs and pulled him to his feet. Then the three searched for India's diary, which was nowhere to be found. It had been buried and/or destroyed.

Meanwhile, the two mummies drifted on, unfazed by the storm.

"They're totally ignoring us," Buffy said, intrigued.

"Yeah. I'm so insulted." Faith clapped her on the shoulder. "This is a good thing, blondie." She said to Giles, "Does your car, you know, work?"

Giles, as always, looked mildly offended by the question. "Yes."

He led the way through the ruined courtyard to the parking lot where he kept his car. Palm trees had toppled; electric wires were snapped and sparking. Someone was shrieking in the wind, or else it *was* the wind.

They got in the Gilesmobile and freighted it to the hospital. When Buffy got out, the wind was blowing so hard it felt like it might rip the skin right off her face. Around her, people were batted by the fierce gusts like Ping-Pong balls tossed at a jet engine. Those who could move under their own steam were staggering toward the entrance to the medical center, while a woman who had lost her walker slid to the ground next to a gray Toyota Camry and buried her head against her knees.

"We've got to help these people," Buffy said, as she held onto one of the poles supporting the awning over the front of the entrance. Or rather, where the awning used to be. It had been ripped away.

"We're not going to be much use," Faith pointed out. As if to demonstrate, she lurched to the pole opposite, then unwrapped one hand from the column and held it out to her side. The wind caught at it and spun her around the pole like a tetherball.

"This could be fun if it might not also kill us," Faith shouted, as she flung herself back against the pole and gripped hard with both hands. She dropped down to her knees, then scooted out backwards as she slid down her hands to the base of the pole. Carefully she pressed first her right palm and then her left against the concrete walkway. She made herself as flat as she could, and then she inched her way toward an old man who had slammed back-first against a stand of bushes. His back was bowing and his right shoe had been blown off his foot.

Buffy copied Faith's motions and the two worked their way toward the man. Then with a squeal like a wounded humpback whale, the Camry at the curb upended. It teetered for an instant, then crashed right on top of the old woman crouched beside it.

The three were shocked into motionlessness for a few seconds. Wide-eyed, Buffy stared at Faith, who had not stopped moving. Buffy said, "Get inside with Giles. I'll see what I can do."

Faith nodded. Slowly, arduously, Buffy slithered in extreme slo-mo toward the curb. Beyond, in the parking structure, cars began to rock and shift. Metal scraped metal.

There was an enormous *zzzizzing* sound behind her, then a strange, overpowering pop. Buffy hazarded a glance over her shoulder.

From the looks of things, the power in the Medical Center had just gone out. The large glass windows in

front revealed a very dim lobby, and people milling
haphazardly around, some clumping away from the
windows, while others started pushing on the doors.
Faith and Giles were gesturing for them to get away
from the sheets of glass, which could be shattered
at any moment by any number and type of wind-
powered projectiles. No one paid them the slightest
bit of attention.

Buffy kept crawling to the Camry.

The woman's arm extended from beneath the car.
Buffy checked for a pulse. There was none.

The poor lady was dead.

"Well, gosh, can things get worse?" Buffy shouted
over her shoulder. As if in answer to her question,
smoke and flames billowed from the roof of the building. The glass entrance doors burst open and screaming
people poured out. Someone shrieked, "The hospital's
on fire!"

The panic was immediate and riot level. Buffy
shouted, "Stop!" as men and women ran blindly forward, slamming into the columns and trampling a
young Asian man who had the bad luck to fall.

More arriving ambulances joined the din, swarming
onto the streets surrounding the hospital, at least six
screeching up to the curb while others poured around
the side to the emergency room entrance.

Faith grabbed Giles and pushed her way through the
stampede, slamming her fist into the face of one man
who was pushing her from behind, side-kicking another,
and barreled like a front end for the Raiders the rest of
the way to the entrance. Buffy joined them; they were
all definitely fighting upstream as they got closer and
closer to the surgical waiting room.

"Yo! Touchdown!" Faith cried, as they stumbled through the crowds and landed inside.

"Come on," Buffy said, leading the way, since she knew the hospital layout better than Faith.

They ignored the elevators and took the stairs. Giles kept up, despite the fact that he was bruised and limped slightly. As they rounded a stairwell containing a couple of vending machines, one of them burst apart. Fruitopia and Mountain Dew geysered into the air.

They kept going, coughing through thickening smoke, and popped out of the stairwell onto the intensive care unit floor. Things were not as chaotic here; the medical personnel wore masks to filter out the smoke and moved quickly, efficiently, but there was no panic.

The walls were lined with patients waiting to be evacuated. Buffy, Faith and Giles took a moment, then Buffy nudged Giles as Cordelia, who had gone ahead with Xander, waved at them from a doorway.

Buffy was about to protest that she had to check on Willow, when Cordelia said, "Willow's fine, meet this guy," and herded her forward into the crowded room.

"Hello," said a young, dark-haired man, standing beside a couch. He was wearing dark brown cords and an Irish fisherman's sweater.

Buffy instantly knew who he was.

"Christopher Bothwell," she said.

He held out her hand. She took it. Buffy regarded him steadily, but she felt very dizzy. This was the Watcher of the girl whose death had activated her.

"We haven't much time," he said gently, though in a loud, steady voice. "There is a creature called the Gatherer, and—"

"We know some of it." Buffy looked at Giles. "We know a little bit of some of it."

Faith said, "If you guys don't need me, I want to go to the fire department to get the axe. Nice to meet you," she said to Christopher Bothwell. "I'm Faith. Bye." She turned her head to see Xander appear with an armload of vending machine food. "I'm taking him."

"Right," Giles said. "Xander, are you up for it?"

"Sure."

"Good luck," Buffy said, giving him a hug.

He nodded, kissed her cheek, winked at her. "You, too, *chica*."

Faith and Xander headed out, and Buffy shifted her attention to Christopher Bothwell.

"You may have realized that all of this . . . " He paused and gestured around himself ". . . revolves around the four elements, Earth, Air, Fire, Water. What you may not realize is that one of these qualities dominates the being of a Slayer. You, Buffy, are a Slayer of the Air."

"No airhead jokes," she admonished. She looked over her shoulder. "I want to check on Willow."

"In a moment," Bothwell said authoritatively. "We need to go over this."

Buffy looked at Giles and pursed her lips. Giles shrugged and said to Bothwell, "She isn't keen on taking orders. I told you she was unusual."

"Hey." Buffy looked affronted.

"Let me continue. *Please.*"

Buffy nodded impatiently, trying to give her attention. But her heart was really in Willow's room, and she was getting more and more impatient to check on her.

"The Gatherer has two assistants in this dimension, the Servant and a woman named Cecile." He flushed, and Buffy had no idea why. "Cecile is a remarkable woman, accomplished in the Black Arts, very cunning. Also beautiful. She's been alive for centuries. She's the real mastermind behind the plot to liberate the Gatherer."

"Liberate it from . . . " Buffy said.

"It lives in a pit. It's a sort of created being, absorbing the essences of the people and animals it consumes. It found a way to merge, or join, with a single strong personality—the Servant—and that person became its eyes and ears, its very body."

"Following," Buffy told him.

"Good. Once the Gatherer was given a Slayer to absorb, it realized that the primal force each Slayer carries within her gave it new life, new consciousness, and new integrity. It has absorbed many Slayers. The First Servant, ibn Rashad, gave it its very first Slayer, Shagrat al-Durr. During the ensuing chaos as it experienced her power, ibn Rashad was released from his tenure as Servant, and a Second Servant was called.

"That was a French knight named Chretien de Troyes. This was in Jerusalem. He was eventually lured to the Southern colony of South Carolina, where he was dispatched by the current Servant, Cameron Duvalier."

His face puckered as if he had eaten something sour. "But Duvalier is quite mad, and was an unsuitable choice for Servitude. Cecile, who in her homeland of Jamaica, had been a voodoo queen, had managed to follow the Gatherer here, and willingly allowed herself to be treated as a slave so that she could be near it. She remained with Duvalier for over a century, but his insanity eventually proved his undoing."

"Who is the Fourth Servant?" Buffy asked.

Bothwell shrugged. "I'm assuming we shall soon find

out. Cecile and the Gatherer are on their way here, even as we speak."

"How do you know all this?" Buffy asked.

"Runes," he said simply. "I've made a life study of this. Because . . . because my Slayer was absorbed by the Gatherer. But something went wrong. She's been able to somehow break free of the Gatherer and act independently."

"That's not wrong, that's good." Buffy started walking toward Willow's room.

Bothwell caught up with her. "The Wanderers have each been given an axe that will destroy a Slayer so that her essence can be absorbed by the Gatherer. That's why they pursue you so vigorously with the axes. One supposes," he added. "As the Slayer of Air, you must be killed with the Axe of the Air, by the Wanderer of the Air."

"This is too much like math," she said.

She walked into the room, to find Oz sitting with Willow. Both had on white masks, but they looked relatively unaffected by the smoke.

"Will," Buffy said warmly. "Oh, Will."

They embraced. Buffy gave herself the luxury of this moment, of reconnecting with her very best friend in all the world.

Then she smiled at Oz, who said, "Check it out. Willow made a warding spell, keeps the smoke from bothering us."

Willow said, "Pretty neat, huh?"

"Very neat," Buffy agreed.

"Buffy," Bothwell persisted. "I need you to travel the Ghost Roads. Kendra and . . . India . . . will meet you there. You'll perform a ritual."

"That does what?" Buffy asked, frowning slightly.

Instead of answering her, Bothwell looked at Cordelia.

"I need to ask something of you. Something very dangerous, and very important."

"Oh, yay," she said, grimacing. "Let me guess. You want me to allow one of the dead Slayers to take over my body so we can join forces for the final battle and kick the Gatherer's ass."

Buffy stared at her in amazement, then Christopher Bothwell, who nodded.

"That's exactly right," he said.

Cordelia sighed. "Okay."

Buffy blinked at her. So did Giles. Cordelia looked up, saw everyone's expressions of astonishment, and snapped, "I told you, I'm really nice. No, it wasn't any of you, it was Xander, and he'd better find out I did this."

"Okay, then," Christopher said, putting his hands on his knees. "I've got the herbs we need, I have the incantation—"

"And you need four Slayers," Willow said. "Buffy, Faith, whoever Cordelia becomes and . . . one more."

"No way," Oz and Buffy said at the same time.

Giles stepped forward. "I agree. She's recovering from surgery. If we need a fourth, I shall fill in."

"Or me," Oz said.

"Slayers are girls," Cordelia said with an air of authority.

There was silence, and in that silence, Buffy understood that Bothwell was agreeing with Cordelia.

"She will possess Slayer strength and healing abilities while she is filled with a Slayer's soul," Bothwell observed, his voice kind, reassuring. "It may actually benefit her in the long run."

"If it doesn't kill her in the short run," Buffy snapped. "No. I won't let you do this to her."

"We must, Buffy," Bothwell said.

"Use Faith." Buffy scowled at him.

"Math class, Buffy," Cordelia trilled.

"Faith's got to be there as well. There must be four Slayers, one of each elemental sign," Bothwell explained. "That will be you, Faith, Cordelia and Willow." He took a breath. "As Kendra, and as India."

Everyone took a moment. Then Cordelia said, "Who am I gonna be?"

"You are an Earth sign. As was Kendra."

Cordelia looked bemused.

"I'll be India, then," Willow said softly.

"This is insane." Buffy crossed to Willow. "You don't even have any hair."

"I shall bolster her with magick." Bothwell regarded Willow, who looked bravely up at him. Oz was holding her hand. She looked small and easy to kill, and Buffy was not about to lose another friend to death so easily.

The Watcher continued. "A Wanderer hacked India to bits right in front of me. She was so happy to have a real home at last. I'd gotten her a dog. Her father was going to stay home from the sea and she would finally have a real family."

"Slayers die," Buffy said, crossing her arms over her chest.

"If this thing devours the force of two living Slayers at once, there is an excellent chance that the line will not be able to recover," Bothwell continued. "In other words, we will have no more Slayers. Ever."

There was silence around the room, at least among

those directly concerned. Finally, Cordelia said, "That would be bad."

"Then don't fight it," Oz said.

"It will keep coming for Slayers. It will pursue you relentlessly," Bothwell told Buffy.

She threw back her hair and crossed her arms. "Then I'll fight it relentlessly."

"It will have Cecile, and whoever the Fourth Servant is. You won't know whom to trust. Whom to kill." He shook his head. "It's on its way to Sunnydale as we speak. It's here to challenge you.

"You—all four of you—must fight the Gatherer."

Buffy looked over at Willow and murmured, "No. It's too much to ask."

"It's okay. It's a sacrifice I have to make," Cordelia said importantly.

Christopher Bothwell took both of Buffy's hands in his and walked her away from the others.

"You will see India." He hesitated. "I-I love her," he said. "Tell her that. She sacrificed herself for me, not because she was the Slayer, but because she loved me in return. I would do anything to be able to see her again, except risk your friend's life."

Tears welled in his eyes. "If we had another option, I would take it in a minute. But we need all four of you. Together, you are Four. Everything to do with the Gatherer is made up of the Four Elements of the Arcana Mystica: Earth, Air, Water, and Fire."

"Us," Buffy said.

"You. You are air, Buffy. India, water. Faith, fire. And Kendra, earth."

"Who's the rainbow?" she asked, thinking of her dream.

"I'm sorry?"

"Nothing." She bowed her head.

"It was wrong of her to sacrifice herself for me," he said. "A waste of her potential."

"Well, she was a Slayer," Buffy said. "We do stuff like that."

"Not for your Watcher. Nor one good friend," he said giving her the eye. "Nor for a lover. I certainly hope Rupert Giles trained you better than that."

"I did," Giles said sternly, coming up beside them.

Buffy remained silent.

"For that reason, in terrible remorse, I withdrew from Council matters. Since then, I've devoted my life entirely to the study of magick, to find her. . . ." He trailed off. Tears welled in his eyes.

"Because you wanted to bring her back," Buffy guessed.

He lowered his head. "I wanted to bring her back."

"That's understandable," Buffy said quietly. "Do you have a picture of her? So I'll, like, recognize her?"

He slid his wallet out of the back pocket of his corduroy pants. Then he plucked a photo the size of a school picture out of the credit card section and handed it to her.

A beautiful AmerAsian girl smiled back at her. There was a startling intensity in her almond-shaped eyes. She had beautiful features and shiny hair. She looked smart. And brave.

"I've seen her," Buffy told him simply. "I've been dreaming about her."

Kit took the picture from her and studied it. "I think she contacted me once, in a dream. I think to tell me not to grieve so. I began casting spells practically day and night to strengthen the connection."

THE BOOK OF FOURS

He ran a hand through his hair, looking tired yet determined.

"I suppose my spells threw off magick residue, which might be why you were affected and had those dreams. Or maybe India needs to talk to you, and has been trying to find ways to do that."

"And she walks the Ghost Roads?" Buffy asked.

Their gazes locked. She realized he had wanted very much for her to ask that question.

"I believe so, yes."

"There were four shooting stars on Friday night," Giles said. "They were spotted in England, and Jamaica, and all over the globe. It signifies something of enormous significance that has to do with the number four."

"It's time," Buffy said.

"It's time," Christopher agreed.

Buffy said, "Okay, before I go, debrief. Each box contains—or used to contain—an axe. But somehow there's two axes that got away from the bad guys."

"One is the axe of the Air," Bothwell said, "and one is Fire. You are Air, and Faith is Fire."

"Yay," Buffy said.

"Each axe will kill only a Slayer who corresponds with the Wanderer of her element. Otherwise, it can only seriously injure a Slayer of a different element."

"Not following," Cordelia said.

He turned to her. "Each Slayer is rooted in the fundamental magickal matter of the universe. India was a Slayer of Water. You can usually find evidence in their life histories which helps identify their element. For example, every place India ever lived was by the sea."

"There are two living Slayers." Bothwell's eyes shone. "Think of it. It's never, ever happened before.

The combined essence of your two beings attracted the Gatherer to you. It's an incredible amount of magickal energy.

"That's what it wants, both Slayers. If it takes you and Faith both, it will rise from its pit and walk, like a man. It will terrorize the earth."

He grew somber. "And there will be no more Slayers, ever, to stop it."

"But why?" Cordelia asked. "Why won't another Slayer be called?"

"Because there are always consequences to actions," the Watcher replied. "The consumption of so much Slayer essence would deplete the source, to be sure. It would probably end the line."

"Feeling too special," Buffy muttered.

Kit put a hand on her shoulder. "One can argue that each Slayer leading up to this moment has been special. And yet, India sacrificed herself in part because she didn't believe she *was* special."

Buffy nodded. "I read some of her diary. Slayer easy come, Slayer easy go." She grimaced. "Been there, thought that."

"It's not true." Kit rose and pushed up his sleeves. "Who can dare to say which of the millions of acts undertaken each day, will lead to something that will benefit the entire human race for millennia?"

Buffy smiled wanly. "Has anyone suggested a career as a motivational speaker for you?"

He let that pass. "I want you to talk to India. Find out if she knows precisely how to defeat the Gatherer. I believe she contacted me because she knows."

"Talk to India . . ." Buffy echoed.

She looked at Bothwell, and he looked at her.

"I can open the portal in Willow's hospital room. So

that Willow goes, too. And Cordelia," Kit said urgently. "I'm an experienced sorcerer, Buffy. I'll do everything in my power to set things right once we're done."

Buffy walked over to Willow's bedside, closing her eyes against sudden tears.

"I have herbs," Bothwell said. "In my pockets."

Each person held herbs as Christopher chanted. Lights filled the room, then thinned out to a barely noticeable line, but as he retraced the space over and over, it thickened. Like a miniature aurora borealis, the colors changed from white light to blue to green, and glowing shapes and shadows began to move within the ellipse. It hung in the air, prisms of light refracting in formation like a kaleidoscope.

It was fully formed. Buffy took Willow's hand, and then Cordelia's, they entered the Ghost Roads together.

This time, there was no middle ground, no gray limbo while they oriented themselves to the land of death. As soon as they reached the other side, they were overrun with phantoms running in frenzied disarray, completely lost to panic. Buffy fought back, with jumpkicks and hard punches. Each time a specter was hit, it shattered. Before her first trip on the Roads, she had never thought of ghosts as brittle. Her assumption was that they would be misty and insubstantial, like dry ice.

Or memories.

"What are we supposed to do when we find them, whistle?" Cordelia said. "Hold up little signs with their names on them?"

"No," said a figure ahead, on the road.

Buffy recognized her from her picture.

It was India Cohen, as solid as if she were alive.

Chapter Two

On the Ghost Roads, Slayer regarded Slayer.

Then India said, "How is Kit?"

"Good." Buffy nodded eagerly.

India's eyes welled. "He's mad at me for saving him."

Buffy was taken aback. "No," Buffy said. "India, he's not angry. He . . . he loves you."

India closed her eyes. "Oh, God, Kit," she whispered. To Buffy she said, "He contacted me, you know. A couple of times. I shouldn't have done it, but I would do it again. To save Kit, I'd . . . I'd give my soul." She closed her eyes. "I think that's what I did. I think that's why the gatherer couldn't absorb Lucy."

"Listen, we're in big trouble back on Earth, or whatever," Cordelia said. "The Gatherer—"

India nodded, her features hardening; Buffy saw the Slayer resolve there and knew instinctively that she and India were part of the same line. At a very deep level, they were closer to each other than blood relatives.

"Don't underestimate it, Buffy," India said. "It

wants you and Faith especially. Because you're alive. Somehow, it couldn't completely take my essence, and it missed Kendra altogether. But you two are fair game."

"So, it like, spit you out," Cordelia ventured.

"Slayer," said a familiar voice behind Buffy.

Kendra was there. Approximately Buffy's height, with her regal bearing, her hair in its customary pony tail. Dear Kendra, still with the slash on her neck where Drusilla had sliced her with her fingernails, and killed her.

"We are four," she said to Cordelia. "If you'll allow it, I will take over your body."

"Yeah. Okay," Cordy said unhappily.

India held out her hand. "I was proud to die for love, Buffy. But it was very wrong of me. Slayers must be braver than that." India looked hard at her, and her expression was one of pleading.

"I died, Buffy, and you became the Slayer. Help me make better sense of my death. Let me become the Slayer I wasn't."

The air on the Ghost Roads filled with the scents of herbs—rosemary, for remembrance. Lavender, for hope. Buffy smelled candle wax. She thought she might be able to hear the soft, low chanting of male voices.

Giles, she thought. *Kit Bothwell. And Oz.*

Her mind filled; she knew the incantation, though India's Watcher had not told her the words:

We are the Four. We are One, and we are the Four.

India joined her, then Cordelia, then Kendra. Buffy felt energy crackling around her, inside her. She smelled the herbs, and her body prickled with sensation.

We are the Four.

Then it happened, slowly, as the two dead Slayers grew faint. Willow caught her breath, then Cordy, and then they smiled at Buffy.

Willow was India, and Cordelia had become Kendra.

Chapter Three

On the Ghost Roads, the three Slayers embraced. Buffy was overwhelmed; India began to cry. Cordy/Kendra merely looked uncomfortable.

India said, "Hey, I was a tomboy. Never cried on the job."

"Me, neither," Buffy lied.

"It couldn't take my soul," Willow, as India, said. "It was really pissed about it, too. Starting with Lucy Hanover, it just couldn't get it right. I think it was because Cameron Duvalier is so insane," she concluded.

Buffy took a breath. "What was it like . . . you know . . . when the Gatherer tried to absorb you?"

Willow regarded her steadily. "I wouldn't wish it on my worst enemy. Which is the Gatherer, I guess." She laughed harshly. "Going in and coming out, it hurts like crazy. In between, there's nothing. I just . . . wasn't."

Buffy swallowed. "No, um, afterward?"

"I'm thinking not, but only because I was with the Gatherer," she told her honestly. "It timeshares you, sort of. If it's using your life force, you can't use it yourself."

She touched Buffy's shoulder. "It wants Slayers. It's coming for us. If it gets what it wants, it will be worse than being nothing. For every single living being on this planet. Pain is its god. And it worships at the altar every chance it gets.

"Agony is what makes it feel alive."

"Then we will give it agony," Cordelia announced. "Come. We must find Faith." She swept past Willow and Buffy. "No more tears. Are you Slayers or little babies?"

Willow raised her brows and looked at Buffy, who grinned.

"I had forgotten about her Spockian tendencies," she said. "She goes by the book."

"The Slayer's Handbook?" Willow/India asked. "Or the Guide to Military Correctness?"

"See, you got the Handbook, too," Buffy groused. "Giles never even bothered, because—"

"*Come,*" Cordelia said impatiently.

"Yikes," Willow whispered.

Buffy smiled. It felt good to smile.

She hoped to be smiling for years and years and years.

Chapter Four

The Slayers announced that they needed time together, and added that they had to go in search of Faith. Giles was loathe to let them go out into the storm, particularly as Willow—temporarily India—looked so fragile. But things were not solely up to him, and what they were doing now extended beyond his realm of experience, Watcher training or no.

Very reluctantly, he let them go.

Bothwell told him they had things of their own to do to prepare, and Giles realized that the most accessible location for books and occult equipment was the school library, as his condo had been destroyed. Again.

Giles and Kit fought the elements as they made their way from the hospital to the parking structure, where Kit had a car.

Giles bellowed to Kit, "It's remarkable, what you've managed to accomplish with your magick. I do hope you'll consider rejoining the Council. Our numbers are sadly diminished these days." He thought of Roger Zabuto.

"Perhaps."

Then Giles said, "I'm glad you've a car. Mine was—"

He stopped, suddenly acutely aware of danger. He stared at Kit and said, "You're . . . *wrong*. Something about you is terribly wrong."

Kit smiled. "I'm a time bomb," he said. "And I've just been detonated."

A woman stepped from the stairwell facing them. She was beautiful, with black, curly hair and exotic features.

"Hello, Watcher," she said. "I'm Cecile." She smiled at Kit. *"Bon soir, mon amour."*

Giles blinked. *Cecile Lafitte! The Sorceress!* To Kit he said, "She's . . . Watcher, snap out of it! You've been enchanted. By the Powers of Light, I command you to be free—"

"I'm the Fourth Servant," Kit announced triumphantly. "I will set the Gatherer free. And she and I will sit at his right hand."

"This has all been a setup," Giles said slowly. "Bothwell, you bastard."

Cecile laughed. She moved her hands and a ball of blue energy formed between her palms. Giles knew it for a weapon and ran straight toward her, before she had a chance to hurl the sphere at him. He slammed into her, sending her onto her back, and raced for the stairwell.

Energy exploded where his head had been, just seconds after he threw himself down the stairs, tucking his head as best he could. He was no Slayer, but he had trained one.

Explosion after explosion slammed into the stairwell. Somehow, they all missed him. Giles ran from the structure into the storm, turned, and saw the entire thing go up in flames.

Chapter Five

"Is it my imagination or has the wind died down a little?" Faith asked, as an entire tree shot past her and Xander. They had just hightailed it away from their battle at the fire station, and were now sauntering—*insert irony,* Xander thought—through the hurricane that was Sunnydale. Faith had stashed the axe in her belt and he thought she looked quite jaunty.

"Har har," Xander said drolly. "You just slay me, Faith."

"But we got the axe. Kicked major butt to get it, but hey, we got the sucker." She held it up.

The Sunnydale Fire Station was nothing to write home about, unless one's home was Sunnydale, in which case one might send a postcard that read, *You so do not want your house to catch fire in this town.* The engines were really old and didn't hold half as much water as the new kind; plus the firefighters were all guys who had left other jobs around the Los Angeles basin, usually for dereliction of duty.

Some of this Xander and Faith knew going in, but the part about the smaller water capacity they had to listen to while they snuck up on the double-wide that served as the firefighters' home away from home while they were on duty.

They spied on the occupants for about two minutes while they surveyed the scene, curious about why the Master's vampire fan club had not shown. As soon as they high-fived each other that they'd made it to the fire station ahead of the other team in the Scavenger Hunt of the Apocalypse, the vampires had jumped off the top of the double wide and hijinks had ensued.

To his dying day—*which could be any minute*— Xander would be sorry that Buffy had not seen him kicking butt alongside Faith. He usually came off as kind of a handicap in the sweepstakes, or so Giles and Buffy claimed. Also, it would have been nice to show off for Cordy. *So, dysfunctional.*

But in the big fight, he was a helper, and when Faith whooped and said, "Man, I am so horny! You horny?" he actually staked a vampire by accident because the very stiff, ah, stake he was holding kind of jerked forward in his grip and slammed into the heart of a bad boy who was leaping at him.

Bam, slam, kicks, and counterkicks; Faith executed a totally mouth-dropping backflip over two vampires while Xander located and retrieved the axe, which had been put into a padded mailer addressed to the Sunnydale History Museum Curator.

Now, nursing a sore jaw from the battle, Xander grinned at Faith. "We are so cool."

"Hey." Faith stared across the street, which was the cross street for the hospital.

Before them in the driving rain stood Cordelia, Buffy, and a half-bald Willow, who was wearing baggy jeans and a sweater. Oz was with them.

Xander and Faith crossed the street. Faith took a step forward. "I know who you are," she said to the newcomers.

Cordelia and Willow nodded. "We have come back from the dead."

"Oh." Xander looked confused.

"I'm India Cohen," said Willow.

"*Oh.*" Xander's eyes widened.

Cordelia said, "I am Kendra."

"Nice to see you again. Not. Not that it's not nice, but that it's not really you. But it is, isn't it?" His voice was high and squeaky. He looked at Buffy. "This is creepy."

"We need to go to the summit," said Willow. "To prepare." She looked at the other girls. "Kendra and I should go first. Alone. To get our bearings. Give us some time and then follow."

"I can go with you," Xander offered.

"*Alone,*" Cordelia said.

"That's dumb," Faith piped up. "It doesn't make any sense. We go together, as a group."

Cordelia shook her head. "Then we will be the Four. If the Servant summons the Gatherer, we will be engaged in battle too soon. And India and I need to learn to use our bodies."

"Teaching?" Xander asked, raising his hand.

Willow chuckled, and Cordelia glared at her. "We have no time for jokes," Cordelia snapped. "This is serious. We must concentrate."

"You're right," Buffy said, trying to smooth things over. *Boy, am I glad we're not going to have a slumber party after this. Or go bowling. These guys do not get along.*

Willow said, "Okay. So, you guys, we'll gather at the battleground, okay?"

Buffy translated for Xander and Faith. "We're going to the lighthouse. Giles knows where it is. He and Christopher are going up there together to get some magick stuff in place for us."

"I'm checking around for Angel, see if he got that other axe," Oz filled in.

"All right. Sounds like a plan." Xander hugged Buffy. "Good luck." He hugged Willow. "Good luck." He hugged Cordelia, and yearned for the old days when he got to hug her all the time, and a few other things. But now she was Kendra, and he was afraid she was going to faint dead away. Kendra had not been around boys very much in her short, sheltered life.

Oz made his farewells and headed out toward Willy's Alibi. Xander smiled ruefully and gave the two newly reanimated dead Slayers a wave.

Then he joined Faith and Buffy. "I still don't get it," he said. "Why the splitting up?"

"We're Gatherer magnets if we're all together," she told him.

"Aw, the Gatherer's just a user," Faith quipped. "Guys are all the same. He'll show, beat us up, eat our souls, and forget to call."

"You are so cynical," Xander observed drily.

"Just smart," Faith responded.

After a few more minutes, they were in the forest, which was currently still on fire, but not in the section they had snuck into. Snuck, because the authorities had declared it unsafe and posted CLOSED UNTIL FURTHER NOTICE signs all over it—most of which had been blown off whatever they were nailed to and were sailing around like kites.

Not on fire in their section, because there was nothing

left to burn up. The trees were columns of cinders and ash, and the underbrush was gone.

Suddenly Buffy heard a low groan. She focused in on its direction, waiting for another. As she cocked her head, she slid her gaze toward Faith, who nodded.

"Heard it too," the dark-haired Slayer murmured.

Xander looked around. "Heard what?"

"Over there." Buffy pointed to some stubbly bushes on the other side of a shallow incline.

Faith nodded, and the two Slayers started bounding down the ditch.

"I didn't hear anything," Xander grumbled, stumbling after the agile girls.

He fell on his butt and slid a couple of feet, then regained his balance and continued on. Then the wind picked up, hard, and a dervish of ash whipped up around him. Before he had time to react, some of it blew in his eyes. It burned like crazy.

Xander swore and bent forward, reflexively pressing his fingertips against his eyelids. That hurt worse, but the swearing helped a little, so he did some more of that and cupped his eye sockets with his hands. The gritty ash washed over him; he thought about his Aunt Rhonda, who had been cremated and had her ashes spread in the woods—not these particular woods, but still, gross—and grimaced.

"Hey, guys?" he called. There was no answer. "Buffy?" He squinted, trying to open his watering eyes. "Um, gals?"

Then he heard a sound. He listened hard, trying to figure out what it was, a rustling of leaves? Or the movement of some kind of fabric? He cocked his head. It was unnerving.

"Buffy? Faith?" he called. His voice was shrill.

The sound came closer. Xander swallowed, wondering if he dared move when he couldn't see.

"Guys? This isn't funny anymore. Okay, it wasn't funny in the first place, but now it's really not funny. Because, um, guess what? I can't see. My eyes are full of ash. You know, like when you stick your head up your—"

Closer.

Maybe it's not my best idea to advertise the fact that I'm standing here basically helpless.

On the other hand . . .

"Help!" he screamed, as loud as was possible.

Buffy and Faith had been following the groaning noise. Buffy stopped and turned around, catching her breath. "Where's Xander? I thought he was right behind us."

Faith leaned forward, planting her hands on her thighs as she caught her breath. "I coulda sworn I heard him behind me." She wiped her forehead. "Of course, the fact that you wanted to win the fifty-yard dash more than anybody may have had something to do with losing him." She grinned. "You must have been a killer at doorbell ditch."

"I was a TP-*artiste*," Buffy drawled. "Nobody could toilet paper a front yard like me. A cheerleader thing, y'know?"

"I keep forgetting you were a socialite in L.A. Weird. Cuz you're pretty much an outcast here." Faith rolled her shoulders in circles as she stood up. "The slaying thing screwed you over, huh."

"No news there," Buffy replied, glancing around for Xander.

Faith looked down, kicked a pile of ash, and made a

face. "Oh, God, that used to be something in the Bambi subspecies."

Buffy was grossed out, but she kept silent.

Then she pushed aside some scorched pine tree branches as they flapped back and forth like the wing doors on a saloon in a John Wayne western. She moved between them and looked down at the highway about fifteen feet below the incline on which they stood.

"Faith?" she called.

"What?" the other Slayer asked, coming up behind her.

Wordlessly, Buffy pointed.

Like most of the roads, it had become a river. Debris and greenery swept along—boxes and shopping carts, and . . . a familiar car. The water was already to the bottom of the windows.

Buffy's eyes widened. "That's Xander's mom's Subaru. Oh, my God, Faith, she's inside!"

Sure enough, Xander's mother was behind the wheel, pounding frantically on the window and paying no attention to the road because, what was the point?

At that precise moment, Buffy heard a scream of such intensity it probably ripped out the vocal cords of the person who made it.

"That's Xander!" Buffy shouted.

"Okay. I'll get the mom," Faith said. "You go for the big guy."

They nodded at each other and parted ways, Faith heading for the river, and Buffy back into the forest.

"Hold on, Mrs. Harris!" Faith bellowed, but she didn't know if the terror-stricken woman heard her. Xander's mom had let go of the wheel and was slamming her fists against the closed window.

Why doesn't she just roll it down? Faith wondered.

Then the answer came to her: *It's electric. The water's shorted it out.*

The water rushed around Faith's thighs. Then there was a dip—*pot hole?*—and she was up to her hips. She gave up walking and dove in, swimming as hard as she could for the car.

What am I gonna do when I get there?

She thought about the months she spent in Albuquerque. *With Carl the Total Dweeb Loser of All Time, but no need to dwell on the past during a 911 situation.* What she was thinking about was flash-flood warnings, and people get swept away in their cars and drowning, and the fact that Xander's mom was in trouble but not the biggest trouble yet, because there was no . . .

—*Damn it, yes there is!*—

. . . Water *inside* her car.

There was lots of it: Mrs. Harris was up to her waist in swirling water. Faith reached the driver's side. She held onto the door handle and gave it a yank and *Hey! Presto*! it came off in her hand.

Faith swore and tried to put it back. No good.

Faith put one of her own palms up against Mrs. Harris's and decided she'd better look for a different escape route. The door behind the driver's door was locked, too.

Mrs. Harris was panicking. Faith gestured for her to stay calm, but Xander's mom didn't seem to notice her. Faith slogged around to the passenger door in the front. Her hand brushed open space. The window was gone, and that's how the water was getting in.

"Unbuckle your seat belt," Faith said.

Mrs. Harris was shaking her head. She was completely wigging out. She yanked her arm away and pointed with both hands behind Faith.

Faith turned.

Yikes.

"Xander, you have got to lay off the junk food." Buffy grunted, as she and he walked along the highway bank. The "river" had become cluttered with floating debris—a couch, a bunch of cardboard boxes, and more than a few cars. *Fortunately,* those *are empty.* She was searching for signs of Faith and Mrs. Harris, but there was an awful lot of stuff bobbing around.

She had found Xander prone on the smoking forest floor, the fabric on his right leg and arm burned away, the skin beneath a charred mess of *ow.* Xander was in so much pain that he didn't make sense; he kept talking about Boris Karloff, the actor who had played Frankenstein. What Frankenstein had to do with Xander's burns Buffy could not figure out, unless there were some very quiet villagers with torches skulking around Sunnydale Forest.

His arm was draped across her shoulders. In fact most of him was. He said, shakily, and to the accompaniment of many gasps, "I'm not heavy, I'm your brother."

"Wrong and wrong," she said, with a faint smile. "Your arm weighs more than my entire body. And by the way, what's with mumbling about Boris Karloff?"

"The Mummy. He starred in it," he told her. "After you vixens took off, our own personal Sunnydale version came gliding along, singing a song. I touched it, and it burned me." His eyes widened. "And it was just a touch."

Buffy processed that while scanning the water. In the short time Faith and she had parted ways, more had rushed into the ravine created by the road, until it was an actual river. The top of the Subaru was all she could see of the Harrises' car.

There seemed to be an awful lot of churning going on beneath the surface.

Distracted, she murmured, "Maybe Faith had to race her to the hospital. Or she's behind one of those dumpsters, giving her CPR."

"Huh? Who? Where is Faith, anyway?" Xander asked.

She blanched; she hadn't told Xander anything, especially not that his mother was down in that water, probably dying by now.

It won't do any good to tell him. It will be of the bad: He'll freak out and try to save her, and he'll get in Faith's way.

"And my way . . ." she said slowly.

"What?" Xander turned his head. "Holy moly, Buff. What's that?"

The waters were bubbling like a witch's cauldron. Then the wrapped head of a mummy broke the surface, blowing out an enormous stream of wind that scattered the clouds and wind above its head.

Then Faith's head appeared beside it. She was gasping for breath. "Buffy!" she cried.

"Stay here," Buffy ordered Xander, undraping his arm. She ran toward the submerged highway as fast as her Chosen One legs could carry her.

On the bank, Xander waved with his good arm.

"Buffy!" he shouted. "Wait! Right behind you, boss."

"No!" she insisted.

Farther on down to the right, he noticed a woman's body bobbing against what looked to be a crate of clear plastic boxes in fashionable designer colors. She was wearing a dress just like one of his mother's, and her hair was the same color, and—

"Oh, my God!" Xander shouted. "Buffy, save my mom! My mom's in there!"

Maybe later, I won't know how I did this, he thought, as he ran-walked as fast as he could to the water and splashed in. *Or maybe later, I'll be laid out in my coffin wearing one of my dad's cheesy sports jackets, the final humiliation of my life.*

The water on his burns hurt like hell, but physical pain and abject terror evaporated as soon as he reached his mother's side. Her current condition was hideously ambiguous. She might be alive, barely alive, or very dead. He set her chin in the crook of his arm to keep her face above water, begging her not to be behind Door Number Three.

He got to what had become the shore and staggered out, carrying her all the way out of the water. Her face did not look good. Her chest was not moving. Xander dropped to his knees and felt for a pulse. Nothing.

I brought Buffy back with CPR, he told himself, as his heart triphammered against his ribs. His panic was so intense he began to hyperventilate. *I made her live again. I can do this.*

Choking back his fear, he leaned over his mother and started pumping on her chest. *One, two, three, four, five. Breathe. Listen. Check for pulse. One, two, three, four, five. Breathe.*

No pulse.

Oh, God, Mom. How long was she under?

His arm and leg hurt so badly he wished they would fall off. With every compression of her chest, pain bulleted from his wrist to his shoulder and sent a fire alarm through his brain.

As he counted, a portion of his mind left the building and wandered down the hall of old medical TV shows. Up until *E.R.,* CPR usually did the job. A more optimistic era of doc shows. Hair-raising snippets of Dr. Green and Dr. Carver grimly announcing "Let's call it" made him redouble his efforts. Retriple, even. After all, this was his mom.

Xander didn't know if the water rolling down his face was tears, highway river water, or sweat. All he knew was that he had turned into a machine that went *onetwothreefourfivebreathelistenbreathepulse— pleaseGodplease.* The pain in his arm had gotten so bad that his brain had given up trying to tell him about it, and he had begun to shiver almost uncontrollably. *Maybe I'm going into shock. I wish I hadn't skipped health and safety all those times to make out with Cordelia in the closet. If my mom dies because I was a stupid, horny truant, I'll repeat high school so I can become a doctor.*

"Mom," he called. "Mom, damn it, wake up!"

Doggedly he pushed on her chest, doing his utmost to ignore the searing pain shooting through his arm. Perhaps just as stubbornly, she did not breathe. Then with an abrupt, choking cough, her stomach contracted and water spewed out of her mouth. Xander rolled her onto her side and more water came up. She kept coughing, and then she vomited.

Kneeling, Xander curled protectively over her. "It's okay, Mom," he said. "I'm here. It's okay."

"Xander, what?" She gazed around with a terrified look on her face. The whites of her eyes were bloodshot and her face was mottled and scratched.

"Mom." Xander swallowed down his emotion. There

was more going on inside him than he knew how to express, either to his mother or to himself. "Looking for a catchy bit of ironic self-reflection, here," he blurted, knowing he sounded goofy.

"You saved me," she said. Tears spilled down her cheeks. She gasped and closed her eyes, coughed a few times, and tried to clear her throat. "You dove in and saved me."

"No, it was . . ." And he realized he couldn't tell her about Faith. Well, he could, but doing so would open the door to a lot of questions in the category "Slayers for $200" that he didn't want to answer. Figuring silence was not the same as telling an outright lie, he cleared his throat and stood up to see what was going on.

Whoa.

Buffy was pummeling the hell out of the mummy that had attacked. His mother turned her head and saw as well; she began to scream at the top of her lungs. "What's happening? What is that?" she shrieked.

"Store mannequin," Xander told her. "It must have washed in from the drug store." He hurried down to the edge of the water. "Buffy? Do you need a hand? With the store mannequin?"

"Xander, stay back!" Buffy shouted. "You just might lose a hand!"

"Thanks for your faith in me," he muttered, and, saying to his mother, "Stay," he limped toward the water for what he sincerely hoped was not his own personal grande finale.

"Xander, you're hurt. Back off," Buffy yelled, as she thrashed in the water with the thing from another nightmare.

Faith, clinging to a buoyant piece of wood, was groaning. She put her hands over her midsection and drew up her knees. Her face was gray.

"Oh, God. I'm dyin'."

Buffy was alarmed. "Hold on, Faith, okay? Just lie still while I take this thing out. We'll get you some help."

Faith said, "Try the axe. I've got the axe. In my jacket."

"It's the Axe of Fire, right?" Buffy asked. "If the Wanderer gets it away from me, it'll kill you."

"Then don't let it," Faith groaned. "God, I'm dying anyway."

Buffy moved into action mode, slogging over to Faith and feeling for the axe.

She pulled it out, and gave it a summary glance. It looked evil. It felt evil. She didn't like touching it.

The mummy stared at her. Its gaze traveled down her arms to the axe in her grasp. It came toward her, rising above the water, gliding, its bandages bursting into flame. It became a torch, headed toward her; steam gushed beneath its feet and the water nearest it began to bubble.

Where Buffy stood, the runoff was quickly heating.

It's the Wanderer of Fire, all right, she thought anxiously. *So it can't kill me, right?*

She began to swing the axe at it. It didn't hesitate, just kept coming for her. She half-swam, half-ran through the water, making huge arcs. It kept coming, hands outstretched, just as Xander had said—Boris Karloff.

Then she leaped forward and brought it up over her head, then down, and sliced it down the center of its face.

Flames gouted out of the wound, spraying her; she ducked under the water before any significant damage was done. Looking up through the murky, rushing water, she saw blurs of gray and orange; when she breached the surface, she realized it had frozen in place, burning.

Hands around the axe, she doubled her fists, locked them together, and rammed the axe blade into the wound once more. Flames geysered out, peppering the water. Buffy backtracked as fast as she could, bashing into Xander, and grabbed him around the waist.

She hit shallow water and flung him toward the bank.

"Sit. Stay," she ordered him.

Xander taken care of, Buffy sloshed over to Faith, as the mummy blazed above the surface of the water.

"Buffy, I think I'm dying," she muttered. "The mummy touched me and something's inside me now. Something that's hot and burning and making it really hard to breathe."

Buffy didn't know what to make of it, but it sounded like what had happened to Xander. She grabbed hold of the plank and gently pushed Faith to the side of the road. Xander reached down to give Faith an assist. Xander's dark hair hung in his eyes, and his brows were glistening with water droplets. As he cleared himself a viewing space through his bangs, Xander looked at Buffy and said, "My mom's on shore. She's okay."

"Does she need a doctor?" Buffy asked, quickening her rescue mission as together, she and Xander eased Faith to dry land.

"I don't know. I gave her C.P.R. When I gave you C.P.R., you didn't go to the hospital afterward, but you're the Slayer. My mom heals slowly. Always has."

Xander ran his hand through his hair. "And, speaking of healing, may I say ouch. And possibly, ouch again."

Showing his teeth in a grimace belying much pain, Xander gestured to his burned arm, which was really looking bad. Very cooked, with long strips of skin peeling off and at least a dozen blisters rising.

"Which is an indirect way of saying," he concluded, "that I could use some medical help, too."

"And a meat thermometer," Faith said, making a face. "What'd you do, try to broil yourself for lunch?"

Faith had curled back up in a fetal position, clutching her stomach. She added, "That looks extremely painful. Not to mention gross."

Buffy gazed at him. "That's two people you've saved with your mighty breath. Maybe you should consider a career in medicine."

"Or blowing up balloons and making 'em into funny toy animals. Like poodles," Faith zinged. Buffy was impressed that the dark-haired Slayer could make with the funny when she was in such terrible pain.

She looked back at the rushing water.

The mummy was gone.

"We'd better get the heck out of here," she said. "Who knows where that thing went?"

Faith nodded.

Ahead, Xander's mother was slowly getting to her feet. Xander race-walked over to her. Buffy watched her put her arms around her son and was glad for Xander. She often got the feeling that Xander's parents didn't put much thought into the day-to-day existence of their lives as parents. Xander never complained, but

Buffy felt that he and Willow were both ignored by their respective families.

"Can you walk, Faith?" Buffy asked.

Faith moaned under her breath. "Buffy, I'm so messed up inside. My guts are on fire." She gasped.

"We'll get help," Buffy promised.

But help is not on the way, Buffy thought, as yet another vehicle passed them.

"I can't understand it," Xander's mother said. "Can't they see we're in trouble?"

"Everybody's scared, Mom," Xander told her, hunched over and hurting. He was sitting on the curb. "Things haven't exactly been normal around here. Or what passes for normal in our fair town."

"I know."

Behind and to the left of Xander, Faith groaned. She was lying on the grass divider between the sidewalk and the curb, all curled up, and her color was not good. It was the gray of recycled cardboard.

"Is she okay?" his mom said under her breath, too loud, the way she did when they were at the mall and somebody really hot walked past. She'd roll her eyes and whisper at the top of her lungs, "That girl dresses like a hooker!"

"No, Mom, she's really not okay," Xander replied.

"Oh, dear."

"Yeah."

At a loss, Xander silently surveyed the ruins of Sunnydale. What surprised him most about the aftermath was the amount of trash. Trash that was now burning, in fact. There were huge piles of fiery paper and battered, smoking cardboard boxes and dozens of reeking pieces of plastic and melting glass.

Flashfire tumbleweeds and rust, everywhere he looked.

His mother murmured, "All this freakish weather. It's such a mystery."

"Yup. That crazy weather," Xander bit off. He was angry with his mother for not noticing all the other stuff that went on in Sunnydale—eviscerated animals, missing children, the number of fatalities at his school.

Highest in the nation.

But her life was narrow, and unfocused, and despite the fact that Xander's view of the world had been broadened not by travel but by his secret life as Robin to Buffy's Batman, he resented her lack of interest in the bigger picture.

Truth be told, her eggshell imagination frightened him. He didn't want to end up like her. The only time she read anything was when she went to the doctor's or stood in line at the grocery store. So much of life seemed to be about conforming and fitting in; how did you find a way to be different from your parents?

"I need to talk to you about something," his mother said. "Maybe after we get your burns treated."

Xander smiled grimly. *If I don't die waiting for a ride first.*

"Tell me now, Mom. What is it?"

She took a breath and plunged in. "Kevin's mother phoned, just before everything went kerplooey."

"Yay." Those were the rich relatives, the ones who shunned Xander's branch of the Harrises.

As well they should.

"Your cousin's very sick."

That didn't register. Nothing ever happened to the golden boy of the San Francisco Harrises. Unless you counted totaling a classic Mustang Xander would have sold his soul for.

Or at least possibly rented my soul out, with a limited number of centuries. "Yeah, and?" he asked, his mind now wandering over to the topic of cars he'd like to own. At the moment, any car would do, but if he could have anything he wanted . . . maybe a classic red-and-white Studebaker Hawk.

". . . match you as a bone marrow donor," his mother said.

Xander swung his head back around to look at her. "Excuse me?"

His mother huffed. "His parents had that tropical fever or whatever. . . ."

"Mom, it's called hepatitis. They got it from that restaurant they sued."

"Right." She nodded vigorously. "So they can't donate. And your father has the high blood pressure. They want to see if you can be his donor."

Xander was astonished. "They need something from us?"

Her lopsided grin spoke volumes. He knew she was pretty tired of all the in-your-face wealthy-people snobbery of the upstate, upscale Harrises of San Fran. Better yet, mention Dad's brother in front of him and the big guy let out a belch and asked you to pass the corn nuts in that wacky I-fix-cars-for-people-like-my-brother way of his.

"They'll pay for your airplane ticket and you'll stay at their house." She looked excited.

"And they'll owe us big time," Xander observed.

"Well, I don't like to think about it that way." His mother's eyes gleamed. "But yes, they will."

"May I say again, yay."

His mom touched his arm. "Honey, he might die without new marrow."

A car approached. Buffy reached out her arm and waved, and the sucker screeched onward.

"Jerk," Xander's mom said. She ran her hand through her hair. "I wish I had some gum."

"I wish I had some skin." He looked down at his arm. "I'll bet I get some scars out of this one. They won't look good with my swim team gig."

"Oh, are they going to lift the ban?" she asked.

He was pleased that she even knew about the ban. He hadn't realized she paid attention to anything that had to do with him and high school. Or him and anything. "Possibly. Snyder wants the teams back."

Another car sailed on past. Xander watched Buffy's temper wind up for the pitch.

"Your dad likes Principal Snyder," she said. "He's got a firm hand."

"Not, however, a firm grasp on reality," Xander muttered.

She cocked her head. "What?"

"Nothing." He was really hurting, and it was getting harder to talk. If they didn't get a ride soon, it was going to get harder to live.

"Not that many cars come by here," his mom said.

"Nope." He grimaced. "Mom, do you have any aspirin or anything?"

She shook her head. "My purse is in the car." Her hair hung around her face and she looked doughy and confused. "Your father is going to be so angry about the car."

"Insurance money," Xander said.

"We haven't paid it off yet."

"Jeez, Mom, it's like, fourteen years old."

"We spread the payments out." She scanned the horizon. "I don't think things like this happen in San Francisco."

Plan A was not working.

Buffy said loudly, "Screw this," and stepped into the middle of the road. She made sure the axe, which she'd taken from the mummy, was wedged securely inside the back of her pants. No sense freaking out a potential free ride by looking like an urban legend axe-murderer.

The oncoming truck blew its air horn and kept racing toward her. Through the windshield, Buffy saw the driver. It was Christopher Bothwell, and a hot-looking woman was next to him.

"Wow. This is amazingly cool," Buffy said.

The truck rolled to a stop and Bothwell got out. He smiled and said, "Well, I'll be."

She looked around. "Where's Giles?"

"Would you believe it? His car broke down," Bothwell told her. "He told me to go on ahead, and I hitched a ride."

She frowned. "Then why are you driving?"

Then the beautiful woman climbed out. She opened her hands slowly. A large sphere of energy glowed between her hands. Bothwell walked over to Faith and yanked her to her feet.

The woman said, "We're going to the summit. Get in, or we'll kill that boy and his mother."

"You're Cecile," Buffy guessed.

The woman only smiled.

I have the axe, Buffy thought. *I can fight.*

The woman's smile faded. "Get *in.*"

"Are we going to the summit?" Buffy asked.

The woman nodded. Faith groaned and said, "B., we should do it."

Cecile looked at Faith. "We have to find that axe before she dies," she said to Bothwell. "If she doesn't die by the axe, the Gatherer won't be able to absorb her."

Buffy started sweating. She resisted all temptations toward heroics and meekly climbed into the truck. Faith and Xander did likewise, injured as they were.

Mrs. Harris was left by the side of the road, screaming and stomping her foot.

"You go, Mom," Xander said hoarsely. He gave Buffy a half-smile. "Wish I could start screaming, too."

The Book of One

Prologue

They were walking along the beach, Kit and India, and he was staring up at the stars. When he realized she was looking at him, he smiled shyly and said, "Some people believe the stars are the souls of fallen warriors."

The Slayer asked him if he believed that, and he nodded and said, "Yes, I do. Have you heard of Lord Dunsany? He wrote a marvelous poem. It begins, 'She like a comet seemed . . .' " Then he trailed off, looking uncomfortable.

He loves me, she thought. *He doesn't want me to know, but he does. Oh Kit, Kit, if I do die, wish on my star, and I will make your wish come true. I will do anything for you. Give my life, my soul . . . yes, even my soul.*

Chapter One

They reached the summit.

When Christopher Bothwell opened the back of the truck and told them to get out, Buffy saw that the others were already there. In the howling wind and rain, the stormy seas and the spurting fires, Willow and Cordelia stood waiting. They looked unnaturally calm, astonishingly focused.

They looked like Slayers.

"Join them," Bothwell said, pushing Faith brutally out of the back of the truck. The rogue Watcher left Xander there, and Buffy was content to let her friend remain off the radar in his condition.

Faith groaned and limped forward, rolling her eyes as if to say, *Pain's a bitch, ain't it, B?*

Angel. Buffy looked for him, but didn't see him. Had he gotten the axe? *Oh, God, don't let him be hurt. Don't let him be dead.*

Cecile said to Bothwell, "The Gatherer's body is in a safe place. But it won't need that oozy mess much longer."

They smiled at one another, radiating victory.

"You don't have to do this," Buffy said to Bothwell. "You're under her thrall. You don't have to."

"He does," Cecile said. "And speaking of alternatives . . ."

She made a ball of energy between her hands. It spun and glowed, and then something hard and solid appeared within it. It was the head of a dark-skinned man who looked very much like Cecile.

Leaving its owner's body had pretty much ended its life.

"Simon, thank you," she said. "I'm sorry, but the position of Fourth Servant has been filled." She clapped her hands, and the head disappeared.

Christopher Bothwell laughed and kissed her. "You had a list," he said.

She smiled. "I have worked for centuries to produce the proper Fourth Servant," she said.

"I'm honored."

Cecile smiled first at him, and then at the sky. She closed her eyes. "I can feel the Gatherer," she shouted. She reached up her arms. "I can embrace my god!"

"O-*kay*," Buffy muttered.

Then Giles pulled up, with Angel and Oz. Xander slowly tumbled out of the back of the truck to join his friends.

"Four friends," Cecile said brightly, pointing to them. "Four Slayers."

"And Four Wanderers," Kit said.

The mummies coalesced from the Elements around them, the four swathed creatures from the dreams of Buffy and Faith—and Willow's. One was dripping wet; one burned. The Wanderer of the Earth was covered with mud. And the bandages on Buffy's Wanderer flapped in the wild wind.

Then Cordelia gasped and said, "I saw this. In my slumbers."

So Kendra *had* dreamed on the Ghost Roads.

That was encouraging, Buffy thought, to someone hoping for an afterlife.

The sky darkened and more lightning jittered across the thunderheads, reminding Buffy of fingernails against a chalkboard.

Buffy and the others stayed lined up. They stood firm.

The Wanderers advanced on the four Slayers.

The world went into overdrive. If there had been a storm before, it was like nothing now.

The Four stood together.

The Wanderers drew near.

Out of the corner of her eye, Buffy saw Angel. He nodded at her, patted his jacket.

Yay, Buffy thought. *He's got my axe. The axe of Air.*

That was when Kit Bothwell fell to his knees.

And that was when Cecile Lafitte ran to the truck and flung open what Buffy now realized was a false bottom. A hinged lid swung down, and Cecile plunged her arms into the box, shrieking with agony and triumph.

"My king!" she cried. "It is I, your Servant!"

Kit Bothwell raised his head and stared at her. "What are you doing? I'm the Servant!"

"You fool," she sneered as she stumbled back toward the others. Her arms were coated with ooze. "Do you think I would allow you, a mere man, to serve my god? I am now the Fourth Servant! All has been accomplished, and I am my master's body on this earth." She whirled with the wind. "And when he eats these Slayers, then he shall be transformed!" She pointed to the sky, and enormous streams of energy emanated from her body, shooting into the sky and puncturing the clouds with magickal brilliance. "He comes!"

Christopher Bothwell kneeled and began to chant. Then the air around him shifted.

Cecile laughed and said, "He is taking you. He will engulf your rotten soul."

He continued to kneel. She pointed at him, shaking. "Stop your magickal babbling. It won't save you. You wanted her. Part of you knew what I was, and what I was doing. And you thought I would let you have India, if you helped me."

"No, Kit! My love!" Willow shouted, breaking ranks. "Take me instead! Take my soul!"

She sailed over the cliff as Buffy screamed; and then the sky burst with the light of a thousand stars, a hundred thousand: All the souls the Gatherer had consumed; the spirit-matter of innocents, and wicked men, and Slayers, whose deaths had been hideous.

And now, it had back India Cohen.

The brilliance blinded Buffy, and then it exploded. Clouds, or smoke, or gases formed a face that was alien, repellent. Miles wide, it stretched across the sky. Stars exploded inside its features like fireworks.

"I walk," it thundered.

"And talk!" Faith yelled at it.

"I destroy worlds!" it boasted. Lightning flashed in at least a dozen parts of its features, igniting the muddy ground. Frenzied gale forces sliced the lighthouse in two pieces; as the halves hit the ground, the ground tossed the warring sides into the storm and pitched them into the sea.

The three Slayers stood resolutely in a row, their

friends behind them. Angel had taken cover, Buffy assumed her axe had gone with him. Buffy was grim-faced, reeling. *Willow's dead. India's gone. But it wasn't enough. Now we're not the Four. We're going to lose.*

The Wanderers glided forward with their boxes. As Buffy eyed them, the skulls and bones writhed and groaned; the sound was terrible: the souls of dead Slayers, tormented inside the Hell that is the Gatherer.

My Wanderer doesn't have my axe, she thought. *And I have the Axe of Fire. So for the time being, I'm safer than the others,* Buffy realized. *And I can do some damage.*

I have to take the lead.

Like the Four Horsemen of the Apocalypse, the Wanderers hovered about twenty feet from the three Slayers. They seemed to be waiting for a signal. Buffy took the time to plan strategy.

Should I kill myself, too?

Chapter Two

The plane lurched and pitched as Micaela closed her eyes and attempted to reach out to Giles's mind again. Neema watched her anxiously, twisting and untwisting her hands. She had no psychic skills of her own, no supernatural abilities.

She did, however, possess the well-trained mind of a Watcher, and it was she who had deciphered the pages of The Book of Fours, which Roger had kept in his diary:

It comes down to souls, and their integrity. For who knew, back in those ancient days when the Gatherer was first born, that human souls can become fragmented? That good and evil war even there, and such has happened to the Gatherer? I, of all people, should have known, for that is precisely why I, Cecile Lafitte, was able to create so many zombies. In like manner, the Gatherer has absorbed fleeting bits of souls, such as a part of my descendant, Tutuana Lafitte's evil soul. He has also managed to capture the part of India Cohen that pushed her to suicide. This lack of purity has weakened the Gatherer; and he must have

coherence. I will join with him on the Night of the
Stars, and the force of my strong, intact soul will give
him freedom. Then I will feed him the primal soul-
force of the Slayer, and my god will ravage the earth
with evil.

"Giles," Micaela murmured. "Giles, hear me. I know
what to do."

On the ground, Rupert Giles looked up and around.
He frowned, touching his head, staggering and lurching
through the ferocity of the storm. Xander, whose full
attention had been focused on the Slayers, took note,
and stumbled over to him. Oz was lost, staring and
frozen, as if unable to process what was going on
around him.

"It's . . . it's Micaela Tomassi!" Giles shouted. Xander blinked, and Giles waved his hand. "She's in contact . . . never mind. She's going to help—"

At that precise moment, a spectral woman's form
shimmered into being beside Xander, who yelped and
jumped away from her. She was white-skinned and
dark-headed, and her chest had been sliced open with a
knife.

"I am Mirielle," she proclaimed.

Another form shimmered beside her. Before it took
solid form, it left them, soaring over to Buffy. Suddenly
it was a girl dressed like someone from the Civil War.
She handed Buffy something and gave her a nod.

"Lucy Hanover," Mirielle shouted over the wind. She
opened her arms. "My soul is partly his. Sacrifice a portion of your souls as well. Let the Gatherer have them, but
only part. You will weaken him. You will fragment him.
The Slayers can fight him then."

Giles nodded. "There's a ritual," he told Xander. "We must perform it."

"Giles?" Xander yelled. "Um, soul-donation? Are you sure about this?"

Giles nodded impatiently, clearly on a mission. "Get Oz. Quickly."

Xander raced for Oz. He grabbed the poor catatonic guy and led him back to the Watcher.

Giles stationed Oz across from himself and put his hands on Oz's shoulders. He put Oz's hands on his own shoulders. He said to Xander, "Face her and do the same."

They made a square. Mirielle said, "We are Four."

"Four," Giles said.

Xander echoed, "Four."

Tears streamed down Oz's face. "Four." He wept.

The ghost of Lucy Hanover had given Buffy the Axe of the Air, which Angel had had before. Buffy knew there was no time for questions: she had the Axe of Fire, and her own axe, and it was time to rumble.

The Wanderers put their hands in their boxes. Two pulled out axes: the Wanderer of Earth—for Kendra; and the Wanderer of Water—for Lucy, whose death had been by water, when Cameron Duvalier first created the Wanderers.

"On your mark!" Buffy shouted.

Without consulting each other, Kendra took on the Wanderer of Water, while Lucy went after the Wanderer of Earth. As the Air and Fire came for Buffy and Faith, Buffy yelled to Faith, "I've got 'em both, okay?"

"Check." Faith grinned crazily and started pummeling the Wanderer of the Air, groaning with each movement, each hit, as she smashed fists and feet into the mummy's steel-solid form. She looked to be in terrible pain, but it wasn't slowing her down. Buffy was proud to fight beside her.

She was proud to fight with all of them. Kendra, as Cordelia, though clearly beginning to tire, was rabbit-punching the Wanderer of Water in the midsection, and actually forced it to give ground. Lucy had ripped her long skirt off at the thighs; and she was an amazing fighter, her legs whipping like pistons as she beat back the Wanderer of Earth.

Suddenly Giles blinked and said, "No. This is wrong."

The others looked at him in surprise, but he knew the secret was not in giving up a part of their souls; India had tried that and failed. It was in taking away the soul of the Gatherer itself.

The Gatherer who was now manifest.

He turned his full attention to Cecile Lafitte, who was watching the battle between the Slayers and the Wanderers. Her eyes gleamed a demonic, evil red; she was lost in the glory of the struggle. Giles began to chant in Latin: "I take thee in, dark one; I take thee in . . ."

Cordelia, as Kendra, looked straight at him. Though she was perhaps forty feet away from him, she locked gazes with him. She nodded, signaling her approval.

"Repeat after me. Say precisely what I say," Giles told the other three. "We must fragment it!"

Xander and Mirielle followed suit. Oz's lips moved, and then he seemed to snap out of his shock, and began to chant with the other three in earnest.

*   *   *

Flying through the storm, Micaela felt the change in Giles's psychic energy. "Break it. Cleanse it. Make it anew," Giles was thinking. She understood what he was doing, and she knew he was correct. She closed her eyes, and began to chant as well. "I take thee in, dark one . . ."

Neema, who spoke Latin, joined her.

Cecile whirled around, aiming a sphere of energy at Giles and the others and shouted, "No! What are you doing?"

The Gatherer roared. All hell screamed with delight. It threw back its head, and it rose so high into the black sky that it curved against the atmosphere, glittering like the Milky Way.

"This is my night. The Night of Stars!" it exulted

Human faces appeared in it, shrieking in pain and terror. Its maw widened; Buffy saw cities going up in flames; whole chunks of continents washed by tidal waves; skyscrapers tumbling during violent earthquakes. Whole forests and mountain chains blasted away by winds. Lightning fires raging on the cliff shot miles into the air. Below, the ocean skyrocketed ever higher, then crashed down as hard as exploding skyscrapers. The ground shook so hard that Buffy was certain she would be jostled to pieces.

As she watched the others battling, a bolt of lightning flashed from the center of the Gatherer's forehead and slammed into her body. She fell.

Then India appeared before Buffy, as herself, but very much a phantom. Light streamed from her body and filled the space on the cliff. It gathered and thickened into a column, which assumed the zigzag shape of stairs. "Come together," she said in Willow's voice.

Staggering to her feet, Buffy took a step on the staircase made of stars. Someone came up behind her. And behind her. And behind her.

All the Slayers who had ever walked—Faith and Kendra, and hundreds of others—moved past Buffy up the stairs of light. Wind, rain, fire assailed them, and not one could be moved.

Buffy reached the huge, gaping mouth of the Gatherer and looked in. Oblivion stared her in the face.

Not pretty, she thought.

"You have to enter willingly, accepting the absence of yourself forever to kill it," India said. "You must allow it to eat your soul!" She swallowed, her eyes widening. "I'm disintegrating. We must all go as one. We will conquer it." She began to panic. "Hurry!"

Buffy took a breath. She had no choice but surrender, and oblivion. "I'm the Slayer."

Buffy had spoken, but she realized the voice was not just her own, but the voice of legions, each Slayer renewing her vow, her covenant. Slayers of the ages—tall ones, short, light-skinned, dark. From all nations, all peoples, all times and places. As each made the decision to accept the end of their lives, their spirits, and their souls to fulfill their duty, they turned and saluted the one behind them.

Until Buffy found herself turning and staring at a vague form that shimmered, unformed and as yet uncalled. *She's the Slayer after me. The one who takes my place after I die.*

No, the form replied. *Your place will never be taken, Buffy. It is your place, and yours alone.*

Buffy stepped forward.

Into all the other Slayers.

As one, all the hundreds of Slayers put their hands one over the others, magickally forming a handprint. As Buffy watched, the print began to glow. Then the Gatherer took the shape of a huge box identical to the four the Wanderers had carried, skulls and rib cages and spinal cords hanging off it, dangling for miles down from the heavens themselves. The bones whipped and clacked in the wind and the rain; lightning struck, charring long strings of them. The box shifted and changed, revealing more skulls, more empty eye sockets, more jaws pulled back in a screaming rictus of tortuous death.

Screams climbed up and down the matrix of relics, the martyrs of good in the battle; thousands of captured, living things that had been absorbed into the Gatherer. Animals, birds, tiny organisms, little children; women and blind men and old men, warriors and lovers, kings and rebels and Union boys, and Slayers.

I will absorb the world, it exulted. *There will never be enough. I will never have enough. Sufficiency does not exit. I will swallow the universe, and all the dimensions within and without it.*

I will swallow oblivion.

I will take everything away, into myself.

Then everything became chaos, an orgy of evil, as demons and djinn and devas flew from the mouth of the Gatherer. All the evil creatures and monsters and demons the Slayers had collectively fought, during all their years and lives and battles. They were countless, and almost overwhelming.

Buffy, Cordelia, Faith, and the others fought like demons themselves.

The battle raged, across a sky of burning orange and violet and crimson; through acrid smoke and frigid water; through tornado winds that had once ripped through the deserts as sandstorms, burying the living and the dead. Through sunrise, when all the creatures of night—including the vampire with a soul—found shelter. Through another sunset. Through time and space, out among the stars, foreheads sopped with sweat as they clashed close to the sun.

To places that might never be.

To places that might one day exist.

Slayers rose, and fell, and rose again. They chanted and shrieked battle cries, and prayed and laughed and screamed in fury. Like banshees, or Valkyrie, the Slayers rocked the scales of good and evil.

Then Buffy snapped back into consciousness, aware that she was one of four Slayers fighting the Wanderers, and that Cordelia—Kendra—was trying to get her attention.

"Look!" Kendra said, pointing.

Cecile Lafitte was pummeling Giles, Xander, and Oz with magick, and yet they stood steadfast. At some point, Angel had joined them, and the ghostly Mirielle had vanished. Angel was taking most of the magickal blows, and he glanced over at Buffy, and nodded once at her.

Buffy frowned, then looked at the Wanderers, two of them still armed with their axes.

Did I dream the mouth-thing? she wondered.

Oz was moving in a haze, but he understood the danger he and the others were in as they dodged the magickal assault weapons of Cecile Lafitte. They were drawing her soul out of her body and into themselves. *Not a good feeling,* Oz thought as the damned, seething bits of her evilness spread throughout his being. *But we'll kill this thing and someday, somehow, I will get my Willow back.*

Buffy looked at the three Slayers, who were still fighting the Wanderers. She ached from the top of her head to her toes. She had been fighting the entire time she had imagined herself on the staircase. *Come together.*

And suddenly she knew what to do.

"Give me the axes," she shouted at the others. "Don't worry about the Wanderers. Just get the axes."

Cordelia and Faith body-slammed the Wanderer of Water together, and Faith grabbed the axe out of its grasp. She threw it to Buffy like a third baseman throwing it to home. Then Faith and Lucy went after the Wanderer of Earth, kicking, lunging at it; slamming their fists into its blank face and wrapped arms and legs; into its torso and midsection.

Then, crying out, Cordelia joined them, ducking wildly as the axe swiped at her. She turned and looked at Buffy and—

They were in the library again, just the two of them. Kendra lay in Buffy's arms, her throat slit, and Buffy whispered to her, "I'm sorry, Kendra. I can't save you."

—And the Axe of Earth sliced into Cordelia Chase's body, severing limbs, cutting out her

Heart

Brain and

Spine.

Then she shimmered into nothingness.

Faith jerked the axe out of the ground and threw it to Buffy as the Wanderer of Earth came at her, swinging. And Buffy, moving faster than she had ever thought possible, racing against time and space, as the world began to fall apart, raced over to Cecile with all four axes in her hands. Two were in each hand, crossed over her chest.

The voodoo queen's full attention was concentrated on stopping Giles and his group. She never saw Buffy run up behind her; did not hear the warning bellow of the Gatherer; maybe never even felt the four blades as they became one, and sliced off her head.

The Gatherer threw back its huge skull, made up of thousands of skulls, and a horrible blackness poured out of its mouth. From its eyes, vile, green flames erupted, spraying the sky until parts of it began to burn away.

It's my dream, Buffy thought. *It's ending the world.*

Pieces of the sky fell like huge mirrors, crashing; behind the sky was a gray field. Gray figures reached forward, groaning as if to pull the covers back over themselves.

Buffy felt something wash over her; it was terrible pain, horrible, deep wounds that never healed. Sorrow, and jealousy, and hatred, worse, self-hatred, and loneliness, and guilt, and shame, and loss. It was like Pandora, spewing all that was not born from love back into the world.

Buffy cried "No!," stepped forward, and every single atom of all that vileness washed through her, tearing her into tiny pieces as the others looked on.

* * *

Then it was done.
Sacrifice accepted.
Balance restored.

Angel rushed to Buffy, who lay inert on the ground. She looked incredibly peaceful.

Then she opened her eyes and said to him, "Oh, my love, you are my soul."

Epilogue

Los Angeles

In the Church of Our Lady of Mercy, Natalie's memorial service was over. All Buffy's old friends had gone ahead to the Hernandez home for the reception.

Xander was at Cedars-Sinai, undergoing the harvesting of his bone marrow, said to be quite painful. A lot to go through for a cousin he couldn't stand—nothing, for a fellow traveler on the planet. Willow, who reappeared in her hospital bed as if she'd never left, and Cordelia, found asleep in a chair beside Willow's bed, didn't remember a thing.

Buffy sat quietly in the pew, gazing at a statue of the Virgin Mary. The figure, a pale, rose-cheeked girl wearing flowing robes of white and blue, stepped on a serpent and held out her arms for all those who were troubled and weary-laded.

Then Christopher Bothwell touched her shoulder. He wore the brown robes of a monk, and the gentle sunshine streaming through the stained glass cast pale colors on his tired-looking face.

Buffy brushed her mother's hand to let her know she was leaving the pew. She joined Kit, who turned and led the way out of the church. Outside, a low white-washed wall lined an exquisite rose garden of pink, yellow, and white roses. In the center of the garden, a white statue of St. Francis was decorated with bird seed, and small bluebirds and pigeons—tremendous numbers of pigeons—were taking advantage of the church's largesse.

Together they walked along the tile floor. Frescoes of doves and vibrant flowers decorated the walls of the rectory and the parish hall.

Kit looked out over the roses. "I can never forgive myself for what I almost did."

"Cecile was controlling you," Buffy said. "Forcing you to do things against your will."

"I wish I could believe that, too. But deep down, Buffy, something in me knew. Something prodded me to go along with it, pretend I was unaware. For India. I thought I could finally bring her back." He closed his eyes. "I don't know how I will ever find peace."

"Maybe you will someday. After you've punished yourself enough."

He put his hands into the sleeves of his robe and walked slowly, looking first at her and then back at the roses. "I think the Gatherer took her with it when it was destroyed. That she has no being, anywhere. I no longer sense her. She's gone, completely gone. As if she had never even existed."

"No, she's not gone," Buffy said. She took her hands in his. "I'm here."

Kit Bothwell looked at her, and for the first time since India's final sacrifice, he smiled.

"Maybe it's love, and not some primal force of supernatural strength, that keeps the legacy of the Slayer going," he said softly. "Because I feel great love for you,

Buffy, not as a man loves a woman—as I loved India—but as a living being who needs saving from the dark. And who recognizes in you something that cares so much that you will protect all of us until you die."

The tears streamed down his face. "If that's not a legacy . . . something she passed on to you, and that never dies, then what is it?"

"Just call it Buffy." She smiled back. "For now."

This is the Book that is called Les Livres des Quatres, *the* Book of Fours. *Much has been spoken about the stories that went on after this Book was shut. Of the quest by the Three to find India, of the Water. Of the constant yet humorous discord between Kendra, of the Earth, and Faith, of the Fire, whose Slaying styles could not be more in opposition.*

Of their leader, Buffy, who, moved by love, resolved that she would not die until India was found, and freed.

But that is for another Book.

This one has told its Tale.

The Watcher of the Fifth, as told to Nancy Holder.

About the Author

Nancy Holder is the award-winning, *Los Angeles Times*–bestselling author of forty-two novels and more than two hundred short stories, articles, and essays. She has won four Bram Stoker Awards for her supernatural fiction, including Best Novel for *Dead in the Water*. Her work has been translated into more than two dozen languages. With her frequent collaborator, Christopher Golden, she has written many Buffy projects, including *The Sunnydale High Yearbook*, *The Watcher's Guide, Vol. 1,* and *Immortal*. Her solo Buffy-Angel efforts include *The Evil That Men Do* and *Not Forgotten*. She is currently finishing the first Buffy-Angel crossover novels with Jeff Mariotte and the official *Angel* companion with Jeff Mariotte and Maryelizabeth Hart.

Holder is an avid swimmer and lifelong horror aficionado. A native Californian, she lives in San Diego with her brilliant and beautiful daughter and their intrepid dog Dot.

Buffy the Vampire Slayer™

"Well, we could grind our enemies into powder with a sledgehammer, but gosh, we did that last night."

—Xander

As long as there have been vampires, there has been the Slayer. One girl in all the world, to find them where they gather and to stop the spread of their evil...the swell of their numbers.

LOOK FOR A NEW TITLE EVERY MONTH!

Based on the hit TV series created by
Joss Whedon

2400

Prue, Piper, and Phoebe Halliwell
didn't think the magical incantation
would really work. But it did.
Now Prue can move things with her
mind, Piper can freeze time, and
Phoebe can see the future. They are
the most powerful of witches—
the Charmed Ones.

Published by Simon & Schuster

2387